About SOLSTICE

After eighteen years of endless summer, Earth is dying a slow, hot death. Oceans are wastelands of dead fish, deadly heat bubbles threaten to wipe out entire cities, and the soil is so desiccated that plants are in danger of extinction. This is Piper's reality, and her domineering, overprotective mother makes it even more suffocating.

Piper's best friend Chloe is her only outlet from the bleak reality within and without. However, when Piper rebels by secretly opening a mysterious birthday present and getting a tattoo with Chloe, she just exchanges her Global Heating Crisis nightmare for a mythological one.

Suddenly, Piper's world teems with murderous, deceitful gods, legendary monsters, and criminals damned to suffer eternal torments in hell. A creeping moss that only Piper can see coats the skin of the people around her, and a woman with fog-filled eyes stalks her, insisting that Chloe is about to die. As if all that isn't enough, two gorgeous guys show up at her school, both claiming to know her, and they both pursue her. And, strangely, they might be the key to this mythical mystery.

The trouble is, Piper can't resist either of them, even though they seem to be sworn enemies. She's falling for brooding, passionate Shayne and for seductive, rebellious Reese. Piper needs to make a decision, and the stakes are high in ways she can't even begin to guess.

Choose the wrong guy, and the uneasy boundary between the mythological world and the human world will disappear, Piper will never learn the truth about herself or her family, and … all hope for the future will be lost.

SOLSTICE

P.J. HOOVER

For Mom and Dad,
who raised me to believe I could do anything.

Chapter 1

Disaster

Mom says, "Watch the heat today."

I nod and hug her and go to school like normal. Her concern's nothing out of the ordinary. And neither is the heat.

At school after lunch, I walk through the breezeway, keeping my head down so the mist doesn't get in my eyes. The vapor sprays out from above, causing a layer of green gel to settle on my skin and hair. I reach up and run my hands through my hair to try to smooth it, but the cooling gel only makes the curls get wilder; it's no use. My clothes stick to me, and under my backpack, I'm coated in sweat. Out on the old parking lot, heat waves ripple over what remains of the black tar, only disturbed by a random cactus here and there. Still, I take my time before Social Sciences, soaking in the heat. Every other kid at school complains about it, but to me, the heat finds a way to sink into my soul and give me strength.

For the school to be spraying gel, the heat has to be extreme. Just before I walk back inside, I glance up at the bright red numbers of the thermometer. It blinks one hundred and twenty-one degrees Fahrenheit, which definitely falls into the extreme category. The temperature hasn't climbed this high since we moved to Austin four years ago. It rarely goes above one hundred and sixteen. I pull out my FON to double check it, and it registers the same. One degree more and…

The sirens start blaring in an earsplitting pattern of high and low, up and down. One degree becomes a reality. I step inside, and for a second, all the kids just look around at one another, like the sound hasn't yet registered. Like they're all waiting for someone else to move.

"It's another drill," one guy to my left says.

"Didn't we just have a drill?" someone else asks.

I shake my head because I know this isn't a drill; I'd seen the thermometer. But I don't want to cause a panic. The principal comes on the intercom system and does the job for me.

"Report to your designated cooling areas immediately. This is not a drill."

Realization sinks in, and the hall erupts in chaos. The crowd effect's going on, so movement just stops. But I'm on the Disaster Student Council. I need to help out. I push my way through person after person until I escape into the science hallway; the emptiness makes the sirens seem even louder as the sound bounces from one wall to the next, then off the floor and ceiling and straight into my ears. I rush toward the end, checking in each classroom to make sure it's empty, and from there,

I circle around until I'm close to the gym—the designated cooling area for our high school. I take up my position at the door on the far left and start directing kids inside.

We have drills every month, but one degree makes everyone go crazy. Drills consist of kids walking, talking, and making stupid jokes about the Global Heating Crisis. But there aren't any jokes now. Just a whole lot of pushing and screaming and everything they tell us not to do during a real disaster.

My job is to make sure everyone who comes through this door is accounted for. I stand to the side of the door and try to scan each person with my FON as they walk through. But the crowd's too thick; I'll have to wait until they're inside.

Of the ten doors leading into the gym, only me and three other student council members are already in position. Chloe's supposed to be next to me, but she must be trapped behind everyone. I don't want to think about her getting stuck outside in the heat. The last time she got too hot, she passed out.

"where r u?" I text her.

She responds in under five seconds, "b there in a sec," and when I look out across the crowd, I catch her waving.

My FON is almost back in my pocket when it vibrates again. I don't have to look to know who it is.

"Hey, Mom." I cover one ear with my free hand and

yell into the FON over the sound of the sirens.

"Piper. Why haven't you answered? I've called you five times today."

She's actually called me seven times, and I've ignored each one. "I'm at school, Mom."

"You have to come home right now." My mom is always oversensitive that the earth is going to swallow me whole or something ridiculous like that, but this time her voice has an extra layer of worry on top.

"I can't," I yell back. Two kids in front of me start pushing to get to the door faster, but one of the teachers breaks it up. I motion them inside with my free hand.

"You have to. Please." Her pleading comes through even amid the disaster. But she has to hear the sirens in the background. Does she think I'm going to just cut out in the middle of the crisis?

"I'll be home when this is over."

"Now, Piper." Instead of worry, she uses her authority voice. But it only makes me want to do the exact opposite of what she's asking.

"I'm not leaving now," I say.

"It's a heat bubble. The whole city is covered in it."

I don't speak as her words sink in. A real heat bubble means we could be stuck with deadly temperatures for weeks. The last time one of the pockets of hot air formed, the city was evacuated, and even then, almost a thousand people died. An evacuation is going to be nothing short of a disaster.

"Piper?"

"I'm here," I say, but a sick feeling forms in the pit of my stomach. Heat bubbles are the newest, worst threat of the Global Heating Crisis. Cities all around the world are testing different ways to get rid of them, but it seems like the more done to combat them, the more frequent the bubbles become. Three months ago, one formed over Central America, and a third of the population died. They'd suffocated from the heat. Scientists called it the most horrible natural disaster since the tsunami fourteen years prior that had wiped out most of Indonesia.

"The city's going to disperse the bubble. And activate the domes," she says.

Disperser missiles have never been tested on a real bubble. There's no telling what's going to happen. "But—" I start.

"Take cover. And get home before they seal the domes. Please," she says, and then she ends the call.

I'm still holding my FON when Chloe shows up next to me. My mind is spinning over what my mom said, because there's no telling what a missile will do to the heat bubble. They've only been tested in the deserted regions of western Texas.

I give Chloe a quick smile to reassure her—or maybe myself—but we don't get a chance to talk because at least thirty freshmen are trying to get my attention. I give up entirely on scanning them and just motion them all inside. If the city really is going to try to disperse the heat bubble, we need to get everyone behind the sealed doors.

It takes another few minutes before the hallway finally clears. Anyone stuck outside now is going to have to find some other shelter. The thought of being stuck outside during the disaster sends a wave of dread through me, but I try to suppress it since I'm supposed to set an example.

I mouth to Chloe, "Let's talk later," and she nods. And then we both go into the gym and pull our doors closed behind us. One of the teachers swipes his FON in front of a scanner, and thick walls of plastic start lowering to the ground, forming a shield to protect us from the outside. My entire body relaxes when the shields touch the floor. We're going to be safe.

The freshmen are supposed to be in a single file line, but most of them are sitting next to their friends, crying and consoling each other. I'm not going to stop them; most people do think the Global Heating Crisis will end the world. If the heat doesn't stop sooner or later, everything on Earth will die except maybe the cockroaches. Already most of the smaller vegetation is gone.

Overhead, the giant industrial air conditioners kick in. The city has mandated they can only be turned on in times of disaster, and only then, set to cool to eighty-nine degrees. Otherwise, most of humanity has to settle for eco-friendly A/C, which cools to a toasty ninety-three degrees.

I take out my FON and scan each kid's identifier until it beeps. One by one, I make my way down the line, but I stop when I notice a girl sitting against the gym wall with her knees pulled up against herself and tears running down her face. Her arms are covered in red blisters, and standing over her is some empathy-challenged freshman girl and her boyfriend who even in the midst of disaster tries to act like he's above it all, the heat be damned. There's just something about the whole situation that gets under my skin. I detest bullies. I detest when people are flat-out mean and get away with it. And I detest when people take advantage of bad situations.

I walk over, and when they see me coming, the girl and guy scoot away to Chloe's line. Chloe catches my eye and winks. I know my best friend will set them straight. I turn back to the girl on the ground, but she doesn't look up. Instead, she scratches her blisters and stares straight ahead.

"Hey, it's going to be okay," I say and squat down beside her.

She bites her lip, but her tears are still coming.

I reach out and run my hand over her blisters. "You're allergic?"

She nods and then pulls her arms away and tries to move them to the inside of her legs.

She shouldn't be embarrassed. One out of every ten people is allergic to the cooling gel they use, but this was deemed acceptable by the city council since it helps more people than it hurts. My mom was furious about the decision, but her vote was in the minority.

"I'm Piper," I say.

The girl's eyes finally meet mine. "Everyone knows who you are," she says.

I give a weak smile to help relax her. "Only 'cause my mom's on the city council."

"Yeah, maybe," she says. And she smiles back.

"You know my mom swears fennel tea will help reduce the allergic effects of the gel."

Hope fills the girl's eyes. "Fennel tea?"

I nod. "It's supposed to counteract the chemicals they use. We grow all sorts of it at home."

"At the Botanical Haven?" she says.

"Yeah. The Botanical Haven." Apparently everyone knows where I live, too. I guess that's the price of living in the largest private greenhouse in town. Chloe had told me once that people refer to it as the Flower Fortress behind my back. "I'll bring you some on Monday if you want to try it."

"Really?" Her face lights up like I've told her I'll be her best friend.

"Yeah, really," I say. I give her a final smile and stand up and am about to start scanning more kids when, over the wail of the sirens, there's a boom so loud I feel it deep in my bones. It sounds like a bomb has dropped just outside the school walls. The ground rumbles, and the A/C overhead gives a final clunk and turns off. Any sense of order that might have been taking over the gym vanishes.

Someone shouts, "we're all gonna die," and people start screaming and crying. The sirens are still blaring, and the thermometer on the wall reads ninety-two. As I watch, it creeps up to ninety-three. Ninety-four. Everyone's eyes are fixed on it, like it's some electronic symbol of their fate. I hold my breath and wait for something to change. The sound from outside could only be the disperser missile. If it doesn't work, maybe everyone else will be right. Maybe this will be the end of the world. Ninety-five. The temperature keeps rising. Ninety-six. And now, having twelve hundred kids and ninety faculty members stuck in a sealed-off gymnasium doesn't seem like such a good idea. Maybe they should have been testing the air conditioning more regularly.

I'm just about to let despair consume me. The thermometer clicks to ninety-seven, and I think this is it. This is going to be the end.

But the temperature holds.

And the sirens go silent.

And the thick plastic walls lift.

And then there's the sound of the doors to the gym unsealing, and twelve hundred kids start cheering, myself included. Whatever the missile was supposed to do to disperse the heat bubble, it must've worked. And I think maybe we will be able to survive this global warming disaster after all.

The principal comes back on the intercom and tells everyone school is canceled for the rest of the day. He instructs everyone to return home "in an orderly fashion" and await further instructions. Since I already talked to my mom, I know that the domes are about to be sealed. I hurry over to tell Chloe, but she's caught in the crowd and being pushed out the door. I'll text her once I get outside.

One step outside, with no cooling gel, and it's like an inferno. Even if the bubble's dispersed, it could take hours for the hot air to drift away. I don't wait for a shuttle because everyone is trying to take one; the wait will be eternity. So I start the walk home.

Overhead, the steel struts of the dome structure extend into the sky. Thirty domes are being built over Austin, but only eight are supposed to be operational so far. Our Botanical Haven isn't inside one, and I don't want to be caught on the wrong side. My mom would freak.

I have to admit the thought of being away from my mom for a weekend is appealing. I could stay with Chloe. We could stay up late and watch ridiculous videos on the tube and eat popcorn and talk about which guys are hot and which ones she'd never date even if they were the last guys left on earth. But I keep walking.

I'm hardly past the last strut when the glass starts to grow between the beams of steel. I can't pull my eyes away. Inch by inch, the glass forms like the shell of some sea creature. The Global Heating Crisis will continue to destroy the atmosphere, and cities around the world will create their own new atmospheres, and maybe life will go on; at this point, nothing is a guarantee. I watch until the glass seals fully into place, and then I walk home.

Chapter 2

Social Sciences

From what my mom and I watch on the news Friday and Saturday, the domes work just like promised. The eight functioning ones sealed shut and blocked the worst of the heat and UV radiation, which was great. What wasn't so great was the fact that, in the areas which weren't domed, the crime rate skyrocketed. Reporters estimate a record high of thirty rapes, fifteen murders, and an uncountable number of burglaries throughout the city. Hotter days always bring more violence to the city, but this is the worst it's been yet.

The steel struts retract the glass of the domes late Sunday, reabsorbing the sand and lime for use the next time the domes are needed, and now everyone's allowed out again. My mom tells me the GHC council has an emergency meeting after school Monday—that she might not be here when I get home. I try to keep the smile off my face; I'll have a little time to myself. My mom is smothering in large doses, and this weekend of her doting on my every movement hasn't helped matters. I only saw one other person the entire weekend when my mom went out to collect some seeds. One of our customers, Melina, came by to talk and drop off a birthday present. On a normal Sunday, I look forward to Melina's visits, but this time, the whole vibe felt wrong. I figured it was the heat.

The next day at school, all anyone talks about is the Global Heating Crisis. Everyone's trying to outdo one another with stories about how crazy or scary or awesome their weekend was. I mull over the fact that I spent the entire weekend inside the Botanical Haven with my mom while my eighteenth birthday came and went. To her credit, she tried to make it special, making me a vanilla cream cake and molding tiny flowers out of fondant for the icing. But even the cake couldn't erase the fact that I didn't get to see Chloe.

After lunch, my mom calls me, making sure I remember she has the council meeting to go to. I assure her I remember and try to get her off the FON, but she keeps talking like she just wants to hear my voice. She starts telling me about the latest crop reports from the Midwest, how this year farmers estimate yields of corn will be at an all-time low. I normally latch on to this kind of information, but I'm already late; I have no choice but to hang up on her and head to class.

When I walk into Social Sciences, there's a new guy sitting right where I normally sit near the windows. His face turns to me, and his eyes are the first thing to catch my interest. They're dark like chocolate and filled with shadows. His lips move into a flicker of a smile, and a piece of his dark hair falls across his forehead. He makes me think of mysteries and secrets. In short, he sums up every single thing my mom tells me to avoid. So I sit down in the empty seat next to him.

"You're late, Piper." Mr. Kaiser's already started class.

I pretend not to look at the new guy and drop my backpack onto the ground. "My mom called."

I wait for the idiotic crack from Randy Conner which I know will come. He doesn't disappoint. "Making sure you got between classes okay?"

The class snickers, and I shoot Randy my best glare. But my peripheral vision catches the new guy, and my heart tightens into something resembling a Gordian knot; he's staring right at me.

My face heats up, and I wish I could fade into invisibility. Jokes about my mom's over-protectiveness are rampant at school. It's not until I turn back around, get my tablet out, and Mr. Kaiser starts lecturing that I feel the new guy's eyes shift off me.

"Global Heating Crisis." Mr. Kaiser prints *GHC* in giant letters on the board in bright orange dry erase marker, underlining it three times. "We'll finish the year with a month-long series on it." Mr. Kaiser caps the marker and turns to face us.

I chance a sideways look at the new guy and catch his mouth curve into a smile when he sees me looking.

"How was your weekend?" he says. His voice pulls

my thoughts away from Mr. Kaiser and the Global Heating Crisis, and my heart pumps into overdrive. It pushes its way through the filters in my brain and stirs up images of freedom and fun. And darkness.

Breathe. Must remember to breathe. Okay, so he's perfect, but if my mom finds out I actually talked to a guy like this she'd probably yank me out of public school and homeschool me for the rest of the year. She's completely over the top when it comes to guys.

"I hung out with my mom all weekend," I say.

He smiles, and I know it's a good thing I'm already sitting because, with the blood pumping out of my legs and into my heart, I'd never be able to stand.

"Seriously? You should have asked to go out or something," he says.

At this, even with my reluctant vocal cords, I actually let out a small laugh. There is just no way he has any idea what living with my overprotective mom is like. It took me running away one weekend for her to ever let me go to public high school in the first place. I was fourteen at the time, and I'd tried everything. Not eating. Not doing my homework. But it was only when I resorted to running away that she finally let up a little.

"That would be pointless," I manage to say. I glance at Mr. Kaiser, but he's busy writing the top ten reasons global warming will kill Earth on the board. It's interesting that his number one reason is the disperser missile because it's my mom's top reason, too. She claims the chemicals used to puncture the bubble strip layers from the atmosphere.

The new guy leans in and lowers his voice, and the classroom seems to fade around us. "So you go on, feeling like you have no control? That doesn't seem fair."

I stare at him because I have no idea how to respond. He's looking into my soul and seeing my exact thoughts. It's like he knows me. But I have no clue who he is.

"Piper?"

I turn at Mr. Kaiser's voice, remembering where I am. "Yes?"

"I asked how long Earth has been in an official catastrophic state."

It's an easy question—the same amount of time I've been alive. The same amount of time everyone in this room has been alive with the exception of Mr. Kaiser who's ancient. "Eighteen years."

Mr. Kaiser smiles, and I notice out of my sideways vision the new guy isn't looking at me anymore. He's looking out the window at a gym class on the soccer field. Misters spray cooling gel into the air, forming a green haze under the UV shade coverings, but the thermometer outside the window is clocking in at one hundred and seven. The new guy watches the game, ignoring Mr. Kaiser. And ignoring me. I vow that the next time I'm in a conversation with the hottest guy on the planet, I will actually say something more engaging. In all fairness, I haven't had much practice.

Mr. Kaiser picks on a couple of other kids, and then goes into some lengthy explanation of atmospheric stripping. I've heard it all before from my mom, so I sit back and let the new guy enter my daydreams—the one place I know my mom can't get to. I convince myself his eyes still look my way. I imagine he asks me to go out with him, and I even smile when my mom agrees—ignoring the absurdity of this. That's the nice thing about daydreams—even the impossible can happen. I wonder what it would be like to kiss him, what it would be like to be with someone who understood me. I can almost feel his lips on my mouth. I want to savor the moment forever.

"Did you have a fun birthday?"

I snap back to reality and peek over. At least this time, he's whispering.

"How did you know it was my birthday?" I ask. As far as I know, he's never seen me before today.

"You told me last week," he says.

I stare at him and try to form coherent words because this is ridiculous. I've never spoken to him in my life. "Do I know you?"

He looks at me like I'm crazy. "I'm Shayne. Remember?"

I shake my head because he must be messing with my mind. "Not really." But I decide to play along with it.

He gives me the cutest little smile like he's got a secret he's dying to tell me. Like we're co-conspirators in a plot to take over the world. And I believe for a second we are. He flips a stylus in circles over his fingers—a skill I've tried a hundred times and never been able to master. He makes it look easy.

"We've been sitting by each other all year," he says.

I glance around the room and notice half the girls in the class staring at him. But he either doesn't notice them or doesn't care. It's like he only has eyes for me.

"So what's my name?" I whisper back, and this time I manage to smile at him even though my throat feels like it's about to lock up.

"Piper," he says. When it comes out of his mouth, it's like he's trying to taste it.

"Mr. Kaiser just said it," I say, realizing it wasn't a very good question.

"That's true." And then his eyes meet mine, and I see red specks inside the brown irises. They almost seem like they're moving, but it's just the fluorescent lights from overhead playing tricks.

I swallow and hold his gaze. And something creeps through me from my ears all the way to my little toes, stopping and settling around my middle for so long I know my heart's about to thump out of my chest. It only takes me a second to name it. Desire. Like I've never felt before. Like I'd do anything for him. Which makes absolutely no sense; I've spoken all of three sentences to him—well, at least as far as I remember. But yet it's there.

His hand moves like he's about to reach over and set it on my desk. But then he bites the side of his lip and stops. "Don't let your mom get you down. You have a whole future ahead of you."

Can he know I dream of a future without my mom?

I try to respond but find I can't open my mouth. I tear at my mind, wishing brilliant words would form there, but I come up empty. And Shayne seems content to let the conversation go and sit in the awkward silence. After a minute, I force myself to break his eye contact. My mom will kill me. I should get up and move somewhere else. My mom would want me to change seats. She's told me a million times that guys can't be trusted. But he seems convinced I've been sitting by him all year, so what's the harm in one more day?

I look back over at Shayne. He smiles, and the red specks are gone from his eyes. I blink a few times, but they're still not there. I must have imagined them. Just like I've imagined not knowing him. He turns back to look out the window and starts flipping the stylus again on his fingers. Mr. Kaiser drones on about the conspiracy theories behind global warming which range from normal things like people not recycling plastic to the more absurd ideas like carbon dioxide being pumped into the atmosphere by an alien race trying to take over Earth. I sit back and listen to all the craziness about the Global Heating Crisis and wait for class to end.

Chapter 3

Study Hall

When class is over, I shove my tablet in my backpack and stand to leave, wondering if Shayne will talk to me on the way out—not sure what I'll say, though anything will top the wonderful conversation I carried on earlier. I'm not actually sure it qualifies as a conversation. But when I look over, the chair next to me is already empty. I glance toward the door, hoping I don't look obvious, but there's no sign of him. He either ran from the room or disappeared into thin air.

My heart regains a normal rhythm as I head to the library, but as I walk down the hallway, I can't help but look around, hoping to catch his eye or even a glimpse of him. I stop at the water fountain, swipe my FON, and drink until the fountain turns off. I swipe my FON again, taking another turn. The water is warmer than the air around me, but my throat's dried out over the last hour, so I don't mind as long as it's wet. I wipe my mouth and stand up, glancing around. Shayne is nowhere. But I do run into the girl with the gel allergy from Friday. Her blisters have dried up to the point that they've crusted over which makes me glad I thought to bring the aloe salve for her also. She thanks me like a million times and then heads to the bathroom to put it on.

Chloe's already waiting for me in the library. Her dark hair's shorter than it was on Friday, and she's got it pulled under an emerald green bandana so just the ends stick out. She's worn a bandana every day of the four years I've known her. I remember asking her why on the shuttle home from school the first day I met her. She'd laughed and said, "Because it looks good on me." And Chloe was right, though the bandana has nothing to do with it. She's got the body of someone who hasn't missed a day of exercise in years, and blue eyes the color of stormy water.

"You got a haircut."

She touches her hand to the bandana and smiles. "It was getting out of control."

I laugh and sit down. "I don't want to hear it." As if she knows out-of-control. My blond hair grows curlier and longer by the day, and getting it cut only seems to make it grow faster. My mom always says it's like the plants we sell in the Botanical Haven: thick and full and gorgeous, and she combs it for me each night. I view it as a burden and stick it in a ponytail as soon as I get to school each morning.

"You're late," Chloe says. She reaches into her backpack and pulls out a box wrapped in red-striped paper and tied with a bright red ribbon.

I smile when she pushes it across the table to me. I look at the present, itching to open it, but also bubbling over to tell her about Shayne. She beats me to the punch.

"I have a total new crush," she says, and instantly my heart tightens. What if she's talking about Shayne? I think I'd crumple in on myself and die on the spot.

"Who?" I ask.

"Reese. From Physics. I can't believe I've never noticed how smoking hot he is until today, but we got teamed up in this lab activity, and I swear he flirted with me the entire time."

"Who's Reese?"

Chloe rolls her eyes. "You know who Reese is. Tall. Blond hair. Looks like he could squash an army tank." The blue of Chloe's irises deepens when she talks about him. I've seen her act this way before. She crushes on someone new each week.

I shake my head because I can't place someone named Reese. "I don't think I know him."

"Totally your loss."

Maybe my memory is just slipping. Or maybe I'm losing it. "Do you know someone named Shayne?" Just thinking about him sends a chill straight down to parts I don't want to mention. At least not to anybody but myself.

Chloe purses her lips. "Sure. I mean, I think. What's he look like again?"

31

I give Chloe the PG-13 rated version. I tell her about his thick black hair, and about his brown eyes. I mention his perfect build. I even tell her about how we talked. But I leave out the part about how he made me want to run away from my contrived life and do something exhilarating. And I certainly don't tell her about the overwhelming urge I felt to be with him like I'd never wanted anything before. I may tell Chloe almost everything, but some things are way too personal to even tell your best friend.

Chloe shrugs. "I think I know who you're talking about. He's okay."

My chest relaxes. My mom may never let me go out on a date with a guy, but that doesn't mean I want my best friend dating someone I could fall in love with on the spot.

"Anyway, this all seems kind of perfect if you ask me."

"In what way?" I ask, pretending I don't know.

Chloe smiles and grabs my hands across the table. "I could date Reese, and you could date Shayne."

A weird, queasy feeling moves into my stomach, and I realize I have butterflies. The thought of actually going on a double date. I could sneak out when my mom wasn't looking. But then reality asserts itself and squashes the butterflies. It's a life I've dreamed of since I knew the difference between boys and girls. But it's also a life my mom will never let me lead. In no uncertain terms, my mom has told me I can't date. Like not even work on homework together with a guy. Ever. Though more and more I wonder how long *ever* really is. Does she seriously expect me to live my entire life with her and never do anything for myself? As much as I love my mom, she's psychotically oppressive, and each day that goes by makes her issues all the more evident.

"Good idea, right?" Chloe's testing me.

I look down and pull my hand away, pushing some of the unruly hair that's come out of my ponytail behind my ear. "Please."

Chloe fixes her eyes on me. "Please what? You're eighteen now. You have a life of your own. Your mom does not own you."

I know it's true. And I love Chloe for saying it. She's always trying to get me to venture out. To escape from the stifling force which is my mom. But I always do what my mom says. I always have.

"She's just got this way," I say. A way of laying on the guilt of how she raised me alone my whole life. Of how she kept me hidden from a criminal father who wanted to steal me away. A father who'd gotten close a few times; nearly succeeded. But my mom had protected me. Made sure I was safe.

"You need to get over it," Chloe says.

She's right. I am eighteen now. I have a whole life ahead of me. Chloe wants me to go off to California for college with her, but my mom insists I should stay here in Austin, go to UT, live at home. Chloe and I laugh and plan, but I never really think it's possible. Still, maybe being eighteen will make a difference.

"I wouldn't even know what to do with myself," I say. I may want to explore new horizons, but I've never done it before. I motion to the present on the table; it's so thin it's hardly a box at all. "Can I open it?"

"Of course." Chloe gives me her best bubbly smile. "Happy birthday!"

"You didn't have to get me anything." Not that I'm complaining. With being homeschooled, I never got many presents from friends growing up.

Chloe rolls her eyes. "Whatever, Piper. How was your birthday? God, it sucked that I couldn't come over. But we were stuck in that stupid dome all weekend."

"My mom made me the greatest cake," I say. "You would have loved it. And then, you know how my mom always goes out scavenging seeds?"

"Doesn't she have enough yet?" she says.

"Not according to her." My mom has seeds stored up to keep us with live plants for three hundred years. If I ever have grandkids, their children's children should always have fresh flowers growing. "Anyway, when she left, you know that girl Melina I've told you about?"

"The one who hardly wears any clothes?"

"Yeah," I say. "She brought me this old box. Told me she saw it in a flea market and bought it for me."

I don't tell Chloe, but it was weird, because as soon

as Melina handed it to me, I couldn't wait to open it—like it was wired right to my brain. The second she was gone, I locked the door and ran my hands over the etched surface of the box. It was small and round with a background of coal black, but around the entire perimeter, painted in red, were images of birds and flames.

I lifted the rounded lid and looked inside, and there amid the ebony interior, sat a single red feather. It called to me, beckoned me to pick it up. It knew my name. I felt like it was a part of me, tugging at my heart, and I set the box down and picked up the feather, and letters started swirling around in my mind. A jumble of Greek characters, blending together and forming words; I had no idea what they meant, but it was like they were trying to tell me something. Trying to give me some sort of message. But all I could see was a red feather and an empty box. And before I could catch them, the letters drifted away, and the feather burst into flames and burned to ash.

I don't tell Chloe about the feather because it's just too freaky, but I give her all the other details.

"Did you hide the box?" Chloe asks.

"Under the bed," I say.

"That's a horrible hiding spot." She slides her present over to me, and I pick it up and begin untying the grosgrain red bow, running my fingers over the ribbed lines. When I finish untying it, I knot it around my ponytail.

I unwrap the paper and open the lid of the wafer-thin box. But when I look, I'm not sure what to make of the piece of paper tucked inside. I pick it up and unfold it. It's about an inch wide and has a bunch of Greek letters on it. Greek letters like I saw when I held the red feather.

I hold it out to Chloe. "What is it?"

Chloe licks her lips and smiles. "The design for our friendship tattoos."

"Tattoos!"

Chloe nods. "Yep. We're finally going to do it."

Getting a tattoo has been my ultimate dream. A permanent sign of rebellion against my mom. Something that will last forever, like my friendship with Chloe. We've talked ad nauseam about the tattoo—where we will get one, how much it will hurt, what it will be. But I've always doubted that I'd truly follow through. "Get real," I say. And I fold the piece of paper and put it back in the box.

Chloe grabs it. "I'm serious." She holds the paper open to me. "It's Ancient Greek."

Goose bumps rise on my skin even though the eco A/C is anything but cool. "What does it say?" I feel like I should be able to read the letters, to piece them together into a word that won't quite come to the forefront of my mind.

Chloe shrugs. "*Giving* or *surrender* or something like

that. I looked it up."

I squint at the design, still trying to read it. "How'd you decide on it?" As much as we've talked about tattoos, we've never been able to agree on exactly what to get.

Chloe smiles, and I lift my eyes to meet hers. "I saw it in a dream. Last night after we talked. And as soon as I woke up, I scribbled it down just like I remembered." She holds the piece of paper up. "It's perfect."

Chloe had a dream with Greek letters. And I'd seen Greek letters yesterday when I'd opened the box. It seems a bizarre coincidence, but I push it aside.

"I'm not getting a tattoo," I say. But the thought of Shayne comes back to me, and the life I want to lead flashes before my eyes. I play a vision in my mind of actually getting the tattoo. Of defying my mom. Of living my dreams.

Chloe draws an invisible band around her bicep. "Here. We're getting them here."

I roll my eyes. "I could never hide that." With every day being over a hundred degrees, tank tops have become the school's standard uniform.

Chloe looks like she's just eaten the last piece of chocolate in a Valentine sampler, and I realize she's been planning this for a long time. "I know."

I blow out the breath I've been holding since I saw the piece of paper. I can't get a tattoo. I won't get a tattoo. "I wouldn't even know where to go to get a tattoo."

"But my brother does," Chloe says, and I remember her brother who graduated last year has at least twelve tattoos, some in places I've only heard about and never seen.

"Chloe…"

"What?" she says. "You need to do something. Something for yourself. Not for your mom. Not for me. Do it for you. Make a decision for yourself."

I let the heat of the world soak into me and think about my future. With the Global Heating Crisis, some people aren't even convinced there will be much of a future. What would I do if I only had days to live? Where would I go that my mom would not be able to follow?

"When?"

Chloe smiles. She knows she's won. "We're skipping the rest of the day. I set up an appointment for us in a half hour."

Chapter 4

The Parlor

I've only been to the Drag once before. My mom needed some special seeds for a plant she wanted to grow, and the only place in Austin which claimed to have them was some hippie shop located behind the college bookstore. We took a shuttle there, and she left me on a bench to watch the world while she ran inside. Which says something about how horrible the shop must have been. The Drag was a world I'd never seen. One I hadn't even imagined. The kids walking around hardly seemed older than me, but none of them had their mothers with them. Looking around now, it's kind of hard to believe my mom actually wants me to go to college here. Does she plan on coming to classes with me?

Chloe jumps the three steps down from the shuttle, and I follow. She grabs my hand, and we start weaving our way through the crowd, backpacks in tow. Within two steps, I'm immersed in a sea of tattoos and body piercings, shaved heads and bare chests—at least on the guys. And based on the fabric of tattoos surrounding me, It seems the Drag is the right place to come for permanent ink. The misters spray down on us, and a slick of gel forms on my skin. I imagine the tattoo there on my bicep—forever.

The steel struts are in place overhead though the glass is long gone. The university was the first dome to be built. I guess the city figured since the college was dumping tons of money into researching solutions for the Global Heating Crisis, they should be the first to get protection. But even at that, the domes are nothing but a temporary patch; it's one of the few things my mom and I agree on. If temperatures keep rising, not even the special glass they grow will keep out the heat.

The clenched-up blob in my stomach increases in size with each step I take. I let go of Chloe's hand and shove both my hands into my pockets, hoping to steady my nerves. I can't believe I'm actually going to go through with getting a tattoo. Instead, I focus on the campus and try to imagine myself walking around here like one of them.

There's a group of three girls sitting on some rocks off to one side. They've got a canopy over their heads, and a large sign is staked into the dirt in front of them.

Only YOU can stop Global Warming, the sign reads, and it's covered with pictures of dying animals washed up on the beach and human corpses on city streets.

I guess I've stopped to watch because one of the girls stands up and walks over to me. She's dressed in cut off jean shorts and a tank top, and she's got tattooed snakes and scorpions curling up her legs and arms. Her black hair hangs down over her white shoulders like snakes, matching the tattoos on her legs. I think to look around for Chloe, but my vision is glued to the girl. Her eyes hide behind sunglasses, but when she gets in front of me, she flips them up and makes eye contact.

That would be if she had any eyes.

Her sockets are empty. Filled and puffed out and rimmed with lids, but there's just nothing in them. Not even skin behind. Just a void. I shift backward, hoping to break her visual grip, but she's got me. And then she reaches out and grabs my wrist, securing my bond to her. I swallow and try to calm the shaking building up inside me, but she blinks, and I see the emptiness of her eyes all over again.

"Give her the pitch, Tanni," one of her friends calls over. I can't look to see who because my eyes won't move; they're locked on this freakish empty-eye-socketed girl.

"Make her know she's responsible," the other girl calls.

Tanni tightens her grip on my wrist. "Only you can stop Global Warming, Piper."

When she says my name, she lets it drawl out, nice and slow, like every single letter is coming out of her mouth one at a time.

I can't tear my eyes from her face even though shivers run up my spine. "How do you know my name?"

She grins and closes her empty eyes. "Did you hear me, Piper?"

"I read your sign," I manage to say. I think I sound braver than I feel. Because I feel like I should turn and run away—if only my body would comply. But I hold my ground. "How do you know my name?" I say again. I've never seen this girl before in my life. She's certainly not the type of person my mom ever mingles with. And I don't ever remember her coming into our shop.

And where the hell is Chloe?

Tanni opens her eyes again and lashes out, grabbing my other wrist, and she pulls me so close to her, her features blend together into one big blurry spot in the middle of her face. When she opens her mouth to talk, her hot breath pours into my own open mouth, tasting sweet. "Do you know your fate?"

My fate? Until I left school to get this tattoo, I thought my fate was to live under the compressive thumb of my mom forever. To hide from a father I've never met. To change cities every time he gets too close. But now I'm not so sure.

I pull back and shake my arms loose. Tanni lets go and takes a step back, and her friends start laughing. Every muscle in my body is tensed up like skin stretched over a drum, and when I feel another hand on my wrist, I whip around.

"Chloe!"

"What happened, Piper?" Chloe says. Sweat beads all over her face and neck. "I thought you were right behind me."

I let my breath out, and my muscles try to relax. "I stopped to look." I motion at the group of girls. Tanni is back on the rocks with her friends, sunglasses over her eyes. She's not even looking my way. None of them are, in fact. It's like they never talked to me. Almost like they never even noticed me. One of the girls takes a long sip from a water bottle, and I realize my throat feels like sawdust. Maybe I imagined the whole thing. Except I can't get the image of the empty eyes out of my mind or the taste of her sweet breath out of my mouth. And I wonder if I do know what my fate is.

"They're just a bunch of freaks," Chloe says. "The Drag's full of them."

Freak seems like the perfect word to sum up Tanni. Or maybe me, seeing as how I'm the one imagining things today.

Chloe starts walking again, and this time, I vow to stick with her, casting one final glance back at Tanni and her friends. They're already talking to someone else, pointing to their Global Warming sign. To them, I don't even exist.

"The tattoo parlor is right around the corner," Chloe says. And she leads me the rest of the way.

I've never seen one, but there's an image in my mind of what a tattoo parlor should look like. It's a dirty dark place run by a guy wearing nothing but leather and chains. And bonus points if the crack of his ass shows when he sits down. So when we walk into a waiting area, smelling of bleach, with stenciled dots of red and purple on the walls and a water cooler off to the side, my butterflies settle down enough to walk over and get a cup. It's one of those tiny conical cups, so I stand there and refill it five times before I finally toss it in the nearby recycler.

"How'd you find out about this place?" I ask.

Chloe fills her own cup now that I've moved aside. I think the A/C unit's stopped working because even though the place is shiny and bright and filled with vibrant colors and the ceiling fans are on full blast, it's roasting hot. A drop of sweat trickles down my face, and I lick it when it hits my lip. It's bitter from the misting gel we got sprayed with earlier.

"My brother's dating the owner. It's how we got ahead of the waiting list." Chloe fills her cup three times before recycling it. And then we both sit. On cue the butterflies start up again.

My fate. Tanni, the eyeless girl, asked if I knew what it was. Whatever my fate was, with every second that ticks by now, it careens further and further off course. My mom pops into my head. No surprise since I'm sure the school's called her by now. With taking a shuttle down here, we've been gone almost an hour already, which makes us officially late for our tattoo appointment and definitely missing from school. But the tattoo artist hasn't come out yet, so there's nothing to do but wait.

"I've heard it doesn't hurt that much."

I shift my thoughts at Chloe's words. "I hadn't really thought about the pain." And it's true, even though we've talked about it in the past. Of all the things going through my mind today, pain hasn't come into the equation. Until now. "But thanks for mentioning it."

"The arm isn't supposed to be that sensitive. At least not the outer part."

If she's trying to make me feel better, it's not working.

"Where is the owner?" I stand up and look around, walking over to a board covered with designs. Our Greek letters are nowhere to be found; it's mostly dragons and snakes like Tanni had on her legs. "You know, maybe we should forget it. If we get back to school fast enough, I could say I've been in the bathroom sick or something." The butterflies are back, and my arms shake. I won't even have to fake the sick part. My stomach is clenched so tight, I'm sure I could throw up on cue if needed.

I hear Chloe stand and walk up behind me. She wraps her arms around me and squeezes. "Don't worry about it. You need to do this."

"Having second thoughts?" someone says.

We both turn at the sound of the voice, and Chloe lets me go. I put my hands in my pockets and try to take deep breaths but find it's harder than I thought. When I get home with a tattoo, my mom is going to kill me. I won't have to wait for Global Warming to do it. That will be my fate.

"Nope," Chloe says, pulling the piece of paper with the Greek letters out of her pocket. "We're ready."

The Asian girl who's walked into the room smiles. Her head is shaved, and Polynesian tattoos cover it. Tikis of all sizes and shapes. I can see the top of it because she's probably under five feet tall. But the strangest thing is that for just a second she seems to be covered in patchy mold. It's mostly got an orange hue, but spots of dark fill in gaps here and there. I watch it shift and grow on her skin because it's among the oddest things I've ever seen.

When I blink, it's gone.

She doesn't make eye contact with either of us. "Good. Tattoos are easy," she says. "They heal fast these days. Used to be they caused all sorts of scabbing and infection. But now we seal each puncture once the ink's inserted."

I nod and decide the orange mold was just the lights flickering. It had to be.

Chloe's brother once told us that tattoos had been used to mark slaves, and that they were used now to barcode criminals. I wonder if my dad got tattooed when he was in prison.

"So who's first?" the girl asks, turning and walking into the next room. The red tiki on the back of her skull watches me as she goes, daring me to follow.

I look to Chloe, who smiles. "Piper is."

Chapter 5

Botanical Haven

I am right. My mom wants to kill me. As soon as I walk into the Botanical Haven, I know she knows. The Botanical Haven is enormous, with glass walls and ceilings that reach so high entire trees grow straight into the air, and the entire lower level is filled with growing things: flowers, fruits, and herbs just to name a few. But my mom's anger finds me, even amid all the vast space, and focuses. A dampness settles into the air around me, and the Easter lily next to me seems to wither as if even the plants can sense her anger. She's still in the back near the rows of sinks we use to water the plants, and I have a last minute urge to try to cover my newly tattooed left arm before she gets to me. But I know she'll still find out, so I don't bother.

I start for the stairs to the apartment we live in above the shop. One step. I feel her getting closer. Another. She's about to turn the corner. The tile floor echoes with her footsteps. Deep breath. I take another step. I'm almost to the cash register.

"Piper."

Her voice sounds calm. Too calm. Like it's water

that she's placed inside a copper pot, but it hasn't yet boiled.

"Hi, Mom."

She comes around the corner and smiles when she sees me. But it's not her normal smile which makes me feel safe and secure, although a bit smothered. This smile is thin. Calculated. School only let out a half hour ago, but she definitely knows I've skipped.

"How was school today?"

I shrug, keeping my left arm away from her. I can't help myself. I sling my backpack so the strap hangs over the tattoo and lick my lips. My freshly inked skin protests against the strap, but I hold my position. "Fine. Aren't you supposed to be at your meeting?"

She looks to one side, and another plant seems to wilt under her gaze. I swear when she's mad my mom can kill plants with a glance. Apparently, it offsets my eternal green thumb.

My mom catches my eyes with hers and holds them. I can't tear them away, and I think of Tanni from the Drag, taking me captive with her empty eyes. I force myself to maintain my mom's gaze.

"Did it hurt?"

Her voice is still calm, but the anger is inside, seething just below the surface. She walks closer to me, brushing past a fern, and brown leaves fall to the ground.

"You're going to kill all the plants."

Another leaf falls from the fern, and purple flowers on a nearby iris crumple.

"I asked you a question. Did it hurt?"

I nod and tears spring into my eyes, but I fight to keep them back. "Yeah. It hurt. It hurt like hell." But it also felt blissful. Like every stick of the needle was setting me free. Giving me hope for a new life.

"I'm glad," she says.

I look around. Dead leaves litter the floor. "It's a mess in here," I say.

My mom undoes the clip holding her long black hair. It falls around her shoulders, and she smoothes it down. "You can clean it up. I'm already late for the council meeting."

I don't bother arguing, and I don't reply. I've gotten through the worst of it, and once I hear the front door shut, I look down at my arm and smile. The black ink smiles back at me. I actually did it. My very own tattoo. Complete rebellion. I sweep some of the leaves out of my way and move behind the register, dropping my backpack. I think about Shayne and how he'd singled me out in class. Not some other girl. Me. Talking to him was total rebellion, too. I want that rebellious life.

I brush my tattoo with my hand. The skin's raised underneath the black ink. The tattoo artist, Morgan, told us the skin would stay that way for months. Maybe even forever. She also mentioned the pain would persist at least a week, but mine's diminishing with each minute that passes. I move my hand over it and close my eyes. It's like having Braille stamped into my skin. I decide I like the bumps, and I hope they never go away. Even in the dark, I'll be able to see my tattoo. My first sign of freedom. And a permanent reminder of my friendship with Chloe.

I turn on the news so I can listen to it while I clean. The team of global weather experts is predicting another heat bubble. They flash to an image of the city council chambers where a press conference is just starting. Councilman Rendon is up front, and in the background are the other members of the council including my mom. They must've waited for my mom to get there. She sits just to the left of Rendon, and even though it's impossible, I feel like her eyes find mine across the broadcast.

Councilman Rendon calls for the first question.

"Is it true that the domes are now inoperable?" a reporter asks.

Rendon looks equal parts charm and concern. My mom's told me he plans to run for the state Senate next term. "The glass within our dome structures needs eighteen days to regenerate between activations," he says.

"That means the domes can't be used for the next eighteen days, correct?" someone calls out.

"Yes, that is a correct statement," Rendon says. "Next question."

I grab a bottle of soy juice off the shelf and sit down to watch the broadcast. As long as I can see my mom on the tube, it means she won't be home.

"We've heard rumors the disperser missiles are negatively impacting the environment. Is this true?"

This is the same rumor that came up in Social Sciences today. The one about the chemicals inside the missiles tearing layers from the atmosphere.

Councilman Rendon tries to laugh. "Who here in the audience felt relief from the heat on Friday? Raise your hand if you felt the bubble disperse."

Everyone in the audience raises his or her hand.

"If we relieve the heat, we are helping the environment," he says.

Behind him, I see my mom stiffen. She glances away from the eye of the camera, and the council leader takes the next question. But as he talks, green the color of seaweed seems to ooze down him, starting at his head, until it covers him in a sheet of blackish fungus.

He pauses and shifts under the lights of the council chambers. Can he feel it? Can no one else but me see it?

I tap on the tube, thinking it's a problem with the reception, but the color remains.

"How many missiles is the city equipped with?"

Rendon is about to answer when he presses a hand to his ear to listen to a private message. Then the greenish-black color oozes off him, sinking into the ground, and he returns to normal. Rendon smiles out at the crowd. "I've just been updated with a new count. The city of Austin has produced five fully loaded missiles. And as we speak, three more are under construction. We will use missiles as needed to keep the threat of the heat bubbles away. And I can guarantee you when other cities around the world see the success we're having, they'll be begging for our technology."

Once the press conference is over, the tube cuts back to the global experts who rebut the use of the missiles, claiming the chemicals create instability and will cause a global disaster. It seems to me we're already in a global disaster in every way possible. Shortages of crops are causing starvation on colossal scales, and most coastal cities are now underwater. Half of the population of Africa now lives in subterranean cities, growing food in massive underground hydroponics bays. But the experts claim the missiles will bring the end faster, if in fact the end is coming, and destroy all life on Earth, not just in Austin. I make a mental note to talk to my mom about it when she gets home.

The bell on the door rings, signaling someone's come into the warehouse, and I snap my eyes away from the tube. I didn't lock the door behind my mom, and she didn't lock it either, which reminds me of how distracted she must have been. Still, I'm not expecting any customers. We do most of our business through mail order and corporate accounts. Except for the rare customer like Melina, who brought me the box yesterday. But at the door now is most definitely not Melina. A blast of heat pushes through the door when it opens, and the fans cut on to spread the heat evenly across the plants.

My heart gives a few extra beats when I see the guy there. I know even before he reaches the counter who he has to be. He's just like Chloe described. No, even better. His blond hair is rolled into tight curls which fall around his sculpture-worthy face, and from the way he's staring at me, I'm guessing he's not here to ask about any plants.

He smiles when he reaches the counter, sets his elbows down, and leans toward me, swiping some dead leaves out of the way. "Hey, Piper."

I've never seen him before, but when Chloe talked about him nonstop during our tattoo sessions, she swore he'd been here all year. I decide to pretend I've known him all along because I don't want him to think I'm crazy. "Reese, right?"

He nods, and his arm muscles flex as he pushes against the counter. "I saw you and your friend talking in the library."

I hold my hands at my side and attempt to remain composed. "Chloe was talking about you earlier today." And Chloe had been the one going on and on about how awesome he was. But I don't think he's here to talk about Chloe either.

"Yeah, we have some class together." His response

totally matches his attitude.

"Physics," I suggest.

Reese nods. "Physics."

I dare myself to meet his eyes, and when I do, I find I can't read anything about him. His irises are like ice; all I see in them is myself reflected back.

I inhale, and even above the fragrance of the entire Botanical Haven surrounding us, I can smell Reese. It reminds me of the thick, red wine I drink with my mom, dry with just a hint of sweetness, and it's so strong I can just about taste it.

"Is your mom here?" Reese doesn't bother looking around.

I shake my head, but at the same time realize maybe I shouldn't admit to being alone. Reese looks like he could devour me. "She'll be back any time."

He seems to let his guard down. With his fresh smile, his scent fades until the plants in the Botanical Haven take over again. "She's pretty controlling, isn't she?"

"Maybe a little." I manage a nervous laugh. When I hear it come out, I realize I'm kind of shaking, so I sit down in the chair behind the counter and try to get ahold of myself.

"My mom used to be like that," Reese says. He pulls a stool up to the counter and sits on it, facing me.

Everyone always tells me this, but no one really understands. "I doubt it."

Reese crosses his arms over his chest. "Seriously. There was this one time I was out with some friends, and when I got home, she grounded me for like ten years."

His voice is helping settle my nerves, even if he is exaggerating. But I can't get over the fact that we're actually having a conversation. That for the second time in one day, a gorgeous guy has shown interest in me. A gorgeous guy that everyone else seems to know except me.

"Ten years?" I give him the obligatory eye roll which makes him laugh.

"Fine. Not quite ten years. But she flew off the deep end. Told me never to see those friends again. She threatened to have them impaled if they ever showed back up."

It's like he's telling me the male version of my own life, and, for a second, I think he might actually be able to relate. "So what'd you do?" I ask.

Reese uncrosses his arms and sets his hands down on the counter, and he leans closer which makes my nerves start up again. "I ignored her. Snuck out behind her back."

"I've never been quite that brave," I admit, though the word *quite* doesn't seem adequate.

"You should try it sometime."

I shake my head. "You don't understand—"

"With me."

My breath catches at his words. *With him*. He's suggesting sneaking out with him. And I'm the worst friend in the world because even though Chloe told me she likes him, a horrible part of me deep inside wants to do it.

Reese hops off the stool and walks around the counter so he's right next to me. The rest of the Botanical Haven seems to vanish around us until there's only me and him and an intense silence, which increases with each passing moment. Yet I don't pull away, even when his arm brushes up against mine and I feel the slick sweat on his skin. I don't want to move.

"I'm not sure," I say. There are a million automatic excuses running through my mind.

"We're perfect for each other. I knew it the day we met." He points at me. "You and me…we're the same. Misunderstood. We're like soulmates."

Soulmates. The word hangs there in the hot air between us. I laugh at the thought, and Reese smiles in response. But I wonder if somewhere out there I do have a soulmate. Is it really Reese? Or could it be Shayne? Will I ever be able to find out with my mom controlling my every move?

"What do you have to lose?"

"My mom—" I start.

Reese makes a dismissive gesture with his hands. "Sneak out. Come on." And when he says it, his eyes fill with an excitement that makes me think it might actually be possible. Like I could have a shred of adventure. With Reese.

I open my mouth, but I'm not sure what to say. Reese is still right next to me with our arms pressed together. I guess my body tenses up, because the next thing I know, he backs up and walks to the other side of the counter. I can almost see the gears turning in his mind.

"I never let being grounded get in the way," he says.

I let out a breath now that the distance between us has grown. I think about Chloe—how she suggested double dating—her with Reese and me with Shayne. I try to bring Shayne to my mind, but it's futile. All that my mind seems to be willing to focus on is Reese and the thought of disobeying my mom. It's a kind of freedom that tempts me every time I hear about other kids going to parties and hooking up and staying out all night. "My mom doesn't let me date."

"Who cares? What time does your mom go to bed?"

"Nine o'clock," I say before I can stop myself.

"Perfect. Friday night. Sneak out once she's asleep." Then he gives me a final look, but instead of conveying adventure, his eyes are peeling me apart layer by layer starting with my clothes. I shift under his gaze, but don't turn away. And then he turns and leaves, slamming the door behind him.

It takes me a good five minutes to be able to think about anything else. Reese is gone, and all that's left are dead leaves scattered around my feet. I play the conversation over again in my mind, thinking I've missed some vital part of it. But it's all there. Reese wants me to hang out with him—alone. And without even really meaning to, I think I've agreed. Which just can't be. Chloe wants to date him.

I rub my hand over my arm again, feeling each Greek letter of the tattoo underneath, until Reese's presence is gone. I wipe the sweat off my forehead and rub it on my shirt, and I grab a broom and a dustpan and start cleaning up the mess.

Chapter 6

Hallway

When my mom finally comes home, I start for the stairs. I want her take on the news conference from this afternoon. But I stop when I see her sniff the air and look around. Can she smell Reese? Just thinking about him draws the intoxicating scent back into my nostrils though I try to ignore it. She starts toward the counter, taking one slow step after another, eyes alert. Past where she walks, fresh dead leaves drop to the ground. Maybe it's the news conference that's got her upset. Or maybe it's my tattoo. Or maybe she somehow knows a guy's come over to visit.

After what seems like an eternity, she moves away from the counter and starts back to her work. I watch for a few minutes as she begins her routine, spraying leaves and packing in dirt. But she doesn't say anything and doesn't even call out to me. Maybe it's not such a good time to ask her about the council meeting, so I tiptoe away. When she finally comes upstairs, she heads right for her room, shutting the door behind her. She doesn't offer to comb my hair or even say good night. She's never been this mad at me before. I'm sure she'll tell me we're moving in the morning. That I'll be home-schooled until I graduate. That I'll never see Chloe again. My eyes fill with tears.

I think about calling Chloe, but decide against it. I don't want to tell her about Reese asking me out. Not just yet. I'll tell her tomorrow in person. I get up and move to the window, looking out at the blackness of the sky. Even in the dark, the clouds are thick, and the promise of rain hangs in the air. Rain which is something we desperately need but causes flooding every time it comes because of the hard-packed ground.

Out back are greenhouses I spend hours reading and taking naps in. And our nearest neighbors are Randy Conner's family a quarter of a mile away. But when it's dark like this, the greenhouses and the neighbors fade into black, and it's like we're the only people in the world.

I lift the screen so it's just me and the darkness, and I let the heat pour through me, inhaling the humidity. Wondering if another heat bubble will really come and suffocate the city.

And then I feel someone watching me.

I peer down into the darkness, but with the trees growing beyond control in our eternal summer, I can't see anything. But I know I'm not wrong. Someone is out there.

My mind shifts to Shayne. He'd been pushed to the back of my mind when Reese was here earlier. But now, with the memory of Reese fading, Shayne begins to resurface. He's a total mystery. I've spoken so little to him but have this burning desire to get to know him better. Like the red specks in his eyes hold secrets he wants to share with me. I want the eyes out in the darkness to be his. I want him to beckon me out in the darkness. I imagine he touches me, and I don't stop him. I want to find someone I can be with forever, and I wonder if Shayne is the one. Or is it Reese? A shiver runs down me when I think about him, and I don't try to force it away.

As quickly as it came, the presence vanishes, leaving me once again alone with the darkness of the night. I shake my head. Whoever was out there is gone. And I'm left with only my daydreams.

I head to my bed, but a slip of paper on the nightstand catches my eye. I pick it up, unfolding it, and then hold my breath.

I read the letter three times through until the paper is shaking so hard, I can't see the words anymore. My father. He's found us. He's been searching for us since he broke out of prison, and now he finally knows where we are. He's come into our house. Come into my room. He could come back at any time, even when I'm here. Dread punches me in the stomach as I think about it.

I fold the paper and prepare to head to my mom's room and tell her, but I stop when my hand touches the doorknob. My mom isn't talking to me. She's upset about my tattoo. And if that upsets her, this letter from my father will push her over the edge. My pseudo-normal life will end. Right here and now.

It frightens me way more than the letter from my terrorist father.

I tear the letter into tiny little pieces, wash it down my sink, and head to bed. I hope for sleep to take over, but my brain seems to have a different idea. I wish for dreams of mysterious guys, but my night is sleepless. Girls with empty eye sockets fill my mind. Heat bubbles smother the city. And when I try to imagine my father, he has no face.

The next day I walk into Social Sciences, but my heart sinks when I see Shayne's not there. I head to my normal seat and sit down, forcing myself not to look at the vacant seat next to me. At least today, I'm on time; my mom hasn't called me all day, which gives me a weird feeling of guilt mixed with independence.

I catch movement near the door out of my peripheral vision; it's him. I stare straight ahead and pretend I haven't noticed, which is about as easy as pretending I'm blind. My heart is pounding, but I look directly ahead.

Please let him sit next to me. It's a silent prayer, and I'm not sure whom I'm even praying to, but whoever it is doesn't listen. Shayne sits far to the left against the wall. My face burns, but I try to keep any sign of emotion off it. The last thing I want is him thinking I am looking for him, which I am; let's face it. When I dare to glance over, he's not even looking at me. Instead, he's staring straight ahead with a look on his face like he wants to kill someone.

Mr. Kaiser starts the lecture by talking about the missiles. He's been in contact with the members of the International GHC Committee who have conclusive proof that each time a missile is detonated, it strips a thin layer from the atmosphere. He tells us he's written a letter to the city council and encourages us each to do the same. But given Councilman Rendon's attitude, I doubt a letter will have much impact.

Mr. Kaiser then makes us come up with reasons why Earth is in a crisis state, but the sad fact is no one really knows. Sure, there are plenty of theories, but they're only that. Theories. None are proven, and there are new ones every day. The fact is winter has stopped coming. Leaves never fall from trees. The earth is in a dying cycle of drought and flooding with sea levels rising around the world. I've heard summer used to be a good thing. But all I've ever seen it as is a death sentence for Earth.

It's why my mom starts a greenhouse wherever we move. She says it's her contribution to keeping the earth healthy. To keep the smaller species of plants from going extinct. To replenish them after the trees grew big and blocked their water and sun. To help preserve the big trees for when they eventually die out, too. My mom really does care about the earth. Sometimes, she talks like eternal summer is something the world should embrace, but at the same time, she does whatever she can to help things return to normal. A normal that I've never known, since it's been summer my whole life.

I manage to zone out for the rest of lecture, and blessedly, Mr. Kaiser doesn't call on me. When class ends, I look toward Shayne, hoping he'll be looking at me, but he's already gone. He must have been the first one out of the classroom.

"Nice tattoo."

I look up and see it's Randy Conner. He's standing there with his girlfriend, Hannah Reed, who's got one hand wrapped around his arm and the other crossed over her stomach.

"Don't tell me your mom really let you get one," Hannah says.

"Not quite." Randy and Hannah don't normally talk to me; I never knew getting a tattoo would get me attention from the in crowd.

"No way," Randy says. "You actually went behind her back?" Randy lives next door to the Botanical Haven. He of all people knows how overprotective my mom is. Four years ago, when we first moved in, he tried to come over and talk to me. My mom ended that before it started, threatening to peel the skin from his back if he so much as set foot near the brick fence. Needless to say, Randy never again came by to talk to me. And he told the entire school my mom was a psychopathic lunatic which, whether it was true or not, wasn't cool at all. It certainly didn't make starting at a public school very easy.

I nod, loving how his words reaffirm my rebellion. I did go behind her back.

"And you got away with it?" Hannah turns to Randy. "I want to get one."

"Your mom would kill you," he says.

Am I really not the only one in the world whose mom is overprotective?

"There wasn't much she could do once I got it," I say, and I realize the power of a tattoo. Unless I get cosmetic removal, it's there to stay.

"Awesome," Randy says. "But you're not getting one now," he adds to Hannah, and they move on out of the room.

I pick up my backpack and head for the door.

"Yeah, nice tattoo."

Shayne is there outside the classroom. Waiting for me. I almost drop my backpack I'm so shocked by the sound of his voice. The way he says *nice* sounds like it holds a thousand different meanings, all of which I like. But the best part is he's saying it to me.

"Thanks." I attempt to think of something else to say, but nothing comes to mind.

"I waited for you," he says.

He waited for me. I record the words in my mind so I can play them over and over later. "I see that."

His smile makes me want to just stand there staring at him, but then he gestures with his head down the hallway. "Can I walk you to class?"

"I have Study Hall," I say before I can think about how irrelevant that is.

Shayne reaches out and takes my backpack off my shoulder. "Okay, can I walk you there?"

"Sure." I work to keep my voice calm, like I'm not over-the-moon that I'm being walked to class by the most gorgeous guy in the world. We turn the corner, and at least seven other girls stare our way. I pretend I don't notice though I can't believe he's actually picked me to walk with. I keep wanting to glance over at him to make sure he doesn't disappear, but manage to control myself.

I wrack my brain and finally think of a conversation starter. "What'd you think of the lecture today?"

God, that's so lame.

Shayne shifts the backpack so it's on his other arm. This leaves his hand dangerously close to mine.

"Tedious," he says.

"Tell me about it," I say. "If I have to hear Mr. Kaiser discuss conspiracy theory for this entire month, I'm going to pull my hair out."

Shayne stops walking, so of course I do, too. And he reaches up and takes a piece of my hair between his fingers. "Please don't. It's so beautiful."

And I'm left speechless once again.

He lets go of my hair. "I hear you have plans on Friday."

He's heard about my plans? Reese must've told him. Maybe they're friends. I nod and avert my eyes, hoping he doesn't see what I'm really thinking. I want it to be him instead. I want him to be the one who's asked me to sneak out.

He touches my tattoo, and the shock from his touch travels up my arm and through my body, sending chills to places I only think about once the lights are out.

"It's Greek," Shayne says.

"Chloe says it means *surrender*. We both got one." My heart is pounding so hard, I'm sure he can hear it.

"Sacrifice," he says.

I look down at his hand. "What?"

He traces a letter with his index finger. "It says *sacrifice*."

"You know Greek?" Is that the best thing I can think of to say?

Shayne nods, and his black hair settles on his shoulders. "Sure. Doesn't everyone?"

"It's not really the most common language to learn."

"Well, it should be." He rubs his thumb across the tattoo, and I know he's feeling the raised skin underneath.

I stop breathing and try to keep the light smile on my face though my knees are about to collapse.

"I like it." He rubs the tattoo a final time and gives

my arm a squeeze, and then he lets go. "Have fun on your date," he says, and the happiness evaporates from his face.

"Thanks." I'm not sure what other response I can possibly give. The electricity from his touch still pumps inside me, and I hope it will never go away.

"Be careful. Okay?" His brown eyes darken, and the look on his face from class returns like he wants to tear someone limb from limb. But then he blinks, and it fades.

Careful? "Do I need to be?" I say it half in jest and half not.

Shayne nods. "Yeah, Piper. You do."

Anticipation and nerves blend together and flutter in my stomach. "Oh."

He opens his mouth as if he's about to say something else, but then shuts it again.

"What?" I say.

He shakes his head. "Nothing."

So I start walking again, but I'm not two steps forward when he puts his hand on my arm and stops me.

I turn and face him.

"Maybe we can get together sometime." His eyes don't leave mine as he speaks.

My heart's going crazy inside my chest. I'm about to pass out. "That sounds nice." I focus on each word, making sure they come out clearly.

His mouth turns up at the sides. "Maybe coffee."

I nod and decide against using my mom as an excuse. I skipped school to get a tattoo. I can certainly find a way to sneak in a cup of coffee. "Coffee is great."

I hope he'll suggest right now, but he doesn't. He only turns and starts walking again. And we walk the rest of the way to Study Hall in silence.

Shayne hands me my backpack at the door, and I sling it over my shoulder. I wonder how he'll say goodbye. I wonder if he'll name a time for us to get together.

He doesn't. He makes it simple. "See ya," he says. And in his simplicity I can't help but feel I ruined my chances with him. Maybe it was up to me to suggest a time.

"Yeah, see ya," I say, and I watch as he turns and walks away. I don't move until he disappears from my sight.

Chapter 7

Bathroom

Before I head into the library, I duck into the bathroom. There's no way I can handle Study Hall yet. My legs are about to collapse under me, and I'm sweating so much, a trickle moves down my cleavage. I drop my backpack and lean against the sink, scanning my FON to turn on the water. There are two temperatures. Warm and hot. I go with the warm and splash it on my face, closing my eyes, letting it wash over me. When it times out, I turn it on again, doing this until my heart slows down. I don't care that water has gotten in my hair. It's pulled back anyway and tied with the red ribbon.

"Do you know your fate?"

I freeze at the sound of Tanni's voice, and my chest tightens. I look up, but there's no one in the mirror. Only me, water dripping off my face, staring back. I don't stop looking, and my calmed heart has started beating so hard I feel the pulsing in my neck. Her soulless eyes are on me, staring at me. I feel them even if I don't see her.

"Do you know your fate?"

I turn, whipping around to see Tanni, empty eye

sockets and all, staring back at me. She's been there the whole time, behind me as I washed my face. Watching me with those vacant eyes.

"Why are you asking me that?"

Tanni shrugs, and bracelets on her arms jingle, the sound filling the emptiness of the bathroom. "It's my job. It's what I do."

"Does this have something to do with your global warming protest?" I ask even though I know it doesn't. Why would my fate have anything to do with the Global Heating Crisis?

She smiles and shows her teeth. They're white—almost glowing. I can nearly see through them, but I try not to stare. But not being able to look at her eyes or her mouth, I'm running out of places to focus.

"Not today," she says, licking her lips. And she takes a step closer to me.

I back against the sink. There's nowhere left for me to go.

"Who are you?" I manage to say. My throat's dry, and the water I splashed on my face is gone, replaced by a thin layer of sweat.

She takes another step toward me, and I think she's going to grab me again. I pull my arms behind me and use them to prop myself up on the sink. I could jump up and kick her and run out. But my feet are rooted to the hard tile floor compelling me to stay.

"I'm your friend," Tanni says, and she rests her hand

on my shoulder. "I want you to always believe that."

She's close enough now I can stare into where her eyes should be, and I see mist swirling behind the half-closed eyelids. She opens her lips, and mist churns inside her mouth. She leans toward me and tilts her head, and for a second, I think she's going to kiss me. But then she exhales, and the mist pours out, filling the space between us. Filling the bathroom.

I can't help but breathe it in. It's sweet, like cotton candy, and it enters my lungs, and I feel myself grow weak. I almost fall, but Tanni catches me and holds me by both shoulders. My knees wobble under me, and I can't take my eyes off her face.

"Chloe will die."

She says it as she breathes out the mist. It echoes around the room, though it's only a whisper. *Chloe will die. Chloe will die.* Around me, it bounces off the walls, taunting me.

"No," I say. Chloe is my best friend. Young. Healthy. Chloe is not going to die.

"Chloe will die."

The echoes continue, like a chorus of dead souls taking turns with a riddle.

This must be some kind of joke.

"Chloe will not die." I shout, even though it's only me and Tanni in the bathroom. Me and Tanni and the chorus of voices around us.

"Chloe will die."

Why won't she stop saying it? "No!" I scream, and instantly, the voices stop, and the fog disappears. Tanni lets go of my shoulders, and I collapse to the floor, hitting my head on the sink as I fall. I'm all alone.

Chapter 8

Opportunity

I'm not sure how much time passes before some freshman finds me in the bathroom and takes me to the nurse's office. The nurse bandages my head, and he sends me home on a school shuttle. I spend the whole time convincing myself that Tanni doesn't exist. She's just some far-fetched part of my mind playing out my worst fears. I tell myself Chloe won't die.

When I get home, my mom rushes over and hugs me. I fall into her arms, and I can't hold back my tears. I let them come, flowing out of my eyes with sobs so loud, the gash on my head pounds with each one. She holds me, never saying a word. Never asking a question. She locks the front door and leads me upstairs, takes my ponytail out, and helps me get into the chem-shower and change into my pajamas.

It's only when I finish getting dressed, and she pours me a deep glass of red wine and we sit in the family room that either of us speaks. I take a sip, waiting for the familiar relaxation in my veins. My mom has been proclaiming the life-giving powers of wine for as long as I can remember. She claims it's a gift from the earth herself and grows grapes downstairs just to be able to make it. My mom watches me, never taking her eyes off me.

"I'm so sorry." I don't even try to explain or make excuses. "I'm so sorry for everything." I feel the tears threaten to start again. I'm not even sure what I'm sorry for. I just know that I am.

"Shhhh…" She comes around and sits next to me on the rattan sofa. I lean into her and let her put her arm around me.

"I'm sorry." I say it again, this time managing to control the tears. It just feels so good to be here with her, knowing she still loves me.

She doesn't say anything, and I realize she's rubbing my arm, moving her fingers over my fresh tattoo. I tense up, but none of the plants in the room seem to be dying which I take as a good sign.

"It's nice," she finally says. "I like it."

I wipe my face and turn toward her. "You do?"

She nods. "It makes you even more beautiful."

I sniff, feeling relief course through me. I've done it. I've done something for myself and my mom isn't mad. "Chloe got one just like it."

"It says *sacrifice*," my mom says. "Interesting choice."

I nod, wondering if I'm the only person on the planet who doesn't know Greek, but a sob catches in my throat when I remember Tanni from the bathroom. *Chloe will die.* She'd said it over and over.

"What?"

My mom's eyes are fixed on me, but I don't want to tell her about Tanni. She'll think I'm too weak to handle the world without her. How could it have happened anyway? It's not natural. It's not possible. And I'm not losing my mind.

"Do you believe in fate?" I ask.

My mom's face freezes, and her eyes look away from mine. "What kind of fate?"

I'm not really sure even though I asked the question. "Do you think people can know the future?" It's the best I can come up with.

"Your future?"

I shake my head. "No. Anyone's future. Do you think there are people who know what will happen?"

My mom hesitates before answering. "No. The future's uncertain. People are too complex and can act in too many different ways."

I let out the breath I've held since I asked the question. I don't want to believe in fate either.

"I saw you on the tube yesterday," I say.

"The council meeting." My mom stiffens next to me. "They're going to destroy the earth."

"It's the missiles, isn't it?"

My mom stands and walks over to crack open a window. The heat filters through, but now there's a cross breeze in the room. "It's everything. Councilman Rendon is lying. He's deceiving the city for his own personal gain."

"I could tell," I say. I don't mention the green fungus I saw covering him, but I think that's what the fungus was showing me—his selfish desires for power. "He avoided the question."

"He's suppressing the results," my mom says. "His only concern is the election and to hell with the fate of the earth."

"Why don't you say something?" I can't stand by and watch everything I love be ruined by lies.

My mom leans back against the counter and runs her hands through her hair, and in that moment she looks so vulnerable. "Don't you think I have, Piper? I've brought my concerns to the mayor, but he won't listen either. It's like they can't see beyond the boundaries of Austin. As long as they shove their city under those stupid domes, they could give a rat's ass what else happens."

I pat the sofa beside me, and my mom sits back down.

"I'm sorry," she says. "I shouldn't get so upset."

"Yeah, mom, you should. If there's anything worth getting upset about it's the fact that they're killing the earth." Not about tattoos, I think to myself, but I leave that unsaid. "So what are you going to do about it?"

My mom studies me. Her eyes scan over me from the gash in my hair to deep into my soul. And then she finally answers. "There's nothing I can do, Piper. I think we just need to resign ourselves to our fate."

It's a peculiar answer considering she just told me she didn't believe in fate. And something about the way she looks away makes me think she's keeping something from me. Like maybe she has some sort of idea how to fix things that I'm not privy to.

I suddenly let out a yawn I don't even know I've been keeping in and realize I can hardly keep my eyes open.

"You're tired, Piper Rose."

I nod and curl into her embrace. My eyelids are reminding me I didn't sleep last night.

We sit in silence, and the wine does its job, relaxing me, calming me. Here, with my mom's arms around me, I believe things are once again as they should be. And with her accepting my tattoo, I believe she will actually let me make more choices in my life.

"You'd never leave me, would you, Piper?"

Her words reach my ears clearly, but it takes a second for my brain to process them.

"What?"

She rubs my arm, and holds me closer. "You're all I have, Piper. You're everything to me." Her hands stop rubbing and press into my shoulder. "I'd die without you."

All at once, every muscle which the wine had previously relaxed tenses up. And I realize my mom will never let me make my own choices. "Why would you ask that, Mom?"

As if she's caught herself, her hand starts rubbing again. "I just want you to know how much I love you, Piper."

I try to settle back into her arms, but my muscles still feel tight. "I know you love me, Mom."

"I do, Piper."

I don't respond. There's nothing to say.

"And you'll never leave me, will you, Piper?"

Her question makes me want to run away and leave her right then. To open the door and never come back. "Of course not, Mom."

"I'm glad, Piper."

I'm about to drift off when my mom's voice stirs me.

"There's one more thing, Piper."

"What?"

She gets up and walks over to one of the cabinets, and when I notice her hands shaking, I sit up. She opens the door and gets something and sets it on the coffee table in front of me. It's my box. The one Melina gave me. My face freezes, and I stare at her. I'm wide awake now.

"Where did you get this?" She asks it slowly, not taking her eyes off me.

I hold her gaze. Sure, I've hidden the box, but I haven't done anything wrong. "It was a present." I look at the box, reach over for it, but she pulls it away.

"A present from whom?"

My first reaction is to lie. To tell her Chloe gave it to me. But I'm a terrible liar. "From one of our customers."

She presses her lips together and looks down at the box, drawing her hands back as if she doesn't want to touch it.

But I, on the other hand, really want to touch its black surface. To run my hands over the engraved red symbols on the top and sides. The hammer and the birds and the flames, which seem to sparkle under the fluorescent lights.

"Which customer?"

I shrug. "You know—that girl with all the corn rows."

My mom looks back up at me. "Have I met her?"

I know the answer is no. Melina comes on Sundays and only when my mom's out getting seeds.

"I guess not. But she's really nice and always takes the time to talk."

My mom scowls.

"What's the big deal anyway? Why shouldn't I get a present?"

My mom reaches down, but instead of keeping her hand away from the box, she rubs it, almost caresses it. "Did you open it?"

I nod, glad she's going to accept it. "Yeah."

"And…?"

"And what?" I reach for the box, and this time, she lets me take it, sliding it over toward me. It warms under my touch, and the etched birds seem to shimmer and come to life.

"Was there anything in it?" She's looking at me like she knows the answer. But I don't want to tell her about the feather.

I shake my head and lie. "It was empty." I lift the lid, and she flinches, but I hold the box open and show her the inside. It is void of anything except its ebony interior.

For a moment, my mom has stopped breathing, but she does look inside. "Are you sure?"

I nod. "Yeah, sure." Why is my mom so interested?

"Okay, then." My mom is apparently going to let this box thing go.

I relax and scoot it away, not wanting to put it aside, but at the same time, not wanting my mom to see my interest in it.

"I need to go away this weekend," she says out of nowhere.

It's nothing new; we've gone on trips before, sometimes for the council, sometimes to buy plants. "Where are we going?"

But my mom shakes her head. "I'm going alone."

"What about me?" My mom's never left me alone before.

She gives me a weak smile. "You'll stay here."

My heart stops in my chest. She can't be serious. Me. Stay alone? Without my mom? Is it some kind of test? Is she trying to see what I will do given the chance?

"I'll make sure there's enough food so you don't even have to leave."

"When?" I manage to say, hoping that, of all the mixed feelings going through me, she doesn't hear the anticipation in my voice. I force my face to remain calm, though I'm not sure if I succeed.

"Friday morning," she says. "I'll get back on Monday."

Friday. It's the night I'm supposed to sneak out with Reese. And, like the Fates are rearranging my life, now I won't even have to sneak out. I can do whatever I want. Thinking about it makes my palms sweaty. My mom would kill me if she knew what I had planned.

"You'll be fine," she says like she's trying to convince herself. "If you need help, you can go over to Chloe's."

"Where are you going?" I'm not sure I can think of a situation extreme enough for my mom to leave me alone.

My mom looks away. "I have business to take care of."

"What kind of business?"

She doesn't want to tell me; I'm sure of it. And the more she doesn't want to tell me, the more I want to know.

"You better get to bed," she says.

"What kind of business, Mom?"

"Why does it matter?"

"Because I want to know."

My mom looks at me a final time then looks away. "Family business."

"What family?" My chest tightens. It has to be my father.

"I have things to talk about with your father."

I act surprised. "My father?"

She nods.

"Where?" I'm trying to keep my voice calm.

"It doesn't matter. What matters is that he doesn't find out where you are. And I plan to make absolutely certain he doesn't."

An eerie chill runs though me. The father I've never known. My mom said he'd left when she was pregnant. That he got involved in some terrorist group and got thrown in prison after they blew up some giant water still being built in Nevada. Hundreds of people died in the explosion, and he was the person named responsible. He went to prison without even trying to deny his actions, and then he escaped less than a year later. And now, my mom's planning to run off and meet with him alone?

"I should go with you," I say, though the thought makes me queasy. His note had been nothing short of cloaked threats.

"No. You shouldn't."

"But he could hurt you," I say.

My mom gives me a small smile. "I'm the one who's supposed to protect you. Not the other way around."

I open my mouth to argue again, but my mom stops me.

"Go to bed. You have school tomorrow."

Chapter 9

Plans

Even though I'm running late, I take my time, walking through what used to be the parking lot when I get to school. A couple years ago, the city council finally tore up the blacktop and attempted to plant some native greenery. Global Warming kills the atmosphere, so cars are taxed and restricted, and now most people don't drive, which means a parking lot at a high school is no longer necessary, especially one made of blistering, black asphalt. Sometimes Chloe waits for me here in the mornings, but today she must already be in class like I know I should be.

I check the thermometers before I go in and resync my FON to match it. At one hundred and nine, we shouldn't have to worry about another heat bubble today. Maybe not all weekend. The reporters must be wrong. And I can hardly believe my mom is actually going away. I mean, this has never happened. I head into school and pass the bathroom, thinking of Tanni, wishing she'd been a figment manifested from the deep recesses of my mind. But I touch the tender bump on my head. The blood's scabbed over into a thin line which my curly hair hides—even in a ponytail. But it still hurts, and I know the bathroom—and Tanni—were real.

Shayne's not in Social Sciences. I try not to spend the entire time wondering where he is. And in truth, I'm thinking more about Chloe. I haven't talked to her since the tattoo parlor. I can't get the words *Chloe will die* out of my mind. Or the image of Tanni's empty eye sockets. And so, as soon as the bell rings, I look at no one, stop nowhere, and head to Study Hall.

Chloe's there, waiting for me.

"What happened? I must've tried to text you a hundred times." She jumps up from her chair and rushes over before I even get to the table.

I push the image of Tanni out of my mind. But her horrible words won't budge. *Chloe will die.* "Nothing."

"Nothing! I heard you got sent home yesterday. That you bumped your head."

I nod. "I slipped in the bathroom. It was nothing." I pull aside my hair so she can see the scab.

Chloe looks at it. "They sent you home for that?"

"Yeah. I think I passed out. Some freshman found me."

Chloe lets go and walks back over to the table. "I'm so glad it wasn't something serious."

I smile and nod, but Tanni's haunting eyes come back to me, burned into my mind, and I think it was serious. "Yeah, me too. How'd you find out?"

Chloe's eyes get a dreamy look. "Reese told me. This morning in Physics."

How did Reese know? I haven't talked to him since he came by. My chest spasms; I need to tell Chloe about my plans.

"My mom's leaving town this weekend." I say it casually, but as soon as the words are out, my stomach starts flipping.

Chloe drops the stylus she's picked up. She hasn't started studying. Neither of us gets much studying done during Study Hall. "No. Way."

I nod and bite my lower lip. "Yeah. She leaves Friday morning."

"Oh. My. God." Chloe's excitement is infectious.

But I don't want the whole school to know. "Shhhh!" The kids sitting two tables over have stopped writing and look at us.

"Piper, do you realize how huge this is? What are we going to do?"

The flipping in my stomach continues. "She told me to stay home all weekend."

Chloe rolls her eyes. "I didn't ask what she told you to do. I asked what we're going to do."

"Chloe…"

"What?" Her eyelids lower, and her eyes narrow. She knows I don't plan to sit around watering the plants all weekend.

"I have to tell you something. I swear I don't know

how this happened and I have no clue how to get out of it." Or if I want to get out of it.

"Out of what?" she says.

I sigh and make a silent wish she won't hate me forever. "I think I got asked out for Friday night." I whisper it because I really can't believe it myself. And even if it's not Shayne, I've still never been anywhere with a guy alone.

"Like on a date?"

"Shhhh!"

"Shayne?" At least she lowers her voice.

I shake my head, though now that she voices it, I'm torn between wanting it to be Reese and wanting it to be Shayne. I can't believe Shayne wasn't in class today.

"Then who?"

"Reese." I can barely get the name out, and I watch her face to gauge her reaction.

The smile stays on Chloe's face though it falls into a shadow of itself. "Wow. Reese."

I realize Chloe is giving me the excuse I need because, as each minute brings me closer to Friday, my stomach tightens from nerves. Or excitement. At this point, I'm not very clear. "I'm going to tell him I can't go. I'll tell him I have other plans."

Her eyes are moist, but she's fighting to hold back her hurt. "He talks to me the entire class. He seems so interested," she says.

"He should be," I say. "He's an idiot if he's not."

Chloe sits there, looking down at the table. I squeeze her hand, but she doesn't return the gesture.

"I'll tell him I can't make it."

But finally Chloe shakes her head, and her face brightens back to some semblance of what it was before. "No. No, you need to go. You've never been on a date."

I lean close. "I don't mind. I don't really want to go."

"You have to go." Her smile is halfhearted, but still there.

"No, really. I'll tell him I have to study."

Chloe blows out a breath. "Please, Piper. Do you realize how huge this is?"

I nod, realizing also how much trouble I'll be in if my mom ever finds out.

"I'll come over beforehand. I can help you get ready."

I look and see Chloe's eyes have returned to normal, happiness shining through her. Like she really is happy for me somewhere inside. And Tanni's horrible words come back to me hard.

Chloe will die.

It can't be right. Not now. Chloe's only eighteen like me. She's got her whole life ahead of her. The whole thing was a dream. Or a nightmare. And just not real.

I smile. "Are you sure? Because I don't mind—"

Chloe puts up her hand. "Don't say another word about it. So how about Saturday?"

Saturday. I haven't even thought that far in advance. "How about it?"

"Let's go somewhere. Let's do something fun."

"Like what?" I ask.

Chloe shrugs. "Leave that to me. So where's she going?"

I lower my voice and spit it out. "She's going to see my father."

Chloe's eyes shoot open. "Your father?"

I nod.

"You know where he is?" she asks.

"No. But apparently my mom does. And she's not bringing me along."

"So will you get to meet him?"

I shrug, because even though everything I know about him tells me I should stay far away, I do want to meet him. "I'm not sure." And then I tell her about the note. Even though I've destroyed the piece of paper, the words are etched in my mind.

"He asked what frightened you? God, that's creepy."

"Yeah," I say.

"Piper, the whole note sounds creepy." She brings her hand to her tattoo and feels the skin underneath. The same way I've been doing. "He'll be seeing you soon?"

She's confirmed my exact thoughts, and heaviness pushes into my mind. "Why can't I just have a normal family like yours? Why is it that, after eighteen years of running from some phantom father, he really does have to turn out to be as bad as my mom's told me?"

Chloe grabs my hand. "You don't need him. You've been fine without him this long. Let your mom go away, do whatever she needs to do. We'll go off and have our fun, and then things can just be normal."

I laugh. Like things have ever been normal. Still, Chloe can be pretty convincing when she wants to be.

"So she'll be back…?"

"Monday," I say.

Chloe clasps her hands together in front of her. "We are going to have so much fun."

I know she's right. My mom will take care of my father. He'll stay out of our lives. And Chloe will not die. Tanni was a figment of my imagination. People don't walk around with fog in their eye sockets spouting gloom and doom fortunes. It's just not the way life is.

Chapter 10

Date

I peek outside at ten o'clock on Friday night and see Reese staring up at my window. The fact that he knows exactly which window is mine is both creepy and flattering. I try to focus on the flattering part.

I open the front door and call to him. "Hey."

His eyes shift in my direction. "Hey."

"My mom's gone for the weekend," I say. Maybe it's not the smartest thing to tell him, but my rush of freedom is controlling my mind.

A grin forms on his face like he's just found a way to fix the lottery. "That is perfect."

He walks up the steps to the door, and I notice he's carrying a bundle of pink calla lilies. At first, I think he's brought me a potted plant, but when he moves his hands forward, I see they're clipped at the stems. I can't help the shock that registers on my face. There are huge penalties for being caught with cut flowers. Not to mention if my mom sees these, she'll freak.

But my mom's not here.

"I brought you flowers." He looks past me into the Botanical Haven like he's making sure I'm really alone.

Chloe left fifteen minutes ago; I don't know if I should invite him in.

"They're illegal," I say, which I know sounds so goody-goody, but he's breaking the law. Once they're cut, they don't help the atmosphere.

"No one will see them." He looks down at the flowers. "And they reminded me of you."

"Dead?" I say before I can stop myself. Because that's what cut flowers are. Dead flowers.

Reese cups one of the blooms with his hand. "Fresh. Vibrant. Exciting." And the way he holds the flower hints at how he feels about me.

"Thank you," I say. "I love them." And in that moment, they become more than just cut flowers. They become a symbol of something forbidden. I move aside, and he takes this as his cue to enter.

Reese passes the flowers to me, and I catch their scent. With it, I catch his aroma. Same as before, but stronger. Red wine. Thick and dry. Powerful yet velvety smooth. Like a Merlot or a Cabernet. I close my eyes and take a deep inhale, pretending I'm smelling the flowers. But really it's Reese I want more of. His overriding fragrance that's making me forget everything but his wonderful presence. I take another breath and know I need to open my eyes. When I do, he's staring at me.

I find a vase for the calla lilies and set them on the counter. When I turn, he's behind me, close to me. So close I can hardly move.

"God, you look gorgeous."

Chloe told me the same thing. Well, maybe not in those exact words. She helped me pick out the dress— thin spaghetti straps holding up black cotton fabric which reaches to just above my knees. Red designs swirl on the black from the waist down.

Reese takes a step back and looks at me—up and down. He takes in each part of me, and I feel like I'm being savored. One piece at a time. It makes me feel like I actually am gorgeous and exciting like he said. By the time he reaches my feet, even in the humid air, I'm shaking, and I never want him to take his eyes off me even though they're revealing something almost feral.

He steps close and brushes my cheek with his hand. "You're nervous."

Nervous minimizes how I'm feeling. "Not at all," I say.

"I like that you're nervous."

Before I can respond, he leans his face forward and brushes his lips against mine. Just a hint of a kiss, but it sends all sorts of crazy shivers down through me. My very first kiss.

This is life without my mom around.

It's exhilarating.

He pulls away and increases the distance between us, and his smile reaches his eyes.

"So where are we going?" I place my hands on the counter behind me and try to calm the quivering emotions running through me. I decide I should breathe through my mouth until I can get the scent of Reese's body out of my nostrils.

He shrugs. "Anywhere."

"That's a start," I say.

"We could climb the steel struts of the dome," he suggests.

I don't know if he's serious, but I don't want to fall to my death at the age of eighteen. "I'm not sure I'm up for that."

"Okay, then. How about we break into the city planetarium and have a picnic under the stars?"

I laugh because I know he must be kidding. "Tempting. But maybe something less…"

"Illegal?" he suggests.

"Yeah. Less illegal."

It's like Reese actually has to consider this. "Legal is normally boring."

"How about dinner?" I say. "Will that be too boring?" I've eaten little to nothing in the last week, and I've never been out to dinner with anyone besides my mom or Chloe.

"Dinner," Reese says. "I can work with that."

Reese has a car. I'm not sure how he got the permit for it; they're mostly reserved for CEOs, and senators, and even some of the members of the council though most of them opt out. I've been in cars a handful of times but haven't set foot in one for at least five years.

Reese opens the door for me and helps me get in. His car's low to the ground, black, and kind of reminds me of a cockroach. But the leather seats inside engulf my body, and I try to relax.

"It won't start unless the belts are done." He reaches across me, and his arm brushes my chest as he clips the belt secure.

I try not to flinch, but shivers run up my neck, and I think of his kiss. Then he moves his arm away and shuts the door. I feel eyes on me as he walks around to the other side. Not Reese's eyes. Someone is watching me. My mind flashes to Tanni and her soulless eyes. Her words come to me. I try to push them away, but they're too fast. *Chloe will die.*

"What?" Reese is already in the car and fastening his own belt.

I try to erase thoughts of Tanni from my mind. "What what?" I say.

"You look like you saw a ghost."

I shake my head. I'm half-tempted to tell Reese about Tanni, but I know anything I say will sound crazy. "I guess I am a little nervous."

Reese puts his hand on mine, and his warmth erases Tanni's words. "And gorgeous."

Driving on the streets of downtown Austin at night is a far different experience than taking the shuttle during the day. For starters, his car is self-powered and doesn't have to stay on any kind of track like the shuttles. Reese turns down streets I've never even seen, taking us through the park and behind the theatre which is lit up like a torch despite energy restrictions. And second, it seems on Friday nights, every person who lives here is outside, walking in the streets, heading into bars. Reese swerves around pedestrians until he finally pulls onto the bridge that takes us across the river. The city thermometer reads ninety-nine, and I can understand why there are so many people outside. With as hot as the days are, relief from the sun is a gift.

Reese stops on Sixth Street in front of a valet station, which clues me in to the fact that we're not headed to your average restaurant. We get out, and he tips someone to take the car. Given it's such a primo opportunity, two guys argue over who gets to drive it until Reese finally points at one of them. "You."

The argument drops. The kid Reese pointed at jumps in the driver's seat, and the car disappears around the corner. We walk into an old hotel and take an elevator to the top floor. The air's probably fifteen degrees cooler in here meaning they must have real A/C. Or illegal A/C. I try not to look around and stare at everything. But I notice every detail's been precisely chosen. The black and white tiles. The golden walls. The bronze statues of Greek gods on pedestals in the middle of the walkway.

Before I know it, we've reached a hostess stand. The hostess tries to tell us the restaurant is full, but Reese pulls out a bill and hands it to her; she smiles at him like he's an angel and tells us a spot just came open. The sardonic smile she gives me tells me I'm not good enough to be here with Reese. Like she should be the one on a date. But she's not. She's only the hostess. Still, I don't want to blink and wake up. I want to continue to defy my mom. And even though Chloe should be here in my place, a horrible part of me loves that I'm out with Reese. That he's chosen me.

The hostess takes us to a table in the back near a window overlooking the city where I can see the Capitol and four of the dome structures extending into the sky. I wonder how different it looked last weekend when the domes were sealed.

"Nice view," I say. "Good thing they were able to fit us in."

Reese sets his elbows on the table, interlacing his fingers. "Bribery works every time. Watch. They won't even card us."

Sure enough, a sommelier comes over with a wine menu and begins to make some suggestions, but Reese puts up his hand and orders a bottle of aged Chianti. I know the wine must cost a fortune; grapes are so rare these days. But, like everything else, this doesn't seem to be an issue with Reese. The sommelier nods and moves away, taking the wine menu with him.

I've certainly had wine before with my mom. But when the sommelier comes back with the bottle, shows it to Reese, and then uncorks it, I still can't believe we didn't get carded. Reese samples the bottle, nods, and tips the guy. I'm starting to notice a pattern. Large tips get you treated like a god.

Reese pours a glass and pushes it my way. I pick up the tall glass by the stem and dare to sniff it. It mixes with the aroma coming from Reese, and I realize I want to relax—to quench the flurry of excitement running through me, so I take a sip and sit back.

The wine does its job. It inches its way through my body, mixing with the butterflies in my stomach until the butterflies mellow and the wine settles in. I have a hard time making eye contact with Reese or even with the waiter, but I don't mind. Just being out and away from my mom is intoxicating by itself.

Reese keeps trying to ply me for information about my life. When I try to explain my mom's compulsive nature, he nods. "Like my mother."

I shake my head. "No. My mom is way worse. She never lets me do anything."

He raises an eyebrow. "Anything?"

I smile and take a bite of my steak, licking the juice off my lips. "Nothing." I point to the steak. "She doesn't even eat meat."

"So I'm your first date."

"You're laughing at me," I say.

He feigns shock. "Never." He raises his hand, calling the sommelier over, and orders another bottle of

Chianti.

I ignore the stray thought that runs through my mind. That I wish I were on a date with Shayne instead. But he hadn't asked me. Reese had. And here I am.

"I'm not allowed to date," I say.

"Why? What is your mom afraid you'll do?"

"Maybe have fun?"

Reese laughs. "Because having fun is bad, right?"

I shrug. "She just doesn't want me to be away from her. She's kind of possessive that way."

Reese nods. It's a truthful if not complete answer. But I see no need to mention my father or go deeper into my dysfunctional family situation.

"There was this time when I was little," he says. "My sister and I got into this fight."

"You have a sister?"

"Yeah. Unfortunately. She's been a pain in the ass since the minute she sprang into existence."

I'd be happy to have a sister, pain in the ass or not. "What did you guys fight about?"

Reese shifts back in his seat, and I can almost see him recollecting in his eyes. "It was when she was first allowed to do things without our parents. She was always tagging along. Wanted to do every single thing I wanted to do."

"That doesn't sound so bad." Chloe had told me how she'd been the same way when she was little.

He lifts his glass and takes another sip, so I do the

same. "Yeah, at first it was kind of cute. But then she stole all my friends. Turned them against me."

"I hardly believe that."

But he's not smiling, and I realize he's not kidding.

The memory seems to shift back to one of humor. "So we started this whole practical joke thing."

Which again to me sounds like fun. "My mom's not big on jokes. She probably hasn't laughed in ten years."

"Be thankful," he says. "First my sister took every single one of my toys and melted them. She was brutal. She burned down my tree house and blamed it on lightning."

With global warming, fire is so against the law, the smallest penalty is five years. I arch my eyebrows to encourage him to continue.

"So I shaved her head one night when she was asleep."

The image is a bit on the severe side. "Okay, so that does go beyond normal sibling rivalry." Chloe's brother had never shaved her head. But then again, she'd never burned anything of his.

Reese sets his glass down, and his eyes almost tear over. If I wasn't seeing it, I would never believe it. "I haven't talked to her in years. Some days it feels like forever."

"I'm sorry," I say because I'm not sure what else I can offer. My dad springs to mind. "It's hard being alienated from family members."

Reese refills my glass, and if there were any tears, they freeze in his eyes. "Trust me, in this case, it was totally necessary. Our house was a war zone. And my mom freaked."

The idea of his mom freaking makes me realize I never want my mom to come back. And I never want the night to end. This date is way better than I ever thought possible. Reese is so easy to talk to, and I never would have thought it, but we have a ton in common.

"You're smiling." Reese reaches across the table and takes my hand. I've set my wine glass down, freshly filled and only a sip taken.

He's right. I am smiling. "Is that okay?"

Reese flashes his teeth, and in his face, I see Shayne. I try to bring Shayne into my thoughts, but he won't come. He's slipped out of my mind; there's not room for both of them, and right now, I'm totally occupied with the overpowering presence of Reese.

"You are totally sexy when you smile."

I know my face must be bright red, but his comment only makes me smile more. "You're not so bad yourself." And it's true. Reese has been perfect. Funny. Gorgeous. Reckless.

"I love you."

His words stop my breath.

"I swear I'm in love with you."

My eyes manage to find his and lock onto them. I'm sure he's joking. But his eyes aren't laughing. The blue's darkened, and the emotion behind them makes me hold my breath until I realize I've stopped breathing.

"You've known me less than a week."

His eyes continue to hold mine, not letting me go. "Just let yourself feel it, Piper. Let yourself believe in love at first sight. Think how good we would feel together."

He's chipping away at the wall inside me. "But love…" I say.

"I feel like I've known you forever."

I'm not sure why, but I feel the same way. Like part of me has known Reese since before I was even born.

"I would do anything for you, Piper. Anything you want." Reese won't take his eyes off me. "If I can't have you, it'll kill me."

My mind tells me this is not standard first date conversation. I try to lighten the mood. "Isn't that a bit extreme?"

"Maybe. But I see nothing wrong with being extreme."

I can hardly form a response. "You probably say that to all the girls you date."

"Only girls named Piper who take my breath away."

I smile but stand and pull my hand away. "Can you take me home?" What I need is some fresh air. I can hardly take my eyes off Reese. He's permeated my soul and moved deep into me. I feel nothing like myself, but I absolutely love the way I'm feeling.

Reese's smile returns and quells the edgy atmosphere. "Do you want to finish your wine first?"

"I've had enough." Actually, I think we've both had enough.

Reese stands up, leaving a few bills on the table. Large bills. "Like I said, anything you want."

We don't speak as we take the elevator down, though his arm is around me, pulling me close as if he wants the world to know we're together. When we reach the bottom floor and the doors open, Reese walks out first and then takes my hand.

My heart pounds, drumming in my ears so hard I'm surprised I hear anything else. But I listen to the doors shut behind us and the elevator gears start up again. Reese keeps hold of my hand, and sweat forms between our fingers. I move to let go, but he grabs my other hand, and with a single motion, he pulls me close to him. The wine's thick and sweet on his breath, mixing with his already exotic fragrance. I can't help but breathe it in, and I let it fill my lungs. But once again, I think of Shayne, and the image of his face finally comes to me. His black hair covering his forehead. His golden shoulders and mysterious eyes.

I shake my head.

"I'm just asking you to give me a chance, Piper," Reese says. "That's all."

He leans forward like he's about to kiss me. I freeze, and my mind spins. I'm searching for the right answer.

Trying to decide if I should kiss him. But before I can decide, his mouth is on mine. His full lips press into my own, and I feel them separate, his tongue slipping into the space in between. Even with the image of Shayne in my head, Reese's presence takes over, and my own tongue meets his. I kiss him in return. I put my arms around him, pulling him into me with ferocity equaling his own. He tastes even better than he smells, and my mind plays out infinite scenarios of what the future will hold. What our future will hold.

I never want the kiss to stop, but I force myself to pull back.

Reese is breathless as he stares at me. "Just give me a chance."

The valet runs as soon as he sees us, and within minutes, Reese's sleek, black car crawls around the corner. He helps me in and again buckles me up. His arm feels warm when it touches me, and part of me wants it to stay there. But the seat belt clicks, and he moves it away.

The car barely makes a sound when it comes to a stop outside the Botanical Haven. I've only left a single light on in the place—upstairs. Even the plants need nighttime to grow. Especially with unending summer.

I unclip my belt, and Reese does the same.

"Thanks for a nice evening." And I'm suddenly wondering what will happen now.

Reese smiles with just a touch of humor that tells

me he's not ready for the night to end. "You're not going to invite me in?"

The part of me that feels like an imposter is screaming to invite him in. To explore life a little. But I think if I invite Reese in right now, he'll never leave.

I think I don't mind.

"Maybe for a couple minutes." I'm aching to see what the next level feels like.

"Right. Just a couple minutes."

Reese opens his door and starts to stand up, but five seconds later he sinks back into the seat, and it's like he's transformed. He grips his hands on the steering wheel and looks straight ahead. "On second thought, I better go."

"Really?"

He takes a deep breath, holds it for a couple seconds, and then blows it out slowly. "Yeah, really."

"Why?" Have I done something to upset him in the last two seconds?

"It doesn't matter." His words are clipped, and there's no question in them.

I put my hand on the door handle and pop it open and try to pretend I don't care. "It's okay. I'm tired anyway." Which is a lie. My mind spins as it tries to figure out what happened.

In case I was worried about Reese trying to kiss me again, I'm assuaged. He reaches over and pats my hand. "I'll see you around, Piper."

Just like that. Like we hadn't kissed back at the hotel. Like he hadn't told me he loved me.

I push the car door all the way open. "Yeah, I'll see you around." And then I get out and shut the door behind me.

Chapter 11

Desire

I'm not two steps away from Reese's car when it drives off. He's left me, and now I stand alone in the darkness. I can't help the tears that spring to my eyes. It's like I've been dumped. He really left.

I wipe away a tear, and that's when I see Shayne. He's sitting on my front doorstep waiting for me. Had Reese seen him? Could that be the reason why he went away?

Our eyes meet, and Shayne stands.

"Hi, Piper."

"Shayne?" I stop in my tracks and stand there and try to wrap my mind around the fact that he's here waiting for me.

He leans against the railing and gives me a crooked smile. "You're home early."

My face heats up, but I don't want to talk about my date—not with him. So I nod. "What are you doing here?"

He runs a hand through his hair and looks out past me at the road where Reese had just been. "Making sure you got home safely."

My heart's pounding at this point, and my head is spinning from the wine, and what I really need to do is sit down, not have some guardian angel figure hovering over me. As if my mother isn't overbearing enough. "I'm fine."

His face falls the smallest amount. "I was just worried about you," he says. And then he waits, like he's not sure what to say next.

"I'm sorry," I say because I know I sounded bitchy. "The last week has just been a little crazy." It's a mild way to put things. I fumble in my purse for the keys and pull them out, but I drop them on the porch.

He picks them up. "No, I'm sorry. I shouldn't be checking up on you." He hands me the keys, and I put them in the lock, and the door swings open.

"Do you want to come in?" I ask quickly before I can think too much about it.

He looks into the warehouse. It's still dim, but he takes his time looking around. "Maybe not. I should probably get going," he says.

I step to the side and try to calm my heart when I answer. "I could make coffee." The night has been nothing but hazy, and coffee should help. Coffee is safe. Plus he'd suggested getting coffee sometime.

Shayne hesitates, shakes his head, but I motion for him to come in, so he finally does. The door swings shut behind him leaving the two of us alone in the dark. He stands a couple feet away looking at me, and then shifts his eyes down.

"I'd love some."

"What?" I say.

"Coffee. I'd love some."

In the space of seconds, I've forgotten all about it. "Oh, yeah. I'll run upstairs and make it."

I turn before I say something stupid and ruin the entire moment. But my hand catches on the counter, and the pink calla lilies Reese brought me fall to the ground. The glass vase shatters on the tile below, and water splashes my feet. Reese's cut flowers lay crossed over each other, staring up at me.

Not only had I gone on a date with Reese, I'd enjoyed it. And I'd kissed him like there was no tomorrow. When I think back, it's like I'm watching actors on stage. Like it was someone else and not me. And what about Chloe? She's the one who likes Reese. I haven't even thought about her since I got in the car. For the last few hours, all semblance of common sense has vanished from my mind. What kind of friend am I? It must have been the wine.

I close my eyes and blow out a breath. "Ugh."

"You broke your vase."

I can't help but laugh at his matter-of-fact tone which totally simplifies the whole night. "Yeah, I'll clean it up later." And I head upstairs to the kitchen.

I make the coffee as fast as I can. Shayne is downstairs—waiting for me. I hardly believe it's real. But I don't want to jinx it, so I hurry and go back down.

He's near the counter, bent over with a broom.

The bulb from upstairs casts enough light to see his outline. I set the coffee on our small ice cream table and walk over to him.

"You don't have to clean that up." I grab the dustpan off the ground, but his hand reaches out and covers mine. In seconds, he loosens the dustpan from my hand. It falls to the floor and makes a clattering sound which probably would wake Randy Conner's family next door.

I feel something move through me, starting at the hand he's holding. The sensation is moving up my arm and into my torso, and when it settles in the center of my soul, I have to work to make sure he doesn't hear my breathing.

"I don't mind," he says.

"It's my mess," I say. Kind of like this whole situation between me and Reese and Shayne is becoming. A tangle in my mind.

Shayne shakes his head and finishes cleaning the glass off the floor. He reaches for the flowers, but I take them first.

"I'm not a big fan of cut flowers," I say.

"I know." And his words echo truth, like he really does know. Like he can see behind my eyes. Which makes me a bit insecure. My thoughts have always been my own.

I move around beside him and set the flowers in the sink, and when I turn, he's looking right at me. I don't say anything. And I don't move. His eyes settle on my face, and unlike Reese, Shayne has no confident outer shell. He's wearing his inner self on the outside. Like he's baring his soul to me.

The silence grows with each second until he reaches up and touches my hair.

"You have it down." He twirls a piece of my curly hair around his finger and then lets it go, watching it bounce back.

I feel my face flush but know with the darkness he can't see it. "Yeah, I—"

I see his outline nod. "I know. Your date. Did you have fun?"

"I wished it were you instead."

And the second the words are out, I can't believe I've said them. He's going to think I'm a pathetic, desperate girl. He probably has girls flocking around him at every turn.

Shayne lets go of my hair and brushes his fingers against the skin of my tattoo. "I wish it were me instead, too."

My face betrays me, because a grin starts to form there no matter how cool I attempt to act. And Shayne must see it because he smiles, too.

"The coffee's ready." I walk back toward the ice cream table. I'm not looking behind me, but his footsteps echo on the tile floor. He's following me. Which still seems unreal. I sit in the purple seat and leave the yellow one open for him. Both face the forest of plants I grow. I slide one of the cups closer to him. "Do you like it black?"

"It's the only way to drink it," he says. When he sets his mug down, I notice his eyes travel back to Reese's flowers, but he doesn't say anything.

I'm so tempted to reach out and touch Shayne's face. He's so close—just across the table from me. "Are you guys friends?" I ask.

Shayne takes another sip of his coffee. "Reese and I?"

I nod and set my hands on the table to keep them from shaking.

Shayne's hand moves toward mine, as if he wants to take it. But he doesn't.

"It's a complicated situation," Shayne says.

I open my mouth to ask more, but his hand lifts off the table and his fingers move to my lips. "And not the conversation I want to have with you."

I don't move a muscle because I don't want his hand to leave my mouth, but it does, so I take a sip of the hot coffee to again clear my mind. "What conversation do you want to have then?" I ask.

Shayne leans back into the heart shape of the chair. "Tell me the funniest thing that ever happened to you."

My mind starts churning as I attempt to piece out

something funny that's happened to me in my life. "How about a different topic."

"There must be something."

"I haven't led a very funny life." Between home-school and moving, humor's been a low priority. But I don't want him to think I'm a total bore.

He purses his lips. "You have a whole lifetime ahead of you to change that."

My heart skips at the thought of my future. And I'm reminded I am eighteen now. I need to get away from my mom. "How about you?" I say. "Tell me something funny about your life."

Shayne seems to consider this for a moment. "You'll think I'm horrible."

"No way," I say.

"Promise?"

I nod.

"Okay," he says. "There was this time when I was little. I was hanging out with my best friend. And, well, my father had this one clock that he just loved. It was huge."

"Like a grandfather clock?"

His arms circle way up toward the ceiling. "Way bigger. It was as tall as this room. My father's got this fascination with time. Can't get enough of it. He has about a million clocks and spends every waking hour making sure they're perfectly synchronized."

"Sounds like a fun hobby."

"More like an obsession," Shayne says. "Anyway, this one day, my dad was gone, and my best friend was over, and we climbed to the top of the clock and changed it so it would be a few seconds off."

I can almost picture Shayne at the top of a huge grandfather clock. "That doesn't sound so bad."

"You wouldn't think so, but the first time it chimed after all the others, my dad couldn't believe it. He checked and rechecked all those clocks for days. And then he finally got them synchronized up again."

I know where this story is going. "So you changed it again."

Shayne nods. "The first time he thought it was a malfunction. But then, after the second time, he set up security everywhere. And then he waited."

"So what'd you do?" Every word draws me in and connects me to him. I wish I'd been a part of the experience.

Shayne shrugs. "We changed it again."

"But what about the security?"

He finishes his coffee and sets the mug down on the yellow table surface. "Sure, it got harder, but that only made it more of a challenge."

"Did he ever find out it was you?"

"Nope. In fact, it kind of drove him crazy until one day I went into the room and the clock was in a million pieces." He seems to consider this for a moment. "He's probably still working on fixing it."

"There's no way I can top that." It's a way better story than Reese shaving his sister's head. I trace my finger around on top of the coffee mug and say a silent prayer Shayne won't leave.

But he pushes his chair out and stands up. "It's really nice here. Kind of like your own private oasis from global warming."

The Botanical Haven is a nice place to live with the vivid colors of all the living things around me and the peace of the greenhouses out back. But I know I'm not meant to live with my mom for the rest of my life. I stand up also, and though we're still across the table from each other, it's like we're only inches apart.

"I want to move out."

His muscles visibly tense. "Where do you want to go?"

"California maybe. To college with Chloe. I want to study law. But my mom wants me to stay here and go to UT." Without even realizing I'm doing it, I take a step closer to him. And he does the same. And then we really are only inches apart.

"It's beautiful here," he says and touches my arm.

My breath catches in my throat. "Maybe when my mom's not around."

His eyes meet mine, and each second that passes stretches into eternity. I hold his gaze, and even though my heart is pounding out of my chest, I don't look away. And then Shayne leans in and kisses me. His lips brush mine for only a second, and it's so soft, it's more like a whisper. The kiss is exquisite—a perfect moment tucked into my oppressive life. Reese's kiss had been all about the physical, but Shayne's is empathic. Like in its simple motion, my soul is bared.

He pulls back and looks at me. And I'm sure he's trying to gauge my reaction. I stand still but my mind is going a million miles an hour. Before tonight I'd never kissed a guy, and now I've kissed both Reese and Shayne. I remember my conversation with Reese about soulmates. And I'm hit with the overwhelming sensation that Shayne, not Reese, could be mine.

"Your mom should go away more often," he says.

I laugh in an attempt to relax, which isn't going to happen. "My mom should go away permanently."

When I say it, his face falls into a cynical grin. "If only life were that easy."

"Do you want another cup of coffee?" I want him to sit back down and stay here forever.

He shakes his head. "I need to go."

I open my mouth and am about to ask him to stay, but then I remind myself that I don't want to sound pathetic. "Are you sure?" It's not like my mom goes away every weekend.

He looks at me, and his eyes tell me he's not sure. That he wants to stay here as much as I want him to. But his words disagree. "Yeah, I'm sure." He grabs my hand and gives it a squeeze, and I know I can't stop him from going.

He lets go of my hand and walks to the door. I watch him from where I stand, and then he's gone. And I'm left in the dark alone.

I walk to the cash register, move behind the counter, and sink to the floor. It's only after I sit there for ten minutes that I'm able to clear my head. Sweat pours off me, but I can't stand up and put the fans on. My legs won't hold me, and my dress sticks to me around my thighs.

I don't move until his presence evaporates, and only then do I head back to the sink where the pink calla lilies rest. I still feel life within the exposed stems. Weakening, but they can last longer—if I want them to. An odd urge to smash them hits me. To throw them in the compost pile and pretend my date never happened, but I can't do that. Moving around the Botanical Haven, I look for the perfect vase. And I move into my routine, there in the dark, watering and taking care of the plants.

Chapter 12

Creek

After Shayne leaves, I hardly sleep; Tanni keeps invading my dreams. I toss around on my cotton sheets, hoping to find a position to keep her out, but she comes back each time with her empty eye sockets and words of doom.

I know her words aren't true. But they repeat over and over in my head—a haunting mantra. I will see Chloe tomorrow. We have plans. She'll call in the morning.

I wake before the alarm, clicking it off and checking for messages. My mom hasn't called, which is so far from her normal overbearing nature, I wonder if she lost her FON. I think about texting her to make sure she's okay, but I don't want my father to see any messages I send. Maybe I'll text her later, or maybe even tonight after bedtime.

I relax and think about the night before. Thinking of Reese leaves me disoriented. I know it's wrong to cut flowers and drink under age, but I loved breaking the rules. It was intoxicating and frightening all at the same time, and made me want to do more. He offered up a reckless freedom, one that my mom would kill me if she knew about. Not that she'd be any happier about Shayne. When I think of him, a comforting warmth runs through me, and I keep him in my mind the whole time I'm showering and getting dressed, hoping the memories never fade.

It's not until I push the button on the coffee machine that Chloe calls. I mute the tube and answer.

"We still on for today?"

The sound of her voice sings into my ear. I know she won't die. She's my best friend. I touch my tattoo with my free hand, and run my fingers over the imprint. But as much as I want to get out, all the reporters have been talking about this morning is the heat bubble they're sure is going to form around the city.

"Have you seen the news?" I say. "Maybe we should stay inside."

I can almost hear Chloe shake her head. "No way, Piper. We are not staying inside the first day of your freedom."

I glance at the tube and see Councilman Rendon talking with an image of a disperser missile inset behind him. I don't have to hear him to know he's convincing the world the missiles are safe.

"You could just come over," I suggest even though I don't want to stay in either.

"Turn it off," Chloe says.

"What?"

"The tube. Turn it off now. You need to stop watching the news," she says.

"But they're predicting the bubble will form before noon." And my thoughts go to my mom. Will she be safe from the heat wherever she is?

"So it gets hot," Chloe says. "It's hot every day. Just turn off the news and get ready."

"Fine." I click off the tube, and my mind quiets down instantly. Maybe I should watch less bad news.

She says she'll be by in a half hour; shuttle routes don't make it much easier than that. I have so much to tell her. About Reese. About Shayne. I can hardly wait. But when Chloe hangs up, Tanni's voice returns.

I push it away, and grab a nectarine, cutting it with a knife and pulling out the seed. One benefit of owning the Botanical Haven—we grow lots of fruit, so even with the Global Heating Crisis, shortages are never a concern for us. It's sweet and juicy, and when I take a bite, the juice runs down my chin. I think of Shayne barely kissing me, but he's quickly replaced by Reese. Had he really told me he loved me? Had I really enjoyed his kiss so much?

When I see Chloe walking up, I check the temperature. One hundred and thirteen. Still in the safe zone. I can only hope the reports are wrong. Still, the second I step outside, the heat punches me like a fist.

"It feels hotter than a hundred and thirteen," I say.

Chloe shoots me a look. "We're not staying in."

"Right," I say. "We're not staying in." I clip my water bottle on my shorts and hand Chloe one of my mom's herbal heat suppressors. They're brown disks that look like cow patties, but my mom swears they help the body process heat better.

Chloe wrinkles up her nose. "Those things are disgusting."

"They aren't that bad," I say, and force it into her hand. I already had two this morning. Chloe's right; they taste even worse than they look.

Chloe takes it but puts it in her pocket instead of eating it. I opt against pressing the issue. She's pretty good about taking her sunscreen pills, so I don't have to worry about that.

I lock the door behind us, but the shuttle has already pulled away. So we sit on the bench to wait. It's not three minutes later when Randy Conner and his little sister head over to the shuttle stop to join us. As little as my mom lets me out of her sight, I'm like a phantom, but I do know Randy has a sister.

"Hi," I say, and I smile and wave.

The little girl's only about seven. But instead of the normal brightness I'd expect to see on a seven-year-old face, her eyes are hollow and don't meet my own. Randy pulls her close, and they stand off to the side, not joining Chloe and me on the bench.

"She's kind of shy," he says. And whether this is all the explanation necessary or not, it's all he gives. "So where are you guys off to today?"

I think Chloe used to have a crush on Randy even though he's kind of a jerk. But that was like two years ago before he'd started dating Hannah. "We're going exploring," Chloe says.

Randy lets out a low whistle. "Your mom is letting you out of the penitentiary today, Piper?"

I nod and stop staring at his little sister. "She's out of town." I say it like it happens all the time, like my mom leaves me to make my own choices and hang with my friends all I want. But Randy's not an idiot.

"The prison warden is really gone?"

"Yep." And even I can't keep the smile off my face.

Randy laughs. "So when does the party start?"

I laugh, too, and shake my head. "No party." I haven't even considered a party. In truth, the only person I'd want over is Shayne, not counting Chloe of course. With the wine now out of my head, I'm so glad Reese left before I could invite him in.

Randy turns more toward us but keeps his arm around his sister. "Oh, come on, Piper. This is a once in a lifetime opportunity. How about just me and Hannah and a couple of the guys from school? We'll bring our own beer and everything."

Would my mom be more upset if I drank beer with a bunch of kids at our place or if I ventured out into the city with Chloe when a heat warning had been issued? "Tempting, Randy, but Chloe and I are just going to hang out."

"God, that's boring."

I'm saved from further banter by the shuttle. Its brakes whistle, too loud to hear anything else Randy may say. He moves in front of us when the door opens and helps his sister up the steps, watching to make sure her FON gets scanned. And then he steps back down and lets us by.

"You're letting her go on the shuttle by herself?" Chloe asks.

Randy shrugs. "She'll be fine."

But Chloe turns to him. "That's stupid, Randy. She won't be fine. She could be abducted or something."

Randy waves at his sister who's found a seat already. I have yet to scan my FON. "I told you she'll be fine," he says. "She's pretty independent."

Chloe points at Randy's sister. "Independent? What is she? Six?"

"Seven," Randy says.

I've been watching, listening, but decide to open my mouth. "Randy, seven is not independent. There are bad people out in the world." Bad people, like maybe my father, who prey on kids and steal them away. Who ask what frightens them and then turn around and use it to do just that.

Randy fixes his eyes on me. "Piper, there are bad people everywhere. She's going to be fine." And he ends every bit of question and conversation by turning around and walking back in the direction of his house.

Randy walks away, and I continue up the steps to the shuttle. Chloe joins me, though not until I've scanned my FON. Randy's sister stares out the window, looking at her house and Randy's departing form.

"Randy is crazy," Chloe says, stepping up behind me.

I catch the driver's eye and point to Randy's sister. "She's riding alone," I say.

The shuttle driver nods. "She always does. She'll be fine. I'll keep an eye on her." And he smiles to reassure me until I move back and take a seat.

"Where are we going?" I ask once Chloe's swiped her FON and sat down next to me. Aside from her cryptic exploring talk, I'm not sure what Chloe has in mind.

"The Greenbelt."

I don't even try to keep the smile off my face. My mom's never let me go to the Greenbelt before. She tells me it's a breeding ground for vagrants and criminals, but all the kids at school go there on the weekends since it's fresh water and hasn't yet run dry.

"How was your date?" Chloe asks.

My date. "Which one?" I say, deciding to stall a bit.

Chloe rolls her eyes. "Puh-lease, Piper. You only had the date of the century." She puts her hand on my arm. "Tell me about Reese. I want to hear everything."

And I want to tell her everything—eventually. "I'll

tell you when we get there."

"You better," Chloe says.

The ride takes forever because for some reason everyone in Austin is riding the shuttle today. Or at least it seems that way. Randy's sister gets off at her elementary school, and I relax when I see hundreds of kids there, too, waiting to go inside. They let all the younger kids go to school on weekends during heat advisories to take advantage of the air conditioning. The thermometer on the side of the school reads one hundred and seventeen in bright red numbers. Four degrees more than when we left. I push away thoughts of the heat bubble and try to focus on our day.

When we get off the shuttle at our stop, the change is immediate. The shuttle has eco friendly A/C, which may not be the greatest, but outside we're now at the mercy of the atmosphere.

"Maybe we should—" I start.

Chloe puts her hand up. "Don't even say it." And like she's trying to make a point, she takes the herbal heat suppressor out of her pocket and smashes it under her foot.

Sweat trickles through my thick hair and runs down my neck. "Aren't you hot?" I say.

She kicks at the dirt with her toes. "I feel great. Like today's the start of a whole new future."

And despite the heat, her enthusiasm infects me.

We make our way down a rocky path until I can't see

the road anymore. Ahead of us is the Greenbelt complete with trees and rocks and a trickle of water—fresh and clear—and we take off our shoes and dip our feet in. It's still early, and though I'm looking around for either vagrants or criminals, I don't see either. No one is around besides the two of us. Chloe and me.

I look at Chloe, and Tanni's words hit me in the head causing the bump there to throb. *Chloe will die.* I push the words out of my mind, but they're persistent.

"What?" Chloe's looking at me. She still has a smile, but only half-sized.

I'm not about to tell her about Tanni's prediction, so I smile in return. "Nothing."

"No really. You've been looking at me funny all week."

Have I been that transparent?

"You're imagining things." I reach up to her arm and feel her tattoo. "I'm just excited we got these." But I pull my hands back when I touch her. With the temperature as high as it is, Chloe's skin should be burning, but it feels cool.

"Yeah. I can't believe you really did it," she says.

My mouth falls open. "You thought I'd chicken out?"

"Let's face it, it's really the only rebellious thing you've done since I've known you."

"Yeah, I guess so." I think about Reese and Shayne and the mixed-up night before. Will Chloe be mad I kissed Reese? I'll figure out a way to bring it up slowly and then I'll tell her I have no interest I him.

"So what gives? Why are you looking at me so funny?"

I'm not going to tell her about Tanni. But still…

"Do you believe in fate, Chloe?" As I say it, the heat seems to press down on me.

She kicks the water with her foot. "Like whether we were fated to be friends?"

"Kind of." I splash some water across onto the rocks, watching it dry almost as soon as it hits. I see a tiny pool of fish, swimming circles and trying to reach the next part of the creek. So many fish have died off; only the tiniest ones still live here.

Chloe rubs my tattoo, and again, I'm struck by how cold she is. Like her body isn't processing the heat at all. She's not even sweating. "Yeah. I think we were destined to be friends," she says. "I felt that way from the first day we met."

I felt that way, too. On my first day of public school after being homeschooled my entire life, I was sure I'd talk to no one the entire day. In fact, I vowed I wouldn't. Since my best friend Charlotte had died in sixth grade, I kept my distance from people.

I decided I wouldn't make friends, and my mom would be happy. And if my mom was happy then I could keep this small semblance of freedom. But no sooner had I found a seat on the shuttle than Chloe plunked herself next to me.

"You aren't going to hog the whole seat, are you?" Chloe asked.

I shook my head, and down she sat.

I did my best to keep my mouth shut, but Chloe had been persistent.

"Are you new?" she asked.

I nodded, still trying to keep my vow of silence.

"So where did you move from?" she asked.

"Chicago," I finally said, thinking I could end the conversation even though this girl seemed kind of cool. "Homeschooled."

"Wow. Your whole life?"

"Yeah. Even before that when I lived in Virginia," I said.

Chloe offered me a Life Saver then, giving me my choice of colors. I reached for the one on the top, trying to be polite.

She scrunched up her nose. "You really like the green ones?"

I hated the green ones. They reminded me of fish scales. "No, but that's okay."

She grabbed the green Life Saver out of my fingers and pitched it out the shuttle window, which shocked me since littering was way illegal. "Pick your favorite color," she said.

I took a red one. And we'd been friends ever since.

Movement off in the tall trees catches my eye. I look

through the barren trunks but see nothing. Not even leaves rustling. I slowly realize the whole world is still. And hot.

"How about death?" I say. My chest tightens even as the words come out. But I can't stop myself now. "Do you believe fate determines ahead of time when someone will die?"

Chloe turns my way, and our eyes meet. She stares at me, not saying a word. I notice her orange bandana holding back her hair, matching the burning sun overhead. She's stopped smiling, and I know she's thinking about my question.

She stands up and moves farther down the creek. It narrows to a trickle here, hardly moving over the rocks. They say the creek's been drying out for years, and once it stops flowing, the clean water source to Austin will be cut off. Chloe squats down and puts her hands in the water, bringing it up to her face, but instead of drinking it, she lets it slip through her fingers.

Chloe will die.

The light shifts, and I imagine her there, lying dead in the creek, facing downward, looking toward Hell.

Chloe will die.

I close my eyes and suck in a breath. I smell the earth around me—the rocks and the soil and the tree bark. And I smell something else. Pungent and odorous. The thick smell of rotting flesh.

"I don't know," Chloe says.

I've forgotten she hasn't answered. I try to push the smell away. "You don't know if you believe in fate?"

"I don't know if death is known ahead of time." She reaches down again, scooping more water with her hands and letting it slip away.

Far off, in the distance, the sirens wail. I pull out my FON and confirm the deadly temperature of one hundred and twenty-two. The heat bubble has come.

I jump to my feet. "We need to go, Chloe. We need to get out of here."

The rotting smell is even stronger. I look at the trees, and this time I see a man, short and strong, and when he moves to the side, I see wings attached to his back. White as clouds, and so long, the tips nearly touch the ground behind him.

He ignores me. He's looking right at Chloe.

Chloe will die.

The man takes a step toward Chloe. She's looking right at him but doesn't seem to notice he's there. From overhead comes the thump of the disperser missile being fired. I brace myself. All I know is I need to get Chloe away from here.

"Chloe! We need to go now!" I move to take a step toward her, but the heat presses in on me. The air's so thick, I'm having a hard time finding oxygen.

Chloe opens her mouth to answer me, but her words won't come either. And for the first time, panic crosses her face.

"Run, Chloe!" I know the man approaching her is Death. He's coming for Chloe.

She doesn't move; it's like her mind has stopped processing the world around her. The winged man takes another few steps, gliding so smoothly across the earth, it's like he's flying. His rotten smell permeates the air. The heat descends, and Chloe falls to the ground.

Chloe will die. The voice in my mind chants over and over.

"Shut up!" I can't take it. I need to reach Chloe before Death does. I suck in the hot air and begin to run. But the winged man is already there, by her side, and he's grabbed her wrist.

Her face tightens, and the color drains out. I've almost reached her when I stop in the wet bed of the creek and see Shayne. I don't wonder why he's here; right now, I don't care.

"Help me!"

He hears me. I know he does. The winged man shimmers and begins to fade. Chloe's fading, too. I cross the distance and break their arms apart. The man fights me but lets go with a glance over my shoulder. And then he stands there watching. I manage to get my hands under Chloe's armpits and drag her from the water. She's pale and cold, but she's still breathing. My face is covered in tears, but I don't take the time to wipe them away as I sink down next to her.

"I can't." Shayne says, standing next to the winged

man.

I look up, meeting his eyes.

"Can't what?" I say.

"I can't help you. She's supposed to die."

"No! She's not. She's alive." Chloe has to be alive. I know it. Why did she have to ignore the heat advisory anyway?

He shakes his head and places a hand on her limp chest. "She shouldn't be." Under his palm, I see her chest rise and fall, erratic. She's not breathing enough. And she's pale. Way too pale.

I stand and punch at him with my fists, but he catches them.

"She can't die."

Shayne lets me cry. He doesn't argue with anything I'm saying. He doesn't try to explain.

The breath is moving in and out of her body. It's shallow but still there. And the man with wings has vanished.

"She's alive," I say.

Shayne reaches out and wipes my face. His fingers come back covered with dirt that's mixed with my tears. "She has to die, Piper. It's the way things are."

I shake my head and try to stay my tears, try to look fierce. "I won't let her die."

Shayne doesn't speak. He looks to Chloe, pale on the ground, but breathing. I bite my lip to keep from saying anything, trying to piece out why Shayne is even here. Why would he be here anyway?

It's only after we stand there in our silent deadlock for over a minute that Shayne finally responds. "If you had a choice, would you want her to live?"

It has to be one of the stupidest questions I've ever heard. "Of course."

Shayne looks to the trees and seems to consider something.

"I would always want her to live," I say again just in case he didn't hear me the first time.

He turns back my way and nods. "Will you come with me somewhere? Please?"

On the ground, Chloe's stopped breathing, and I'm about to say something when I notice everything else has stopped too. Not even the water is moving. Every single drop is frozen in time. The fish I saw swimming earlier are still. It's like the entire world hibernates. I squat down to Chloe.

"She'll be fine." He knows what I'm thinking.

"I should get her to a hospital. She could have heat stroke."

Shayne shakes his head. "I swear, she'll be fine."

"How can you possibly know that?"

"She'll stay just like this until we get back. No one will bother her. I promise."

"What if she wakes—?"

"Seriously, Piper. Trust me. Just this once." His voice is layered with frustration, and his eyes plead with me.

I want to trust him. And I want Chloe to live. And if one is tied to the other, I'm willing to take the chance. Somehow Tanni and the winged man of death and Shayne being here now are all linked.

I move into Shayne's outstretched arms, and he wraps them around me and fills me with hints of a courage that wasn't there seconds ago.

"It'll be okay," he says. "Right?"

Maybe there is still some fear in my eyes. "Right." Even I hear my voice shake.

"Good."

We don't walk like I think we will. Instead, we start sinking into the ground. I clench my fingers into Shayne's sides because the movement is so sudden.

"It's okay," he says again. "Remember?"

I can't answer because, in the next second, I'm swallowed by the earth. But instead of dirt and grit, I'm in a silvery void of flowing liquid mercury which seeps into my mouth and ears and nose.

I'm going to drown.

I hold my breath, sure the liquid will kill me, and in seconds, my lungs feel like they will collapse. I try to hold out a little longer. Maybe the silver fluid will be over soon. But the seconds pass, and I can't stand it anymore.

I take a breath.

Instead of gagging me, the liquid fills my lungs, and

they expand and contract as if with normal air. And in that moment, I finally believe Shayne. It will be okay.

I shut my eyes and hold tight onto Shayne, and we seem to float in nothingness. Nowhere on Earth. Like a world all its own. Again I breathe in, searching for a taste in the silvery liquid, but it's like formless ether, liquid and gas and nothing all at the same time. Though we are floating, a current pulls on us, downward and upward, right and left. Pulling us toward our destination. When I feel cool air on my face again, I dare to open my eyes.

We're in a cavern made of rust-colored rocks. Silver fluid trickles down the walls and pools on the hard-packed dirt floor. Light seems to come from the pools of silver and casts all kinds of weird shadows on the walls and ceiling above. Next to us is an underground river, and it's so dark, the water looks black. But it's bubbling, and voices come from it.

The hum of voices is freaking me out, but Shayne hardly glances at the water. He pulls a large gold coin from his pocket and spins it around on his fingers. It flashes in the dim silver light of the cavern, and I see a boat coming across the river toward us.

I haven't moved, and I realize I'm gripping Shayne's arms so hard my fingers hurt. So I loosen my grip and grab his hand instead. "Where are we?" Unlike our hot Earth above, there's a breeze blowing through the cavern that smells of burning sweetness and cools the temperature down way below ninety.

He turns to me as the boat pulls up to the dock. "Haven't you figured it out by now?"

I have, but I don't want to say it. And he doesn't press me. I can't believe it, because it can't possibly be true. Because if it is true, does that mean I am dead in place of Chloe?

The boat's tied up now, and a man jumps out onto the long dock extending into the river and walks toward us. The black water behind him seems to extend forever.

"You have company."

Shayne nods, and with his lips pressed together, he looks as nervous as I am. "She said she wanted to come."

The man lifts a thick hairy eyebrow. "Let's hope so."

Shayne looks toward me, and I nod. My hand hurts from grabbing his so hard, but I'm not letting go. The water's still bubbling, and the voices sound more like cries. I swear I see things swimming around out there in the black water. Things with horrible faces and sharp teeth.

Shayne flips the gold coin off his thumb with his finger, and the man catches it.

"Really. You know it's not necessary." But the man pockets it anyway.

"I don't ever want anyone to say I don't pay my fare," Shayne says.

The man's face cracks into a broad smile. "No one

would ever say anything of the sort." His skin looks as thick as leather, and his smile lines are so pronounced, they look sculpted. And his hair's mostly missing with the exception of a few tufts above his ears and his giant, bushy eyebrows. The smile makes me think if I weren't around, the man would be tempted to muss up the top of Shayne's hair or cuff his shoulder or something equally as endearing.

"That's what you say. But not everyone agrees." Shayne begins to walk toward the dock, and since I'm holding his hand, I follow, trying to take in my situation without totally freaking myself out.

The man talks about the boat as we walk, like it's a favorite family member, and he's so friendly, I can't help but feel I've known him my whole life.

"My name's Piper." I figure I better go ahead and introduce myself if Shayne's not going to. The dark walls of the cavern shift and flicker around me, and the water's still moving. But the darkness wraps around me and cools my skin from the world above.

The man stops walking. "Piper." He presses his lips together. "It's a good name."

"What's yours?"

The man looks to Shayne, who I see gives a small nod.

"Charon. I'm Charon."

My breath catches. I've studied enough mythology in my life to know who Charon is. He's the ferryman. I turn to Shayne. "Then that means…"

His eyes meet mine, and I see the red specks in his brown irises again, but now they're flickering. "You're in Hell."

I ask the question that has to follow. "And you are…"

"Hades. Lord of the Underworld."

Chapter 13

Acheron

I'm not sure what to say. It's like I'm a part of an elaborate hoax, but there's no way Shayne and Charon could make up this world. I want to turn and run away, but I can't imagine where I would go; I sank through the ground to get here. But the image of Chloe's pale body haunts me.

"I should get back. Chloe needs me."

Shayne puts a hand under my chin and looks me directly in the eyes. It's like he wants to draw my discomfort away and into himself. Like he would relieve my burden at the cost of his own. He rubs my chin with his thumb, and chills spill down my neck. "I stopped time."

"You can do that?" My anxiety begins to dissipate at the edges.

Shayne releases my chin. "My father's the god of time. It's an inherited thing."

"So you stopped it now?" I ask. I ignore the father-being-the-god-of-time thing, because it's just too much to process right now.

"Yeah, I stopped it now. I need to show you what Chloe could have."

I look out at the frothing river. "You mean if she dies."

Shayne nods. "You can see her place here in the Underworld, and then you can decide."

"Decide if she lives or dies?" I shake my head. "I don't need to see the Underworld. I want Chloe alive."

"It's not all monsters, Piper. Just give it a chance. That's all I ask."

I've already made my decision. If I really do have a choice here—if this isn't some bizarre dream—I won't let Chloe die. And I did see time stop. Chloe is fine, and Chloe will live. But…

The Underworld beckons me and draws me toward it. I want to see it. It wraps its tendrils around my body and calls to me with a voice I can't ignore. So I smile at Shayne. "Okay. I'll give it a chance."

And his smile brightens the darkness around me.

We walk to the boat, and I get in. It's large enough to carry at least ten people, and I move to a seat at the front—next to Shayne. Charon follows us in and heads to the back, picking up a long pole which leans against the smooth black wood. I watch Charon, and he catches my eye and smiles. The lines crinkle around his face again, and it infects me, forcing me to smile back. Letting me accept the mythical world around me and live in it for the moment. Helping ease my mind of worries about Chloe.

Charon unties the boat, and it begins to drift.

Though the light brightens as we move, I can't see the opposite shore. The water bubbles and laps against the sides, and something jumps out of the water, catching a bubble in its mouth and swallowing it.

Hell. I'm in Hell. And Shayne is the Lord of the Underworld.

"Are you the devil?"

Shayne puts his hand on the inside of my bare leg, below the line of my shorts. Goose bumps break out on my legs, and he grins. "Do you want me to be?"

Charon chuckles from the back of the boat, and Shayne laughs, too.

It seems like a reasonable question to me, and I know what answer I want. "No."

Shayne rubs my thigh, smoothing the goose bumps. But it's futile. His rubbing only causes more goose bumps. I separate my legs the tiniest amount, giving his hand more room.

"Good. I am not the devil."

"You get asked that a lot?"

"Almost every soul who comes here. It's that whole Hell and devil association thing."

I put my hand on his, and he stops rubbing my leg. "So is there a devil?"

Shayne sighs. "Piper, let me tell you something. The devil is everywhere. Above ground. Down here. He's evil. And he's always looking for a way in."

Just when my goose bumps were about to disappear.

"A way in where?"

Shayne lifts his hand, waving it across the river. "A way in anywhere. Hell. Earth. Souls. Any tiny crack or crevice. Evil is trying to seep inside and take over."

I've been fortunate so far that evil has stayed away from my life, but I think about how the crime rate exploded during the last heat bubble. I turn back to the water to where he's pointing—to the voices I hear there.

Send me back to my baby.

At last.

Please don't let me fall.

I'm so young.

I can almost picture faces behind the words. The water bubbles with the sound of each one, and soon they blend together. I lean over and try to get a closer look, to see the things swimming below the surface.

I didn't do it.

My daughter. Don't let my daughter die.

Each voice is different but the same. It takes me a few minutes to realize why, but then it hits me. Sorrow. Anguish for a life which will never come back.

Help us.

I want to reach in. To release the grief in the voices. I lean over and put my hands on the side of the boat. Water splashes up and sprinkles my face. I stand and try to reach further, but my hand slips, and I fall.

A hand grabs me on the arm and catches me, guiding me back to my seat.

"Careful, my love."

I face Shayne. Or Hades. But he looks straight ahead, like he hasn't said a thing.

My love. The words had been as soft as a whisper, and I wonder if I made them up. I hope not.

"What are they?" I ask.

"Voices of the dead. The last thoughts and wishes of those leaving the land of the living. They stay here in the River Acheron."

They continue to call out to me, as the monsters devour them with their long snouts, some with a single gulp, some slipping through the teeth of one only to be grabbed by another. They jump out of the water every so often exposing spikes on their backs and fins that look sharp as razors. "How can you stand to listen?" I ask.

Shayne shrugs. "Better for the dead to leave their sorrows here than live with them for all eternity. It helps keep evil away."

"You mean they aren't sad after this?"

Shayne smiles, and reaches up, brushing his fingers against my tattoo. It's hard to see in the dim light around us, but I feel his fingers stopping on the scar of it. "The sorrows remain here, and the souls are free to go to their place of eternal rest. Why be burdened with dying thoughts when no one can ever go back?"

"Ever?"

"No. Never."

And Chloe had almost died.

Shayne puts his arm around me, and I lean against him because his presence makes me never want to be anywhere else. I push the sorrows of the dead from my mind.

But then I hear Charon clear his throat.

Shayne turns back and looks. "Do you have something to say, Charon?"

I swivel around also so I can see him there in the back of the boat, poling us across.

"It just seems you may want to explain." And then Charon looks at Shayne, and a lazy smirk covers his big, weathered face.

"Explain? What?" I ask.

Charon raises an eyebrow. "The exceptions. I just think they should be mentioned."

"Charon. My rule follower."

I look at Shayne, waiting, knowing he'll go on.

He puts up his hands. "Every rule has exceptions. It's the way of the world. One or two exceptions do not mean people can come back from the dead." Shayne's eyes blacken, and I see the red flashes. "People cannot leave Hell. That is the rule. But of course, as Charon has been so kind as to point out, there have been a couple exceptions over time." He looks back at Charon. "A long time. And we never make a habit of it. And there are always consequences."

I begin to ask the question I've been thinking, but

the words won't come out. I think it's because I'm not sure I want to hear the answer.

"What?" Shayne tilts his head.

I shake my head. "Nothing. It's nothing."

But he persists. "Tell me."

I take a deep breath and force the words out, realizing even as I say them I will be in the Underworld forever. Even if I haven't died, I will remain here. No one leaves. And the thought hardly fazes me except I'll have to leave Chloe. "Am I dead instead of Chloe? Will I be able to leave?"

Shayne surprises me. I figure he'd break it to me gently. But he starts laughing. "Do you want to leave?"

I glance back again at Charon who's also smiling. "Maybe," I say.

Shayne stops laughing. "Maybe." He licks his lips and squeezes my hand. "Well then maybe you can leave. Unless we decide to keep you here forever."

I'm not sure I'd mind. Anywhere forever with Shayne sounds like paradise. But I think of Chloe. How close she came to dying. And Shayne had saved her.

"But why Chloe?"

"It was her time."

"No!" I push his arm off my shoulder and turn toward him. "It was not her time."

He meets my gaze. Again, I see the red flashes in the brown of his eyes; they've started back up. Fire behind the darkness of Hell. "Yes. It was. Fate told you so herself."

"Tanni? So she is real?"

Shayne nods.

"But you saved her."

He nods and glances back at Charon. I look back, and Charon turns away. He's avoiding the conversation.

Shayne's voice is quiet. "I know."

He did save her. "So what happens now? What if I choose to have Chloe live?" Which I know I will. It's not even a choice.

"It will be an exception," Shayne says.

What would Chloe's sorrow have been had she died? What would she have left for the monsters to devour?

Shayne pulls me back toward him, erasing the distance I've put between us. "Just give the Underworld a chance, Piper. Letting Chloe die may be the better choice."

"I doubt it."

Shayne cocks his head. "Maybe so. But try to be open-minded."

There's a magnetic ball in the pit of my stomach drawing me to the Underworld. I want to see it and I want to be with Shayne. But as I sit there, something else about mythology doesn't settle. Something I'm not sure I want to ask about or even face. Everything I know about the Underworld has made one thing clear. Hades is married to Persephone. And they rule the Underworld together.

I open my mouth, but I'm not sure how to bring it up.

"What?" Shayne says.

"It's nothing," I say.

"No really," he says. "You were going to say something."

I let out a long breath and finally let the question come. "I've studied mythology in school. I always thought…"

"She's gone," he says. "She's gone and she's not coming back."

And I don't know how to respond because whatever happened, it's obvious he doesn't want to talk about it.

"I'm sorry," I say.

"I was, too," he says. "But I've moved on."

With the interest he's showing in me, I have to believe he's telling the truth. I decide I won't question him anymore and risk him changing his mind. Maybe he's left his sorrows here in the river, too. I settle against him and watch the feasting of the monsters, and push Shayne's past romances out of my mind.

We travel from the dark cavern and then through a swamp so hazy and gray I can't see the front of the boat. The haze dissipates, and we're out into the middle of an ocean with a sky overhead that sparkles like a crystal. Two suns pound down from above, but unlike my Earth, the heat they generate finds that perfect in between space of warmth and cool. It's like what my mom told me spring used to be like, back before the Global Heating Crisis started. She'd said autumn was a season of dying and winter brought horrible temperatures so cold people froze to death, but that each spring, life returned to the earth.

I don't realize we're approaching the far shore until clouds form in the crystal sky and the monsters in the water diminish. The voices weaken, as if no sorrow is permitted to reach the banks. And then I see the trees and feel the humidity. Limbs twist over the water, dripping below, and as we pass under the weeping willows, droplets rain down on me, falling in my thick hair. Far above, crows call out, talking amongst themselves, jumping from branch to branch. And when I see the cerulean blue sky complete with clouds, I know we're no longer in a cavern but in some other world entirely.

Shayne jumps out first when the boat pushes its way through the reeds and cattails and hits up against the dock. He grabs the rope and loops it around a post. Above him, the canopy of trees holds back the light from the suns of Hell, and shadows play on the hard wooden surface. Then Shayne extends his hand toward me, and I grab it, letting him help me out.

Charon flips the gold coin which Shayne catches high in its arc. "I can't take your money," Charon says.

Shayne laughs and puts the coin back in his pocket. "I know." And their exchange makes me wonder if Charon is like a father to Shayne.

"You're going back already?" I ask.

"My work is never done. And when I say never, I do mean never." Charon laughs, and I imagine him crossing the river thousands of times each day. The same routine over and over again.

The image of the gold coin flashes in my mind. "You must make a lot of money."

"Not as much as you might think," Charon says.

"Nobody buries people with money anymore," Shayne says. "We've had to start a donation fund within the assembly of gods."

"There's an assembly of gods?" I ask. And I wonder if it's filled with the same corruption the city council has back home. Does someone like Councilman Rendon lead it and make every decision based on his own gain?

"Everyone needs rules and government," Shayne says. "Especially immortals."

"And you're on it?" I ask.

"Yeah," Shayne says. "I'm on it." He unties the rope and tosses it back in the boat. Charon uses the pole and turns the boat around, already pushing it through the reeds, toward the other shore, away from the overhanging branches and back into the river of sorrow.

Chapter 14

Crossroads

I'm totally unprepared for what happens next. Something bounds out of a tunnel ahead of us and leaps for Shayne, knocking him flat to the ground and landing on his chest. It's a black dog the size of a bear with three heads, all of which are licking Shayne's face, shoving each other out of the way. One begins to growl at another, and pretty soon, Shayne's pushing the dog off him.

"Cerberus! Be careful!" He looks to me and laughs. "One of these days, he's going to get carried away and bite my ear off." He stands up and reaches out with both hands, scratching two of the dog's heads. The other head nuzzles against his arm until he scratches it behind the ears.

"You have a dog?" I know I'm stating the obvious, but it's just such a bizarre scene, I'm not sure what else to say. And the word *three-headed* does not seem to be a necessary descriptor.

"Cerberus guards the entrance to the Underworld."

Cerberus looks my way, and his tail goes into overdrive. He turns, and I know he's going to run for me and knock me over. I imagine the three heads licking me, and my lips curl up into a smile I can't hold back.

But Shayne moves first, grabbing the neck in the middle. "Not yet, Cerberus. Let her get acquainted first."

Cerberus wriggles and tries to break free. He whines and pulls and tugs, but Shayne holds firm, and I see the muscles in his arms flexing, veins showing, sweat covering them.

"He likes you."

My smile grows, and I walk toward Cerberus. "And I like him." I scratch him behind the ears of his left head—like I'd seen Shayne do. His tail flaps back and forth, moving so hard his backside slams into Shayne, knocking him away. And then Cerberus jumps up, placing a paw on either of my shoulders, which sends me flying to the soft, muddy soil. All three heads begin a licking frenzy.

"Cerberus!"

Cerberus keeps licking. I'm laughing so hard, I can't do anything but move my head from side to side, trying to evade the three sloppy tongues. Completely unsuccessfully.

"Cerberus! Stop right now!"

Cerberus stops licking, but his paws stay on my shoulders. One of his heads swivels in Shayne's direction. I manage to stop laughing long enough to speak. "It's okay. He's a good dog."

Cerberus wags his tail, and moves his heads back to start licking again.

"Cerberus!"

Shayne grabs hold of Cerberus around the middle and lifts him. I can breathe again with the giant dog now off me. Shayne walks to a rocky wall, still holding Cerberus, and takes something out of one of the wooden supply chests stacked there. He tosses it across the way and releases Cerberus who bounds off after it, disappearing into a pitch black tunnel. Shayne comes back over to me. I've managed to stand up and brush some of the dirt and slobber off myself. It's gotten everywhere, even inside my ears.

"Nice dog." I laugh when I say it, trying to shake my ears clean.

Shayne combs his hand through my hair. A clump of dirt falls to the ground. I must be covered in it. How can he look so clean? He's been slammed in the mud, also.

"He's a bit on the excitable side. But there's no better dog," Shayne says.

I look into the dark cave and then take a few steps back so I can see more of the rocky wall. There are ten tunnels cut into the rock that look identical.

"Where do they go?" I ask.

"Different parts of the Underworld."

I point to the one where Cerberus just disappeared. "So this one leads to…"

"My home. But not anymore." He reaches for my hand and moves it so it's pointing to the tunnel on the far left now. "Now my home is down that one."

"So it changes?"

He nods.

"Why?"

"Security. Only I know where they lead at any given time."

"You and Cerberus," I venture.

Shayne laughs. "Yeah, me and Cerberus." He points one tunnel over from where we stand. "And now it's down there."

I step up to the tunnel he's pointing at and look inside. A chill of excitement runs though me. My eyes adjust, and I see there's nothing but blackness ahead, and I know that's the way we're going.

We start down the tunnel. There's a breeze blowing through it, and each time it touches my arm, it caresses me. Even though I can hardly see him, I feel Shayne walking next to me, almost like he has some sort of energy field. I sidle closer to him, and he stops walking, and then I'm up against the cave wall in the darkness.

"Piper." His voice catches when he says my name.

He's pressing against me, his warmth at my front, and the cold, hard stone wall behind me. His breath covers my face, and I'm tempted to move forward and kiss him.

But he puts a hand on my cheek. "I need to ask you

something."

"What?" I wrap my arms around him and pull him closer. I run my hands up his back, under his shirt, feeling his hard muscles which shiver at my touch. Shayne puts me in a place of comfort I've never known existed.

"Do you want to be here?"

I nod in the darkness.

"Do you want to see my world?"

I do. For reasons beyond my explanation, I am drawn to Shayne. To Hell. Even the stones in this tunnel seem to draw me in, making me feel like I belong.

"You have to answer me. Even if you weren't here for Chloe, would you want to be here?"

"Yes." And I lean my head forward again, and this time, our lips meet, and we kiss, and his mouth tastes like burning sweetness. There is no way I've only known Shayne a week. Our kiss screams volumes in my mind, making me sure I've known him forever. I trace my fingers up his spine, and he lets out a small groan. I wouldn't have thought it possible, but he pushes himself closer until every bit of our bodies touches. Against my chest, his heart beats, joining the pounding of my own. His hands are at my shoulders, then my neck, then down at my waist.

They start to travel downward to my hips, but then he stops, pulling his head away and pushing back from me, leaving me unsatisfied and wanting more. He gasps and steps backward, taking deep breaths matching my own. I can't move, because I can't get enough air to make my mind think, and we stand there in silence in the dark of the tunnel.

"That's nice," he says when his breathing has slowed.

I still can't move, though if I could, it would be back to him. "Yeah, nice."

"Thank you," he says.

"For what?"

"For trusting me. And being with me."

"I might never leave," I say.

He lets out a laugh. "And I might never let you."

He takes my hand, and we again walk down the tunnel. The warmth grows with every step we take, but the breeze continues, making it almost balmy. Soon the tunnel begins to grow lighter, and I see flickering, like flames of a fire, ahead in the distance.

"We're almost there." His hand snakes up to my neck, and he gives it a quick squeeze. And then we turn a final corner, and the world erupts in light ahead of us.

I turn to Shayne and laugh. "You live here?" When I thought of Hell in the past, I always figured it to be black and fiery.

He leads me down a couple steps into the room before me. The smooth, white walls look like they get polished hourly. The pristine floor is decorated with a giant mosaic in tiny black and red tiles stretching the entire distance of the room. It's a design of red flowers growing off black vines. A design which reminds me of drawings I made as a child. In the center of the room sits a coffee table with cut gems inlaid in the circular top and red and black chairs surrounding it. The colored gems of the table are arranged in bouquets of flowers—lotuses and orchids, with stems twisting around each other, forming a continuous design.

"Did you expect something else?" Shayne asks.

I turn to him, dragging my eyes away from the table and the amazing mosaic floor. "Well, yeah. Look at this place."

He looks around. "You don't like it?"

"Of course I like it. How could I not like it? I mean, it's fantastic."

Shayne smiles and sits on a black chair. "Someone with impeccable taste designed it."

An enormous pang of jealousy rockets through me when I realize he must be talking about Persephone. And I think that even if she is gone like he's said, I may never be able to compete with any memories of her. I close my eyes and stem the envy running through me.

He gestures at a red chair, and I sit down, sinking into the plush leather, letting it swallow me like I want this whole world to do with each second that passes. Shayne waves his hand over the table, and a bottle of wine and two glasses appear on the bed of colored flowers.

"Isn't there some myth about eating or drinking in the Underworld?"

Shayne picks up the bottle. He uncorks it and fills the two red crystal wine goblets halfway. At this point, I don't mind drinking it if it means I could stay here with Shayne forever.

"Yes, a myth." He smiles and hands me my glass.

I take it but don't put it to my lips. "Is it true?"

"Do you want it to be?"

I smile and put the glass to my mouth, taking a long drink. "Yes. I want it to be." I think about my mom for some reason, right as I drink it, and try to imagine her reaction to what I'm doing. Sitting with Hades in the Underworld drinking wine. And she told me to stay in all weekend.

"Something funny?"

It's not really funny. "I was just thinking about my mom."

Shayne takes a sip of his own wine. "Your mom has issues."

It's funny he should realize this after knowing me for such a short period of time. But it's not like I can deny it. "She's not that bad."

"Maybe we shouldn't think about your mom."

Shayne's right. Thinking about my mom and what she would do if she saw me now is laughable but also a mood dampener. So I push her out of my mind.

I motion down to the floor. "I love your mosaic."

It's complicated, and the flowers sort of shift depending on what angle I look at it from.

"I can't take credit for the design." His eyes meet mine when he says it, and my jealousy resurfaces. He seems like he wants me to ask more about it, but I decide against it. I vow not to think about Persephone again because I'm here and she's not.

"Well, it is beautiful." I look around the room, away from our chairs. The far wall holds a bookcase stacked with volumes of leather bound books. I stand and move toward it, bringing my glass of wine with me. It's so different than the wine I had with Reese last night. Sweeter and warmer.

When Reese pops into my mind, my heart races. I turn to Shayne who's looking at me but doesn't say a word, and I pray mind reading is not a skill the Lord of the Underworld possesses. I look back to the books.

"You have a nice collection."

Shayne gets up and joins me. His hand touches me at the nape of the neck, sending a shiver down to my toes. "I like to read."

It's an amazing response from an amazing guy.

Inset in the bookcases is a framed map. "What's that?"

"The Underworld." Shayne traces his finger over the network of rivers on the map. "There are five rivers in the Underworld. Boundaries between the lands." He points across one of the rivers. "And here are the

Elysian Fields…"

"The what?"

"Elysian Fields. They're kind of like the nice place," he says. "The place you get to go when you've been really good."

"Like Heaven?"

"Some people call it that."

A lump forms in my throat before I can stop it. "Is that where Chloe would go?"

Shayne's hand settles on mine, and he nods. "Of course."

"I don't want her to die."

"I know," he says. "But you promised you'd at least consider."

The lump stays in my throat. Chloe is my best friend. But I did promise. "I want to see it."

"Anytime you're ready."

I reach for my glass and take a final sip of wine. It seeps through me, tickling as it goes. "I'm ready."

Shayne sets my glass on a shelf along with his own—two red glasses on a shelf of black. He reaches out his hand, and I place mine in his. His hand is so large, it wraps entirely around mine, reminding me of Reese's hands. But I push Reese far from my mind. Shayne brushes my cheek with his other hand. "Then let's go see paradise."

Chapter 15

Paradise

When we come out of the tunnel and reach the shore, tree limbs hang low, covered in ice crystals which sparkle everywhere, bouncing off the snowy ground under our feet. Dampness is thick in the air. This river is frozen, and even though we've entered a winter wonderland, I look at Shayne, now bundled in a sweatshirt and jeans, and frown.

He waves his hand in front of me, and my clothes change. I'm now dressed in jeans, boots, and a Shearling wool coat covering to my knees. They say there used to be stores that carried nothing but winter clothes, but now the only places that sell them are indoor resort areas. Back when I was like eight, my mom took me and my friend Charlotte to a resort in Virginia. Once I got past the awe of seeing fake snow fall from the ceiling, we spent the day skiing and skating and making snowballs. My mom even skated though she spent most of her time falling on her butt. It was only years later that I realized the day must have cost her a small fortune, but she never said a word about it.

Shayne takes a step from the snowy ground out

onto the ice. "It's solid. You can jump on it if you want."

I look down at myself and then stare at him. "You can change my clothes?"

He laughs. "I'm a god, Piper. I can do anything."

I narrow my eyes. "Anything?"

Humor plays on his face. "Well, there are rules, but it's fun to find ways to break them."

I don't answer. My mind flickers back to the earlier conversation about rules in the Underworld. There are apparently some rules Shayne isn't willing to break. But I decide against bringing it up. All I want to do right now is enjoy this icy paradise with the guy I want to be my soulmate.

I reach a foot out, barely touching it to the slick ice. But my foot slips out from under me, and I fall on my butt.

Shayne laughs.

"What? It's not like I've had much time to practice ice skating in Texas." Austin used to have a public rink, but it went private when energy rates got too high, and then it closed entirely. Even with solar power, the cost of the A/C was exponential. I put my hands on the ground and try to get up, but I fall again, and Shayne only laughs harder. So I kick my leg out and swipe it against his feet, sending him falling to the ground next to me.

"That's not fair," he says. But his eyes sparkle even as he reaches out and tries to grab me.

I slide backward and push myself up on my hands. "It seems fair to me."

Overhead, a breeze comes our way, rustling the frost-laden branches and sending handfuls of frozen crystals raining down onto the ice. It sounds like a symphony of bells and continues for over a minute. I look upward at the trees, letting the chill in the air and the warmth of the sky hit my face, and I suck in the fresh air. I know Shayne's watching me. But I don't look, instead closing my eyes and enjoying the song.

When it's over, I try to move again, and within a few steps, I remember how to walk on the stuff. Standing there, stable, I actually have time to look out across the ice. "Why is it frozen?"

Shayne slides over to me. "It's Cocytus. The river of lamentation. But there's nothing to be sorry about when you're going to the Elysian Fields, so it's frozen over to make crossing easier."

The ice is thick, and far below I see the monsters, trapped but still moving. If there was no ice, what would these monsters feed on with the sorrows all gone?

I shift my eyes away from the monsters and back to the shimmering world in front of me. "I never thought there would be ice in Hell." And certainly not an icy wonderland, especially since my mom's always talking about how horrible winter used to be. But even in my coat, I shiver when a blast of cold air hits me. Shayne moves closer and wraps a warm arm around me.

"So you thought it would be all fire and torture?"

I nod, and he laughs.

"So there's no fire and torture?" I ask.

"We have our share of that, too. But we're not going to Tartarus today."

"What's Tartarus?"

Shayne leans close and whispers in my ear. "It's where the bad people go." And then he turns my face toward him and smiles. "It's what gives Hell such a bad reputation."

"Sounds intriguing." I laugh when I say it, but part of me does want to see the fire. To see if it really is as scary as all the images of Hell I've been fed my entire life. I want to see everything in Shayne's world.

"Intriguing is a good word for it," Shayne says. His exposed skin's picked up an icy layer which makes him look like he has smoke curling off him.

"I'd like to see it."

His face falls a bit though he tries to hide it behind a quick smile. "Let's just keep you out of Tartarus. It's a nasty, dirty place." He says it casually, but his voice tells me it's not a suggestion.

Which makes me want to see it more. Does he really think I'm so weak I can't handle it? "It's part of your world. You said you'd show me."

"Not Tartarus. Not this time."

He drops it, so I drop it. And soon, we're on the other side.

Shayne slides up to a dock, implanted in the thick ice, and gestures with his arm to the shore—to the people there. "Piper, this is paradise."

Every single person in the Elysian Fields looks like it's the best day of their lives. I guess really it would be the best day of their deaths, since everyone here is dead. But if a single person is sad about being dead, they aren't showing it. I spot three beach volleyball games, at least fifteen couples making out, and enough sandcastles being built, it's like an entire kingdom made of sand. And all I can think about is how much Chloe would love it here. We could play on the beach and not have to worry about the scorching sun overhead.

But I wouldn't be here with her, and I don't want her to leave me.

"So what does it take to get here?" I know billions of people have died over the course of history, but paradise isn't that crowded. There must be some sort of entry requirements.

Shayne laughs. "Well, getting on my good side can't hurt."

I tilt my head, trying to look sweet. "Am I on your good side?"

Shayne brushes my cheek with the back of his hand. "Definitely."

I motion with my hand at the beach. "And all these people got on your good side?"

"Sort of." Shayne links my arm, and we start walking

on the long dock. It's slick with the frozen ice of the river, but my booted feet grip the grainy wood underneath. "It's the people who've done something to help others that mostly get here. The ones who don't only think of themselves." He turns, and his eyes meet mine. "People like Chloe."

I nod but don't trust myself to answer. Even if this is paradise, it's not time for Chloe to die. She can live the rest of her life, and then, when she's old and gray, we can come to the Elysian Fields together.

I step down from the dock, and my feet warm at once, making my boots unnecessary. It seems the boundary between the icy cold of Cocytus and the warmth of the Elysian Fields is immediate. I look at Shayne. "So…"

He looks back. "So what?"

I motion down at my clothes: the jeans, boots, and coat. "Are you going to change my clothes again?"

He gives me a look which makes me want to both kiss him and punch him in the stomach at the same time. "Are you coming on to me?" he says.

I start to pull off the coat. "Whatever." I wonder what I have on underneath the clothes, but I never get the chance to find out. Shayne waves his arm again, and I'm back in my tank top and shorts.

I close my eyes and let the heat of the two suns warm my skin. Shayne walks over to me and touches my arm, brushing my tattoo, and a chill runs down my body.

The tattoo catches my eye. It looks lighter, like it's vanishing, but the skin is still raised underneath.

"It's fading." I'm not sure what it means. "Is Chloe—?"

"—fine." Shayne rubs the tattoo again, and the color returns, each Greek letter darkening at his touch. "She's just like we left her. I gave you my word."

I stare at the tattoo. "Have we been gone long?" Is the fading a bad sign for her? Is she dying—again?

But Shayne shakes his head. "No time has passed." He holds my chin with his thumb and forefinger, and his eyes meet my own. In his eyes, red flashes within the chocolate brown.

"Thank you," I say. His words settle the lump that's been surfacing in my throat every time I think of Chloe. The image of her and the horrible, beautiful winged man.

"Piper!"

I turn at the sound of the voice, and I see a child running toward me on the beach. She's wearing shorts and a T-shirt, and her long brown hair trails after her as she runs.

"Charlotte?"

She laughs, and when she reaches me, I let go of Shayne and grab her into a giant hug because I can't really believe she's here. She was my best friend from childhood, but Leukemia came along with a fury and took her away from me in sixth grade. But now that she's here, I never want to let her go.

"Piper! You're so pretty. So grown up."

"Charlotte…" I'm not sure what to say. I feel like I'm back six years ago, running around, watering plants in our shop. We were inseparable—my mom even approved, and then Charlotte left me. Like Chloe almost left me today. "I'm so sorry."

Charlotte pulls back from me and reaches up to my eyes. "Piper, you're crying." Her face is soft, and her hand moves up and touches her mouth as if she's trying to make sense of my words.

I realized I haven't been clear. "You were so young. You had your whole life ahead of you. And then it was over. Just like that."

Charlotte's face lights up, and her smile returns. "Don't cry, Piper. I'm so happy. Even my dog is here with me." And on cue, the Yorkie she used to have is next to her, pawing at her leg for attention.

I scratch him behind the ears. "Remember how sad we were when he died?"

Charlotte shakes her head. "He never died, Piper. He's here. See?"

It takes me a few seconds to process her words, and I realize she only remembers good things about life.

I bend down, and Charlotte wipes my cheeks, and I gather her again into a hug. "Everyone missed you so much. You had the loveliest funeral. It was perfect." I think of her funeral, the only one I've ever been to. I told my mom I'd seen Charlotte there, up by the altar. Like a ghost and an angel blended into one. So small, but shining and looking right at me.

My mom told me I'd imagined it, and she made me promise never to talk about it again.

"Your parents missed you, Charlotte. Everyone did. Even my mom." I'm rambling now, but I want her to know how much I cared. What an impact she had on my life. If not for Charlotte, I may never have had a true friend before Chloe. And seeing Charlotte, I know I can't let Chloe go, even though I know Chloe would be happy here. I may be the most selfish person in the planet, but she's the only friend I have.

But Charlotte shakes her head. "It doesn't matter."

I feel a hand on my shoulder and turn to see Shayne. "Humans can't escape death. The best they can hope for is to leave their sorrows behind at the River Acheron and come to live here," he says

I look around at the world I've come into and wonder what Charlotte's sorrow was. Does someone that young have a true sorrow? "But everyone doesn't make it here," I say.

Shayne shakes his head. "And everyone doesn't deserve to either."

Charlotte's dancing back and forth on her feet like she can't contain herself. "Are you coming, Piper?

I look to Shayne who gives an "I don't know" shrug.

"Coming where?" I ask.

"The sculpture contest," Charlotte says. "Meet me there." And then she runs off before I can say another word. I'm struck by how different our reactions are. She's acting like we were just hanging out yesterday, and I watched her be buried and have lived six years since.

I turn to Shayne. "Can we go?"

He nods his head toward a giant dune. "We need to check in first."

Chapter 16

Rhadamanthus

We walk over the dune toward a house I haven't noticed until now. In fact, the more I think about it, the more sure I am that it wasn't here two minutes ago. Maybe in paradise, things can appear out of nowhere.

"Who lives here?" I ask. As we get closer, the beach clears until it's just Shayne and me walking side by side. He reaches for my hand and holds it. I pretend my heart isn't beating like crazy.

"Rhadamanthus," he says, like it's a name everyone should know.

I guess he sees my blank look.

"Overlord of the Elysian Fields." Shayne smiles and gives my hand a squeeze. "And one of my best friends."

My stomach fills with jitters when I think of meeting Shayne's best friend, and I guess Shayne can tell.

"You'll love Rhadam," he says. "Of the company in the Underworld, he's the best. Though I'll be honest—the competition isn't too tough."

I grin, and the thought that Shayne wants me to meet his best friend warms me. Like he wants to show me off, when, in fact, it's me who would want to show him off. Though, aside from Chloe, I have only my mom to show him to. And I can imagine her reaction.

"What's so funny?" Shayne asks.

"I'm not sure *funny* is the right word," I say.

"What?"

I laugh again at the absurdity. "I was just thinking of how my mom would react if I brought you home to meet her."

Shayne's face goes deadpan. "Your mom would try to skewer me." But then he gives me a playful smile. "So can I take that as an invitation?"

I figure the question doesn't even need an answer. Ahead of me in the sand, I spot something dark, and when we reach it, I bend down to pick up a black oyster shell.

"So much of the fish life is dying…" my voice carries off, and I look upward. I'm not sure how to phrase it.

"Above ground?" Shayne finishes for me.

I nod. "It's hard to find any shells at the beach." The beach back in Virginia scarred me. Dead fish littered it, and the birds that fed on them coated the sand like filth. It was one of those images that never goes away. I can still remember when the alarms sounded, signaling that the sea level was rising. Everyone was supposed to evacuate the beaches. And most people did. The bodies of those who didn't washed up for weeks afterward. But the sea life never had a chance. Contaminants rushed in with the rising water and killed armies of species. My mom and I had walked the beach for hours, and all we saw was death.

Shayne must be able to read some of the horror on my face. "Your mom took you to the beach when you were younger?"

I reach down, picking up another shell which curves in on itself until I can't see anything but a single dot in the center. I try to focus on it instead of the memory of dead fish. "We used to live by a beach. Back in Virginia, when I knew Charlotte."

"I never knew that."

"Why would you? Are you omniscient?" The thought of Shayne knowing everything sends a rush of adrenaline into my chest.

"If only." He shakes his head, and for a moment, he looks so vulnerable. So normal. "Omniscience is not within the power of the gods."

I laugh. "That's a good thing, I think. Anyway, my mom never wanted anyone to know who we were or where we lived."

"So why'd you move?" He's casual, reaching down, grabbing a handful of sand, letting it fall through his fingers. Each grain sparkles in the sun, and it's so white, when it hits the ground, it reminds me of powdered sugar. But he wants the answer. I hear it in his voice.

"It was right after Charlotte died." My heart starts

pounding when I begin to tell him, catching me totally off guard.

"What happened?" He's looking at me now, coaxing the words out with his eyes.

"Nothing." I throw up my arms. "I don't know. I mean one minute we're there going to her funeral. And the next thing I know, my mom's telling me to pack my bags. That my father had shown up at the funeral. That he was coming to take me away. And we're leaving that night."

Shayne takes the hand not holding the black oyster shell. "Did you see him?"

I shake my head, and though my heart is still pounding, it feels good to get it out. "My father? No. I was only eleven. I don't even know what he looks like. But I've heard it my entire life. That if my dad found me, he'd take me away and never let me see my mom again. That he was a dangerous terrorist and was wanted by the government. She told me we needed to be more careful. It was always the same old story."

"So you never met your dad?"

"No. My parents got divorced when I was a baby. Or maybe they weren't even married. Sometimes I wonder if I can believe my mom." I flip the oyster shell over with my other hand, studying the pearly gray of the inside. It's reflecting a thousand different colors, and I wish I could keep it forever. Keep part of the Underworld forever.

Shayne smiles and reaches up to my cheek. "Sometimes you shouldn't believe her."

I know he's right. But still, it's not like I want to hear him say it. She's my mom. My problem.

He starts walking, still holding my hand. "What do you think of the house?" he asks.

I look up to where he's pointing and try to make sense of what I see there. "Is it really a house?"

I guess in the most technical sense of the word, it is a structure. There are four walls, a roof, and probably a hundred windows, but none of them touches. Each piece floats in the air of its own accord.

"Rhadam is a bit unusual."

This turns out to be a huge understatement. Rhadamanthus looks like a knight getting ready for a jousting competition. It's not just the leather pants and undershirt he's wearing. It's the fact that when we walk into the atrium of his home, he has a sword in each hand and is fighting off two invisible opponents.

"I'll take your spleen this time." Thrust. He whips around, his long brown hair flying. "You think you can sneak up behind me." Stab. Back around. "The spleen wasn't enough? You've come back for more." Thrust.

It's like he's totally unaware of our presence. Shayne clears his throat, but it doesn't help.

"Your head comes off this time." Swipe.

I can almost see a head rolling away into the corner of the atrium. Turn. Kick. Thrust. Twist.

"Is he fighting anyone?" I whisper to Shayne, wondering if there are actually ghosts he's battling or something else invisible to me.

Shayne shakes his head. "Rhadam just has a really good imagination." He clears his throat again.

Still nothing. "You can join your companion." Swipe. And I can almost see the head flying through the air, landing with a thud next to the other one.

Maybe I just have a really good imagination, also.

Only when both invisible opponents are defeated does Rhadam turn around and smile at us.

"I hope you came to fight. It's impossible to find good competition these days." Rhadam's face cracks into a grin that makes it obvious he does a lot more smiling that frowning. And he looks like he lives life exactly how he wants to, kind of like Chloe. She'd go nuts over him. I can almost picture them together.

Shayne—or Hades, I have to keep reminding myself—lets go of my hand and walks over to Rhadam, where they do some handshake thing that makes me think they're trying to kill each other.

"No fighting today," Shayne says.

"Scared?" Rhadam asks.

"Please. If I kill you, who am I going to get to watch over Elysium for me?" Shayne punches Rhadam in the shoulder, but he's so solid he hardly moves.

Rhadam punches Shayne back. "And if I killed you, I'd have to take your place ruling the Underworld." His eyes flash over my way, and he smiles. "But maybe that's not a bad thing. The Underworld seems to have nice spoils."

Blood rushes to my face, and I know I'm turning seventeen different shades of red. I smile back, hoping I don't look like too much of an idiot in front of Shayne's best friend.

Shayne purses his lips. "Spoils. I like that." He walks back to me and takes my hand, leading me over to Rhadam. "This is Piper."

Rhadam lifts my hand to his mouth and kisses the back of it which, even though I'm sure I'm already at the stage of infinite red, still makes me blush deeper. "You're even prettier than Hades said."

I look at Shayne. He rolls his eyes and looks away, so I turn back to Rhadam.

"He's mentioned me?"

Rhadam laughs. "Gods, he hasn't talked about anything else all week. It's been 'Piper this' and 'Piper that.' I feel like I've already met you twenty times over."

My eyes flicker back over to Shayne. It's his turn to be embarrassed. I can't resist. "I had no idea the Lord of the Underworld could blush." But the mere fact that he's been talking about me this week to his best friend is making my stomach flip around in all sorts of ways I never thought possible.

Shayne clears his throat and gives Rhadam the evil eye. "Rhadam may be exaggerating just a bit."

Rhadam takes my hand away from Shayne's. "Trust me, I'm not exaggerating." And he starts walking with me following at his side.

I look at Shayne who, though still bright red, winks and follows on after us.

Rhadam leads us out of the atrium and into the house. With the structure of the house, we slip between where walls should join, move through doors that don't come close to shutting, and walk up onto the roof on individual stairs that don't connect.

"I moved the house because of the view." He motions out to the river which now looks like it has waves big enough to capsize the Titanic. But behind the ocean, like a giant monolith, a glacier fills the horizon. It's blue and green and white, and the suns above reflect off it, making it look almost neon. It's so much ice all in one place and like nothing I've ever seen on Earth.

"I don't blame you." Shayne stands next to me, so close our legs touch. He takes my other hand, leaving me standing between him and Rhadam. Shayne gives the hand Rhadam still holds a suspicious look, and Rhadam lets go of it.

"The ice," I say. "There's so much of it."

Shayne traces his thumb along the back of my hand. "Sometime we should visit the polar caps."

I love that this implies there will be more of *us* in the future. "I'll hold you to that," I say.

"Good," Shayne says.

Rhadam clears his throat. "Of course. I'd love to come. Thanks for asking."

"You can leave?" I ask.

He sighs. "No, not really. It's one of the funny things about paradise. I can't ever leave, but whatever I want, I get." He glances away from the glacier and turns back toward the beach, but instead of being up high, we're again on ground level. We leave the house and start walking back in the direction of the beach party.

"So how did you die?" Rhadam asks.

It takes a second for his words to make sense. I look down at myself to make sure I'm all still there. "I'm not dead."

Rhadam laughs, and I realize he's joking. "Don't worry. You don't look dead. You don't even smell dead."

It makes me wonder how dead people in the Underworld smell. I haven't noticed anything, but then again, I'm not sure I'd know what to smell for.

Rhadam purses his lips and then looks to Shayne. "It's too bad, you know. You should do something about it."

It's like Shayne is actually considering it. But then he replies. "I'm not sure that's the best way to win a girl's heart."

"Definitely not," I say. Though he's already got the heart part under control.

As we walk, people fill in again until the beach party is back in full swing. Shayne is like a rock star. People rush up to him constantly, telling him how happy they are here in paradise and how their only wish is that he would visit more often. He glances at me out of the corner of his eye as if to apologize, but he doesn't push them away. In fact, he lets go of my hand so he can have more space.

I'm fighting stabs of jealousy because so many of the girls are gorgeous when Rhadam leans over and whispers in my ear. "They love him here."

I smile and pretend I'm totally fine with all the attention Shayne is giving them in return. "I can tell." I can't help but wonder if that's how Chloe would act if she were here, all fawning over him and stuff, but I push the thought aside since Chloe will not be here.

As we walk, I decide to ask Rhadam everything I want to know about paradise. Like where people live and if they get married and do they have to work. He tells me about how people fall in love all over again and how weddings are held barefoot on the beach and how everyone has some purpose for his or her existence, whether it's constructing sand sculptures or trying to get their golf swing just right. He talks about friendships that bond over eternity and children that are reunited with their parents once they pass on. And even though he answers my questions endlessly, what I really can't understand is the judging criteria. What makes one person better than the next?

"What if someone is kind of good? What then?" I

ask.

Maybe I ask too loudly because Shayne pulls away from his most recent group of adorers and comes back to my side. "They get judged," he says. "Just like everyone else."

I press him. "Who judges?" I glance to Rhadam, but he has his lips pressed together like he doesn't want to be part of this conversation.

Shayne stops walking and turns me to him. "I judge."

"Everyone?"

He nods. "Every single soul that comes across the River Acheron gets judged."

Rhadam clears his throat. "How about I catch up with you two later?" And before either of us can answer, he simply vanishes. It's hardly the strangest thing that's happened today.

"Isn't that kind of a big job?" I ask once Rhadam's gone. I've never heard the exact numbers, but I know tens of thousands of people die each day. And that number's only increasing each day the Global Heating Crisis continues. I can only imagine how world disasters affect the death toll.

Shayne's eyes get a faraway look, and they aren't meeting mine anymore. "I've had help. But it's still a big job."

"And an even bigger responsibility," I say. After all, trying to decide who gets paradise and who gets stuck with eternal torment could probably keep someone up at night.

"Don't you ever get a feeling about people?" he asks.

"Like what?"

"You know. Like you can look into their soul and see what they've done wrong."

I grab his wrist. "All the time. I swear. My mom tells me I'm imagining things, but I just have this way of knowing who's to blame." It's the reason I want to go to law school once I get out of college. Whether it's bullies at school or criminals on the tube, I get so sick of seeing people get off with no punishment. I think of the black fungus on Councilman Rendon. For some reason, I'm not only able to sense guilt. Now I can see it.

He nods, and I realize if anyone can ever understand, it's Shayne.

"That's how it is for me, too," he says and motions out across the world. "But it's just on a bigger scale here. And judgments last forever."

We reach the dock, and Charlotte runs back up to greet us. She's every bit of her eleven-year-old giddy self. She grabs both our hands and pulls us. "Come on. They're just about to judge the contest."

We let her pull us, and then we run after her as she moves through the people. I worry about running into someone, but it's like a path has been cleared just for us. People have even stopped flocking around Shayne. And then we head up a dune and down the other side to the contest.

There are about fifteen sand sculptures scattered around the beach. The first I see is a giant head resting on its side with a crown of leaves around it. Its eyes are closed like it's sleeping, and hanging above it is a giant hand pressing it downward. My face heats up when I see the next sculpture. A man and a woman are in a moment of complete ecstasy. The woman sits on top of the man with her mouth wide open, and birds flying out of it. I glance sideways at Shayne who looks over and reaches for my hand. I let him take it, and he gives it a squeeze. I squeeze it back and finally look away from the figures. Charlotte leads us through all the sculptures, and we stop at each one until we finally reach the smallest. My heart almost stops when I see it. It's a perfect replica of the box Melina had given me on my birthday. The lid is wide open, and there's a phoenix flying out. The sun sits just above the head of the phoenix such that the rays of light and the feathers of the bird become one.

"Do you like it, Piper?" Charlotte asks.

I nod. I can't pull my eyes from it.

"I made it just for you," she says.

"For me?" How could she have known I would be here?

Shayne smiles at Charlotte. "It's definitely the best."

And as if everyone in the contest can hear him, they all start cheering. I take this to mean Charlotte's won the contest, and I'm not about to disagree. All the sculptures are amazing, but hers rises right to the top.

Charlotte grabs our hands again. "There's the most wonderful view up from the hills. You have to come see it."

"Of course," Shayne says, and the excitement in his voice seems almost childlike. Like given his choice, he'd spend all his days on hills in the Elysian Fields rather than ruling over the Underworld. His eyes light up, and sunshine bounces inside them, mixing with the red flecks, making them glow. They seem to pour out love. But not just love for me. Love for the people around him. Joy from the Elysian Fields.

It's everywhere, and I can't help but let it touch me, too. From the beach to the trees to the clouds in the sky. And when we reach the top of the hill Charlotte's taken us to, I look up and let out a gasp. The Underworld is a rainbow of unadulterated color.

Trees and bushes grow on rolling hills, and flowers of every size and color fill the spaces in between. Meadows of them—purples and yellows and even my favorite reds. Set underneath the tree tops are tree houses and hobbit holes and stone cottages. It's a world of nature and beauty, and it reminds me of what I imagine our own Earth looked like before it got paved over.

Charlotte heads back to the beach, but Shayne and I stay, watching the clouds while lying on a blanket of daffodils.

"Do you like paradise?" he asks.

I laugh at the incredulity of the question. "It's paradise."

"Chloe would be happy here."

"What if I say no?" There's not really a *what if* about it.

"Then Chloe will live."

It's the answer I want. "And then when she dies much later on, she'll come here?" I think of Chloe and me here together enjoying paradise. Forever.

Shayne's words shake me from my thoughts. "She'll have to be judged again, Piper. She'll live her life tempting Fate, and when her time comes again, I'll have to make that decision."

"But of course she'd come here." I can't see that it's really a question.

"Near death can change people," Shayne says. "Not even I know what will happen if you choose to let Chloe live."

I fall into a half sleep there on the grass, thinking about Chloe and death, but I'm woken by the sound of voices. I pretend to still be asleep, but I crack open one eye so I can see. Rhadam's come back, and he and Shayne are sitting across from each other, talking.

"I'm not trying to tell you your business," Rhadam says. "But you have a serious problem."

"Like what?" Shayne asks, and suddenly I'm wide

awake, though I try not to move.

Rhadam's eyes flicker over to me then back at Shayne. Out of my peripheral vision, I see Shayne nod. He doesn't know I'm listening.

"I talked to Minos yesterday," Rhadam says. "I borrowed help from him to move the house. And he mentioned he had a visitor." His words are staid, and I know it's because I'm just a couple feet away that he doesn't want to speak freely.

Shayne's whole body stiffens. "What kind of visitor?"

Rhadam leans in close. "Okay, he started drinking, and you know how Minos is when he drinks."

"Everyone in the Underworld knows how Minos is when he's drunk," Shayne says.

"Right. So, he started bragging. Saying he knew how to return memories and get souls back across the river."

"He's lying," Shayne says.

Rhadam puts up his hand to silence Shayne.

"Maybe. But then he told me he'd been talking to Ares. That Ares found a way to get through the boundaries of the Underworld. He said Ares knew everything."

Shayne's fingers dig into the ground. "That's impossible."

"Impossible, but it happened," Rhadam says. "And you need to watch out."

Ares is the god of war; I know this from mythology.

His name causes my skin to prickle while at the same time making butterflies form in the pit of my stomach.

Shayne stands up. "Tell me how the god of war has managed to enter my domain." His eyes bore into Rhadam who matches his gaze. "Tell me that."

Rhadam is silent for a moment while I watch. People getting into the Underworld without Shayne's knowledge can't be a good thing.

Finally, Rhadam sighs. "He must have help. Some shortcut in."

I decide it's time to enter the conversation. "There are shortcuts into the Underworld?"

Shayne keeps his eyes on Rhadam and doesn't even blink at the fact that I'm awake. I wonder if he's known all along. "There are no shortcuts into the Underworld," he says. "Everyone has to go by Charon."

Rhadam shakes his head. "Except Ares."

"How?" I ask.

"Ares is working with someone on the inside; he has to be," Rhadam says.

Shayne runs a hand through his hair. "I still say it's not possible. The boundaries should be secure."

"So this is a real problem?" I ask.

Shayne looks at me then and tries to give me a reassuring smile, but I see how white his face has gotten. "It's nothing. Just normal stuff going on here in the Underworld."

He's lying. The Underworld has issues just like the

world above. Maybe the worlds aren't so different after all. And he really wants me to send Chloe here? "But other gods are getting in."

"Yes," Rhadam says at the same time Shayne shakes his head.

"So why now?" I ask.

Shayne's eyes meet mine. "Good question. Why now?"

I glance at Rhadam whose eyes are fixed on me, waiting. Why would others be coming to the Underworld? I figure the Underworld can't be much different from any world. "They want control?" I say.

Rhadam nods. "My thoughts exactly. They want control. Ares wants to claim the Underworld for his own."

"The day Ares takes over the Underworld, I'll tear his entrails out inch by inch and knit them into a chew toy for Cerberus," Shayne says.

Rhadam opens his mouth, but hesitates.

"What?" Shayne says.

"You should go to the assembly," Rhadam says. "Get a warrant out for Ares."

"I'm not taking my problems to the assembly of gods," Shayne says. "We've been over this."

"Why not?" I ask.

Shayne turns to me. "Because it's the ultimate show of weakness. There's no better way to lose control than to admit you need help."

I'm not sure if I agree with this logic, but I doubt Shayne wants to argue about it with me. Besides, he's the one in control here, not me.

He turns back to Rhadam. "Thanks for watching my back."

Rhadam nods.

And then Shayne reaches out for my fingers and intertwines his with them, rubbing his thumb softly on the back of my hand. "Are you ready?"

"Are we leaving?" Not that I mind. As charming as Rhadam is, the conversation has put a certain chill into the air, even here in paradise. A chill of gods and battles over mythical domains.

Shayne nods.

"I'll see what else I can find out," Rhadam says. He looks at me, and his smile from the atrium returns. "Piper, can I just say how great it is to finally meet you?"

I nod, and when he takes my hand and kisses it, I feel like I'm on a stage with a million eyes watching me.

"It was great meeting you, too. Maybe I'll be back sometime," I say.

Rhadam nods and looks to Shayne. "It's a pretty nice place to come visit."

Shayne actually laughs, and a giant weight lifts off my chest, returning the atmosphere to one of fun. He grins at Rhadam. "Especially if you're overseeing Elysium."

Rhadam lets go of my hand. "It's a hard job, but I

sacrifice for the greater good." And then, once again, Rhadam vanishes.

"So what did I miss?" I ask Shayne.

"Nothing," he says. It has to be a lie. He must not want me to know. And, of course, this only makes me more curious. I'll find a way to figure it out.

Chapter 17

Paradise

Paradise is perfect, but Chloe is waiting for me. "Are we going?" I ask.

"Almost," Shayne says, and he leads me down from the hill. I guess he's still trying to convince me to let Chloe come here. He must know by now it's pointless. Or maybe he's just trying to stall for time. If this is the case, I can't say I mind much.

We walk until we reach a path of manicured greenery. Trees have grown along the sides, forming a tall arbor with a grass walkway below. It slopes downward, and water bubbles in a stream at the bottom. The green is so vibrant, so different from the world I know back above ground. That world hangs on the edge of extinction. And this world thrives. It's ironic how the world of the living is dying, and the land of the dead is alive.

Shayne grabs my hand, and out of nowhere bounds Cerberus, who knocks into Shayne and sends us both flying. After I wipe my face from Cerberus's exuberant licking, we get up and stroll down the path, Cerberus leading the way. He stops every so often to snap at a passing bird with one or all of his heads, but either has really bad aim, or isn't trying all that hard to catch one.

Once we're out of the arbor, we reach a stream which flows over rocks in a white froth until it clears them and settles into an even flow. To the left is the source of the water—a waterfall cascading down from a small cliff cut into a hill. The sun catches the water, reflecting a blaze of light around the entire valley. Vines climb up the rocks on the side of the falls, creating curtains that bloom with vibrant flowers. Mist hangs in the air above the crash of the water, forming a cloud of rainbows which holds steady even as the mist within it shifts and settles.

With each step I take, I want to move to the Underworld and stay here forever. To have Chloe actually come to paradise. To make it my new Botanical Haven away from the stifling presence of my mom. To live with Shayne forever. I follow him off into the trees, and pretty soon we come to a clearing which is planted with all sorts of orange and purple and electric blue flowers. Saffron yellow. Cherry red. Vibrant colors. Colors I love.

I look at Shayne. "This is your garden?"

"It's a new hobby. I've only been at it for a few years."

I walk into the center of the garden and look at the abundance of life sprouting out of the Earth around me. "And I thought I could grow things."

He walks over and joins me. "But there is this one that won't grow."

Around me is nothing but life. I smell each plant. I almost hear nectar pumping through stems, feeding them. But then I catch it—the smell of death, here in this beautiful garden. So misplaced that, as soon as I smell it, all other aromas go away. I close my eyes, and begin walking, following my instincts, and pretty soon I find myself in front of a tree which, although still alive, is not in bloom like the rest of the garden. It seems to be coated in a thick layer of yellowish green mucus, though when I reach my hands out to touch it, the mucus disappears. It reminds me of the disappearing mold I've been seeing on people back in the outer world. I wonder if both are an illusion that gives some sense of what is inside.

"A pomegranate tree?"

Shayne nods and reaches up to touch a branch with green leaves. "It won't produce fruit."

I run my hands over the bark. At home, in the Botanical Haven, I can nurse almost anything back to life. I can make fruit grow from even the ficklest of breeds. My mom says it's been that way since I was born.

The pomegranate tree is breathing. I feel it under my palms. But it's missing…something. Something fertile in the soil hasn't made its way to the roots. Or has been removed entirely.

"I built the garden around it," Shayne says.

I hear him but don't turn. "What happened?"

In his voice, I hear the resignation. "It just started dying."

Slowly, I turn. "The soil around it is empty."

"I do fertilize." Shayne seems to be reading my thoughts.

"Then why isn't it working?"

He shrugs. "I figured you could ask the tree."

I again place my palms on the hard bark. It seems to tell me it's missing a vital ingredient, but I soon realize maybe this isn't quite the truth. I recognize something, and suddenly, I feel like falling to the ground and crying. In my mind, I'm walking in a field. And aside from the grass which reaches well past my knees, the pomegranate tree stands alone. Awake. Aware. And bursting with life.

The branches hang low to the ground, plump with fruit. Light radiates from it as I draw close. I take a few steps closer until I can brush the bark with my hand. So healthy. So unlike the reality of what I've felt.

I lift my hand and reach for a fruit. It pulls against my touch, but then it gives and comes loose in my hand. It's the color of red wine, and I peel it until I can see the seeds inside.

And then, all at once, I'm being pulled from the tree. I reach out toward it, but it's moving away, and so am I. Leaves fall and fruit begins to drop. I'm so far away the tree is only a brown shape in the distance. Oppression hits the tree like a fist. And I'm back in the garden of flowers with Shayne.

I take my hands off the tree and turn to Shayne.

"I thought you said there was no sadness here in the Elysian Fields."

"There's not. At least, there isn't supposed to be."

"This tree is full of sorrow." I think of the River Acheron. And deep inside me, the origins of the sorrow twist and form, growing like roots. I grab Shayne's eyes with my own and hold them. "Why is this tree sad?"

I see tears in the corners of his brown eyes; they shine when the red flashes. "A lot of the Underworld is sad. We've been that way for years." He looks away and reaches out to touch a nearby red flower.

A breeze blows through the valley.

"Should we go now?" Shayne asks.

I nod because the initial happy thoughts of paradise have vanished. I'm trying to hold onto them, but the tree's dug its sorrowful roots inside my soul. We walk out of the garden and head back the way we came. It's only when I see Cerberus's three heads looking our way that my sorrow begins to diminish. I push it away, but part of it sticks, as if echoes of the sadness will never leave me. Like it's a part of me I'll never understand.

Chapter 18

Departure

I can tell Shayne's pensive, and so am I. He's got his lips pressed together, and he doesn't even skate when we cross the river. Instead, we walk hand in hand in silence. And when we finally reach the winter wonderland on the other shore, I've decided it's time to head home. Shayne must realize he's been quiet, so he starts to make chit chat, but my mind drifts to Chloe, back above ground, at the side of the creek bed.

"I need to leave."

Shayne turns to me, and his eyes soften. I see the sadness filling them now.

"Please don't go." He brushes my arm. "Not yet."

And I think if he asks me right now, I will stay with him forever.

"Please?"

I nod, and he pulls me in and holds me. My body presses up against his on the edge of the River Cocytus, under the icicle trees. His muscles are hard, and they mesh into mine. I feel the beating of his heart in his neck; my forehead is so close to it. His skin is warm enough to melt every bit of ice around us; I let the heat soak into my body.

He kisses the top of my head, and a chill spreads down me, having nothing to do with the frozen river we've just crossed. He lets go of me and backs up so I can see his face. His soft, gorgeous, dark face. A face of mysteries. A face of secrets. I want to know his secrets. Want to share them with him.

"I really like the Underworld," I say.

"I really like you," he says.

He smiles, and I want to sink back into his warm arms. But he's one step ahead of me. He pulls me to the snowy ground, letting my coat fan out below me, and moves to me. His lips find mine. My arms snake around him, and I let his whole weight fall on me.

His kisses are hard and fierce, and his hot breath explores my mouth. I gasp for air when I can between kisses, but don't twist away because if it's a dream, I don't want to wake up. His hands move to my hair, breaking the ponytail holder with a snap, and he runs his hands through the tangles which have accumulated. Against me, I feel him, and I want him to be a part of me more than anything else.

His hands travel down my sides; I don't want to stop anything with Shayne. I lift his shirt and let my hands move over his skin. Each touch is electric, and his kisses taste of singed sweetness. Being with him here in our winter paradise is more perfect than the Elysian Fields, but Shayne stops way too soon and rolls off me. I try to move back to him, but he pushes me away and jumps to his feet, grabbing one of the supply chests near the dock and throwing it. It smashes into the rock wall, and the pieces scatter everywhere. And then thunder rumbles around us.

I stand up and try to force away the yearning which is pulsing so hard through my body it hurts. His back is to me, and I'm not sure if I should go over next to him or keep the distance between us. "Is it something I did?"

Shayne whips around, and his eyes are flashing. The red beats and throbs inside, and the brown is so dark it looks like ink. His teeth are clenched, and for a second, it seems he wants to kill me.

"Gods no! You could never do anything wrong."

I'm relieved and baffled all at the same time. I didn't do anything, but he also doesn't want to be with me. "Then why did you stop?"

Shayne closes his eyes, and tries to get his anger under control. His hands are balled in fists, but when he reopens his eyes, he relaxes his hands, and the red flashes settle down. "Because it would only confuse you more."

It's like his answer only throws more uncertainty my way. "I'm not confused about anything." Except every single event in the last week.

Shayne shakes his head and whistles, and soon Cerberus comes bounding out of the dark tunnel ahead. He runs to Shayne and stops at his feet. "The time isn't right."

The time seems right to me. But it stings, and even though he denies it, I'm sure it's something I've done.

Shayne smiles and reaches down to scratch Cerberus's left head. Its ears go back, and its eyes close as Cerberus leans forward. "I have to be patient; but it's just so hard." Our eyes hold each other until finally he breaks the contact. "I do think you're right about one thing."

Finally. "What?"

"It's time for you to go. At least for today."

I nod, though at this point, I don't really want to leave—ever. But Chloe's waiting for me back at the creek. "Can I come back sometime?"

"Piper, you can come back any time you want."

"How? Do you have a FON?" I have a hard time imagining that the city issued Shayne his own Functional Operating Node.

Shayne laughs and walks toward me, taking my hand. We start walking back down a tunnel, turning a few times, until we come out of the rock wall, and I see the banks of the River Acheron ahead of us. A boat approaches—Charon, coming to get us.

"No, no FON. But just call me. I'll be around." He gives my hand a quick squeeze.

I find the thought that Shayne will be around both comforting and alarming. He can't possibly be around every second of every day.

"Always?"

"No, not always," he says. "But enough."

I relax. The last thing I want is to move from an overprotective mom to an overprotective boyfriend. And I don't know if this thought means that Shayne is my boyfriend.

Our trip back with Charon is quiet. I sit in the front wrapped in Shayne's strong arms while Charon guides us across the bubbling river of sorrow. I hear the voices as we move through the water, see the monsters feasting on sadness, but I ignore them, instead thinking only of Chloe waiting for me and Shayne's burning warmth next to me and his odd but intense burst of anger back on the shore.

Charon smiles when I get off the boat, and for a moment, I want to reach out and give him a hug. He holds his feet firmly in one place, though, and since I don't see an opening, I brush the weird urge away. I chalk it up to the fact that I've just been in Hell for the day and I think I'm in love with Shayne, who is actually Hades, Lord of the Underworld. Not the most normal day, though certainly it's been the most memorable.

Shayne walks me away from the shore, and I recognize the place where we first arrived.

"Did you decide?" he asks.

Paradise will be waiting for Chloe later. Her time isn't now. There has to be a reason Tanni warned me about it. "I want Chloe to live." And with those words,

I am officially the most selfish person in the world.

Shayne nods. "And I stand by my word. It's your choice."

I move to hug him, but he puts up his hand. "Are you sure?"

"Of course," I say. Selfish or not, it is my decision.

"Okay, then she lives."

The words sound almost like a death sentence.

"Are you ready?" he asks.

I look up, but all I see is packed dirt and rock hovering above us. "How do we get through?"

"Just you this time."

I look away from the hard ceiling, back to his face. "You aren't coming with me?" And all of a sudden, I don't want to leave, which is funny considering I was just worried about him being overprotective.

"Chloe needs you. Not me," he says.

"You'll be at school?"

Shayne smiles, and it lights the dark cavern. At least for me. "School. The only good part of it is seeing you."

"You haven't been there all year, have you?" Maybe it's obvious by now, but I want the confirmation that I'm not crazy.

Shayne shakes his head. "Nope. Only a week. But you're the only one who knows that. I had to enroll so I could keep an eye on Reese."

Reese. I'd almost forgotten about him. My face burns when I think about kissing him. Was it just last night? It feels like a lifetime ago.

Shayne takes my chin in his hand. "Just promise me you'll be careful. Reese isn't what he seems."

It takes me a second, but then it comes together in my mind. "He's Ares."

Shayne nods. "The god of war. And apparently a bigger threat than I've estimated." His eyes darken a final time, and the red sparks flash. "Just stay away from him."

I nod even though part of me doesn't want anyone—not even Shayne—telling me what to do. As long as I don't see Reese, I should have no problem staying away from him.

Shayne puts his fingers to my lips. "And promise me you'll always trust me."

It's a strange request. And my mind flashes to our conversation with Rhadam. The secrets I know Shayne's keeping. "Of course."

Shayne smiles. "Thank you." He moves away from me and leaves me standing there alone.

I look back up at the packed earth above us. I know I need to go, yet I want to turn back and run to Hell. To Shayne. But Chloe needs me. And my mom needs me, stifling though she is. So I clear my mind, thinking only of my return, and soon I'm amid the swirling liquid silver, floating in it and breathing it in. I feel myself drifting back—back to the world above. I'm over-whelmed with the urge to fight against the drift, to kick my way back to Shayne and the Underworld. But I know life is waiting for me back on Earth. And so I continue on, losing myself in the cool fluid until I'm again on hard-packed ground.

Chapter 19

Shock

The world comes alive like a nightmare. I'm back in the Greenbelt; there's a stillness, and the sky is dead gray. And then there's some kind of sonic boom, and the air around me starts to hum and vibrate. Just before I left, the disperser missile launched even though the council knew it was going to destroy the atmosphere. And now it's like there's some rebound effect going on. Some kind of switch has been flipped. A blast of cold wind slams into me, and goose bumps explode on my bare arms.

Chloe's where I left her. Lying on the rock-covered ground. Still unconscious. I blink my eyes a few times, and the smell of the earth around me registers. What just happened?

Hell? I've been to Hell?

I look around, but there's no sign of the winged man who'd come for Chloe. His putrid odor is gone. He is gone. And so is Shayne.

Shayne is the Lord of the Underworld.

Chloe breathes normally, but she's pale. I head to the creek and grab a handful of water, holding it in my cupped hands. When I get back to her, I drop it on her face, rubbing it into her cold, white cheeks. She stirs, but doesn't wake, so I get some more and do it again. It's not until the third time that her eyes finally flutter open. Overhead, rain begins to fall. But it's hard, like tiny pellets being flung from the sky.

"Piper?"

She looks right at me, though her eyes don't see me. But she's alive.

I take her hand. "Hi, Chloe." I wipe the rain from her forehead and help her sit up.

She turns her head and looks toward the creek. "What happened? What am I doing here?"

"I think you collapsed from the heat."

She shudders as another gust of cold wind hits. "It's so cold."

I nod, though I want to forget about the weather. I want to forget about this whole global warming disaster we live in. All I really want to do is hug Chloe. To never let her go again. But she's still so dazed, and I don't want to startle her. "They launched another missile."

I don't think she's even close to feeling the panic that's starting to creep through me. Something is seriously messed up with the weather. The temperature has never dropped this quickly since I've been alive. But it's like Chloe doesn't even hear me. She shivers and wraps her arms around herself, and I notice her tattoo. Fading—like mine had done in Hell. I touch it, and the ebony ink revives under my touch until it's as dark as the day she got it. Just like mine did when Shayne touched it. I take this as a good sign.

Chloe pulls her arms closer, and her teeth begin to chatter. I realize she's in shock.

"We need to get you home." And like the fates are against us, the sky picks that moment to open up and begin dumping on us. Something hard hits my head and then bounces to the ground in front of me. I pick up a thick ball of ice. Hail—that's what we learned it was called. But it hasn't hailed since the Global Heating Crisis started.

I grab Chloe, and we make a run for the shuttle stop. She's like a rag doll but lets me lead her. We dash under the UV covering at the shuttle stop, but it's not UV I'm worried about right now. The hail is coming down like stones. The thermometer at the shuttle stop has dipped to fifty-four. I think there has to be a mistake. It drops as I watch to fifty-three then fifty-one. But fifty never comes because a giant piece of hail smacks into the red LEDs so hard, both Chloe and I jump. I think she's shivering, but then I realize I am too. The world is crashing in on us.

It takes forever for a shuttle to come. When it does, the driver has his hands gripped on the steering wheel because the road is solid ice. We're the only ones on the shuttle, and he instructs us to sit in the middle and not say a word. Chloe's not talking because I think she must still be in shock. I'm about to ask him if we can stop at the hospital because she's still so pale, but the driver looks like he's seen death himself, so I keep quiet. Chloe will be fine. She's alive.

The shuttle makes three more stops before we get to Chloe's house. At the first stop, Randy Conner gets on. He gives us a nod and then sits behind us.

"What the hell's up with this weather?" he says.

Chloe doesn't even look at him. She's pressed against me, but I turn my head to talk to him.

"The missile," I say. "It did something to the weather."

"You think so?" Even in a disaster, Randy's still a sarcastic jerk.

I ignore him and turn back around. The shuttle is sliding everywhere; we can't get around a single turn without almost running into either a tree or a brick wall. Finally, when we get to Chloe's stop, it plows right into the UV covering at her shuttle stop, sending pieces everywhere.

I stand up to help her off, but for a second, she looks normal.

"Thanks, Piper," she says.

"For what?" She can't know I saved her from death.

Chloe reaches her palm up to my cheek. "For looking out for me." And her words seem to convey something deeper, like maybe she does know what's going on. On Monday, I'll ask her about it. I'll tell her about Shayne and the Underworld even though she'll think I'm nuts. Because I feel like I have to tell someone or I'll burst.

"You're welcome," I say. I'm about to ask the driver to wait while I walk her to her house, but Chloe waves me away.

"I'm fine," she says.

"You sure?"

She nods. "Call me later." And she walks down the steps of the shuttle and runs to her house.

The driver backs up out of the debris of the shuttle stop and starts back down the road. I go back to my seat in front of Randy and sit down.

"You think school will be canceled on Monday?" he asks.

Overhead, the hail pounds down on the roof of the shuttle like a storm of bullets. I look out the window to where the ground has already picked up a layer of whiteness. I grip the back of the seat as we slide from one side of the street to the other.

"If this keeps up," I say.

"Let's just pray we make it home alive," Randy says.

It seems we will. The shuttle pulls up to the curb by the Botanical Haven without running into anything and stops. I stand up but notice Randy's still sitting.

"You're not getting off?" I ask.

He shakes his head. "I'm gonna go pick up my sister." And for a second, it's like there's a side of Randy he's never let me see before. He's such an arrogant asshole on the outside, but yet he's going to the elementary school to make sure his sister gets home okay. I blink, and his image shifts so he's layered in blue moss. It covers his face and hair, his hands and arms. I hold my eyes open, staring at him to make sure it's really there, but when I finally have to blink, it vanishes. Just like the covering on the pomegranate tree.

"Keep her safe," I say, because I can imagine what a little kid would think of a storm like this.

"I always do," Randy says.

I wave goodbye to him and then get off the shuttle.

The first thing I do when I get inside is text my mom. Even if she is off with my father somewhere, she's got to be freaking out about this weather. I'm shivering, so I grab the comforter off my bed and wrap it around me. It helps, but all the glass of the Botanical Haven makes the cold seep right into my bones.

"what's going on?" I text.

I make some coffee and wait for a reply, but none comes.

I text her again. "weather's gone crazy."

Still she doesn't respond. It's so unlike her, I can't help but let it put me on edge. I sit at the ice cream table with my coffee and listen to the storm rage on the glass above. It's shatterproof, so I'm not worried about it breaking, and I try to relax. The storm pounds down for the better part of the day until, in a single moment, it stops. Just. Like. That. Dark clouds turn to white, and a blue sky creeps back out from behind them. And then the sun comes, and everything outside starts to melt. Water cascades down our glass roof and pools on the ground outside.

I flip on the tube to see what kind of trouble the storm has caused. Around the city, roofs and walls have caved in everywhere. Downtown, about fifty people are trapped beneath the debris of a building, and most of the coverage centers on this, though reports of wrecks and flooding are sprinkled in. I watch the news as each new horror is revealed. Rescue crews pull dead bodies from the building and flash to family members who find out their loved ones are dead the same time I do. I wonder where in the Underworld each person will go. I wonder how Shayne can handle all the sorrow.

When I can't watch any more of the misery, I turn off the tube. And then I go downstairs and start tending the plants and flowers even though they don't really need it. They've been protected from the devastation outside. Like an oasis.

Reese's pink flowers are still alive, though they've sucked up most of the water in the vase. I move to water them, but then I stop. Should I really keep them alive? This is the god of war we're talking about. I halfway feel like picking them up and tossing them into the compost heap, erasing all memories of him and our date. But that would just be causing more death. I go ahead and add water to the stems because that's what I do. I take care of plants. I can always tell what they need—except for the pomegranate tree.

The pomegranate tree. I realize, with the storm, I've almost forgotten about it. The Underworld is fading into memory, and I want to hold onto it with everything I have. Shayne's pomegranate tree—in his garden— aching for something which isn't there. Something missing from the soil. When I think about it, the sorrow inside the tree hits me, and I sink to the floor. What would make a tree in paradise so sad?

The next day, aside from flooding, the cold spell is a memory. Temperatures are back at one hundred by seven a.m., and the weather station predicts humidity will get to dangerously high levels because of the melting. Precipitation is good in that it helps plants grow, but in such mass amounts, the ground and city can't handle it. I try texting my mom again, but there's still no response. I know I shouldn't worry about her, but something just feels off. It's totally out of her character to not be in touch, especially with the weather issues. I call her FON just to make sure, but she doesn't answer.

I call Chloe next, but her mom tells me she's sick. Her mom doesn't sound worried about Chloe but keeps me on the FON for five minutes to talk about the storm. I assure her I'm fine here alone at the Botanical Haven and that if I have any problems, I'll come over.

But I try to get her off the FON. I don't want to spend my day talking to Chloe's mom, so I ask her to have Chloe call me later. Once Chloe gets better, I'll tell her everything, or at least I'll try to. I think she'll have a hard time believing I traveled to Hell and came back to talk about it. I have a hard time believing it. I want to make sure I tell her about Reese and tell her she should stay away from him. But as the hours tick by, I start to think this conversation will have to happen tomorrow at school.

I'm about to lock the door and take a nap when the bell rings. I glance out the glass to see who's here because, at this point, anyone is better than no one. It's Melina—the girl who'd given me the box last week when my mom wasn't home. When I open the door, humidity pours in like thick gel.

"Piper." Melina's lips lift into a cherry ice cream smile, pink and round and perfect. She peeks her head in and looks around, letting her blond corn rows fall forward over her blouse which dips so low in the middle I see her ribs. Each corn row is capped with a shell which jingles against the others creating a song as she moves. Melina looks like she belongs on the cover of Cosmo, except she's so pretty no one would believe the photos are real. "Is your mom home?"

I shake my head and smile. Maybe I will have some company today. "No."

"She's not out picking seeds today, is she?"

I open the door wider so she can come in. Which she does. "She's out of town."

Melina's eyebrows shoot up her beautiful forehead, making the green of her eyes stand out like emeralds. "Really?"

I nod and can't help the grin which grows on my face. "Yeah, kind of unbelievable, isn't it."

"A bit out of character," Melina says. "What have you been doing? Were you okay during the storm?"

My mind flies to my date with Reese and my journey to the Underworld with Shayne. "I was fine. I made it home before it got too bad." The air from outside reminds me I haven't been out in over a day. "You don't want to go for a walk, do you?" I ask.

A perfect smile forms on Melina's perfect face. Her body reminds me of a minx, sleek and supple, and with her low-cut blouse, I see every curve. She reaches out a golden arm and opens the door, and the sunlight catches the fine, blond hairs, making her arms shimmer.

"Definitely," she says, and I walk outside.

Melina follows me out, letting the door swing shut, linking arms with me as we walk. There's no one around to see us, so even though my reflex is to pull it back from her, I let it be. We pass the greenhouses out back which are steamed up from all the humidity; I can't even see inside. I head for the path in the woods, walking under the trees. There are puddles everywhere from the storm, and no matter how hard I try to avoid them, my feet are soaked in seconds. Outside, I see how sheer Melina's clothes really are. In the sunlight, I can see right through the blouse. Her nipples are hard against the fabric which clings to her, showing the brownness of each nipple perfectly. Her thin skirt falls into the space between her legs, outlining her thighs, and it's clear she's not wearing any underwear. But if anyone can pull off the look, it's Melina. I glance at her sideways, unable to take my eyes off her. Imagining the effect she must have on guys.

"Crazy weather, huh, Piper?" she says. If she's aware her clothes leave little to the imagination, she doesn't show it or doesn't care. She stops near a large crop of limestone and sits on one of the bigger rocks, spreading her legs to let her skirt hang in between. And then she pats the place next to her.

I sit down next to her, pulling my eyes from her chest. "My mom thinks the atmosphere is being stripped away."

Melina draws her pouty lips together. "I guess that's one theory."

"What's another?" I ask.

She seems to consider this. "Maybe the Global Heating Crisis is just coming to an end. Maybe the whole thing has just been the natural progression of weather on Earth."

"Maybe," I say, though I don't for a second believe it. Global warming has been predicted for the last hundred years. It's not just going to disappear by magic.

"Or maybe it's something else entirely," Melina says. "Maybe it's those air diverters they've been trying out in Japan."

"My mom thinks those are just as bad," I say.

"But what do you think?" Melina asks.

I nod. "I think she's right." Everything I've read about the air diverters suggests that all they're doing is redistributing the heat. Nothing really gets rid of it. They just move it around. I pick up a pebble and throw it, trying to hit a puddle. Instead, it lands on a slope, and I watch it tumble down a few feet and stop in the mud. "Thank you for the box."

Melina puts her hand on my forearm which causes goose bumps to form. "You already thanked me."

I shift my arm to get her hand off it. "Yeah, I know. But I didn't realize how beautiful it was."

She sets her hands behind her and tosses her head back, letting her corn rows fall until they touch the rocks. "My husband made it. Did you open it?"

I hardly have time to think about that fact that Melina is married. She looks like she's only a couple years older than me, and I can't imagine a perfect enough guy to be her match; it seems every creature on Earth would feel inferior to Melina. But my sensors go up when she asks if I've opened the box. It's the exact same question my mom asked when she'd found it hidden in my room. "It was empty," I lie.

Melina turns to me, lifting an eyebrow, moving so her breast brushes my arm. I flinch but don't pull away. I don't want her to think she's making me uncomfortable.

"Empty?" she asks.

I sigh and, unable to take it anymore, scoot enough so we aren't touching. After all, she did give me the box; I guess I can tell her. "There was a red feather inside."

Her eyes widen, and this time, they look violet. I shake my head, knowing the sun must be playing tricks on me; eyes don't change color on demand. "Interesting," she says.

"You didn't know?"

Her eyes say no, but her perfect lips disagree. "Yes. Of course." And she settles back on her arms.

"I never knew you were married," I say.

Melina nods. "For a while now." She stretches her arms, and, for the first time, I notice the thick band on her ring finger. Patterns twist on it into knots.

"Was it love at first sight?"

Melina laughs and settles her hands in her lap, letting them fall between her legs, shifting her legs farther apart. "Not hardly. Let's just say it was a marriage of convenience."

I'm not sure what could be convenient about marrying someone you don't love—especially if you're the most gorgeous creature on the planet. "So do you believe in love at first sight?" I ask. I think of Shayne.

Of the first time I saw him in class. And the desire that moved through me. If I didn't fall in love that day, I'm sure I never will.

Melina turns and looks me in the eye. Her lilac eyes glimmer in the sunlight and pick up the iridescence of the shells hanging from her hair. "Do you?" she asks.

I nod.

She smiles but continues to hold my eyes. "So do I. I believe there is some love so strong nothing can stand in its way. Love is the only certainty in the whole universe."

"That's exactly how I feel," I say.

She nods and breaks eye contact, closing her beautiful eyes and looking back up to the sun. "Good, Piper. Always hold onto that belief." She inhales and lets out a deep sigh. "I felt that way about someone once," she says.

"Not the guy you married?"

Melina shakes her head. "No. I was already married. But I loved this guy, and he loved me. The world stopped when we were together."

"So what happened?" I barely breathe the question.

Melina angles her head. "He fell in love with someone else."

"I'm sorry," I say because I can't think of anything else appropriate.

Melina turns to me then and holds my eyes. "Are you really, Piper?"

"Of course," I say. Though I've only known Shayne for days, I'm pretty sure my world would shatter if he loved someone else.

Melina points to her gorgeous body. To her face. "Look at me, Piper."

I'm not sure how I could look at anything else, so I nod.

"It happened to me. It could happen to anyone."

I let out the breath I've been holding. "I'm sorry," I say again.

And Melina lets it drop. We chat for a few more minutes but then say goodbye. I leave her there and head back to the Botanical Haven by myself and lock the door behind me.

I walk upstairs, stopping in the kitchen for a quick drink of water. Outside, it's getting warmer by the second; the thermometer's well over one hundred and five. It's like the ice storm was a fantasy. I want to flip on the tube to make sure it really happened, but I can't bring myself to watch any more bad news. I finish my water, set my cup on the counter, and head down the hallway to my room.

I open the door to my room, and pink flowers are everywhere inside. Cut at the stems and scattered about—on the dresser, the table, and especially on the bed. My stomach knots. Reese had come into my room while I was out and put flowers all over the place. Cut flowers. Illegal flowers. His scent is everywhere, thick on the sheets and hanging in the air.

My chest constricts as I look around. I wonder if he's still near. Maybe even in the Botanical Haven. I stand there for at least a minute, frozen. Each flower has been arranged flawlessly, and I love them and hate them at the same time. They've been severed and won't live through the night, but they're also beautiful.

Anger bubbles inside me, and I walk toward the bed, each step causing the fury to intensify. I'm angry at Reese for violating my home, and I'm angry at myself for seeing beauty in what he's done. I begin to scoop them together so I can trash them but stop when I see a note tucked under the pillow, sticking out just enough that an edge of the crisp white paper shows. My hands shake as I reach down and pull it out.

Remember I love you.

I tear it to shreds, and when I can't tear the pieces any smaller, I feel the overwhelming urge to incinerate it. But my mom would flip if I started a fire. So I content myself by gathering all the flowers and the ball of paper scraps and shoving them in the compost heap, and I hope that helps resolve the conflicts in my mind.

Chapter 20

Death

Sunday night, the city council holds a press conference. The council room looks empty without my mom sitting there. The Botanical Haven feels even emptier. Councilman Rendon gets up to the podium and talks about the rescue efforts downtown and how nearly everyone was pulled from the debris of the collapsed building. He lists only fifteen casualties of the fifty people trapped. His math reminds me of the cooling gel the city uses in the misters. Ten percent allergic to the gel is acceptable. I think he figures as long as he gets the majority of the vote, he'll win the election.

After he's talked on and on about how well everyone responded to the emergency, the questions start.

"How many deaths were reported?" the first reporter asks. It's always right to the worst of the worst.

Council Rendon clears his throat and uses his most serious expression. "Reports as of late afternoon are that two hundred and eighty-seven lives were lost in the ice storm."

Two hundred and eighty-seven deaths. It's a horrible number. I can't help but wonder, of those two hundred and eighty-seven deaths, how many will make it to paradise.

The reporters jump on this response and begin grilling him on the details: how many died from roofs collapsing, how many died from accidents on the road. But the next question is the one everyone, including myself, has been waiting for.

"Is the disperser missile to blame for the ice storm?" the reporter asks. She stands there and stares at Rendon until he gives his reassuring smile and motions for her to sit down.

She stays standing. "We need to know, Councilman. Is it to blame?"

"Of course not," he says. "The university has been doing tests on the missiles for months now. I've stated before and I'll state again. The missiles are not the cause of the atmospheric disturbances. The missiles are helping."

I almost laugh at his simplification of the disaster our world is in. Atmospheric disturbances. Two hundred and eighty-seven dead, and it's a disturbance. I know he's lying, and as I watch, I see the thick green fungus spread over his skin. Every single word coming out of his mouth is false; not even he believes them. And I think this is the kind of man who would never make it to the Elysian Fields. I watch his lies for another few minutes and then try texting my mom again. There's still no reply, so I flip off the tube and head to bed.

When I get to school on Monday, I immediately know something's wrong. Tension hangs in the air like black crepe at a funeral.

"Randy Conner's dead."

Someone whispers it in the hallway.

"What happened?" Another whisper.

"It was the ice storm."

"The shuttle wrecked."

"He died instantly."

Oh my god. I had been with Randy on the shuttle. I'd talked to him just before I got off.

"Is his sister okay?" I ask. He said he was going to pick her up.

No one seems to know.

My stomach flips over, and I almost throw up. I can't believe Randy's really gone. Dead. And unlike Chloe, Randy will not have anyone to bring him back.

When I get to Social Sciences, I see the empty chair where Randy normally sits, and I can't help but notice Shayne's chair is empty, also.

Mr. Kaiser walks in and tells us what he knows. Randy Conner is dead. He'd been one of the unfortunate two hundred and eighty-seven people to die in the city this weekend. I'll never have to worry about any more wise-cracking comments about my mom's over-protectiveness from him. I ask about Randy's sister, and Mr. Kaiser tells the class she is fine. She was with him when he died, and then her parents came and took her away. The funeral's going to be held Wednesday, and anyone who wants to attend gets out of school early for the day.

I haven't been to a funeral since sixth grade when Charlotte died.

Charlotte.

I've almost forgotten her.

It's like little pieces of my time in Hell are escaping me.

And I wonder: will Randy Conner go to the Elysian Fields? Because at this moment, if I had to judge, I would say yes. He'd been taking care of his sister when he died, and if that isn't something that deserves paradise, then I don't know what is. I feel like that's what the blue moss was trying to tell me.

I look again to Shayne's chair, trying to command him to appear, but I don't want to call his name. I want him to be there on his own. So I sit back and try to replay anything I can from the Underworld, letting it all come back to me. Mr. Kaiser lectures on everything needed to construct an underground city, but my heart's not in the lecture. I don't think anyone's is.

When I leave class, I look around, hoping to spot Shayne. He's nowhere to be found, but blood drains from my face when I see Reese, leaning against the lockers. Watching me. His head towers above the other kids milling around, and he looks like he could pick up and throw any five of them together. He looks every bit the god of war.

I can't believe he's the god of war.

Reese isn't in speaking range, but he catches my eye and nods. When our eyes meet, I know he's been standing there waiting for me. I can feel it inside me, tickling in my stomach. But he doesn't come over to talk to me or even move for that matter. He just leans against a wall and watches.

I think of the pink flowers. He entered my room without permission. He left dying flowers as if that would impress me. But instead of the anger I should feel, all that comes to mind is the way they were arranged. They were placed one at a time by his hands, crossing over each other until a blanket had been formed. It's like there's a hidden side to the god of war. A side that would take the time to arrange something beautiful. It's hard to imagine that side coexists with the one trying to take over the Underworld.

I don't even realize a smile's formed on my face until Reese takes a step toward me, and before my face betrays me further, I walk away. I don't want to talk to him. Not now. Because the thought of his lips on mine is just too consuming even though I try to push it away.

I head for Study Hall. I need to talk to Chloe about everything that's happened. She'll help me understand what's going on. But now that I'm thinking about it, maybe I should leave out the mention of Hell and Hades and anything three-headed or dead; I'm not really sure. But when I get to the library, she's not there.

I figure she's late, but five minutes later, she's still not there. So I get out my FON and call her. Nobody answers the first time so I leave her a message, but then I dial again, and she finally picks up on the third ring.

"Piper?"

"Hey, Chloe. Where are you?"

"I'm at home."

"It's a school day. Are you still sick?"

Chloe seems to hesitate. "Maybe. I feel really light-headed, Piper. My brain's in this total funk."

I think of Shayne's comments on near-death experiences. About how they can change people. "I'm sure it'll pass," I say.

Chloe lets out a laugh that sounds like she's about to cry. "I hope so. I keep doing really screwed up things."

My breath catches, and I'm almost afraid to ask. "Screwed up like what?"

A pause. "Like I unplugged everything in the house yesterday."

"That doesn't seem so weird," I say to minimize it, and I try to laugh.

But Chloe only sounds more frantic. "Every single thing. And then when my mom plugged everything back in, I broke the light bulbs."

"All of them?"

"All of them," Chloe says. "There were a hundred and thirty-four if you count the ones in the stove and refrigerator."

"Why?" I ask.

There's panic in Chloe's voice. "I don't know. It's like I keep getting these weird urges, and I can't control them."

"Maybe you're just in shock, Chloe," I say. I'm trying to convince myself, too. "Is your mom there?"

"She just went out to fill a prescription for me," Chloe says. "And all I want to do is get the hammer and drive nails into the mirrors."

"Don't, Chloe." I glance at my watch. There's no way I can get to her house and back before Study Hall is over, but I don't care. "I'm coming over."

I can almost see her shake her head. "No, Piper. I'm fine."

I scowl even though she can't see me. "You're not fine. Just wait there for me."

In the FON, I hear someone talking.

"It's okay, Piper. My mom just got home."

"Can I talk to her?" I ask.

Chloe actually laughs. "No. I'm fine. Really. I'll take some medicine and take a nap, and I'm sure I'll feel much better."

Still, I don't want to let it drop. "Can I come by later?"

"How about I call you, Piper?"

"I could just stop by after school," I say.

Chloe blows out a breath. "I'll be asleep. Seriously."

"Are you sure?"

"Totally. Anyway, I gotta go."

At least her mom is there which is some consolation. She should be able to keep Chloe from doing anything destructive. "I'll see you tomorrow?" I say.

"Yeah," Chloe says. "Tomorrow." And she disconnects.

At least Chloe is alive.

My mom doesn't come back that day. Nor does she call me or text me or anything. I must call her and text her twenty times, but I don't get any response. And other than that I have no idea how to reach her. She didn't even tell me where she was going. And I wonder if somehow, by wishing she'd go away forever, I've made her do just that. Though I know I should miss her, the emptiness of the Botanical Haven fills me with freedom. And if she never comes back, I know I'll have this freedom forever. I'm a horrible daughter for feeling this way, but my feelings persist.

My heart sinks Tuesday when I walk into Social Sciences. Shayne's still not there. I stare at his chair for probably the entire hour, wondering when he'll decide to show up. But wondering doesn't help. Mr. Kaiser spends the lecture talking about alternatives to the missiles and underground groups that are fighting against the city, but the class feels dead; I don't even want to listen, but I force myself to.

He starts with a list like he always does. I manage to

come up with the Japanese air diverter option, and someone else mentions the reverse tornadoes they've been dreaming up in South America. But I swear for each item listed, Mr. Kaiser has at least three reasons why it does more harm than good. Finally, I can't take it anymore.

"So what's your solution then?" I ask. All he does day after day is give us a million reasons why nothing will work.

Mr. Kaiser sets the orange dry erase marker down and leans back on his desk. "For starters, we stop everything we're doing."

"Everything?" someone says.

"Everything." He points at the list. "Let's imagine that none of these tactics had ever been tried. Where would Earth be then?"

"Dead?" someone suggests, and I have to admit it's a valid point. One severe heat bubble and our entire city would have been wiped out.

"Not so." Mr. Kaiser slams his fist down on the desk. "That's exactly the kind of propaganda the city council has been feeding you. But who's to say the heat bubbles would even still be a threat?"

"Councilman Rendon," I say. He'd say the bubbles would still be around.

"Right," Mr. Kaiser says. "Councilman Rendon and others like him will continue doing anything and everything they can without enough long-term experimentation. And when they keep it up, the only viable solution will be for everyone to move underground."

Underground. I actually have to suppress a smile at this. We'll be underground one way or the other. Either everyone will be dead and in the Underworld, or everyone will be alive and living in an underground city. Like somehow the worlds will be merged no matter what happens.

At least Chloe's in Study Hall. She's at our table when I get there, and I pull out my chair, dropping my backpack on the ground.

"How are you?"

She's wearing a red bandana today, crisp and ironed, like she's taken extra care in making sure it's folded perfectly. She looks up, and I notice how pale her face still is. But worse, her skin seems to carry a thin layer of yellow mucus just like the pomegranate tree. It stays there even when I blink.

"My mom told me I was sick."

I smile and try to get her to relax. "Yeah. It was the heat."

Chloe shakes her head. "That's what my mom told me. But I don't remember it. It's like the last three days have been a blur."

I decide not to bring up our FON conversation from yesterday. Maybe if she doesn't remember breaking light bulbs, it's for the best. I take her hands, and the second we touch, the mucus disappears. But her hands feel like dead, clammy fish in mine. "But you're better now. That's what matters."

But even as I say it, Tanni's haunting words telling me *Chloe will die* slam into me so hard the air is punched out of my stomach.

But Chloe didn't die. She's here in front of me. She's cheated death, and Tanni's horrible words will never come to pass.

I realize my face has frozen into a frown, and I'm sure Chloe's going to call me out on it, but she doesn't seem to notice.

"Is your mom back yet?" Chloe's words snap me back to the present.

I shake my head. "It's weird. She hasn't called or anything." And even though my mom and I have our differences, another day has passed, and the thought of her being gone forever has started to grow a lead anchor of guilt in the pit of my stomach.

Chloe purses her lips together. "So no word from your father?"

"Not since the note." Of course, with my mom gone this long, maybe she's convinced my father to give up. Or maybe he's abducted her and is coming for me next.

"Maybe she won't come back," Chloe says.

I laugh, but then stop when I see Chloe's not smiling. "Yeah, maybe."

"What would you do, Piper?"

I know the answer—at least what I'd want to do. I'd go back to the Underworld. But now, a few days later, it seems unreal. Like it almost didn't happen. I decide now's as good a time as any to start telling Chloe everything that's happened, but I'm not sure how to start. "Well, I'd wear really bright colors every day," I say. "Like red."

Chloe smiles and tugs at the ends of her bandana. "Red is the color of blood."

My face freezes. "Yeah. It is." It seems like a whacked-out comment. "And cherries," I add.

"Blood reminds me of death."

Chloe will die. Tanni's words. I ignore them.

Chloe tents her fingers in front of her face. "Remember when you asked me about fate, Piper?"

I nod. "Sure." I push Tanni's words away.

"I don't think someone can escape fate," she says.

Chloe did. Shayne had given me a choice, and I'd saved her. And she'd cheated fate. Stayed alive. "They can, Chloe." But even as I say it, it strikes me as false. Like I'm lying to her and myself all at the same time.

"There's a funeral tomorrow," Chloe says.

I nod. "Randy Conner. Are you going?"

"I want to see it," she says. Which is a weird reason for wanting to go to a funeral.

"Why?"

"I want to see the people." And then she grabs my own hands back with such force, my pinkie finger feels crushed against the rest of my hand. "Do you ever wonder what someone would say at your funeral?" She looks at me, and it's the first time today her eyes meet mine and really see me.

I shake my head and try to break my hands free. But she won't let go, and I can't get them to budge. "No. I haven't."

"Do you think he'll be there?"

"Who?"

"Randy." She says it like it's the most natural question in the world. "Do you think he'll be there watching?"

"Chloe, he's dead."

She doesn't hear me. "Would you watch your own funeral? Would you want to know who came?"

The blood's being cut off from my fingers, so I make another move and tear both my hands free. Chloe's obviously still in shock. Maybe I should tell the nurse so they can send her home.

I shake my head. "No, I don't think I would."

But I see Chloe's answer in her eyes. She'd want to watch. She would be there. Watching over the crowd. And in my mind, I see Chloe's funeral instead of Randy's. Her mom and dad. Her brother with his multiple tattoos. Maybe the tattoo artist, Morgan, would even come.

I look at Chloe's tattoo, and like black worms crawling on her skin, the letters shift under my gaze.

They swirl and twist, and I can't make them out. They seem to slither off her arm, holding on by only a tendril. I'm tempted to reach out and catch them, or try to steady them at the very least. But then they settle into a string of symbols, none of which I can read. Still, my mind knows what they say. It can sense the word even in Ancient Greek.

Death.

I look again, but the letters stay the same. Morphed from *sacrifice* into *death*. I glance down at my own tattoo, but it's stable and solid. And it no longer matches Chloe's. When I look up, Chloe watches me. Her eyes flicker down to my tattoo, and she smiles.

"You know what I love about you the most, Piper?"

I hardly dare to breathe, but I answer her. "What?"

She unties her bandana. Her brown hair falls over her shoulders, and she twists the bandana around in her hands. "You always believe me."

I nod which she takes as encouragement.

"I know no matter what I do, you'll believe me and trust me." She reaches across and takes my hand. "And that means everything to me."

I squeeze her hand in return and chance one more glance at her tattoo, holding my breath. But it still says *death*. A death which Chloe escaped.

I open my mouth because maybe this is the right moment to start telling Chloe everything that's happened. "I never told you about my date," I say. That seems like a good place to start.

Chloe just smiles. "I want to hear all about it, Piper. But can we talk about it tomorrow?"

"Yeah, sure."

"Good." And she spends the rest of Study Hall pretending to do homework, though all she does is trace her finger in circles over the screen of her tablet.

Chapter 21

Funeral

Wednesday after second period, I head to the funeral. I wait for one of the shuttles in front of the school, and I keep scanning the crowd, looking for either Chloe or Shayne, but it's like I'm in a sea of unfamiliar faces. I know almost everyone around me, but I can't focus on any of them. I say hi to a couple of the kids in my classes, but otherwise stick to myself.

My back is already drenched in sweat, and heat presses down. But there haven't been any reports of impending heat bubbles, and, for now, I think the city will be spared any more disasters. This still doesn't keep other kids from talking about it, and someone even starts taking bets on when the next bubble will hit. One sophomore guy claims it will be tomorrow; he swears he's developed some equipment in his home lab that can predict to within the minute when the bubble will form. Given the random nature of the bubbles I've seen so far, I highly doubt he's right, but on the off chance he is, he could make a killing. If nothing else, the kid's got everyone hanging on his every word, juniors and seniors included. I hop a shuttle while he's still talking and head to the funeral.

When I walk into the church, I can't find Chloe anywhere. But it seems the rest of the city has turned up. Every seat is taken, and the standing and greeting areas are packed. I look down the long front aisle and see Randy Conner's family at the front. From the back of the church, I spot his seven-year-old sister with her face turned enough that I can see her eyes are dry and her lips are pressed together like she's holding back a river of tears which she never plans to let loose. I see the backs of his parents, his mom leaning away from his dad, toward his sister, and shaking with silent sobs. And as if he knows I'm watching, Randy's dad turns, and our eyes meet. Anger flashes there, rooted so deep it's wrapped and coiled around every bone and sinew in his body. It tears at him and eats him alive day after day. It's a black mold around him, smothering him and everyone he touches. And, for some reason, I remember Acheron—the river of sorrows.

I shift my eyes, not wanting to empathically share his anger, and spot Randy's girlfriend Hannah Reed there in the front. She sits on the side opposite from Randy's family and won't even look their way. Her wide dry eyes scan the crowd, not seeing anyone; if she notices me, she makes no acknowledgment.

What is Randy Conner's final sorrow? What will he leave behind on his way to the Elysian Fields?

An usher sees me and tries to find me a spot. I end

up standing against a red brick wall tucked into the place where they light candles. I move to the far back corner and wait. I'll find Chloe later, after the Mass.

Mass begins with a song. "Amazing Grace." It's the same one they played at Charlotte's funeral so long ago. Charlotte had been my best friend, but I never really knew Randy at all. He was a face in the hallways and a voice at the back of the classroom. A shadow next door after my mom threatened to skin him. But when the casket begins its trek down the long aisle, the sobs coming from the crowd around me bring an unexpected lump to my throat. I feel like I should have taken the time to know him better.

The priest motions everyone to sit when the song ends, so I lean back against the bricks but turn when I feel someone next to me.

"Shayne?"

He's dressed in black, appropriate for the occasion, and his hair's been combed neatly behind his ears. He squeezes my arm but doesn't smile.

"Where have you been?" I whisper, almost under my breath, forcing the lump out of my throat. I know he'll hear me.

"Busy."

"Will you be back tomorrow?" I can't stand the thought of sitting through another Social Sciences class wondering where he is.

He gives the smallest hint of a smile. "We'll see

tomorrow."

"But you promised."

"Promised what?" He reaches for a pack of matches set near the candles.

"You promised you'd be around."

Shayne nods and strikes a match. The immediate sulfur smell hits the air. The flame flickers as he moves the match to an unlit votive candle. It takes a couple seconds, but the wick catches in a burst of light. Then he moves the still burning match close to his mouth and blows it out. "Do you have any special intentions?" He holds the pack of matches toward me.

I take them, pulling one out of the box. "What was your intention?" I ask.

His hand reaches up, brushing my arm. "I can't tell you."

"Like wishing on a star?"

Shayne nods. "Right. If you tell what you intend, then it won't come to be."

"Then I won't tell you what I want." But I hope he wonders.

I move the match to the box, ready to strike it when a flame flashes out of nowhere and the match ignites. I'm so startled that I drop it into the candle-holder. I stare at it, watching it burn and melt the surrounding wax until it sputters and extinguishes on its own. And then I turn to Shayne.

He's staring at the match, now covered in cooling

wax. His eyes shift to mine, and he smiles. He's playing tricks on me. Using some god power from the Underworld to light the fire. So I take out another match, push the box closed, and prepare to strike it. Yet this time, it doesn't ignite until I pull it across the scratchy paper. I dip it down, lighting the candle and letting the sulfur again enter my nose. And then I blow it out.

"So where have you been?" I ask.

He shakes his head and puts the pack of matches back in the recess. "I've been around."

"But I haven't seen you." And if I haven't seen him, he may as well not be around.

"You haven't called me."

He's right. I haven't, and I'm not entirely sure why. "You're busy." It's the best reason in my mind. I opt not to mention the walk in the woods with Melina or the bedroom full of flowers from Reese. I'll sort out Reese on my own.

Shayne nods. "Never too busy for you."

I smile whether he means it or not.

"I almost came by yesterday," he says.

My heart flutters. "Really?"

"I got to your front door," he says. "I almost knocked."

Had I felt his presence? I'd been so worried about Chloe, I hadn't thought of much else. "Why didn't you?"

His lips tighten. "I thought your mom might be home. I didn't want her to see me."

"You're not scared of my mom are you?" Though in actuality, he probably should be. I'm scared of my mom.

"I'm not sure *scared* is the most appropriate word," Shayne says.

"So why not just come to class?"

Shayne leans close and whispers into my ear. "It's hard, Piper. I'm trying so hard to stay inside the boundaries, but more than anything in the world, I want to tear them down. And I can't. No matter what that ends up meaning."

"What boundaries?"

Shayne only responds by kissing my ear. It comes out of nowhere, and I'm pretty sure I've died and gone to the Elysian Fields. But when I look around, I see we're still here in the church, though a small hidden corner of it. Taking part in Randy's final blessing.

My corner of happiness vanishes when I feel eyes on me; they fill me with dread. Slowly, I turn around toward the back of the alcove. Tanni—Fate—stands next to a statue of the Virgin Mary, her eyes matching the empty eyes of the statue. Her friends stand on either side of her, sunglasses on but watching me.

The statue's hands are extended out in front out her, reaching out to implore those who would listen. Tanni's arms lift to match.

The church around me enters a bubble of muffled

words and fades into background. Outside of the bubble exist only me, Shayne, Tanni, and her two friends.

My body tenses as rage builds inside me. "You were wrong," I say. "Chloe did not die."

Next to me, Shayne stiffens. "Don't talk to her, Piper."

It's too late for that. Tanni's soulless eyes look at me, but it's like she didn't hear me. "It's your fault," she says.

Shayne pulls on my hand. "Let's go."

I pull my hand away from his. I don't need him telling me what to do now. "Chloe did not die," I say. I want Tanni to hear me. I want everyone to hear me. I know I'm yelling, but I don't care. Chloe is alive.

Tanni's eyes shift to Shayne. "You have no reason to be here." And just like that, he vanishes.

I stare at the spot where he was. "What did you do to him?" I demand.

Tanni shakes her head, and her hair moves from side to side in a cascade. "It's all your fault, Piper."

"What's my fault? And where is Shayne?"

Tanni steps forward and grabs my wrist, and her cold steel grip is like a vise. I'm not sure why I bother struggling, but I do, trying to break my wrist free until it hurts.

"Randy Conner is dead," she says.

I nod, and with her grip and her words and the fog circling behind her empty eyes, she's got me. I'm rooted in place.

"And it's your fault."

"What is?" But something's starting to come together inside me. A nasty itching sensation in the back of my mind. I don't want to face it.

"You killed him."

I open my mouth, but nothing comes out.

"You killed Randy Conner. It's your fault."

"How?" It's the only thing I can manage to say.

"Someone had to die. It wasn't his time. It's your fault."

I stare at her now, and I can't pull my eyes from her face. The truth slams into me like a freight train. I saved Chloe. But at what cost? Randy was one of two hundred and eighty-seven people to die. Would he really be alive right now if not for me?

"It's your fault." Tanni says it a final time and then lets go of my wrist. She walks back and joins her friends at the Virgin Mary, and they fade until they're gone.

The bubble around the world slips away, and the church is reanimated. Mass has ended, and six of Randy's friends carry out his casket. No one has heard anything. And Shayne is gone.

My fault. I hear it in my head. Is Randy Conner's death my fault?

I wait for the church to empty, and then I head home.

Chapter 22

Reunion

My mom is home. The second I walk through the door, a giant burden lifts from my shoulders. She's not dead. I can voice this concern in my mind now that I know she's okay. The cold feeling in my gut I've been carrying around since the day she was supposed to come back dissipates. I didn't even realize it was there, weighing on me.

She moves around in the Botanical Haven, cutting dead leaves off plants all over the place. And she's taken the calla lilies Reese gave me and set them on a table at the front of the store. The glass vase shimmers from the sunlight coming through the windows. I'll have to explain why I have illegal flowers. Maybe I can lie and say I cut them myself.

"Hi, Mom."

She gives me a sideways glance and then looks away. Snip. Snip. More leaves fall. Some aren't even dead.

I walk in and decide to go ahead upstairs. Let my mom have her time and then come talk to me when she's done. After all, if either of us should be angry about something, it's me. My mom should have been home on Monday. She didn't call. Didn't give an explanation. Didn't do anything except not show up. Yet, even with all that, my stomach is clenched in fists of guilt.

"Did you miss me?" she says.

I turn, halfway up the steps. She's at the bottom looking up at me, scissors in hand.

"You said you'd be back on Monday."

My mom sighs and pulls off her gardening gloves, tossing them onto the counter by the cash register. "Things got complicated."

My heart skips a beat. "With my father?"

She nods, and I notice her eyes glance to my tattoo. I look down at it and focus on the bumps faded from redness into just the black of the ink.

"Who is he?" I haven't asked in years. A lifetime. Not since I got over the dream of living a normal life with a normal family.

My mom turns away and walks to the door, locking it from the inside. It's early. No one who went to Randy Conner's funeral went back to school afterward, but if my mom knows about the funeral, she doesn't say anything.

"Who is he?" I repeat my question, wondering if I'll ever know.

"It doesn't matter, Piper."

I throw my backpack to the ground, watching it tumble down the five steps I've already gone up. "Yes.

It does. You spin me some story about how he's some escaped terrorist and then you spend almost a week with him? And then you come back here and tell me it doesn't even matter who he is. It doesn't add up, Mom. If he's so bad, why have you been gone so long? What's complicated anyway? What complications could there possibly be?"

My mom's eyes meet my own, and it's like she's begging me to drop the subject. To stop asking my questions. I don't want to stop. I'm sick of living a life filled with her mysteries. Or lies. They seem to blend together.

I start up the steps again, leaving my backpack lying at the bottom.

"It's about custody, Piper."

Her words freeze my feet in place. "Custody?"

"I can't lose you, Piper. Not now. Not ever."

"He wants custody?" How could a father I've never known want custody of me? I'm eighteen now. Custody shouldn't even be a concern. Not to mention an escaped criminal could never even take the case to court.

"He wants to take you away from me." My mom's voice is coarse as sandpaper. "And I'll never let that happen. I won't share you."

Share me? It seems such an odd thing for her to say. Sharing her adult child with an estranged father. The father who'd left me a note in my room. The father who'd said we'd have all the time we need to get to know each other.

"Why did he do it?" I ask. "Why did he leave?"

My mom laughs. "He never wanted to be a part of your life from the very start. We were nothing to him. So he left and got himself in trouble and escaped from the burdens of a family."

My father never wanted me?

"So why now?" I whisper the question, but she still hears it.

"Why now indeed?" My mom walks toward the counter, shuffling through the dead leaves on the ground. More drop off around her as she walks. I glance at them in passing but then move past them in my mind. "Because we haven't been careful enough." She laughs. "I haven't been careful enough."

"Careful? How much more careful could we have been?" I suppose if we completely removed ourselves from the grid that would have been more careful. But even my mom hasn't been that extreme. At least not yet.

"We'll have to move again." She pulls out some junk from a drawer and begins shuffling through it.

"No."

She ignores me. "Yes, that's the only answer."

"No, Mom."

My mom swivels her head and stares through me. "No what?"

I look to her eyes, but she won't meet mine. "No, I won't move again."

She turns back to the stuff from the drawer and

flips thought it like she's looking for something. "Yes, you will."

I won't. I tell myself this over and over in my head. I have a life here. I have Chloe. And now there's Shayne. I don't have to live with my mom forever.

The bell rings. Someone's trying to come in. The knob shifts, but it won't open since my mom's locked the door. I look through the glass to see who's visiting.

Reese.

I look at my mom, and she's staring right at him. He's looking right back at her.

"I wondered where the flowers came from." My mom's voice is so calm it sounds crazy. Each word drawn with perfect precision.

"Open the door," he says. It's a command. And I know this is so very bad that my worlds are about to collide.

My mom faces me again, and I am compelled to walk down the steps until I'm at the bottom, near the counter.

"Think we should have a little fun?" She uses her crazy calm voice again. And more leaves drop from plants.

I only want her to get rid of Reese, not kill him. "Mom, it's no big deal."

She thrusts her finger out and points at the door. "He is a big deal. How dare you try to tell me he's not?"

Reese knocks again and twists the knob. I hear the

metal crunching inside it.

I throw up my hands. "He's nothing. I swear it." I tell this to my mom and myself at the same time. Reese is nothing. It's Shayne my mom should worry about.

Or am I lying to myself? Should my mom be concerned with Reese, also?

"He gave you these." And in a single move, she grabs the pink flowers from the vase and throws them down on the tile.

When she turns back to the door, her mouth twists into a frown. Reese stands there in the door frame.

"Look who it is." My mom narrows her eyes at Reese, and I realize she knows him. They've met before. Maybe he came by when I wasn't here or something. But she can't possibly know he's really Ares, the god of war.

He takes a step toward her. "Did Piper tell you about the great time we had Friday night?"

My eyes almost fall out of my head. I can't believe he's gone and said this.

My mom turns to me, and I know she'd like to lock me away. Forever. Somewhere no one will ever come. "Piper has told me nothing of the sort."

"Do you want me to tell you all about it?" Reese takes another step, and his foot smashes the pink petals of the calla lilies.

My mom picks up her shears, and if they were only bigger, I know she'd cut his head off. "I'd like you to leave," she says.

"How do you know each other?" I say, but neither of them looks at me. It's like I haven't even spoken.

"You can't stop it," Reese says. "You know Piper and I are going to end up together." And he looks at me, and all at once, our eyes lock, and his intoxicating smell pours into my nostrils. God, I could die in that smell and be happy. I totally remember his kiss.

He can tell I remember it; it must be all over my face, and he smiles.

I want to make the thought go away. To force Reese out of my mind. But his scent flows through me like the wine we also shared on Friday. It reaches into the parts deep inside me that tell me how much fun life can be and settles. I try to force myself to look away from him but find I don't want to. So I take a step back to increase our distance and get the smell out of my nose.

"I think you must have misunderstood." My mom's voice sounds certain. She has no idea what's going on inside my head. I don't either.

Reese won't take his eyes off me. Won't free mine. "I didn't misunderstand anything," he says.

My mom moves closer to me and settles her hand to my shoulder before answering him. "Piper is going to stay with me," she says.

I decide they've both gone nuts. I squeeze my eyes shut, breaking the contact. "Would you both just leave me alone?" And I run for the door before either Reese or my mom can react.

Chapter 23

Threat

I run out of the Botanical Haven, past the green-houses, and into the trees, pushing deeper and deeper until I can't see anything but a forest of bark around me and branches high overhead. Even then, I keep running, trying to put as much distance as I can between myself and the craziness of my life. Chloe is totally freaking me out. My mom and Reese know each other. And Tanni claims I'm responsible for Randy Conner's death.

I stop when I see a Spanish Oak in front of me; one of its long branches twists so low to the ground I can rest against it. It's only then that I catch my breath, letting the hot, clear air around me replace the smell of Reese. He's like a drug. I want to run toward him even though I know I should run away. I let the heat of the world soak into me to erase him from my thoughts.

"Shayne," I whisper, praying that wherever Tanni sent him, he can hear. In seconds, he's there next to me.

"I was afraid Tanni killed you," I say.

"Fate can't kill me that easily," he says.

We stand there staring at each other, neither of us moving. I feel like I've betrayed him. I feel like I've been with Reese. But I haven't. I'd run away from the

Botanical Haven before I got too close.

I take a small step, and this is all it takes. Shayne pulls me to him, and I bury my head in his neck. I can feel him breathing in my hair.

"Reese came to visit," I say.

Shayne stiffens. "When?"

I shudder amid the warmth of the world around me. Reese and my mom. Have they started after me yet? Will they even follow? "It's like they know each other," I say. "How can that be?"

Shayne rubs my back but doesn't answer, and then he tenses up, and I know why. I smell Reese. He's followed me from the Botanical Haven.

"Look how precious." Reese's voice sizzles in the air. Taunting.

Shayne lets go though I desperately want to cling to him. "Go away," he says.

Reese puts his hand to his chest is mock surprise. "You're kidding, right?"

"Go away now," Shayne says. "I don't want you anywhere near Piper."

Reese looks at me and catches my eyes, locking them in place. "Piper doesn't seem to mind."

As soon as he says it, his smell amplifies. I fight, with every muscle I have, to stay rooted in place. I lean back on the Spanish Oak and pray it will grow limbs and hold me so I don't go to him. But like it has some power over me, his scent draws me forward.

Shayne turns to me, and I want to die when I see the hurt in his eyes. He's watching the struggle inside me. I don't want to be anywhere near Reese; I want to be with Shayne.

I want to be with them both.

Shayne opens his mouth, his beautiful lips pulled back in a snarl around his teeth. "Piper wants you to leave."

Reese laughs.

"What's so funny?" Shayne says.

"Everything's funny, Shayne."

I hear the bite when Reese says the name.

"What?" Shayne takes a step away from me. A step closer to Reese. And his hands are tightened so hard into fists they're white.

Reese sneers. "I was just thinking how funny it'll be when you're trapped in your own tortures. A suitable end for the ex-Lord of Hell."

Shayne takes another step toward Reese, and I want to reach out and pull him back. The last thing I want is for the two of them to start fighting. I want to run to Reese, but I also want to grab hold of Shayne and leave this place now. The sooner the better.

But Shayne's such a freaking guy. He wants the fight. "Stay away from Piper. Go away now, or I won't wait for permission from the assembly. I'll set Prometheus free and give you his place. Let the birds eat your liver for a few millennia. We'll see how you feel then."

Another wave of Reese's aroma hits me. I turn my face away, trying to block it, but it's not like I can stop breathing.

"Such a delicious punishment. Piper might like that." Reese's teeth gleam under the smile which forms on his mouth. "Not that your threats matter."

"Watch and see," Shayne says.

"The assembly backs me." Reese flexes his fingers and then relaxes them. "But of course you'd know that if you ever came to any assembly meetings."

"I have more important things to do," Shayne says. "Like run the Underworld."

Reese laughs at this. "Maybe you're not doing such a great job. I'm sure you've heard I've been to visit."

Shayne glares at him in reply.

"It's true," Reese says. "But I can tell you want to deny it. I'll tell you what."

"What?"

Reese puts a hand to his chest. "I left you just a little sprinkle of proof. Look for it when you get home."

Shayne takes a step forward, and I'm pretty sure this is it. They're going to kill each other. "You visit, and you die," Shayne says.

Reese just gives a wave with his hand and then turns to me. "Did you hear Randy Conner died in the ice storm, Piper?"

Randy is dead because of me. I might as well have wrecked the shuttle. "I heard," I manage to say.

"Now let's see, Shayne, where would you put someone like Randy Conner?" Reese puts his finger to his mouth as if he's considering the question. "The Elysian Fields?" He shakes his head. "No, that's not what my sources tell me."

But it has to be. I know in my heart Randy belongs in paradise.

"Shut up, Reese," Shayne says.

Another wave of Reese's scent comes to me. I desperately try to push it away and focus on the humidity in the air around me.

"So Randy didn't make it to paradise." Reese snaps his fingers. "Asphodel then."

I glance at Shayne and can tell from his pursed lips that Reese is right. That somehow Shayne didn't see the good in Randy that I saw. There's been some oversight. I haven't been to Asphodel, but I know it's not paradise.

"Shayne." I find my voice and manage to get out his name, trying my best to breathe out of my mouth and ignore Reese.

He turns to me, fists still balled. "What?"

"I need to get out of here. Now." He's got to hear the struggle in my voice. If I don't get away from the two of them, I'll go crazy.

Reese laughs. "I'll see you soon, Piper, okay?"

"Not okay," Shayne says. He scowls at Reese, and before I realize what's happening, he wraps his arms around me, and we start sinking, through the dirt and damp and rock and then into the river of liquid mercury which carries us until we're there on the bank of the River Acheron. Charon's just pulling the boat up to the dock when Shayne and I arrive. Charon's face cracks into a leathery smile which pulls his white eyes almost shut.

But before we walk over to join him, I turn to Shayne. "About Reese—"

Shayne leans over and kisses me, stopping the words, and his kiss erases any desires I felt for Reese.

"It's okay," he says once he pulls back. "You don't have to make any excuses for him."

I'm not sure how to explain it. It's like something uncontrollable came over me. "It's just—"

He shakes his head. "You never have to make excuses for him. He doesn't play fair." And his eyes darken. "Which is precisely why I told you to be careful around him. He can't be trusted. Ever."

I know he's right but wish he weren't. Even though I hate myself for being so weak around Reese, Shayne doesn't hate me, which is some consolation.

"Why won't you talk to the assembly of gods about him?" I ask.

The lights from the silver pools shift causing shadows to flicker on Shayne's face, giving him a more serious look. "Let's just say some members of the assembly and I are not on the best of terms right now."

"Why not?" I ask.

"Because we're not. End of story."

I gather not to press him any more.

I remember what Reese said about Randy. If he'd been trying to get under my skin, it had worked. "Randy should be in the Elysian Fields," I say.

Shayne shakes his head. "I judged him. He's in Asphodel."

I glance at Charon who's watching our conversation but not interrupting. "You judged wrong." I've never felt so sure about anything.

Shayne grabs my hand which I've balled up into a fist. "How do you know?"

I shrug and try to relax my muscles. "I just know. I talked to him before..." I can't believe I was probably the last person to talk to Randy Conner.

"Before he died?" Shayne asks.

"Yeah." I tell Shayne about the ice storm and about how Randy was watching out for his sister, making sure she got home okay. "He just didn't seem like such an asshole," I say. "It was like I could see the good in him." I don't mention the blue moss I'd seen on him, but I know it's a sign. I don't need anyone's confirmation on that.

Shayne purses his lips, but he doesn't say he's going to change it. Instead, he reaches into his pocket and pulls out a gold coin which he flips off his thumb. Charon catches it and pockets it without even looking.

"You know you don't need to pay," Charon says.

Shayne grins. "Don't want anyone to say I don't pay my fare."

I watch the conversation and attempt to relax. Try to shake away life's worries. But I worry I've killed Randy Conner and Shayne's doomed him to Hell for eternity.

Charon flips the coin around in his pocket. "Nobody would dare say anything of the sort."

It's the same banter from before, and I realize this must go on every time Shayne makes the water journey. Eternal friendship.

"Can you move Randy?" I ask.

I hear Charon let out a whistle under his breath.

"No, Piper. I can't. He's been judged. He has to stay there."

"But don't you ever worry that you're wrong?" I ask.

Shayne looks out across the water when he answers. "If I worried about that, it would consume me. I judge and move on."

I process this thought as we get into the boat and decide I'll come back to it. There has to be some way I can get Shayne to move Randy. Charon boards last and picks up the pole to move us.

"How long have you and Charon known each other?" I ask. We sit on the bow of the boat, side by side still in the darkest part of the cavern. I look out to the black water, seeing the sorrows there bubbling to the surface. Seeing the creatures shimmering below the froth, eating what sorrows they catch. Far ahead, the sky brightens where I know the two suns shine down from above.

"Forever."

I laugh. "That's a long time."

Shayne pulls me closer. "An eternity."

"So who do you live here with? Just Charon?"

Shayne glances back at Charon whose face is frozen as if he's trying to not blink. But Shayne quickly turns back to me and smiles. "Don't forget Rhadam."

I smile at the memory of the energetic overlord of the Elysian Fields.

"And Cerberus. Not to mention the billions of dead souls keeping me company."

I think of the sorrows of all those souls, left behind here in the river to be devoured by creatures of the Underworld. "What was Randy Conner's last sorrow?" The question forces its way into my mind. I can't pick Randy out of the chorus. All the voices blend together, shifting in rhythm when one gets swallowed by the creatures. Moving to fill the empty space.

Shayne is rigid against me all of a sudden. "You don't want to know."

"Yes, I do." I think of the shuttle accident. Randy's girlfriend and tons of friends and classmates at his funeral. His miserable family. And I remember Tanni and her friends by the Virgin Mary. I press my eyes closed and try to find his sorrow on my own, but it won't come. "I just want to know."

"Maybe you should just let Randy be."

But I know I can't let Randy be. "I want to know."

Shayne sighs and looks to the river, and I see a bubble rise to the surface. It grows larger and begins to float, and the things under the water stay away from it.

I lean toward the edge of the boat, hoping to hear, but I feel Shayne's hands grab my arms. He's worried I'll fall in.

"I want to hear." I need to hear.

"You'll be able to."

So I lean back into him and close my eyes again.

If I die, who will protect them?

I gasp when I hear it, and images fill my mind. My eyes fly open, remembering his family at the funeral. His little sister with dry eyes. His mom shaking with sorrow, leaning away from his dad, not touching him. And his dad, with a black aura of anger pulsing through his veins. I see his dad's anger in Randy's sorrow. Anger his dad can't control. Anger which makes Randy's dad hit his wife and children.

Tanni's words pound into my head.

"It's my fault."

I don't even realize I say them aloud.

"No, Piper."

The bubble pushes again below the water and disappears. My fault. Randy Conner's death is my fault.

"I made you save Chloe."

But Shayne grabs my shoulders and turns me to him. "No, it's not your fault. You can't think that way."

"Then why?"

Shayne narrows his eyes and glances to the side. "The Fates determine who will die next. Not you. Not me. Chloe lived, and they chose Randy Conner."

It's all tumbling around in my mind. "But if Chloe had…" I can't even bring myself to say it. I don't want her dead. More than anything, I don't want her dead.

"Randy may still have died." His eyes shift back to me. "It's all a game to them, watching lives fall apart." His eyes have narrowed to slits, but the brown irises inside start to stir with flecks of red.

"And you do whatever they say?" I know it comes out harsh, but he's just taken Randy and delivered him for eternity to the wrong place.

His defenses go up. "What do you mean?"

"When they die. You take the soul away from whoever the Fates say."

An icy look runs across Shayne's face, and his arms tense. "I don't take anyone's soul away."

I motion around with my arm. "But this is your world."

Shayne is holding anger just under his skin. "Yeah. My world. And my responsibility. But not my doing."

"But I thought—"

"—wrong." Shayne's eyes won't meet mine. "My job is to judge and maintain control. And trust me, that's a big enough job."

I feel like I've slapped Shayne. My cheeks burn, and I wish I could take it back. "I'm sorry."

Shayne's face softens, and he gives my shoulder a gentle caress which sends a shiver down my spine. "I'm the easy person to blame."

"Doesn't that bother you?"

His lips curl up in a smile. "It does get a bit old having every single death in history blamed on me. But it goes with the job."

"So why is Randy in Asphodel?"

"It's not so bad there, Piper," Shayne says.

Bad or not, if I've fated Randy to die and doomed his family to suffer under an abusive father, then at least I need to see the product of my actions. My choice to save Chloe. "I want to see."

Shayne rubs my shoulder and pulls me close. "I know."

I hardly remember Charon is on the boat. His presence seems to evaporate when Shayne and I argue. When the boat bumps against the dock and Charon jumps out, I remember him, and my heart sinks; I've hardly spoken a word to him.

But he's the one who helps me out this time, and when his hand grabs mine, he gives it a quick squeeze. Something stirs inside me, and I reach out and hug him. He lets go of my hand and grabs me in a bear hug so fierce, my lungs feel like collapsing. When he lets go, his weathered face cracks into its smile, which, even after two visits, I love.

"Have a wonderful time."

I smile back, and Shayne gets out of the boat behind me. "I will." The Underworld feels more welcoming than my real home back at the Botanical Haven, even with all its scary river monsters and haunting sorrows.

Once our feet hit the swampy shore, Cerberus runs over, weaving through the trees, tail thumping so hard it's like his lower half is another head with a mind of its own. He jumps both front paws up onto Shayne, and they wrestle around until Shayne finally falls to the ground.

"Does he wait for you every time you leave?"

Shayne reaches over to rub Cerberus's belly which causes him to flop down, roll over, and expose every bit of his giant stomach. Even with three heads, he's just a dog.

"Pretty much. Man's best friend, right?"

I laugh. "You mean god's best friend."

"I may be a god, Piper, but I'm still just your regular, average guy."

All it takes is one look at Shayne to know there's nothing average about him.

We turn and wave a final goodbye to Charon. He's already far away from the dock, out in the reeds and cattails, but the warmth of his smile even at that distance broadens my own.

"Charon likes you," Shayne says.

"I like Charon."

Shayne laughs. "Now that's one thing not many people will say. Most people aren't happy about dying. Everyone knows they don't live forever, but when it's actually their time, they almost never want to go."

I think of Randy Conner. "Randy didn't want to go, did he?"

Shayne shakes his head. "No. I crossed with him. It was pretty rough going at first. But once he got to the other side...well, it always changes."

We reach the end of the tunnel, and ahead, I can already see the flickering from the fireplace inside Shayne's home. Cerberus curls in front of the fire, and instead of sitting next to Shayne on the sofa, I plop myself on the ground next to Cerberus and start scratching between a couple of his ears. I feel Shayne's eyes on me though I don't turn to look at him.

"Did you miss me?" He tilts his head and pauses and waits for my answer.

I move my hand, scratching a different head. "I missed your dog."

Shayne laughs and comes down to sit on the ground next to me. He touches my earlobe which causes a tingle somewhere which is definitely not my earlobe. And he pulls my ponytail holder out, letting my hair escape from its bonds.

"I'm glad you came back."

My chest is tight, and I don't dare look at him. I know I could melt into Shayne and let him absorb me forever. "I am, too." I lean my back against him, and we sit there, me still scratching Cerberus, and Shayne running his hand through my hair. The fire never dies. It crackles and spits sparks into the air, and with the burnt aroma, I feel more like I'm in Heaven than Hell. And I never want to leave.

"Are you sure you want to see Asphodel? We could go back to the Elysian Fields. Rhadam's been asking about you."

Shayne's words snap me out of the paradise I'm living. It's not that I want to see Asphodel. I need to see it. I look at Shayne; his lips have pressed into a smile. "I'd take paradise forever," I say. Here with him.

"Most people would, when given the choice."

"But they don't get a choice, do they?"

He shakes his head, and orange embers from the fire reflect off the blackness of his hair. "If they did, no one would choose Tartarus, would they?"

I consider this. "Maybe the really bad ones would. They might want a lifetime of torture."

His eyes shift to the side for only a second, but I notice. "No one would choose that life, Piper. Trust me. To end up in Tartarus is like picking the short stick in life. Or death, as the case might be. And the worst part is it lasts forever. There's no getting out."

I sit up. "Never?"

"Never. There are two basic rules down here. Once a person has been judged, they stay where they are placed forever."

Like Randy Conner. Stuck forever in Asphodel. But I'm not ready to accept this yet. "And the second?" I ask.

"No one can ever leave the Underworld."

I raise an eyebrow. "Except the exceptions of course," I say. "And me."

Shayne rolls his eyes. "I'm not talking about you. You haven't died. Not to mention you came here by your own choice, and you are my guest."

His guest. I like that. "Too bad." I'm joking, but only kind of. "If I couldn't leave, I'd have to stay here forever. And my mom couldn't do anything about it."

Shayne's face tightens, and it looks like I've made him mad.

"What? I'm only kidding."

He shakes his head. "It doesn't matter."

But my mind tells me I should know why he's upset. "What did I say wrong?"

"Wrong?" Shayne stands up. "You didn't say anything wrong." He walks away from the fireplace—away from me. I watch his feet step across the red and black mosaic floor—the floor I love as if I've created it myself.

I stand up and follow him. He reaches a table set against the far wall. It's black wood, buffed to such a high polish, I can see his reflection in it. A picture hangs overhead, oil painted on canvas, with souls and angels and demons and Hell partitioned into regions with rivers flowing throughout. "Then why are you upset?" I ask.

Shayne turns and leans against the table which rocks under his weight. All at once, his eyes shift. Flickering, but so fast they're like sparks in a fire. Like the air around him could ignite if he wanted it to. He's holding a helmet of some sort. I hadn't noticed it before, but it's made to cover only the crown of the head, and it shines of pure gold.

He holds it out to me, and the air crackles around him and it. "Piper, do you know what this is?"

My breath catches in my throat. I do. I know exactly what it is. I've seen this object many times before, but I don't remember any of them. "It's the Helm of Darkness."

Shayne's face relaxes as if the weight of the helmet has been removed from his head. "Yes. It's the Helm of Darkness."

My mind forms the words for me. "It makes its wearer invisible."

Shayne nods and turns, setting it back on the table. "Do you know who I am?" He turns back when he says it, and it looks like he's going to take a step closer to me, but he doesn't.

My feet feel planted in the ground; I can't move.

"Shayne. You're Shayne."

"And…?"

I take a deep breath. I'm not sure why I have a hard time saying it—even to myself. "You're Hades. Lord of the Underworld."

Shayne's eyes bore into me, and I take a step back without even thinking about it. "And who are you?" he says.

I don't know who I am. I want to be someone else, but I'm not sure who. Someone who lives a life of tattoos and danger. Someone who doesn't obey every small command her mother makes. I want to be that person, but I know I'm not.

"I'm Piper," I say, but I feel like there's more.

Shayne's eyes stay locked on mine, but something disappears from them. Something hopeful and mysterious. "Yes. You're Piper." He walks toward me, and his eyes return to normal. He leans forward and kisses me on the lips gently. And I know whether he claims to be a god or an average guy, I love him.

"Are you ready to see Asphodel?"

With Shayne, I'm ready for anything. "Tell me about Asphodel."

"It's the place in between," he says. "For the souls who aren't so good and aren't so bad."

"Like Purgatory?"

He seems to consider this. "Purgatory. That's one way to look at it."

Shayne smiles, and I never want him to stop. His smile has a way of filling me with a comfort I haven't felt my entire life. I link my arm around his, and we start walking. "Except no one minds being there. They don't even think about it."

"So Randy is happy?" Maybe I can just find him in Asphodel and say goodbye. Tell him I'm sorry.

Shayne's smile turns wry. "I'm not sure I'd go quite that far. But I'll let you decide for yourself." And then he picks up the Helm of Darkness and clips it onto his belt, and we move out of his sanctuary into the blackness of another tunnel.

Chapter 24

Asphodel

Nice is erroneous. From the minute we reach the barren, red shore, I know this: Asphodel is a hell. Not like the eternal torture Shayne tells me is Tartarus. But a hell all the same.

The thick scent of musty wet clay hits me from the first step. I screw up my nose and look out from the mouth of the cave. "Which river is this?" I motion out beyond the dried up red river banks to the churning rusty water in the middle, and I see monsters again, but they aren't staying under the surface. They're jumping above, baring their fangs, snapping at each other. Their razored fins slice at each other, and if they bleed, their blood blends with the red water.

Shayne presses his lips together. "The River Lethe. Passageway to the Asphodel Meadows."

Clay cakes under my feet, pulling at my sandals until I toss them aside altogether, letting my toes sink into the oozing redness. Along the shore lie skeletons of boats marooned in the thick clay, falling to pieces. It's a dead world and a dead river with nothing alive except the monsters waiting for us. In a way, it reminds me of how my world will look should the Global Heating Crisis continue. And there's no reason to think it won't. I imagine the Botanical Haven as a singular oasis amid a world of barren desert because I know my mom would never move to a city below ground. And I know she'd want me by her side.

Will the world really come to that? Will my life really come to that?

Shayne and I walk to the dock; its piers aren't even submerged until halfway out, and when we reach the water, thankfully the monsters stay away from Shayne. It's like he's got an invisible force field surrounding him, and I happen to be lucky enough to be ensconced in it.

I motion to the monsters. "They never bother you?"

Shayne unclips the Helm of Darkness and holds it out. Around us, the monsters move back, increasing the distance between them and us. "The Helm makes the wearer invisible, Piper, but it also helps maintain control of the evils here in the Underworld. It's one of the final remaining gifts from the Cyclops. One of the only few that still exists." As he moves it, the monsters shift, keeping the distance even.

"They're more active than the others." And I let out a small laugh that even to me sounds like my throat is shaking.

"They're fed well." Shayne steps down into the mud-caked boat, and I follow, not waiting for his hand. I don't want to spend even a second too far from him with these things flying around.

"More sorrows?" Like the monsters in the River Acheron, I figure these monsters must eat sorrows.

But Shayne shakes his head and shoves the boat off from the dock. He hoists the rope in, and it drops on the floor of the boat with a thud.

I scoot away, not wanting a drop of the tarnished water to touch me.

"Memories," he says. "When souls head to Asphodel, they leave everything behind. And the monsters eat it all."

"Everything?"

"Everything. Names. Happiness. Fears. Goals. Every piece of thought which makes a soul what it is stays behind in the River Lethe." Shayne clips the Helm of Darkness back onto his belt. The monsters edge back in, but still stay outside our boundary.

"And that's what happened to Randy?"

Shayne motions back to the red river. "He left everything here. Randy doesn't even remember who he was."

I bite my lip, trying to piece this out. "Then I can't talk to him?"

"Why would you want to?" Shayne asks.

I push the lump in my throat back down. "To tell him I'm sorry."

Shayne shakes his head. "It's not your fault."

But I know it is. Even if Shayne wants to deny it, I cursed Randy to this place as surely as if I've killed him myself. And somehow I'll make it up to him. "Does the

Helm only work here?" I ask.

"It works anywhere. The sea. The Earth. The Underworld." He links his fingers with mine. "And trust me—there are monsters everywhere."

We ride in silence. The only sound is the snapping of the monsters' jaws. They bump against the boat, some hidden below the thick red of the river and some jumping until I fear they may join us in the boat. But none do. Overhead, the sky is as lifeless as the world around me. There's no sun to speak of. No light, but also no darkness. Only that in between gray of a lifeless world.

I lean against Shayne, feeling the muscles of his arm holding me. I try not to focus on the death around me, but my mind can't help the comparisons that keep forming.

"Do you think Earth is going to die?" I ask.

He brushes his cheek against my hair. "From the Global Heating Crisis? Yeah. I do." There's not a bit of doubt in his voice.

"What about the other gods? What do they think?"

Shayne looks out across the red water. "They're divided. They have been for years. Some of the members of the assembly fight to do everything in their power to restore the world to how it was. And others…they think the crisis is a good thing. They think change on any kind of massive scale is needed to keep humanity moving forward. They relish the struggles for power, and they enjoy choosing sides."

"Like Ares," I say.

"Yeah, like Ares."

I turn so I can see him better, but he's not looking at me. "So which side are you on?"

Shayne lets out a low chuckle. "Neither, which is the root of my problems with the assembly."

"Why neither?" Because if I had to guess, I'd have been sure that Shayne wants to restore Earth to how it had been before the Global Heating Crisis ever started.

"Because I have enough problems of my own, Piper. The Underworld keeps me plenty busy. I don't need two worlds to take care of."

I'm not sure this is valid reasoning, but I don't argue. Who am I to tell Shayne he should do more? But maybe he can read my mind.

"You think I'm horrible," he says.

"No. Not horrible. Just…" I struggle to come up with the right word.

"Obsessed?" he suggests.

"Dedicated," I say. "You're dedicated to the Underworld."

"Someone has to be," he says.

I look back across the water, and soon I see the opposite shore, and Asphodel there beyond it. We're almost to the dock, and the souls wait for us. As we pull up to the dock, empty stares surround us. One grabs the rope Shayne throws, tying it to a wooden pier. Another clears the path in front of us.

Shayne walks like he is Lord of the Underworld. He holds his head high, and he doesn't look anyone in the face. I make the mistake of doing so and am met with eyes which seem to penetrate right through me without seeing me. But then one face in the crowd catches my eye, and I gasp when her eyes meet mine.

"Chloe!"

Shayne turns to face me. "What?"

I point into the mass of faces, but she's gone. "Chloe. She was right over there."

Shayne looks, craning his neck over the crowds, searching. "Chloe isn't here, Piper."

I realize I haven't taken a breath since I saw her, so I inhale. "I saw her. She looked right at me."

He shakes his head. "You couldn't have, Piper. Chloe is back above. Alive. You know that."

I do know that. But it had looked so much like her. And there had been recognition in those eyes. It had been Chloe. "She knew who I was."

Shayne takes my hand. "She couldn't have. Even if it were Chloe, people here don't have memories, remember?"

"But she looked right at me."

Shayne narrows his eyes and searches the crowd again. I see the same thing he does. An ocean of empty faces. Thousands of them, pressed in on each other. None of them familiar. And none of them meeting my eyes. I must have been wrong. Chloe is still alive. Back on Earth and waiting for me. And then I catch the scent.

"He's here," I say.

Shayne's face turns away from mine and back to the crowd. He's smelled it to. Reese's aroma hangs in the air like thick, dry acid. I hold my ground, promising myself I will not show my emotions. I will keep Reese out of my mind. And then I spot Randy Conner's face looking back at me.

"There." I point to Randy Conner, but when Shayne turns to look, Randy disappears. And the scent shifts to the right. My head snaps over, and again I see Chloe. But instead of casual recognition, her face is painted with malice. Cold. Hatred. She despises me with those eyes. She blames me for her death. A death which never came. A death I helped prevent. But her face is steel. And her look is poison. It's a look I never want to see on Chloe's face.

Shayne must see it to. "Stay here."

And before I can protest, he's off, putting the Helm of Darkness onto his head; he vanishes in front of my eyes. As I watch him disappear, Chloe's mouth turns into a sneer, and she laughs. And then she's gone also. But the scent remains. Reese's scent.

I'm alone then, in the middle of a growing crowd of empty ghosts pressing in from all sides. I steady my nerves which threaten to send me running for the clay river. But thoughts of the monsters halt me. I can do this. I can wait for Shayne who should be back any moment. I can keep my thoughts from Chloe who is safe back above ground and from Reese who is looking for a tunnel into my mind.

Reese's smell surrounds me and pushes its way into my nose, but it's only teasing me. I shift my feet as if firm footing will steel my resolve. The scent plays with me, coming from all angles, and I squeeze my eyes and hold my breath to keep it out.

"Piper."

The voice is a whisper. But there is no doubt whose voice it is.

"I want you."

Reese sounds like a melody, but I stay in place, not breathing. Not opening my eyes to see if he is really there.

"Don't fight me."

I want to grow my feet into the ground. I want to close my nostrils and live without air. But instead I inhale, trying to get as much of it as I can.

"I can give you everything."

Could Reese give me everything? Does he want me? I don't want to fight him. I want to stop fighting. But I exhale and then stop my breath, seeing how long I can last. Will I die here in the Underworld if I don't breathe? Is it possible to die in the place of the dead?

I'm pretty sure I'm about to find out. I keep my mouth closed and plug my nose. And just when my lungs vow to retaliate if I don't suck in air, Reese's voice fades along with his scent; it disappears into the air above me. And only then do I inhale once again.

All at once, Shayne is at my side. He pulls off the Helm of Darkness and appears next to me.

"Reese was here." I'm gasping at this point from holding my breath, but Reese's smell is a drug.

"It's not possible." His face twists in frustration. "The Underworld may be weakening, but nobody should be able to penetrate it. Not even Ares." He attaches the Helm of Darkness back to his belt and takes my hand. "He's gone now."

"But he was here."

"Only a shadow of him," Shayne says. "He wasn't here physically."

I glance around. "Will he be back?"

Shayne's eyes settle on the mass of dead faces. "Not if I can help it." He motions out to the black clouds. "I need to see how bad things actually are."

I push the thought of Chloe out of my mind, wanting to erase any connection between her and this godforsaken place as fast as possible. It was not her, only Reese...Ares...made to look like her. Chloe is alive, though living on a stolen life thanks to me.

We're on a paved walkway, and ahead are buildings with walls made of gears as big as houses. One connects to another and then to another, and they turn like a perfectly synchronized clock. It's like a giant metal organism. The scent of oil hangs thick in the air, and the gears crunch over and over with clicks and whirls. "What goes on here?" I whisper, but even my whispers draw stares from the dead faces around us.

Shayne tightens his arm around me. "Everything happens here. Asphodel keeps most of Hell running."

"Running? Like what?"

We walk to the largest building in the front. Shayne has to wait until the gears click past, and only then is there an opening we can fit through. No sooner are we inside than the gear moves behind us again and seals out the light. Inside, we're greeted by dead faces which are attached to people who are buffing and polishing metal everywhere. Control panels cover the walls, but they have so many buttons and lights, I can't even distinguish one from the next. Red blurs into blue and green. People sit in front of the controls, and their hands move in the same motions over and over.

"The Underworld is just that. A world," Shayne says. "There's plenty to do. Just because almost everyone here is dead doesn't mean there's no effort involved in running it."

"But look at these people." I motion around at the scene in front of me. The residents of Asphodel stare back at me with their stygian faces filled with only emptiness. It's like they aren't even aware of the tasks they're doing, and yet they have to do them forever. "This is Hell."

Shayne shrugs. "They don't know they're unhappy. They don't know anything. Not even who they used to be."

I can't believe his lack of emotion. "How can you stand this? How can you stand to even come here?" Is Randy just another one of these people, oiling some giant machine?

Shayne considers this. "I have to come here. Whether I like it or not. It's my job, and there's no one else to do it."

I wave my hand across the scene. "But why this? Surely there's some better solution."

Shayne lets out a laugh which doesn't reach his eyes. "Let's face it, Piper. Not everyone deserves to be in the Elysian Fields. Being sort of nice won't get you there."

The dead faces surround me. These faces used to be people. People with lives and families and dreams. People like Randy Conner. "Well, that stinks," I say.

"Maybe. But being sort of bad won't get you sent to Tartarus, either, so it's kind of like a compromise."

It makes sense, though I don't want to agree with him out loud. "How many souls come here?" The dead are packed in like cockroaches; they hardly can move.

"Lots of people have died over the years, Piper. But Hell grows to fit them all." Shayne stands a little straighter when he says this, and I realize he must be proud of his world.

"Isn't that convenient? And when you say lots, you

mean like…?"

"…billions. And most are here."

We leave one factory and then another. I'm pretty sure I've seen all Asphodel has to offer. The entire place seems to be a city paved over with machines. Shayne tries to tell me how each machine has a purpose, but it's all just so industrial. There's no nature and no weather. Asphodel is like a giant void filled with metal. Shayne leads us further into the city, away from the sanctuary of the boat—a sanctuary surrounded by a clay river infested with voracious monsters.

"What are we looking for?" I ask. I don't mention Randy because I know he's not the reason Shayne brought us here. As we walk through the city of factories, they seem to fly by around us. Like they're all in fast forward and we're not. They're a blur in my peripheral vision.

We step to the side as some kind of robotic car comes driving by. It's carrying five dead people who don't even seem to notice us.

"Checking in with the management." Shayne stops and turns his head so he's looking at me. "Do you mind coming along?" The way he angles his head lets me know he's curious what my response will be. Like he's testing me.

Something about his question makes me laugh.

"What?" When he asks, the red flecks in his pupils flash.

"I'd say that I'd follow you to the ends of the earth, but that doesn't seem like enough."

His smile lights up the gray world of Asphodel around us. "No, it's doesn't, but it still sounds nice to me."

"Well, as tempting as it may be, I'm not going to let you leave me here alone."

Shayne raises an eyebrow. "Scared?"

I glance back at the lifeless city. "I'm not quite sure that's the right word." The truth is I want to see what else is out there. I want to see more of the Underworld. And I still want to find Randy—the real Randy—even if Shayne tells me there's no point.

"Good," he says.

And I know I've passed his test.

We start walking again in our fast forward way, and before long, we pass through a flat, metal plane populated with the dead, empty-eyed souls. As soon as I see them, every bit of laughter and happiness is sucked right out of me.

"You get used to it."

I guess it shows on my face. But I shake my head. "I don't want to get used to it."

I don't expect him to respond, but he does. "It's reality, though, Piper. Just like above. Look at Austin. Some parts are nice, and you'd feel safe going out at night alone to walk your dog. But try to do that in the wrong area, and it could be the last thing you ever do."

"Not if Cerberus were my dog."

Shayne smiles and pulls me closer with his arms. "I could loan him to you."

The image of me walking Cerberus around on the Drag fills my mind. Of course, there, he'd probably fit right in. "My mom doesn't give me much opportunity to hit the seedier areas of town."

Shayne leans over and kisses my cheek, making me want to press into him. "So maybe next time Reese comes around, you could employ Cerberus."

The image of Cerberus tearing Reese apart limb by limb is a strange one. Would tearing the god of war apart limb by limb be able to stop him? I almost ask Shayne, but then decide killing gods is a conversation topic I don't want to bring up given our bleak surroundings.

"Rhadam tells me there's been trouble in Asphodel," Shayne says.

"What kind of trouble?" I think of the pomegranate tree dying in the Elysian Fields. That had been trouble for Shayne, also. Things shouldn't die in paradise. And I think about what else Rhadam said. About bad things brewing in other parts of Hell: secrets being kept and plans being made.

"Things not working right. Souls misplaced. Machines breaking. Even attempts to cross the river." Shayne points to a house far off ahead of us. It's up on a hill away from the city, and unlike the rest of the bleak

Asphodel, the air seems fresh around it, and rays of light actually touch it. "And we're going there to find out why."

As to why Shayne decides to take me on this task, I have no idea. He can't possibly think this is some kind of romantic date, and the closer we get to the house on the hill, the less I want to go. Even though it's clear and crisp outside, the house itself seethes evil. But there's no chance I'll venture back through Asphodel without him. And anyway, if he is testing me, I don't want to back down now. I want to prove to Shayne I'm tough like he is.

"Who lives here?" We're at the top of the hill now. Almost at the front door. It reminds me of a retro Hollywood home. Lots of glass windows and steel beams, but the front door is ten feet tall and made of thick black wood—like the door of a fortress.

"Minos."

I guess my blank expression tells Shayne I need more explanation.

"An old Cretan king. He's the overlord here in Asphodel."

"A king from Crete runs Asphodel?"

"An ancient king runs each of the territories. Minos here. Rhadamanthus in the Elysian Fields. And Aeacus in Tartarus."

"Rhadam is a king?" I guess I never thought to ask this when I met him.

Shayne shakes his head. "Was a king. Here in Hell he's only an overlord. They all are. I'm the only king in the Underworld." He scowls. "Which more and more seems to be a point of confusion among the lords."

I remember Rhadam's deference to Shayne, so solid a part of their relationship it could never be in question. "Not Rhadam?"

"No, not Rhadam." Shayne brushes his sleeves, and dirt vanishes off them. "He's true to me through and through. And as it happens, the only one I can trust."

We're at the imposing door now, but Shayne doesn't open it. Can he sense the evil which touches each and every one of my nerves? He lets go of my hand, and I look at him, ready to open my mouth and ask another question. But I stop. In a single moment, he's ceased to be Shayne, the guy I'm sure I'm in love with, and has become Hades, supreme King of the Underworld. A force to be reckoned with.

He lifts his hand and knocks on the thick door—a knock so hard I hear the echoes through the windows inside the house. Nobody answers, but Shayne doesn't knock again. Instead, he waits, and we stand there in silence until, after what feels like eternity, a lock clicks, and the door creeps open. Dead eyes greet us inside.

"I'm here to see Minos." Shayne doesn't ask; he states it.

The man who's opened the door stares at Shayne. He's got sandy blond hair, and from his engorged biceps, it's obvious this guy spent way too much time in the gym back when he was alive. But now, here in Hell, does it really matter how much time someone spent in the gym? I wonder if he spent more time with his loved ones and less time working out if he'd have ended up in the Elysian Fields instead of Asphodel—Land of the Walking Dead.

"King Minos is busy."

It's the first time someone in Asphodel has spoken. Until this point, I'm not even sure they can speak.

Shayne's face hardens, and I almost hear electricity sizzle off him next to me. "Tell Minos that King Hades demands to speak with him." He omits the word *king* in front of Minos.

The man doesn't nod or agree or shake his head. It's only when he walks backward, away from us, and toward a long hallway that I realize he's simply obeying Shayne's command. The command of the King of the Underworld must supersede commands from one of Shayne's minions.

Shayne and I stand there, still on the doorstep, watching him leave.

I lean close to him and put my lips to his ear. "Why don't you go in and find him?"

He whispers back, not turning his head away from the room ahead. "Because even here in Hell, we have courtesies."

"It doesn't seem like Minos is being very courteous

to you."

Shayne gives his head an almost imperceptible shake. "No, it doesn't."

Another ten minutes later, and the blond shell of a man returns. "Follow me."

Chapter 25

Minos

We follow the steroid-ridden ghost man in silence. He has his back to us as he leads us first down a hallway, then through a breezeway to another wing of the house. Every step I take, a sense of dread weighs heavier inside my stomach. I look down and realize I'm clenching Shayne's hand so hard my knuckles are white.

But Shayne doesn't turn to me or comfort me aside from a brief squeeze of my hand. His face is frozen in a hard stare straight ahead. At the end of the breezeway, we stop in front of a glass room overlooking a flat, gray ocean with nothing else in sight.

"King Minos will see you in here." The man moves aside, and gives us a clear view of the room ahead. Every wall is glass, and in the center is a stone chimney so large a Spanish Oak could burn inside without being cut.

Shayne doesn't acknowledge our guide as he opens the glass door. He walks in, and I follow. I can't see anyone in the room, but Shayne doesn't hesitate. He skirts around the giant fireplace and stops at a chair on the other side. Amber liquid sits in a crystal tumbler on a table next to the chair.

"Minos." Shayne's voice sounds like razors slicing glass.

"Hades." Minos doesn't turn to face us; instead, he's facing the windows overlooking the dull ocean. "So you finally decided to grace us with your presence here in Asphodel?" Every word Minos speaks scratches in his throat as it comes out, making it sound like it pains him to speak. A hand reaches from the chair and picks up the glass. He swirls it, making the ice inside clink up against the crystal.

"Unlike you, I have other duties here in the Underworld." Shayne lets go of my hand and shoves the side of the chair around, causing Minos to spin and face us. The drink flies out of his hand and crashes to the ground, and the air is filled with the sweet smell of alcohol.

Minos looks at Shayne, but manages to keep his face impassive. But when Minos's eyes see me, they grow as big as the gold coins Charon collects. He half stands up, but Shayne throws an arm in front of me. "Sit down!"

Minos continues to stare at me but obeys the command.

"To what do I owe this honor?" Minos forces his eyes away from me, but his eyes dart back to me every so often as if he can't control them. Minos gestures toward an empty chair, but Shayne stays standing, and I follow his lead.

"We can start with the escape attempts." Shayne's fingers are unclenched, but he shifts them around like they are prepared for battle.

I'm starting to wonder just what Shayne's gotten into here. What he's gotten me into.

Minos waves a hand. "A couple restless souls crossing the river. So what of it?"

Shayne grits his teeth. "Why are they crossing the river, Minos? They shouldn't have anything to cross back for."

Minos looks at Shayne and narrows his eyes. "You tell me, oh wise ruler of the Underworld. Why would anyone want to leave Asphodel?"

"They wouldn't." I can hear Shayne's breath now, and his presence has shifted to something feral. "Unless someone's been telling them to."

Minos spreads his arms wide, palms up. "Why would anyone in Asphodel tell the dead souls about their past? And besides, as we've seen from the recent attempts, crossing the River Lethe only results in being devoured by the monsters." His eyes shift to me again. I meet them, and he stares at me with such cruelty, I'm forced to look away.

Shayne moves in closer to Minos. "I think somebody's trying to exchange souls. Trying to get people out of Tartarus."

The silence that descends on the room is so real, it

pushes at me from all sides. My heart is beating so fast, I'm pretty sure everyone both below and above ground can hear it.

Neither Minos nor Shayne looks away from each other. The heavy quiet is so oppressive, I feel like something needs to be said, and neither of them is going to say it.

"Nobody can leave Tartarus." I'm not sure how the words manage to escape my mouth, but when they do, Minos turns his head and looks at me. Shayne leans away from Minos, and the silence is replaced with something even worse. Lies and secrets fill the air around us, so thick they're like real creatures.

I'm trying not to look at Minos, but I see him still staring at me, and then he licks his lips. "So the beautiful criminal speaks."

Criminal? He's talking about me? I glance at Shayne and notice his fingers are now balled into fists. And I'm pretty sure by speaking, I've messed everything up.

"It's not her fault." The words come out of Shayne's mouth slowly and clearly, as if he wants to make sure Minos doesn't misunderstand a single one. I have no idea what he's talking about, but I'm smart enough to know now's not the time to ask.

Before I know what's happening, Minos jumps up from the chair and grabs me, pressing something hot and sharp to the softest part of my neck. It's not cutting me, but it's so tight, I don't think I can breathe. Minos holds me like a vise with his other hand. And he spins me to face Shayne.

"You know the penalty for killing a phoenix." Minos's scratchy voice snarls in my ear, mixing with the sound of my pounding heart.

My eyes flash to Shayne, but he doesn't meet them. He's staring at Minos and looks like he's ready to pounce on a kill.

"Let her go." It's a direct command, and the part of me that's not worrying about staying as still as possible wonders if Minos will obey it.

Minos's hot breath seeps into my ear. "You know the penalty." And though I don't think it's possible, Minos presses the knife even closer until I feel it cut into my skin.

"Let her go. Now."

I can't believe how calm Shayne's being, especially when I feel a trickle of blood moving down my neck. The knife is so close, I can hardly get air out, and my heart is pounding in my ears so loudly the room seems to spin.

"Consider this a direct order." And Shayne is every bit the king when he says it.

I feel Minos's muscles tighten, and I know he's about to either slit my throat or let me go. In a single move, he shoves me away, lowering the knife, but not before slicing under my ear with the blade. Warm blood pours from the cut down my neck.

Shayne catches me, but still, he doesn't look at me or talk to me. His grip is like steel, but it also fills me with comfort.

"She belongs in Tartarus." Minos moves away, widening the distance between Shayne and himself. I think he knows he's gone too far.

"It's you who should be in Tartarus, Minos. If I need to come here one more time, I promise you that will be the end result." Shayne turns his back on Minos. I'm not sure if this is a good idea, but Shayne is the king here. I try to convince myself he knows what he's doing. And all I really want is to stop my heart from exploding and get out of here now. I try not to run, but Minos doesn't follow us as we show ourselves out. The blond ghost man waits outside the door, but a single look from Shayne, and he doesn't follow us, instead heading back into the glass room where Minos is. And it's not until we leave the house completely and get down the hill that my heart slows down enough that I dare to speak.

"What the hell was that all about?" I'm holding a hand over the cut in my neck, but I still feel the blood seeping out. I want to stop and rest, but I don't dare suggest it. If Minos really does want to send me to Tartarus for some unknown reason, I don't want to help him.

We stop walking, and Shayne turns to me, taking a deep breath. "Minos is getting power hungry."

I squeeze my eyes shut and shake my head. "No! I mean the part about him trying to kill me and dump me in Tartarus. He said I'm a criminal. And yeah, I may not be the best person in the world, but I certainly haven't done anything worthy of eternal torture."

Shayne actually smiles. "No, you haven't."

"So what did he mean? Criminal?"

Shayne looks back at the house, which is still and haunting, and then back at me. "It means there are things I can't tell you."

"Can't tell me? To Hell with that! I'm sick of hearing that!" I pull away from him and slam my fists down on his chest.

He grabs them and holds me. "Then remember." For all the anger in my voice, his is a whisper. And I want so badly to know what he's talking about. What secrets and mysteries lie in my past? Before I can stop it, the tears come, and I'm sobbing onto his chest. His arms are around me, and he's stroking my hair. Holding me tight. Why does it seem like there's so much I don't know and no one will tell me anything?

We stay like that in Asphodel, and the ghosts avoid us. I'm not sure when I stop crying, but by the time all my tears are cried out, all I want to do is lie down and sleep. I don't even want to find Randy anymore. I just want to find out why my life has gone crazy. But we still need to get out of this hellish purgatory and back across the River Lethe. Back to the safety of Shayne's sanctuary. I don't try to press him or question him on our trip back. I'll figure out a way to get the information I need from him, because whatever it is, he knows it, and I plan to find out.

Chapter 26

Phoenix

Shayne pretends he's got his anger under control, but the red flashes in his eyes so fast it looks like sparks.

It's only when Cerberus pounds through the clay, meeting us on the bank of the river, that Shayne's eyes finally stop their flickering madness and his muscles relax. I, on the other hand, can't stop thinking about Minos.

Criminal. Tartarus. His haunting words keep coming back to me. Killing a phoenix. We walk down the long tunnel, Cerberus only steps ahead of us as if sensing Shayne's unease. We're almost to his sanctuary ahead. Already, I smell the fire burning. Once we're inside, he pours us each a glass of wine. I finish mine in one long sip, and he refills the glass, but already the wine's moving through my veins, flushing the fear out of my body.

Shayne lets out a long sigh. "Your visits haven't gone so well, have they?"

I glance at him, but don't respond.

"I'm sorry," he says.

"What does a dead bird have to do with anything?"

"Nothing. Everything." Shayne gets up and walks to

the bookcase. He pulls a red leather book from the shelf, bringing it back over to me. Flipping it open, he stops on a page with a hand-drawn purple and red bird amid a mass of flames. I suck in my breath when I see its tail: five long red feathers—feathers which look identical to the one I found in the box Melina had given me.

"What?" Shayne has turned away from the page and is studying me.

I shake my head. "Nothing." But images of the box and the feather stay in my mind.

He doesn't press me but turns back to the picture. "The phoenix lives for a thousand years, but when it's time for the phoenix to die, it bursts into flames, burning until it's nothing but ashes. Once the ashes have cooled, the phoenix is reborn again, all on its own."

I look down at the picture, studying it. "Does that mean it can't be killed?"

And why did Melina give me a box with a phoenix's tail feather in it?

Shayne flips the book shut and turns to the fire which crackles when he looks at it. "It's almost impossible to kill a phoenix."

"But it can be done?"

Shayne nods. "Yes. It can be done."

"And for someone who kills a phoenix…" I know how the sentence will end, and I don't want to finish it.

Shayne takes a long breath. "The penalty is eternity in Tartarus."

I've never seen a phoenix, and part of me doesn't even believe they exist. But here I am in Hell drinking wine with Shayne—Lord of the Underworld, and I know it's possible. There was a feather to prove it. Or maybe it was a feather to prove my guilt. "Did I kill a phoenix?"

Shayne moves so close, the warmth of his body smolders next to me. He takes my hands, and the smell of the wine on his breath sends a wave of exhilaration through me, blending in with his sweet burnt taste.

"No. You did not kill a phoenix."

I let out the breath I've been holding, and can't stop the smile that's hiding behind my lips. Finally, an answer. "So Minos was wrong."

Shayne nods. "Yes. Minos was wrong." And then he's leaning into me and kissing me, and I forget about phoenixes and Minos and Asphodel. He traces his fingers up my spine, and I respond by pulling him down onto the floor. Between the embers and Shayne, I feel like I'm on fire myself. I run my hands over his chest, his arms; I just don't want to believe we ever have to be apart.

We stay there forever, and even at that, it's not long enough. I never want to go away, but as the wine leaves me, I know I have to. I need to get back to reality, to take care of Chloe, to deal with my mom. And then, of course, there's Reese. It's only once Charon takes us back across the River Acheron that Shayne mentions him again.

"Please stay away from Ares." The concern in his eyes and voice is enough to catch me off guard.

"I will. There's nothing to worry about." I'm telling myself this as much as I'm telling Shayne because, when I say his name, I remember the kiss we shared and wonder if I'm being honest with myself.

"I'm serious, Piper. Ares will trick you and deceive you and do whatever he needs to do to win."

"To win?" I stare at him. "Is there some kind of competition I'm not aware of? Am I like a prize or something?"

"No, Piper. Nothing like that."

"Then what?" I need to know. "You can only win something when you're competing against someone else."

"Look. Ares doesn't care about the prize. He only cares about the battle and the conquest. He thrives on it. You can think whatever you want, but just remember that. He's the god of war."

I roll my eyes. It's not like this is some kind of amusement park game and I'm the giant stuffed animal up for grabs. This is my life. "I have no plans to go near Reese." And it's true. I can only hope he's gone by the time I get back home and that I never see him again.

Shayne twists up his lips. "Yes, but I'm sure he has plans to go near you."

I cross my arms. "I'll be careful. As long as he

doesn't hold me at knife point and threaten to throw me into Tartarus, everything should be fine."

Shayne doesn't laugh. He caresses my ear, sending a wonderful chill down below my stomach. And then he gives me a wistful smile and walks away, leaving me to return to Earth above.

Chapter 27

Hurricane

I return from the Underworld and find myself by the Spanish Oak. Reese is nowhere to be found. Overhead, the birds flutter through the trees. Birds. Phoenix. I look up and imagine I see a purple and red bird overhead bathed in flames, but there's no fire. There's no sun. A giant gray cloud fills the sky, and the wind picks up and starts blowing leaves off the tree.

I know I need to go back home and see if my mom will tell me what's going on. She's keeping secrets from me about who I am. Who she is. It's like I don't know her. And I don't even know myself.

I try to piece it out in my mind, but there's just nothing that makes sense. I've lived with my mom my entire life. That's all I am. Still, there has to be something more. Otherwise, why would two Greek gods suddenly be fighting for my attention?

A gust of wind slams into the tree, and a cracking sound cuts into the air. I hardly have time to jump out of the way before a branch from the Spanish Oak falls to the ground right where I was standing. Would it have killed me? Would I be judged just like Randy Conner? I try to think of the good things I've done in my life. Are they worthy of paradise?

As I walk out of the woods, the wind starts to really pick, so I run until I'm in front of the shuttle stop. My tattoo aches, and it's turning red again. The ink has faded a few shades, but the raised scar underneath remains. And I think of the face I saw in Asphodel. Like a shadow of Chloe. It had to have been a shade of Reese in disguise, but the ghost Chloe reminds me too much of the fading tattoo. I brush it with my hand, and it deepens again.

When the shuttle stops, I hop on and head for her house. The wind's blowing so hard it pushes on the shuttle, but the driver has his hands tight on the wheel. It's getting dark outside, almost like night, and I think most people will be heading inside. But around the steel struts that reach upward to form the domes, there are work crews everywhere. I get off the shuttle at Chloe's stop, but before I walk the remaining distance to her house, I move closer to one of the steel legs and try to see what's going on.

There's a panel open, and one of the workers is guiding a sand truck that's dumping into it. My mom told me they use sand to help grow the glass in the dome, but I thought the domes needed time to recharge. I walk up to the nearest worker and tap him on the shoulder. He turns around to face me.

"What's going on?" I ask. From above, tiny drops of rain begin to fall down. They're heavy and sparse, and I can see each drop when it lands on the concrete surrounding the steel supports.

"You need to get inside." He looks back at the panel.

"Why? What are you doing with the dome?"

He flips the control panel he's been working on closed and finally looks me in the eye. "Running tests," he says, and I see his lie thick on him, growing like a dark gray fungus.

I wipe the rain off my face. They shouldn't be doing anything with the domes. I pull out my FON and text my mom. I'm still freaked that she knows Reese, but I'm not going to ask her about that now. It's not like I can text the message, "why do u know the god of war?" and get any kind of real response.

"what's going on with the dome?" I text her instead.

She responds in seconds. "get home. talk when u get here."

I start to type out the next message, to tell her about the sand, but then stop. I'm not ready to head home yet. I pocket my FON and sprint to Chloe's house. The wind has started blowing hard enough I have to fight against it as I run. My hair's blowing every single way and getting in my eyes, and anything not tied down is starting to move.

Chloe's sitting outside when I get there, arms

wrapped around herself, legs drawn up into her. It's like she doesn't even realize the wind is blowing. Overhead, a tile blows off her roof and crashes to the walkway where it shatters. The streets are littered, and where any trees still stand, branches snap off and fall.

"It's freezing here." She doesn't even look up at me, but she has to know I've arrived because there's no one else around she could be talking to. "Have you noticed how cold it is?"

I stand over her. "Chloe, we need to get you inside." More tiles pull from the roof. We're under the patio cover, but the way the wind is blowing, one good gust and it could be gone.

"The world feels like ice."

Ice. I think of the River Cocytus between Hell and the Elysian Fields. Frozen over, but still the wraithlike monsters swim underneath, hoping for an opening but never finding one.

She lets me help her up, and then we walk inside. Her mom shuts the door behind me and starts telling me how's she's been trying to get Chloe inside for the last half hour. Chloe's mom is normally a calm person, but she's freaked. Her eyes look bloodshot from worry, and she keeps hovering over Chloe.

The rain comes down in sheets then, pounding on the roof of the patio. I'll have to stay at Chloe's house until the storm relents. My mom may want me home, but she won't want me walking or taking a shuttle in this mess. I text her a quick, "waiting til storm stops" and leave it at that.

Chloe's mom finally goes into the kitchen to make us some coffee which leaves Chloe and me alone. We sit on the sofa, and I try to figure out how to start this conversation with her. There's been so much going on, I don't know where to begin. So much has happened even just today. This hurricane is only the most recent part.

"I missed you at the funeral," I say and put my hand on Chloe's. But I yank it back at the touch. She is freezing. Like she's kept her hand in an ice bin to numb it. I force myself to reach back out and put my hand on hers, rubbing it to warm her. I try to ignore the sound of the wind beating against her house and the memories of Minos accusing me at knifepoint.

"I was there. In the back."

"I didn't see you," I say.

"I saw Randy." She turns to me at this, and her eyes dig into mine, but they look odd. Like her pupils are tiny dots in the center of giant, oversized irises. Irises so big they should touch the boundaries of her eyes. But there's white all around—encompassing them. I remember something I heard once about white showing all around the eye. Something about violent death.

My heart skips a beat, and I'm afraid to look away. Like Chloe might vanish on me or something. Sink down right now into the ground and be swallowed up.

"Randy's dead," I say. "It was his funeral."

And Chloe cannot be seeing ghosts.

But Chloe shakes her head so furiously, I'm actually happy. It's the first bit of emotion she's shown since her near-death experience. "No! I saw him there. He was watching. Listening." And she grips my hand with such force my knuckles feel like they might pop.

Her mom walks back in the room right then and sets two cups of steamy coffee down on the table. She gives me a small smile, but then a boom of thunder hits. We all jump, and Chloe's mom bumps her hand into one of the cups, splashing coffee over the side. I pull my hand away from Chloe's and reach for a towel to wipe it up.

Chloe's mom mouths me a silent, "Thank you."

I nod in response, and then she leaves the room.

Chloe takes a long sip of coffee and then rubs her hands together, warming them. "So what's going on Piper?"

This is it. I can tell her about everything. Reese. Shayne. The Underworld. I can warn her to stay far away from Reese. But as I go over the phrasing, it just feels so off. I'm walking around in a world of mythology; who is going to believe that?

Outside, there's a groaning, like a giant metal monster has just woken up. Chloe and I both jump at the sound because it sounds like something is going to crash in on us. I look to the window, but she has the shades pulled. And then the sound stops.

I wait for my breath to return. "I'm not sure where to start," I say.

Chloe gives me a smile. "Start anywhere. I feel like I've lost the last week." It's like it's the old Chloe. She's back. And Death has left her behind.

I scoot closer to her and relink my fingers with hers. Her hands have warmed up again, and her tattoo is normal. I look to mine and see they match. Black and solid. *Sacrifice*.

For some reason, Minos's words come back to me. *Do you know what the penalty for killing a phoenix is?* I ignore them.

I start with something easy. "My mom got back today," I say, grasping for straws. "She said my father wants custody."

"Custody?" Chloe's voice echoes my own amazement.

"Yeah. Weird, huh?"

The metal outside groans again though not as loud. I think the wind must be hitting against the metal beams.

"Totally weird. You're eighteen. Parents don't get custody at eighteen."

"That's what I thought, too." And then I lean closer though no one is around to hear. "I have to admit I'm a little curious, Chloe."

She moves her fingers until our thumbs press together. "About your father?"

I nod. "I might get to meet him. And he wants me in his life."

Chloe purses her lips. "I don't know, Piper. He got convicted as a terrorist."

"That's what my mom says. But maybe she's lying. Maybe she's just been keeping me away from him."

Chloe doesn't answer. She knows if it were up to my mom, I'd live with her until I was a hundred years old.

"Seriously, Chloe. I want to meet him."

Chloe doesn't seem to hear me. Or she chooses to ignore me. "He was so sad, Piper."

"My father?"

Chloe shakes her head. "Randy. His father beats his mom. And his little sister. Did you know that? She's only seven."

The blood freezes in my veins at her words, and the chill that runs through me knocks the wind out of me. How could Chloe possibly know Randy Conner's final sorrow? How could she know about his abusive father? I lived next to him for four years, yet I had no idea.

"He asked me to help. Wanted me to do something." Chloe looks away, and I can finally blink when her enlarged eyes leave mine.

I believe her. She's talked with Randy Conner's spirit as surely as I've gone to Hell. "What can you do?" When I say it, I'm not really asking her. I'm asking Shayne, but I know he won't answer. His realm is the Underworld, not abusive dealings of the world above. He's made that clear.

Chloe sighs, but she doesn't answer. She wraps her arms back around herself, and turns away. "I did it again, Piper."

"Did what?" I ask. At this point, I have no idea where Chloe's disjointed conversation will take me. And I realize she's not ready for me to tell her anything about my life just yet.

"It was this weird urge," she says.

"Weird like how?"

Chloe actually lets out a laugh; there's not an ounce of humor in it. "I cut my sheets into thin strips."

I try to hold my face steady and act like maybe this is a normal thing. "Oh. Why?"

Chloe shakes her head, making her brown bandana fall askew. But she doesn't straighten it. "They felt so dirty. I washed them but it didn't help, so I cut them up. But I still can't sleep on the bed, Piper, so I moved to the floor."

My breathing has stopped, but I manage to get words out. "Why did they feel dirty?" Out of nowhere, I imagine Chloe sleeping with someone on her bed and then needing to wash the sheets afterward. I know Chloe's slept with two guys before, but there's no one I'm aware of at the present.

Chloe doesn't turn to me and doesn't reply.

"What's wrong, Chloe?"

In profile, I see a tear creep into the corner of her

eye, but her lips stay together. I'm tempted to press her—to ask her again. But the wind slams into the house again, and this time, it hits the window and sends glass scattering into the room. I jump up but Chloe doesn't even move. I hear her mom from the kitchen calling in to ask what happened.

"Are you going to be okay?" I ask.

She nods. "You need to leave, Piper."

Hurt runs through me. I start to ask why, but she talks again.

"Now, Piper. Just please leave now."

Chapter 28

Retribution

I nod and stand up and wipe the tears that spring into my eyes. Chloe acts like she's two different people. But she is right. I need to get out of here. I need to get out of the city. The metal groans again, and all of a sudden, I know what it is. They are opening the growth slats on the domes; they're going to try to grow the glass. Even though the domes haven't had time to regenerate, they're still going to try.

I take a step for the door, but Chloe doesn't even look at me. Maybe the sheet ripping thing was just like the light bulbs—just some near-death recovery thing. It's only been a few days. Chloe just needs time to recuperate. I'm almost at the door when it blows open. From the kitchen, I hear Chloe's mom call out again, but I don't want to talk to her, so I run out the open door.

The sky is furious. Clouds as black as the River Acheron spin in the sky, and rain comes down so hard, it hurts when it strikes my face. The blast of sirens is almost muted from the storm. I glance up at the steel struts of the dome. Glass is growing fast. In the seconds

I watch, it grows downward by a foot. I need to run to get out of the city. I take off and don't look at anything around me. I don't look back at Chloe's house; she'll be fine once the dome is sealed. She'll be fine when she gets some rest. Debris fills the streets, but no one is around. There's no sign of the work crews that had been there earlier. And I'm willing to bet a shuttle won't come.

Litter flies past me and tumbles down the street. Something hard strikes me on the back and knocks the wind out of me, but I can't turn to look. I have to get out of here. I'm vaguely aware of my FON vibrating in my pocket, but I ignore it. My mom's calling, I'm sure, and given this storm, I don't blame her. It's like nothing I've even imagined before.

I'm almost out of the last steel support of the dome when the metal groans a final time. And then shards of glass start to fall to the ground. I dig into my reserves and run like I'll die if I don't. Once I'm free and clear and twenty feet away, I spin around and watch the destruction of the dome the city had prided itself so much on. Glass showers down, mixing with the rain until I can't tell one from the other. My FON is going crazy in my pocket, so I stop under the overhang of a house's roof and pull it out.

"b home in a few," I text my mom. She's probably absolutely nuts with worry.

"please tell me ur okay," she sends back.

"fine," I text.

"i love u so much piper. i never want 2 lose u," she writes, and I surprise myself when a lump forms in my throat and pushes tears upwards to my eyes. Her words are simple, but she cares so much.

I wipe my tears, and wait until the storm begins to subside. I stand there under the patio roof of the house and watch as the clouds first blow away east of Austin and then nearly evaporate from the sky. The rain stops next, and when it clears, I see that most of the glass from the dome is gone, too. All that's left is the shattered skeleton near the sides of the steel beams. The sky transitions first from a dark gray to a creamy butter and then to a denim blue. Then it's back to the color of topaz, and the sun shines down from above, reflecting off every bit of glass littering the ground and the sky. The transformation is so sudden, so complete. There's been a hurricane in Austin, and now, only its destruction remains.

The city is a wreck, but I don't head back to Chloe's house or anywhere near the dome. I need to get home to my mom. Because even with everything that's happened, I want to be near her. I want her to tell me there's been some mistake. That she was just angry and that she has no idea who Reese really is. But as I walk home, my stomach starts to turn queasy. My mom knows I went on a date with Reese; they know each other. And she wants us to move. Again. She's been to see my father, and whatever path we lived on in the past has changed. I just don't know to what extent yet.

The first thing I see when I get home is Reese's pink calla lilies, still smashed on the floor, and nearly every pink petal missing. I pick a single stem up, and before I think about what I'm doing, I infuse life back into it.

The blossom moves under my energy, and even the green stem is given rebirth. Power flows out of my hands into the flower, and it bursts into color and vibrancy. I touch the bottom of the stem, and roots grow and twist around my hand and fingers. In turn, I pick up each of the remaining flowers and do the same, and when they've all reformed, only then do I stop and realize what I've done.

The cut flowers, once dead, are alive. I feel their life with my hands. I've had a green thumb my entire life, but this is paranormal. But then again, so is everything else that has been going on in my life recently. If gods walk the earth, then why can't flowers regrow in seconds? I stick them back in the water-filled vase on the counter.

"Maybe you should just let them die."

I turn and see my mom standing there watching me.

"I can't."

"Throw them out, and tell him to never come back." She shifts, like she wants to say so much more than she is. Like she wants to run to me and hug me.

I set the plant on a shelf next to the sink. "Didn't

you already do that?" I walk past my mom, brushing her shoulder on my way.

"Of course, Piper. But he won't give up." Her voice shakes as she talks. "He'll keep coming back because he thinks he has some right to be with you."

"But why?" I ask.

My mom throws her hands up in the air. "I don't know. I just don't. He showed up here and said he was supposed to take you away. And I can't let that happen."

"Who am I, Mom?" I have to ask the question even though it sounds absurd to my ears.

My mom doesn't even hesitate. "You're my daughter, that's who you are."

I shake my head because her answer's just so frustrating. "No, really. Who am I? There has to be something else."

My mom comes over and pats my shoulder. "Piper, you're beautiful and you're smart and to me, you're the most perfect thing this world has ever created. But that's it. That's all you are."

"No," I say. "There has to be something else. Something special."

She looks at me like she feels sorry for me. "There's nothing else, Piper. There's nothing special about you at all."

Her words sting. I feel them like worms digging into my heart. If she notices she's hurt me, she doesn't show it.

"We need to move. To go away," she says.

"No." I don't raise my voice or argue or even try to make it sound like a compromise. I'm not moving. Not again. If I move anywhere, it's going to be away from my mom—alone.

"Yes," she says. "Your father will find you otherwise."

"The dome shattered," I say because I don't want to talk about moving.

My mom stares at me a second, and I finally let my eyes meet hers. And then she pulls me into a hug. I don't break away, but I don't hug her back.

"I was so worried about you, Piper." She puts a hand on my cheek, and the tears in her eyes tell me how much she loves me.

"I was fine," I say.

"You were out there in the storm. Councilman Rendon called a council meeting to tell us about his plans. He'd gone ahead and activated one of the domes. He said there was a hurricane approaching Austin." She shudders like even the memory is too hard to live with.

"I went to Chloe's."

"The council had a virtual meeting; he said he was going to activate all the domes."

"The glass shattered," I say. "It was everywhere."

Anger flashes into my mom's eyes. "It didn't have time to regenerate. How does he think the glass will sustain a hurricane when the growth proteins haven't had time to bond?"

I don't answer because there's nothing I can really say.

"He's killing the city," my mom says. "He's killing the world. He's pulling it apart with everything he tries."

I know it's true, but it seems a little unfair. "It's not like he started the Global Heating Crisis."

My mom's nostrils flare. "No, he didn't. It doesn't matter at this point how it started, just how we get past it."

I'm not sure I agree, but my mom doesn't leave it open for debate. We head upstairs and flip on the tube. Reports of damage from the hurricane are still coming in. I try to zone out because most of the images they're showing are horrific. People are dead everywhere. The shattered glass from the dome Chloe lives in caused so much destruction, they estimate it will take weeks to clean up. Councilman Rendon is scheduled to give a speech in a half hour to talk about the tragedy. I text Chloe to make sure she's okay, but she doesn't answer, so I call her mom who tells me they're all fine, that aside from some missing roof tiles and the broken window, they got off lucky. I assure her I got home safely and am with my mom.

I attempt to go about my normal routine until the news conference starts. Changing my clothes. Brushing my teeth. It's only when I pick up a comb and begin to yank it through the blond snarls that my mom comes over. She takes the comb from me and sits me down, pulling each and every tangle out one by one until they're all gone.

"Maybe I should get a tattoo, also."

Her words catch me halfway into a trance state. I'm sure I've heard wrong. "What?"

"A tattoo." She touches it. "We could both have one."

I laugh at the absurdity of my mother getting a tattoo. I wonder how *overprotective* would be spelled in ancient Greek anyway. But maybe the time away from my mom was a good thing. Maybe she's starting to relax. To be less protective.

"Maybe we could get matching ones. Mother and daughter. Together forever."

All hopes of my mom relaxing disappear. "That sounds more like something saved for couples," I say. "Not mother and daughter."

She holds the comb steady, feeling each tine with her fingers. "We're an exception, Piper. You'll always be my little girl."

"I'm eighteen now, Mom."

She moves the comb to her own head and runs it through her hair. Even when it catches on a tangle, she keeps her eyes on me. "Eighteen is only the beginning, Piper. We have our whole lives to be together."

I decide not to respond. There's nothing I can say to agree with her. I want my own life, but the impasse is she wants it, too. My silence prompts her to kiss me on the forehead and turn back to the tube. The news conference will start in minutes. But there's something I need to ask my mom.

"Mom, do you know what a phoenix is?"

She freezes, and I see she's stopped breathing. She knows. As surely as I know Randy Conner's death is my fault, she knows what a phoenix is.

"It's a bird." She makes it sound casual like everyone in the world should know.

"What kind of bird?"

"A bird that only exists in legends, Piper."

I don't get a chance to say anything else, because, at that moment, the news conference starts. My teeth grit when Councilman Rendon comes on, standing at a makeshift podium there in Chloe's dome. He's supposed to give some speech about how the domes were activated by accident which I know is a lie. If there was any devastation behind him, it's gone now. The area is lit up like midday, and new trees are planted in the ground. He gives his signature smile and motions with his hand for the crowd to be quiet. He announces he's going to be speaking and won't be taking any questions. Of course, questions come anyway.

"Councilman, how could the domes be accidentally activated?"

"Is it true growth materials were refilled today?"

I think of the sand I saw being poured into the

metal struts.

"What's being done to remove the glass from the domes that didn't shatter?"

The news reports showed these domes. Chloe's was the only one to crack and fall, but the other operational domes only grew about one-third of the way closed. If I lived under that glass, I'd be freaked out, too. One gust of wind, and the glass could all come crashing down.

My mom's staring intently at the tube next to me. Her lips are pressed thin, and I think she hates this man.

He starts a prepared speech, but when the questions don't stop, he gives up and starts with the answers.

"The accidental activation occurred due to a programming error," he says. "I can assure you it won't happen again."

My mom stiffens next to me. "Lies," she says. "Flat out lies."

He goes on to deny growth materials being refilled today even though I myself saw the work crews dumping the sand. But his last lie is the worst.

"I can assure the city of Austin with all faith that there is no risk of glass shards continuing to rain down on the city. Sealant has been sprayed from above." He gives a small laugh like he's trying to win over the crowd. "The real question will be: how do we get the glass down now that it's up?"

"Lies," my mom says again.

The questions from the crowd start fresh, but

they're halted at the sound of metal groaning on metal. I recognize the sound the second I hear it, and I know what will happen even before it does. The groan waxes, and then there's a cracking sound. And we watch as a single shard of glass comes careening down from above and strikes Councilman Rendon directly through the head.

Chapter 29

Dinner

The day after Councilman Rendon's death on national news, school is canceled. Crews have been cleaning up the city nonstop, but for the day, there is not supposed to be any travel to or from Chloe's dome. We text back and forth a couple times, and it's weird because she doesn't even remember the hurricane. She just claims she's tired, that she'll see me tomorrow at school. She acts like she didn't ask me to leave.

When I look outside the Botanical Haven, the Global Heating Crisis is back in full force. Temperatures are over one hundred and eight, and my mom's been called in for an emergency city council meeting.

"Don't let them elect you to be head of the council," I say because I'm trying to gauge her reaction. Is she still convinced we'll be moving? Since the hurricane and Councilman Rendon dying, she hasn't mentioned my father.

"That is one thing you'll never have to worry about." Which I know is true. The head of the council gets far too much publicity.

My mom gives me a kiss on the forehead and makes

me promise to lock the door behind her. She leaves, and I lock the door. I text Chloe again, but she sends me a text that stops me short.

"have a date. tell u about it l8r. ttyl"

A date? She can't be with Reese. My fingers hover over the keypad, but I can't bring myself to respond. Has Chloe been seeing Reese, and I've been too caught up in my own world to notice? I start and stop typing five times, and then give up entirely. Chloe and I need to have a long conversation. But I can't do it if she's with Reese. So I grab my tablet and pretend to read for the rest of the day even though my mind doesn't focus on a single word. Chloe and Reese. I try to put it out of my mind.

My mom finally gets home close to five.

"They're taking down the domes," she says.

"Taking them down?"

"Deconstruction will start this weekend." She walks upstairs and I follow her.

"Why?" I ask.

My mother almost smiles when she answers. "Some underground terrorist group delivered a threat. Said if the council didn't stop destroying the atmosphere, they'd blow up the dome structure."

I put this together in my mind. "So instead of waiting for the domes to be blown up, the city's taking them apart first."

My mom nods.

"What about the missiles?" I ask. If a terrorist group is against the domes, then they're certainly against the missiles.

My mom grabs her hairbrush and starts pulling it through her dark hair. She brushes it first behind both ears, then only behind one.

"The missiles will still be on standby," she says.

My mom fiddles with her hair some more and then moves to her jewelry box and pulls out a necklace I've never seen her wear.

"Are you going somewhere, Mom?"

She clasps the necklace and turns to face me. "How does it look?"

It's a leaf with glittering green gems sparkling against her skin. "Gorgeous," I say.

She gives herself one more look in the mirror and then turns to me. "Get ready."

"Where are we going?"

"We're going out for barbeque, Piper."

My mom hates barbeque. She doesn't eat meat. And we almost never go out. I tilt my head, trying to read her expression.

"Mom?"

Her eyes look past me. "What?"

"You hate barbeque."

Her face is a mask, but there's a certain light in it I never see. "So tonight I've changed my mind."

I bite my lip while looking for more in her face. But

there's nothing there. Nothing she is willing to let me see. "Okay. Barbeque. Who with?"

My mom arranges the jewelry and bottles on her counter and then finally looks at me. "Your father, Piper. He can't wait to meet you."

Everything my mom's ever told me about my dad starts spiraling around in my head. Because if he's such a bad person, why is she bringing me to meet him now?

When we walk into Pok-E-Jo's barbeque, the overwhelming aroma of smoked meat hits me; I focus on it to keep my mind off how nervous I am. I'm going to finally meet my father—something I've dreamed of since I was a little girl. And now it's really going to happen. I close my eyes and suck in the smell, picking out the sausage, the brisket, and even the macaroni and cheese from the air.

I look over at my mom and see her nose is wrinkled up.

"Don't you even like the smell, Mom?" I ask because I need to say something. My stomach is a ball of lead inside me.

"I had a bad experience with meat once," she says. And I wonder if she's as nervous as I am.

It's dark already, and every single booth is taken. My heart skips a few beats as I scan the room, wondering if I can pick out my dad. My eyes settle on a man with a receding hairline and a pair of bright blue eyes staring at me. His hair is spiked and blond and looks like he should wear a hat to keep his scalp from burning. Even with his retreating hairline, he hardly looks thirty.

I turn to my mom and see she's gazing at him, also. The ball in my stomach turns into an iron fist which begins to tighten. My father. The man sitting in the booth is my father. The lines of his face are familiar because they match my own. I open my mouth to say something, but my throat constricts.

My mom puts up her hand. "Let's just get our food and sit down. The sooner we get this over with the better."

I nod, not that I want to get the meal over with. After eighteen years of not even knowing who my dad is, I don't want to rush the meal. I have a father, and he's sitting in a booth waiting for me. He doesn't look like a terrorist or a criminal. And he doesn't look like a kidnapper either.

I manage to walk through the line, ordering my food without even thinking. My mom orders only a salad, holding my arm at the elbow the whole time. Like she's afraid my dad's going to snatch me away or something. It makes me feel like I'm five years old all over again.

I scoot into the booth, across from my father, and my mom slides in next to me. The red vinyl crunches under my legs as I cross them, and already I can feel it sticking to me and sweat forming. If the restaurant has eco A/C, they aren't using it. Or maybe I'm just nervous. Or both.

My father looks over and cracks a grin which reaches far up his forehead. "You like the heat, Piper?"

It seems a funny question to be the first words spoken between my dad and me—simple chitchat about the weather.

I nod. "Yeah. I do. The hotter the better." I reach across the table for the barbeque sauce. The sausage here is too dry without it. My hands shake, but I don't want him to see I'm nervous. I want him to think I'm brave and independent and someone he should be proud of.

My father smiles. "Now that sounds like a daughter of mine." He grabs a different bottle and passes it over to me. "Here, try this instead. It's my own special blend."

Before I can reach for it, my mom's hand shoots out and grabs the bottle. "No."

My mouth drops open. It's barbeque sauce. What's the big deal?

I watch my parents—my father raises an eyebrow and looks at my mom. She stares back, and it's like she's trying to shoot arrows out of her eyes. They stay there, locked in silent combat until finally my mother speaks.

"Piper doesn't need anything from you," my mom says.

My father inclines his head. "And what does Piper need from you? Let's answer that question first."

My mom's eyes flash. "I have given Piper everything

she's needed. For eighteen years, I've been more than she could ever hope for."

His eyes shift to me. "And maybe more than she wants. Too much if I could venture a guess."

It's like he can pick the memories of my oppressed life right from my mind. But I'm not opening my mouth to agree or disagree.

"Piper loves me."

A smile breaks onto his face. "And Piper will love me, too." He places one of his hands on my mom's. "Piper can try the sauce, darling Lucia."

And just like that my mom relents.

It's rare I hear my mom's real name. I never call her anything other than Mom, and we're so seldom around people when we're together. Lucia. It seems way old-fashioned and almost foreign. And I wonder where my parents met.

I take the bottle of sauce and dump it over the sausage and brisket, letting it spill so some dribbles into the casserole. My stomach is clenched hard again, but the sauce smells like ambrosia laced with pepper. I know I'll love it because when it comes to sauce, hotter is better.

"Thanks." I cut a piece of meat and put it to my lips, inhaling the fat and smoke blended together.

"You can't buy sauce like this anywhere," my father says. "I make it myself."

I nod. "It's really good." There are at least three

kinds of peppers in it. Habañero. Chipotle. And something else I can't identify.

He leans forward onto his elbows and stares at me. "So this is the daughter who's been hidden from me her whole life."

Inadvertently, I lean back.

"What kind of father would you have been anyway?" my mom says. Unlike me, her posture matches his. She leans forward and fixes her eyes on him.

I look at my father. White blond hair gelled upward. Led Zeppelin T-shirt with a splotch of barbeque sauce on it. Three-meat platter in front of him. On first glance, it seems to me he'd be a lot more fun as a parent than my mom.

My father holds my mom with his gaze. "Well, for starters, I would let Piper have her own place in the world."

Next to me, my mom shudders. "Piper's place is with me."

My dad stays forward, holding his pose and my mom's attention. They battle back and forth with their eyes, and silence is their battleground. I chew slowly, thinking I shouldn't draw attention to myself even though I am the center of attention. After an eternity, my father sits back and looks to me. "So, Piper, tell me about yourself."

I force myself to laugh, though my muscles are rigid. I'm clenching my fork, so I set it down and think about the difference two weeks can make. If my father had asked me this question two weeks ago, I'd have given some pretty boring answers. Still, I'm not about to spill on my date with Reese and my journeys to the Underworld.

"Oh, you know," I say.

His smile encourages me. "No. I don't. But I'd like to."

I grab my spoon and scoop up some green bean casserole but don't eat it yet. "Well, I'm eighteen. I'm a senior. I have a best friend."

"Eighteen, huh?"

I nod, eating the casserole.

He looks to my mom. "And I see you have a tattoo."

"I got it a week ago." I hold out my arm so he can see my left bicep.

He raises his eyebrows when he reads it. "Sacrifice."

Again, I realize everyone knows Ancient Greek except me.

He reaches across the table to touch it. "It's fading."

I nod. "I think the artist may have messed up. I may have to get it reinked." But my stomach clenches when I say it. I know the fading has nothing to do with the ink and everything to do with Chloe almost dying. I decide not to try to revive it in front of my mom and my father.

My father pulls up the sleeve on his T-shirt. "I have a tattoo, also."

That's putting it mildly. I lean over to get a better

look. It looks like every natural disaster possible has been inked on his shoulder. There are cosmic reds and greens and bright yellows, blended together into a pattern which almost seems to shift and change in front of my eyes.

"Wow. It's the most amazing thing I've ever seen."

He nods and rolls his sleeve back down. "Thank you, Piper." And he winks at me.

"Did you get it in prison?" I ask because Chloe's brother told us about all the people who get tattoos in prison.

He raises an eyebrow and looks sideways at my mom. "Prison?"

My mom remains silent.

"I thought you were in prison," I say. "That you caused the water still explosion out west and you got caught."

My father actually laughs. I think most people would be furious at an accusation like this, but he laughs. "And let me guess, your mother told you that."

My mom twists up her face. "Well, what was I supposed to tell her? That you didn't have time to raise a daughter?"

"You can tell her what you like, Lucia. I'm sure Piper will find the truth on her own."

I know in that instant everything my mom's told me about my dad is a lie.

Next to me, my mom slams her fork on the plate. It

clatters like a bell, such that, four tables over, people turn and look. "Are we done here yet?"

"Done?" My father laughs. "I'm only getting started. So tell me, Piper, do you have a boyfriend?"

I almost drop my spoon at the question, catching it before it lands on my lap. But I do manage to get a giant drop of sauce on my leg. I wipe it off, licking my finger.

"Piper does not have a boyfriend." My mom answers for me.

I open my mouth to protest but then stop. I have Shayne, and then there's Reese. But neither of them are appropriate conversations to have given the present company. So instead, I nod. "Right. No boyfriend." I glance over sideways at my mom who smiles like a fox that's gotten away.

"Oh, come on now. A pretty girl like you? Certainly you have young men declaring their undying love for you every day." And his blue steel eyes meet mine and hold them.

My heart begins to pound; I feel it in my temples. But I hold my face steady and force a smile to my lips. "Only in my daydreams."

He grins, and I feel like we've shared some secret. A secret even I don't know. "Well, you have your whole life ahead of you." He grabs his beer bottle and lifts it to his mouth, drinking the remainder down in one large swallow. Even though I don't drink beer, it's still impressive.

"Piper has no need for boyfriends." My mom spears a cherry tomato with her fork and puts it in her mouth whole. She chews it, and we both watch her, waiting until she's finished. "We have each other and that's all we'll ever need."

My father slaps the table, causing the plates to rattle against the silverware. "Nonsense. Piper, how would you like to come stay with me for a few months?"

My mom rockets up out of her seat. "How dare you? Piper is not going to stay with you."

My father looks at her, commanding her to sit down with his eyes. She glares at him but settles back into the booth.

"Why not, Lucia? You and I both know Piper would benefit from some time away from you."

I guess this means my father is aware of my mom's desire to control me. But I have to admit, the thought of getting away, of getting to know my father a little bit better, is like new flowers planted in a garden. Like tendrils of the life I want to lead are breaking into my world, trying to lay down roots. And I plan to give them as much room as they need.

"Well, for starters, Peter, what would your wife say about that?"

My face freezes at the question. Whether it's the fact that my father now has a name or that he is married I'm not sure. But of course I'm eighteen years old. Why wouldn't he have a wife? And there could be other kids in the mix. Half brothers and sisters I've never met.

"My wife, if you must know, will tolerate it." He waves his hand, and a waitress sees it. He holds up his beer bottle, and she turns to get him another one. "She'll obey whatever I ask when it comes right down to it."

Obey seems such a strange word. But I think of the way my mom relented with the barbeque sauce. Did my mom stop obeying him? Is that why they split up? "How did you two meet?" I take a sip of my iced tea after I ask, wondering if either of them will bother answering. And then I watch their faces.

My mom sneers, and I'm sure she'll start in on some story of how she was horribly wronged by this awful man here at the table with us. But after meeting him, I know in my heart this cannot be the truth.

At the question, however, my father's face softens. "Your mother is quite a charmer, Piper. Did you know that?"

I shake my head and look at her. The sneer falls from her face, and she actually blushes. "No. I had no idea," I say. *Charmer* and *mother* are two words I never would have put in the same sentence.

But my dad nods. "Yes. I fell in love with her the moment I saw her."

My mom laughs, but it's not the snide laugh which up until now has permeated the conversation. "You fall in love with everyone you see."

My father angles his head. "Not untrue. I do admit it. I have an eye for beautiful creatures. But of them, your mom rose to the top. If I weren't already previously engaged, I may have married her on the spot. Instead, the day we met, I took the one moment of bliss I could and left it at that."

The truth hits me. My mom and dad were never married. And beyond that, I was nothing more than the result of a one night stand. My mom. The woman who acts like Earth will implode if I so much as utter the name of a boy at school. She slept with my father the moment she met him and ended up pregnant.

I turn to her and wait. Wondering what she'll say. Wondering if she'll deny it. Or defend her actions. Or anything. But my old mom returns, and she deflects the conversation. "Piper will not be staying with you. You're a bad influence, and besides, she and I have been talking about moving anyway. Having her out and about will not do at all."

My father raises an eyebrow. "Lucia—"

She interrupts. "I'm serious about this. I don't think you want me to be more clear, do you?"

My father shrugs. "Would things be any worse than they are now?"

I have no clue what he's talking about. But I'm not about to interrupt.

My mom nods. "Yes. Things will be worse. Of that you can be sure."

The waitress comes over, holding another beer. My father takes it, but, at the same time, my mom stands up. "Piper, we're leaving."

I look to my father. His grin has come back, and he lifts the beer in a "cheers" sign. "Darling daughter. It's been a true joy meeting you."

I don't want to stand up. To leave. But my mom's eyes are on me. "Will I see you again?" I ask.

"Absolutely." He stands and turns to my mom. "A kiss for old time's sake?"

She scoffs. "Please." But her face is flushed; even I can see it.

"You're still just as beautiful as you were so long ago, darling Lucia." My father reaches out and cups her chin with his fingers. Something inside me stirs as I remember Shayne doing the same thing to me. And then my father leans over and kisses my mom full on the lips. Her body freezes, but her lips relent, and she kisses him back with everything she has. It's a part of my mom I never would have believed existed. But here it is, right in the middle of Pok-e-Jo's Barbeque. And more than ever, at this moment in time, I want to travel back to Hell. To be with Shayne forever. To live a life of love and happiness I've never known before. And I wonder if my mom doesn't crave something similar.

Chapter 30

Tears

Teaching is pointless on Friday. The teachers give it a try, but all anyone wants to talk about is the hurricane and Councilman Rendon dying. I look for Chloe at lunch, and when she doesn't show, I text her.

"will u b in stdy hall?" I send.

Her response is short. Too short. "have plans"

"what plans?"

"crazy. ttyl"

I'm not sure what she's referring to when she says *crazy*: her plans, the world, or herself. I send her a quick response and head to class.

When I walk into Social Sciences, my heart flips over in place a few times. Shayne's sitting there, waiting for me. He moves his arm off the chair next to him so I can sit down.

"Don't the teachers wonder why you're here so little?" In the last couple weeks, he's been in class all of three days. I'd wonder where he was if I didn't already know. But even still, being in Hell doesn't explain why he can't make it to class. Especially if he really does want to see me.

Shayne looks at Mr. Kaiser. He's just uncapping his dry erase marker—purple this time—and the smell drifts through the air.

"Being a god does have its powers, Piper. The teachers hardly notice me. Remember, they think I've been here all year?"

I smile, and in a moment of utter insanity, I lean over and kiss him lightly on the mouth. He tastes like a rustic campfire mixed with something so intense it pulls at every part of my insides.

"I like that," he says when I pull my head back.

"I like that you like that," I say. And this time he leans forward and kisses me.

Mr. Kaiser clears his throat and starts class. It's not like Randy and Hannah weren't always making out before class. But now, with Randy gone, that won't happen again.

"So what are your powers?" I whisper.

Shayne laughs and keeps his head close to me. "Like being near you for starters."

I fix him with a look that tells him he's full of crap. "I hardly call that a power," I say.

A smile plays on his lips. "What would you call a power?"

"Hmmm..." I put my finger to my mouth pretending I'm in deep thought. "Maybe breaking down brick walls. Or climbing up the sides of buildings."

"I'm a god, not a superhero," Shayne says.

I hear Mr. Kaiser clear his throat again. With Randy Conner dead, the class has been drained of all comedic relief, and Shayne's laugh stands out like a wart.

"Would you like to share what's so funny, Piper?" Mr. Kaiser says.

I look around and realize the whole class is staring at me. Now why hadn't he asked Shayne to explain the joke? I shrug. "We were valuing the powers of super-heroes." I glance sideways at Shayne and see he's twirling his stylus on his hand.

Mr. Kaiser raises an eyebrow and then turns and writes the word *SUPERHERO* in large purple letters on the board behind him. He caps the marker and turns back around. "So what power would you want if you were a superhero?" He's not asking me, but the whole class in general.

"How about flying?" someone suggests.

Mr. Kaiser turns and writes *flying* on the board. "What else?"

"Invisibility—cause then I could sneak into the girls' locker room," someone else says.

It's a stereotypical male answer, and it garnishes a stereotypical female reaction of eye rolling, name calling, and laughter. But Mr. Kaiser writes *invisibility* on the board nonetheless.

Most of the answers are funny, even expected, such as my climbing buildings or breaking down walls. There's an enormous sense of release descending on our Social Sciences class, and I look over at Shayne and grin. He reaches out across the aisle, takes my hand, and squeezes it.

The white board is just about full when Mr. Kaiser says, "How about one more thing?"

"I'd like to bring people back from the dead."

It's Hannah, Randy's girlfriend. I still remember her face at the funeral—frozen into a state of repressed sorrow.

Silence falls on the class faster than a flash flood in a dry creek bed. I have no idea what to say, and I'm pretty sure no one else does either. Shayne's still holding my hand, but lets it go and turns around to face her.

"Why?"

It's a simple question but an unexpected one all the same. I can't believe he's asked it.

"Why what?" Hannah's staring at him, and I know their eyes are locked.

"Why would you want to bring someone back?"

Hannah lets out a gasp of exasperation, and, for a second, I think she's going to get up and come punch Shayne. The silence in the class is so solid, I can hear the mercury in the thermometer rising.

Hannah breaks the silence. "I think that's pretty obvious."

But Shayne keeps at it. "What if Randy is at peace? Why would you want to bring him back?"

Hannah jumps to her feet. "How could he be at

peace? He's left his family here with that monster of a father. He's left me here." She glares at Shayne, and I think she's trying to evaporate him with her eyes. "Did you know I'm pregnant?"

When she says it, I realize my heart is pounding in my chest, and I've forgotten to breathe. I don't want to move. Don't want to draw any attention to myself.

"Yes." Shayne's so calm it's like a violent contradiction to the rage and sadness pouring off her.

I'm staring at Hannah, watching her face. It's red, but her eyes are dry—just like at the funeral. And she's carrying Randy Conner's baby.

"Yes what?" she demands.

"Yes, I knew." And whether Hannah, Mr. Kaiser, or anyone else in the class believes Shayne, I do. "But why would you want to bring him back?"

I can't believe he's pressing her. I almost open my mouth at this point and tell him to stop, but my mouth feels pinned shut.

Hannah doesn't speak. Her mouth's opening, but nothing's coming out.

"What if you knew he was happy? Why would you bring him back here?"

Hannah stands there looking at Shayne. Her eyes grow lighter, and soon tears pour down her face. They flow like the River Acheron, full of sorrow, and I know this is the first time she's cried since Randy died. Her hands move to her stomach as she cries, and I think about the baby. It'll grow up without a father. Just like me. But its father will be dead, unlike mine. And its father will not abuse it like Randy's.

"Because I miss him." Hannah manages to get the words out between her tears, and within moments, someone gets up and helps her out of the room.

I'm staring at the place where she was, watching the door swing closed. And when I look at Shayne, he's staring forward, twirling the stylus on his hand. I want to say something to him, but he's not looking at me, and if he knows I'm trying to get his attention, he's ignoring me. So I turn forward and see Mr. Kaiser erasing the white board. With the purple dry erase marker, he writes *GHC: WHAT YOU CAN DO* at the top of the board, underlines it three times, and we get on with lecture.

Chapter 31

Sleep

Shayne waits for me after school. I think he's left, but when I get to my locker at the end of the day, he's there holding it open already.

"I don't know if you helped Hannah or made things worse." I've been going over it in my head since class let out. On the one hand, Hannah finally released her sorrow. On the other hand, she did it in front of the entire class.

"I think I helped."

My mind's been telling me the same thing, but I want to hear Shayne say it. "You're always so sure of yourself," I say.

Shayne gives a small shrug like he's trying to not act cocky. "Not always."

"Lots of the time."

"Yeah, lots of the time," he says.

"I can't believe Hannah's pregnant," I say. "I had no clue."

"Only she and Randy knew," Shayne says. "Randy told me when he crossed."

It's just one more piece of his memory for Randy to

leave behind in the River Lethe.

Shayne shuts my locker and takes my hand. "Can I walk you home?"

"Of course." Chloe's skipping, so I can't take the shuttle with her. I have to wonder if she's with Reese until I catch his scent in the air.

A wave of darkness covers Shayne's face. "Why won't he stay away from you?"

I lift my head and see Reese across the corridor. When our eyes meet, he winks at me.

Shayne's hand tightens like a clamp on mine, and he takes a step in Reese's direction.

Reese's eyebrows arch like he's surprised Shayne would challenge him. I wonder if Shayne will start a fight right here in the middle of school with so many people around. If so, Reese must be up for it because, in five quick strides, he stands directly in front of us.

Reese glances at Shayne and then reaches over and brushes my cheek, sending a flurry of goose bumps down my neck. I'd be lying if I said revulsion was the sole cause of those goose bumps because all I can focus on is his scent. I scoot backward to get out of his reach.

"Have you missed me, Piper?" Reese asks.

I open my mouth to tell him I'm not interested in him, but words won't come out. Shayne's hand feels like it will snap the bones in my fingers in half. I wince, and he lets go though he stays close.

"You need to leave, Reese," Shayne says under his

breath.

I glance around; we've gathered more than a couple stares. Distance forms between our bizarre triangle and the observers who must not want to get caught in the middle.

Reese ignores Shayne and keeps his eyes focused on me. "I've missed you, Piper." He steps forward again—or maybe I do—because his hand moves to my lips, and involuntarily I shudder. "Are you busy tonight?" he asks.

Reese isn't even looking at Shayne, but I glance at Shayne out of my peripheral vision. His face doesn't move, but he's turned so I can see his eyes and the red in them like fireworks.

"Yes, she has plans." Shayne's words catch me. I've started to drift. To succumb to Reese's smell; it's clouding every bit of judgment in my mind. "Now leave, Reese."

Reese laughs. "Leave? Piper doesn't want me to."

My lips part even before I can stop them. I remember the kiss Reese and I shared; god, it was fantastic. The memories and his aroma pour through my whole body. I have to fight every urge to go to Reese; I force myself to take a step closer to Shayne and grab his arm, trying to root myself to him, away from Reese. Reese is screwing with my mind.

"Never. Touch. Piper. Again." Each of Shayne's words is staccato. Not to be misunderstood.

Reese turns to him and glares. "I don't think you can

stop me." His thumb brushes across my lips, sending a chill through me.

In a flash, Shayne swats Reese's hand away. It flies backward, making a sickening crunching sound like bone on bone. And then Shayne punches Reese right in the nose. The odor of blood is immediate and clears my head.

I hear the kids around us gasp which further helps erase the memories of Reese's touch, and I force clarity into my mind.

Reese grimaces and lets his hand fall to his side. There's blood running from his left nostril, but all he does is wipe it with the back of his hand. And then he reaches up and touches my lips again. I step back, out of his reach, and lean close to Shayne. For whatever bizarre reason my body is betraying me, I will fight it. "Can we go?"

"You know Piper wants me." Reese's voice is like nails trying to pierce Shayne's armor. "Her body is aching for me. Just look at her. And it's killing you."

In one step, Shayne moves forward until he's directly up in Reese's face. "Know this, Reese. Come near her again, and I will kill you."

Reese laughs. "You don't have the power." And then he spits on Shayne.

Shayne doesn't flinch. "I dare you to test me."

Reese takes a step back and smiles. "Sounds like a dare I plan to take." And then he turns his back on us and walks away, shoving his way through the crowd, leaving only his haunting scent in his wake.

I'm afraid to move, unsure what Shayne will think. He watches as Reese leaves, and pretty soon, the smell evaporates too, leaving me somewhat in control there in the hallway next to Shayne. And after a few wayward glances, everyone starts to disperse. I don't know what to say.

"I told you to stay away from him, Piper." Shayne's voice is filled with fury.

"I have."

"Then why does he keep coming back?"

I spin on him and unleash my own fury. "Because he's the god of war. You said it yourself. He'll never give up. So stop blaming me."

I kick the nearest locker and then storm toward the doors of the school.

Shayne catches up to me in seconds. "Wait."

I stop. "What?"

"I'm sorry," he says. "That's not fair."

I only nod in response. He's right. It's not fair.

"We never got along," Shayne says. He's clenching his teeth as he speaks. "Not since the first time we met."

"That doesn't surprise me," I say. A friendship between Reese and Shayne seems as unlikely as my mom deciding to let me move out.

Shayne waits until we get outside. The heat hits me, but the misters take over quickly, spraying gel on me until I've cooled to a normal temperature as much as I can with the memory of Reese spinning in my head. I stop for a minute and let the gel and my thoughts collect.

"He's always hated me. Been jealous of everything I've had. He's trying to mislead you to get to me."

I turn to Shayne. I've had secrets and lies and half-truths enough. "It's not like you're bubbling over trying to tell me the truth either." It's not like anyone is. Not my mom. Not my dad.

Shayne tries to take my hand, but I pull it back.

"I want you to know the truth," Shayne says. His eyes pierce into me, but I fight inside, not daring to let myself sink into them, knowing I want to more than anything in the world.

"Really?" It's almost laughable.

Shayne nods. "Look at everything I've showed you."

"But all I have now are more questions." Like why my life was ordinary until two weeks ago, and now I'm being accused of killing mythological birds. And why Greek gods are walking the earth. And why my dad wants custody. I know I'm scowling, but I'm angry at Shayne for not telling me anything. I'm angry at Reese for asking me out in the first place. I'm angry at Chloe for drifting away from me. And I'm angry at myself for letting her. "Everything was fine before. Things used to be normal."

Shayne reaches out again, and I let him take my

hand this time. "Do you want things to go back to how they were?"

I bite my lower lip and meet his eyes. "Maybe." But it's a lie.

Shayne's face falls, and guilt hits me hard in the chest. I don't seriously mean it, but before, at least I knew what was going on in my life. Now, my best friend has almost died, and I'm pretty sure I'm in love with the Lord of the Underworld. And though I desperately wish Chloe were back to normal, I'd never trade anything for knowing Shayne.

But I don't open my mouth and tell Shayne this.

"I can't tell you anything else."

I've been expecting his words, but I still hate them. "Why not?"

"Because if I tell you, it could kill you."

"Then I'll ask Reese." My heart speeds up. Reese will tell me what's going on.

"No." Shayne's words come out like a command, and my face must react because he softens his voice. "I don't want you to die."

"But I need to know what's going on." Even to my own ears, I sound like a desperate child. "What if I'm willing to take that chance?"

A breeze blows through, and Shayne's dark hair moves across his face. The red has started flashing in his eyes. "I can't lose you, Piper."

"I need to know." I have to know.

"I don't want you to find out from Reese," Shayne says.

I ball my hands up in fists. "I don't care what you want," I say. "I'm sick of people telling me what to do." And with that, I turn to run back toward the school. I'll find Reese and make him give me answers. But before I can move, I find myself face to beautiful face with a winged man—not the same one as from the creek with Chloe. Not the one who came to bring her death.

The man reaches out, and before I can even cry out or think about running, he touches me. The world spins, blackness clouds my vision, and I fall to the ground.

Chapter 32

Charon

I wake up in my bed, cool cotton sheets surrounding me, fans on overhead. I look down and realize, even though it's dark outside, I'm still in the same shorts and tank top I wore to school on Friday. I don't remember coming upstairs or falling asleep, or even the sun setting.

I sit up in bed and blink my eyes a few times, waiting for them to acclimate to the darkness. The bright green letters of the clock by the bed tell me it's close to three o'clock in the morning. And then I see the day and realize it says Sunday instead of Saturday. I pick it up, thinking it must be wrong, but unless the geosynchronous satellites rotating around Earth are out of sync, it's really Sunday morning, and I've slept for over twenty-four hours.

"Mom?" Her room is only down the hall, so I don't call too loudly.

There's no answer.

"Mom?" A little louder this time.

Still nothing.

I stand up and find my shoes by the bed, right where I normally leave them, and after I slip them on, I open the door and walk to my mom's room to check for her. Her bed is empty. I stare at it to make sure, but she's really not home. I have no clue where she is. Actually, the more I think about it, the more I realize I have no clue what's going on at all. Like how I got to the Botanical Haven. And how I slept for an entire weekend. Something hazy sits at the back of my mind but won't reach the surface, so I head to the bathroom to wash my face.

I turn on the cold water full force, ignoring the ration rules, and splash it on my eyes, trying to clear the fog moving around in my brain. I look up into the bathroom mirror and reach for the towel. And when I do, I see the red line on the side of my neck, near my ear, and remember Minos in Asphodel. He threatened to send me to Tartarus. For killing a phoenix. Shayne promised me I hadn't killed anything. That I wasn't responsible for Randy Conner's death.

And then it all comes back to me. We were at school. Shayne wouldn't tell me anything, and he didn't want me to ask Reese.

"Sleep," I say to my reflection in the mirror. Shayne put me to sleep because he didn't want me to talk to Reese. He didn't do it himself but had summoned a winged man to do it instead.

I feel wetness on my toes and realize the sink is flooding over. I turn off the water, undoing the stopper so the water will empty. I watch it as it goes down, swirling faster once it gets near the bottom. Shayne asked me not to talk to Reese. And now, being far away from Reese, I don't want to find out anything from him anyway. He makes me think of a hyena searching for scraps of meat.

I walk out of the bathroom, back down the hallway, and head into the darkness of the downstairs. The steps seem to last forever, taking me from the emptiness of our upstairs to the forest that is our home below. Two places so near to each other, but so different. Among the plants, I've always lost myself. Like it's another world.

As soon as my feet hit the cold tiles, I know what I need to do. Shayne asked me not to talk to Reese. But he didn't mention anyone else. I need to go to Hell and talk to someone there. Maybe Charon. Or Rhadam. One of them might tell me something. Minos enters my mind, but I shove him aside. His brutal eyes had caught mine and accused me, and I know I can't go back and see him again. Not alone, and hopefully not ever.

But I will go to Hell. Alone. Without Shayne. And I will get my answers.

I call to the Underworld because I can sense the river of silver skimming under the surface of Earth. It almost seems to reach up and pull me to it, like it could seep into my veins and make me part of it. I'm not sure if it will work, if I'll be able to go without Shayne, but the earth opens up for me. It recognizes me and accepts me, swallowing me whole and holding me close on my journey to the Underworld. Silver liquid fills the void around me, and then I'm there on the banks of the River Acheron, and I see Charon by the docks, waiting. He's got his eyes closed—like he's taking a cat nap, but when I look in his direction, they flip open and grow wide. I guess he wasn't expecting to see me. I'm not sure I was expecting me to make it here either, yet now that I'm here, everything feels as it should be.

I walk to the dock, trying to pretend I belong here. Trying to play my part. I'm not sure if Charon will take me across the river based on his reaction, but he recovers well and waves. Relief floods through me when I see his familiar face, and I know he'll help me.

"I wasn't expecting you." He pulls the boat up against the dock and moves aside so I can get in.

Only then do I remember the payment. My face falls, and I shove my hands in my pockets, trying desperately to find some kind of coin. But my pockets are empty.

"I can't pay you."

Charon takes a step back and bows so low to the ground I see the bald spot on the top of his head. "I could never take a single drachma from you. I wouldn't be able to live with myself."

Relief floods through me; everything is falling into place. For a second, I feel like a co-conspirator. "Does that mean you're really alive?"

Charon stands back up, and his face creases into the smile I love. "It's been up for debate many times."

"And...?" I step into the boat.

He unties the rope, and I sit down, in the middle this time, near enough to Charon so I can talk. After we get out on the water, I plan to ask him my questions. To see what I can learn.

Charon shrugs and picks up the pole, already shoving it in the water to move the boat forward. "Let's just say I don't think I'll die anytime soon."

I see my opening. "Will I?"

Charon looks at me, and our eyes catch. The smile sinks away, and then finally, he looks out toward the water. "The monsters are a bit restless these days."

He's trying to avoid talking. But I've got him pinned like a mouse in a labyrinth with no exit, and I'm not going to lose my opportunity, even if he is poling faster, trying to reach the shore sooner.

"Do you know who I am, Charon?" I figure I can't get much more direct than that.

Charon looks back at me and nods. "You're Piper."

Before I can say anything else, a monster bumps into the side of the boat, sending a spray of water up and drenching me. At the touch of the water, a wave of sorrow overcomes me, and I break down crying. I'm sobbing though I don't expect Charon to come near me or comfort me, and he doesn't. He's probably seen this a million times before.

"It'll pass, Piper. I promise."

"I just want the lies to go away." I'm still crying, but as the water drips off me, the sadness slips away with it.

Charon doesn't say anything, and we cross in silence. Before I know it, I'm jolted when the boat bumps into the dock. But I don't stand up.

"Aren't you getting out?" he asks. He's hopped out ahead of me and has already tied the rope, holding out a hand to help me.

I sigh, but it comes out mixed with a sob. Am I destined to never know anything? "Maybe I should just go back home."

Charon purses his lips. His eyes flicker around—at the shore with the giant trees towering above, toward the empty tunnel in the rocks ahead, then back at the water. The wails of the sorrows tear at me, and each time I hear one, I see a monster jump up out of the reeds and snatch it from the air.

"Piper."

I turn back to Charon. "What?"

He's not looking at me. His eyes are still focused on the tumultuous water. Overhead, the crows call out their song, echoing around from one tree to the next. "Things in the Underworld haven't always been this bad."

I hold my breath. Maybe he's going to tell me what I want to know. "In what ways?"

Charon points to the water. "The monsters are vicious now. The realms are getting out of control.

Even the Elysian Fields. There's talk of other gods gaining entry. Not to mention the overlords are seizing more power every day."

I think of Minos. Of Ares appearing in Asphodel, if only as a shadow. Of Hell not working correctly. "How long have things been going wrong?"

Charon turns, and his milky white eyes meet mine. "Eighteen years."

When he says it, it's like I've been punched in the stomach. It's the same amount of time my Earth above has been in the Global Heating Crisis. A Hell of its own with a sun which only gets more powerful by the day. Eighteen years. There's something connecting my Earth above and this Hell below. Eighteen years. It echoes in my mind.

It's the same amount of time I've been alive.

Are the secrets I crave somehow tied to the physical sufferings of the worlds both above ground and below? And am I somehow involved?

I open my mouth to respond, but I can't think of anything to say.

"Please be safe," Charon says.

I snap out of my thoughts and see him reaching back into the boat. I stand up and give him my hand so he can help me out. And no sooner am I on the dock, walking away from the boat, than I know it's already slipping away through the reeds and the swampy water behind me. And just like everything so far, I only have more questions and still have no answers.

Chapter 33

Sisyphus

I stare at the ten tunnels. I don't know which one to choose. I don't even know where the others go. And Cerberus is nowhere to be found. I think he would have led me in the right direction.

The sixth tunnel is the one we took last time, but when I walk up toward it, I'm hit with hatred. A red fungus suddenly covers the edge of the cave's mouth. I turn from it because the thought of taking that path makes me want to vomit. I step in front of the tunnel to its left, and the nauseous feeling is replaced by happiness. Green ivy covers the opening.

I stare through the illusion of ivy down the dark path. I count my heartbeats.

I don't need happiness. I need answers.

This tunnel must lead to the Elysian Fields, but after Charon's staid words, I know Rhadam won't tell me much either. No one will. I focus on the ivy, which I think is an illusion, but I feed my anger into it until it bursts into flames. I watch it burn. And then I locate the tunnel with the hatred again and take a step inside.

Voices greet me.

Come to us.

Visit us.

I cover my ears and close my eyes but soon realize they're inside my head, like specters floating around, trying to latch onto something real.

We need you.

Each word is a chorus, beckoning me. I haven't moved since my initial step inside the tunnel, and I want them to go away. I turn, thinking I'll leave. Knowing this is a bad idea. But the opening where I came from is no longer there.

Piper.

They know my name. I shake my head and take another step forward, trying to move as far away from the haunting sounds as possible.

"Stop!" I say it aloud, but the voices ignore me.

Piper. It's only fair.

We want to see you.

When they say it, I know where they're coming from. The one place in Hell I haven't been. Tartarus. Hearing the sounds helps me realize why Shayne didn't want me to go there. They're tearing at my insides, devouring my brain. I can't get them out.

Visit us.

It's been so long.

We miss you.

You belong with us.

My heart skips around in my chest, and a hollow

feeling of dread settles on my stomach. I just want them to go away. Squeezing my eyes shut again, I think of Shayne. Of Chloe. Even of my mom. Anything to make them depart.

We'll tell you secrets.

My eyes snap open, and the voices stop.

They know they've got me.

I don't even think about what I'm doing as my feet move me. The voices lead me to Tartarus. The ground feels like gravel under my feet, and the farther I get into the passageway, the less I can smell the comforting banks of Acheron and the more I can smell something close to burning flesh. But I don't care; I need to get there.

I see the flickering redness of the flames and feel the heat long before I round the corner of the tunnel, and when I do come around, the river is on fire. A name rings out in my head from deep in my memories. Phlegethon. The river of fire leading to Tartarus. I tie my hair into a knot, hoping to keep any stray flames from catching it. My mind screams at me to turn around. To run to the comfort of Shayne's home. But I need answers, and Tartarus seems willing to give them to me.

Like the other rivers, the dock extends into the water, but here it is surrounded yet untouched by flames. I want to turn and run, to get away from the flames at all cost, but the voices beckon. I step forward, forcing myself to move until I'm on the hard wood of the dock. The flames hiss up over the sides of my sandals as I walk on the wood, but somehow they don't burn me. I wrap my arms around my middle and step into the waiting boat, and before I can change my mind and turn around and leave, it begins to move, and I'm out in the middle of the river of fire.

Burning souls. I know Phlegethon is an initiation into the place of eternal torture. The flames taunt me, but why they don't touch me, I'm not sure. Even my curly hair seems safe tied up at my neck.

Come to us.

Be with us.

As I move across the burning river, the voices start up again. I open my mind and let them in, wishing I could make the boat move faster. Tartarus holds my answers. I'm as sure of it as I am that there are questions. And that secrets have been kept from me my entire life.

We've missed you.

I miss the voices, too. I've never known them, but I miss them. They are a part of me. And I wonder if I do belong in Tartarus like Minos said. If I did kill a phoenix.

The boat seems to be on fire as it moves on. The wood is red hot like the embers in Shayne's hearth, and around me, sparks crackle. But the heat doesn't harm me, and soon, it's carried me to the dock on the other side. Ahead, all I see is a wall of flames, and for a second, my stomach tightens, and I wonder what I'm doing. Nothing good happens in Tartarus.

Come, Piper.

A single voice calls out, and I know it. I can't place it, but it's drawing me, pulling me through the wall of flames. I close my eyes and walk forward, and then I'm on the other side and immediately the smell of rot and filth hits my nose. I force myself to take a deep breath, and my stomach lurches until I'm on my knees heaving up nothing but bile and emptiness since I've been asleep for over a day.

When I stand up, I wipe my mouth on my bare arm and look around. A desert stretches before me, and I start walking straight, knowing I'll end up somewhere soon. Somewhere besides the rancid smelling barrenness surrounding me.

I walk for miles, and the desert moves by in fast forward, the same way it did in Asphodel, except there's nothing to see around here, and soon I begin to doubt myself. The voices have left me, and there's not a soul around. Maybe I should turn and go back.

Answers. We have answers.

The voice comes out of nowhere, and I shift right, moving in the direction I know it's coming from. Its promises make the ball in my stomach tingle, and with one step after another, I'm soon approaching a mountain range with a medieval castle high on the top. It's where I need to go.

I start toward the mountain, taking another mouthful of the rot around me, and force myself to take breath after breath until my stomach no longer lurches. But as I take my first step, something grabs my foot from behind, sending me flying face first to the hard-packed sand.

I kick with the other foot, and look down, seeing a skeleton hand clenched around my Achilles tendon. Another hand pops out of the earth and grabs at my leg, and they pull me until I'm up to my knee in the gritty sand. A wave of panic rolls over me when I realize I can't even kick my leg anymore. The hands grasp harder, and sharp pieces of bone cut into my flesh. I lift my head and spit out the sand in my mouth and try to grab my leg and pull it out myself. They're cutting and clawing and more than anything, I wish Shayne were here with me. But he doesn't even know I'm down here in Hell. Not to mention in Tartarus. And I can't tell him, or he'll take me away, and I'll never get my answers.

"Let go!" I scream when I realize I'm thigh deep in the sand. I'm going to suffocate, and no one will ever even know where I've been. I can imagine my body hidden beneath the sand forever in Hell.

But at my words, the skeleton hands obey me and let go. I twist around until I've yanked my leg free then get up and run for the mountain, trying to get off the deadly desert. Sand is caked on my sweaty face, and I claw it off as I run. I will not die before I get my answers. I need to know what Shayne knows. Whether he wants to tell me or not.

I'm halfway up the mountain when I see a naked man with shoulders so wide, I'm sure he could pick me up and snap me like a dehydrated stick given a chance. But I have no intention of giving him a chance. He's standing there on the mountainside supporting a boulder nearly as large as he is with only his sheer mass holding it in place.

I move around to the side, trying to hide behind a large pile of boulders. Like my Earth above, there aren't any bushes or shrubs around. Too much heat must kill them off down here, also. From my vantage point, I see the sweat pouring down his dark naked body, tracing patterns through his hairy chest, and my chest tightens when I realize I have no way to get around him unseen. I'll have to wait for him to move.

"Come out and play with me."

His voice is not at all what I'm expecting. Actually, I'm not expecting his voice, but had I been, the sweet, melodic tune is so unfitting the massive man, I don't even try to pretend I haven't heard. I lift my head slowly above the rock pile and see the man is looking my way. His face is covered with a smile so inviting, I find my legs carrying me around from my hiding place and over to him.

"Lovely. Simply lovely."

Heat floods my face when I realize he's talking about me. He turns sideways, propping his boulder up with the side of his body, and I can now see his genitals hanging there between his legs.

He chuckles, and I lift my eyes, realizing I've been staring directly at them. But my eyes keep trying to look back down as if they've got a mind of their own. I pull them away against their will.

"It's okay to look." He shifts, and I catch a glimpse out of my peripheral vision. "I don't mind at all." And he reaches down and holds his penis, cradling it in his hand.

"I'm only here to get some answers." I point toward the top of the mountain, happy to have something to focus on besides his private parts. "I'm heading up there."

"Ah." The man laughs again, and I hear the melody pulling me in.

"Do you know who lives there?" I ask. I'm still looking at the castle, and this close, I can see the orange and purple storm clouds swirling overhead and the lightning striking so close, it must be hitting the stones.

"The master of Hell, of course." The man wipes his forehead and blessedly turns away from me. "Do you mind if we get going? I still have to get this boulder to the top." He doesn't wait for an answer. Instead, he leans over, places both hands on the black rock, and begins to push.

"Do you mean Sha—" I catch myself, "—Hades?"

The man barks out a laugh followed by a huge grunt. The vein on his temple nearest me bulges out so far, I think it might burst. "Not that master." And for the first time, his tone has a hint of disgust in it.

"Then who?"

He turns to me, holding the boulder in place while his eyes gaze my way. But he's still smiling. "You know."

It's not a question. He knows I know. And I realize when he says it I do. "Aeacus." Another of the ancient kings ruling over the domains of the Underworld.

The giant of a man nods and turns back to the boulder.

I motion at the rock even though he's not looking at me. "Why are you doing that?"

"Somebody needs to. And seeing as I've been unfairly accused and left in this place of eternal damnation, I find it's my job."

"Unfairly accused?"

He gives a giant shove, pushing the boulder a good two feet ahead. And he's fast; he moves up before it can slip even an inch. "Accused of killing innocent people. Travelers and guests to my house."

He's got the boulder moving at such a clip, I'm having a hard time keeping up. "And did you?" He's almost jogging behind it.

Out comes another laugh, though, at this point, I notice it's missing most of its humor. "Of course not!"

"So you didn't kill anyone?"

He turns to me, and shakes his head, sending sweat flying in all directions, some landing on my arms and chest. I notice his naked parts shake when he does this, and I avert my eyes, looking instead at the rock. But he catches me looking and smiles.

"What is this? A trial?"

I don't answer. I'm certainly not going to apologize for asking.

"Fine. Yes. I killed many, many people. But every single one of them was trying to kill me first. Or cheat me. Or rape my wife. And so I killed them all." The man turns to me and licks his lips, and his private parts seem to grow in size. "And might I just say I enjoyed it immensely."

My face freezes, and I know without a shadow of a doubt this man belongs right where he is. Here in Tartarus. Spores of evil coat him. I'm ready to leave him, and a weight lifts off me when I see we're only steps away from the top.

His melodic voice sings to me. "I don't believe I caught your name."

I shake my head. "No, you didn't." I don't want to give this monster my name.

"I'm Sisyphus." And with a final push, the boulder crests over the top of a ridge, hitting a plateau. Sisyphus moves it around, making sure it's resting perfectly on flat rocks. He bends down, propping it in place with some smaller rocks to keep it from moving. And then he turns to me, and when he opens his mouth, I smell his breath—foul like he's been feasting on the bodies of his victims. He narrows his eyes, and my skin begins to crawl.

Every part of me wants to run away. But I know I need to finish this.

Sisyphus licks his teeth and smiles. "I know who you are." The melody has vanished from his voice.

He takes a step toward me, and I take a step backward.

"You do?"

Sisyphus nods. "Uh huh. Even in your disguise. You can't fool me. And I know why you're here."

"Why?" My throat's so dry I can barely squeak it out.

"You're checking in for him. I knew you'd come. Aeacus said you wouldn't. Said he'd be lord forever. And maybe that's your biggest mistake. You never should have come."

He takes another step toward me, but my head shifts at a sound. I look past his broad shoulder and see the boulder rock on its pedestal. Sisyphus hears it, too, and turns, but too late. The boulder moves again, shifting around the rocks underneath it. Sisyphus lunges backward, throwing his arms out, but the momentum can't be stopped. His fingernails bend backward as the boulder pulls out from underneath his grip. And then it begins to tumble, picking up speed, until it's a blur on the side of the mountain.

"No!" Sisyphus doesn't even look my way a final time. He's off and running so fast, he blurs into the mountainside, and I'm left alone on the plateau with the dark castle ahead.

Chapter 34

Aeacus

When the slick naked form of Sisyphus disappears, I expect to be able to breathe again. But as I face the dark castle, my chest tightens so ferociously, I can't force air into my lungs.

"Come inside."

"Come to us."

"We've missed you."

The voices again. But they aren't in my head this time. They're seeping out of the walls of the castle, as if a chorus of dead souls has been used to form the stones.

I want to turn and run, but I need to go in. Sisyphus said he knows who I am. And I want to know. Need to know. My answers are only footsteps away. I lift my right foot, forcing the knee to bend, and plant it in front of me. Dust lifts from the ground, swirling at my feet and then growing until I'm standing amid a nebula of dead ground. I lift my left leg and plant it ahead of the right. My feet feel like stones. The dust engulfs me. And all my senses are screaming at me to not go inside.

"Yes. Come closer."

The voices pull at me, and I am a slave to my own curiosity and to their promises.

"We have answers."

"We've missed you."

Overhead, thunder booms, and purple lightning hits a high tower, electrifying it for a moment—outlining it against the stormy orange sky. The castle holds in the electricity as the stones sizzle, unwilling to let it go, but finally the outline of the building disappears, and the tower remains unscathed.

One step at a time, I make my way forward. I'm almost there when a skeleton hand reaches out of the ground. It doesn't grab for me but instead beckons with a long, bony finger. Drawing me forward. Another one comes up beside it, and then another off to the left and closer to the thick doors. All around me, I see the bony hands, palms up, fingers curling inward, making me move. They stay out of my way, and soon I'm at the side of a moat, and a drawbridge slams to the ground.

I jump back but only for a second. Once the dust settles, I set my feet on the wooden planks, my legs trembling under me.

Never leave us.

You belong with us.

The voices come from every part of the castle. The stone walls. The wooden drawbridge. The cobblestones up ahead. I close my eyes, trying not to think about Minos and the dead phoenix, and I remind myself—

they'll tell me what I want to know. What I need to know. And then I'm out on the cobblestones, and the drawbridge rises behind me.

I stand in the middle of a gravel courtyard with only the smell of death to keep me company. Fountains sit in the four corners, but they're dry and cracked like the fountains in my world above ground. I think of Sisyphus. Of him gripping his penis and of his melodic voice. And then there were his words. *I know who you are.*

"Who am I?"

I don't realize I've said it aloud until I hear the echoes of my whisper all around me.

Who am I? Who am I?

It taunts me as it mixes in with the other voices. It blends into their chorus. I put my hands over my ears to hold out the noise, and then another voice takes over. One which drowns out the rest.

"Come join us. We will show you."

To the left, a carved wooden door gapes open. Yellow light pours out from inside, and I know I need to go there. I steel myself against my fears, and walk across the gravel toward it.

I shield my eyes when I walk in, but the door slams, and the blinding yellow light extinguishes. I'm left standing in a room with just enough light from the torches on the walls to see a long wooden table ahead of me and three men seated around it. My eyes move from one to the next, trying to figure out what I've gotten myself into. But before I can take them all in, the man at the head of the table stands up.

He's got a close-cut dark beard, and on top of his thick curly brown hair sits a golden crown covered in gems which send reflections of color across the table and the room. When he stands, I notice he's holding a golden goblet decorated with gems equaling the ones on his crown.

"I certainly hope Sisyphus didn't scare you." His voice is in my head and in my ears, and he raises the goblet to his lips and takes a long drink, leaving a red stain on the hair of his close moustache.

"He did. He did." The man on the right cackles when he says it. "Look at her eyes. Such pretty eyes. Tasty eyes. One at a time. Savor them." His own eyes cross when he speaks, and his lips are so dry, the skin is cracking.

The man—the king—at the head of the table whirls on the man who's spoken. "Tantalus, we shall not eat our guest. It's not polite."

Tantalus, the man on the right, rubs his hands together. "But look at her neck. Like a pearl. And her breasts." He licks his lips, and reaches for a plate of fruit on the table.

I want to turn around and run out the door. I glance over my shoulder, but can't see the door anywhere. It's vanished—blended into the stone wall behind me.

The king slams his goblet down on the table,

sloshing thick, red liquid over the sides. "Can't you see she's scared, you idiot?" He raises a hand and points it at the man, and the plate of fruit moves until it's just out of his reach.

Tantalus screams like he's been wounded, and his fingers claw at the table, snapping against the hardness of the wood. There are scratch marks decorating the wooden planks in front of him. I force my eyes away from him and back to the king.

"Please excuse his rudeness, my lady. We don't make a habit of eating our guests," the king says.

The man on the left laughs. It's the first time I look at him, and my breath catches. He's about my age with light brown hair that reaches past his ears, and is muscular and sculpture-worthy. He's clothed in a toga, and when he looks at me, his green eyes sparkle with humor.

"Perhaps Tantalus would make a habit of it if he could eat anything," he says.

The king picks his goblet back up. The wine is back at the top, somehow magically refilled. "May I please introduce myself and welcome you to my kingdom."

I still don't trust myself to speak, so instead I nod, biting my lip until it hurts. The pain helps stem the fear I feel is about to bubble over.

"I am Aeacus, King of Tartarus." He motions to the right. "You've had the pleasure of meeting Tantalus already."

"And don't forget about me." It's the man on the left talking. The one so good looking I can almost forget Tartarus is a place for the eternally damned.

Aeacus laughs. "How could anyone forget about you, Pirithous?" Aeacus extends his arms wide. "My lady, may I present the honorable Pirithous to you?"

I force myself to flash a brief smile, barely showing my teeth.

"Oh, her teeth. Her teeth. And what of her tongue? Just one glance of her tongue."

I shut my mouth at Tantalus's words and cross my arms over my stomach, trying to hide as much of myself as I can.

Aeacus motions, and a chair at the end of the table nearest me slides out, its heavy stone scratching against the hard floor underneath. "Please sit and join us."

I don't want to sit. I want to call for Shayne. I want to go back and hang out with Chloe. I even want to be with my mom. To let her comb my hair. But I also want answers, and so, against every nerve in my body, I walk forward and sit in the cold, stone chair.

Once I'm seated, Aeacus sits also. Pirithous pours a goblet full of wine, sliding it down the table to me. I watch his fingers as he pours, noticing how long and powerful they look. Veins pop from his arms as he flexes his muscles. Unsure what to do, I catch the goblet when it reaches me and raise it to my lips.

"Her lips. Must have her lips. So red. Always so red."

And Tantalus lunges up, nearly jumping across the table to me. His eyes roll around in his head, and his hand almost reaches my arm. I look down at his skin and notice it's shriveled like a grape left in the sun.

"Tantalus!" Aeacus's voice booms through the chamber, and Tantalus freezes inches from my arm. His chair grows long tendrils that reach out and grab him, yanking him backward so fast it's like he's disappeared and then rematerialized.

Tantalus begins crying. "Just one taste. One small finger."

I curl my fingers under my palms and look away. The only positive part of this is Aeacus doesn't seem to want to let Tantalus eat me.

"The little flower is scared," Pirithous says, and he reaches over what seems like an impossible distance, and his fingers touch my closed fist, caressing it.

Shock runs down my body, and I look away from him, hoping he doesn't notice. But with the shaking in my body, I have about as much control of myself as a feather in a hurricane.

"My lady." Aeacus straightens his crown. "Why have you honored us with your presence?"

My mouth falls open, revealing my chattering teeth. "I thought you knew."

Aeacus forms a lazy smile on his face. "Of course I know. It is my job to know." And then his eyes harden, and he looks into my soul. "But do you know?"

My stomach flips around, trying to settle, but it won't. I lift the goblet and take another sip of wine. I wait until I swallow to answer. "I want some answers. I want you to tell me who I am."

Aeacus's eyes soften. "Good, my lady. You have come to the right place." He motions, and plates of fruits appear along the table with cheese and crackers scattered in, all out of the reach of Tantalus. Aeacus reaches out with a knife, cuts a thick slab of something which looks like Brie, and lifts it to his mouth on the knife. "Do you know what the penalty for killing a phoenix is?"

A rock forms so fast in my stomach it knocks the wind out of me.

"Ah, I see you do." Aeacus cuts another piece of Brie and holds it out to me on the end of the knife. "Would you like some cheese?"

I shake my head, wondering what I've gotten myself into, but can't find my voice to reply.

"Do you see how white her shoulders are?" It's Tantalus again.

I close my eyes to shut out the noise.

"I could feast on just one shoulder forever."

"Enough!" Aeacus's voice pounds across the room, and Tantalus covers his eyes and cries.

"Life in Tartarus."

At his words, I turn to Pirithous.

"With me. Forever," he adds.

Aeacus laughs, then pulls the knife back to himself, eating the moldy cheese himself. "Yes, Pirithous. Life in Tartarus. With all of us."

I open my mouth, but nothing comes out.

"Our flower is so excited, she's not sure what to say," Pirithous says. His hand is still on my fist, and when I realize this, I pull it away as fast as I can.

And then I manage to find my voice. "I didn't kill a phoenix."

Pirithous's face falls, but Aeacus laughs. "Ah, but somebody did. And a price needs to be paid." He motions around the room. "And since you've been so kind as to join us, it only makes sense that I extend the invitation to you."

But I shake my head. "I'm not here about a dead bird. I want answers." I can hear the anger building up in my voice, but I will not listen to this madness anymore.

Aeacus purses his lips together. "It seems your flower has a temper, Pirithous."

"I am not his flower!"

This only causes Pirithous to laugh, and before I know it, my chair is sliding around the table. My goblet falls out of my hand, spilling in a bright red stain in front of Tantalus. He moves his face down to lick it, but the liquid recedes. And then I'm right next to Pirithous, so close our arms touch.

"Ah, yes, that's what Theseus said, also. But I knew

my time would come." And Pirithous grabs my hand, pinning it to the table.

I decide I've had enough, but my feet and legs feel like lead. I can't scoot the chair out and get up.

"Your flower wants to leave." Aeacus watches me closely as if wondering what I'm going to do next.

"Share her!" It's a desperate plea from Tantalus.

I'm directly across from him, and I can't take my eyes off his crazy face and cracking lips.

"No!" Pirithous shifts so his arm is around me now. His other hand snakes out to grab mine, and I'm locked in place.

I need to leave.

I have to get out of this hell hole I've managed to get myself into. I need to get back to Shayne, who doesn't even know I'm in Hell in the first place.

I pick my right hand off the table, and put it on the edge to scoot myself back. My heart is pounding so hard, I'm sure all three of these crazy men can hear it. Three crazy criminals, whose crimes were bad enough that they've been sentenced to Tartarus for eternity. But when I push with my hand, my chair won't move.

"Let me go!" I turn to Pirithous. How dare he hold me here?

Pirithous laughs. "I will never lose you again, my flower."

"Let me go now!" I shove his arm off my shoulder and push again, but even with his arm gone, I'm immobile.

And then all three men around me begin to laugh. I look down at my lap, but instead of the normal flesh and clothes I expect, all I see is stone. Cold, hard stone from my waist down. Panic sets in, and I look to Pirithous's chair. His body is the same way. Flesh from the waist up, and solid rock below.

Their laughter pounds in my ears, echoing through my mind, and it won't stop. My throat constricts, and I can't force a scream or even words out. I'm going to end up in Tartarus forever after all. Penance for a phoenix I didn't even kill.

Shayne flashes through my mind. I'm lost to him and to myself. All the protecting my mom has done my whole life only to end up here. As I sink into the madness around me, my vision starts to cloud until all I see is a dark tunnel ahead of me and red on all sides.

Chapter 35

Retrospection

The room explodes with light. Pirithous screams first, and within seconds, my chair is scooting away from the deafening cry. And then the burning begins. Even with the horror I've just witnessed, I have to turn my head at the sight of the Pirithous. He's covered in flames, and the smell of burning flesh is so strong, I need to wretch. But my legs are still stone. Part of the chair.

Tantalus stands up, as if trying to escape out the now open door. But tendrils from his chair reach out again, and this time, I see they're snakes, hissing and biting him, wrapping around his arms and legs, and forcing him to sit. He's sobbing, but it doesn't help. Fire erupts around him, and through the flames, I see his crossing eyes roving around the room.

"My Lord."

I turn my head to Aeacus. He stands up, ignoring the burning bodies of his two companions. His eyes have grown as wide as golden drachma, and every bit of color has drained from his face.

"How dare you!"

Shayne's voice booms across the room like thunder. The wall to my right explodes, sending rocks flying in all directions. A piece hits me on the arm, slicing into me.

"I was only trying to answer a few—"

But Aeacus doesn't get a chance to finish his sentence. He screams, and the crown on his head begins to melt, gold dripping down his face. A ruby falls into one eye socket and an emerald into the other, and the gold melts and hardens around it, until even his screams can't be heard through the hardening metal. He's clawing at his face, but it's only a mask now. I want to pull my eyes away from him, but with the burning bodies on either side, there's nowhere else to look.

It's only when I feel hands on my shoulders that I snap my head around. And when I see Shayne, I begin to sob.

"It's okay, my love. I'm here."

"I'm so sorry." I sob between every word, and when my tears hit my legs, I realize they are no longer stone but have returned to the soft human flesh from before. "I'm so sorry."

"Shhhh…" He pulls me into an embrace, and holds me. "There's nothing to be sorry for."

"I wanted answers."

"It's okay." Shayne rubs the back of my head. "I understand."

I'm not sure how we get out of Tartarus. All I know is that one minute I'm amid the muffled screams of

Aeacus and the burning flesh of Pirithous and Tantalus, and the next minute I'm on a boat, crossing the flaming River Phlegethon. And Shayne is by my side, holding me the entire time. I can't stop my tears.

When I get off the boat, my legs are shaking so fiercely, I fall to the hot sand. Shayne picks me up, carrying me down the tunnel to his home.

The fire is burning when we get there, and Shayne sets me down in front of it. I prop myself up against a chair, and take the glass of wine he offers me and watch as it shakes in my hand, threatening to spill. Cerberus comes over and licks my free hand until I scratch him behind a set of his ears. Shayne sits down across from me, and Cerberus moves away, closer to the fire.

"So you decided to come visit?"

I am such an idiot. Shayne knows this, and I know it. "How—?"

But Shayne gives a weak smile before I can finish. "Charon told me. If I can't count on Charon, then I may as well pack it up and move out of here completely."

"So you knew the whole time?"

Shayne takes a sip of his wine, licking his lips afterward to get the final drops off. "I was busy in Asphodel." His face hardens. "And almost too late."

I shudder. "Tartarus is a horrible place."

Shayne nods. "The worst of any world. Why do you think I didn't take you there?"

I look down, playing with the crimson stem of my

wine glass, trying to calm my tremors. "I thought you were keeping the truth from me."

Shayne sighs, and then moves over to me until he's sitting next to me. "You're shaking." And he puts his arms around me.

I remember Pirithous's arm and shake even harder. "They're horrible men."

I feel Shayne nod his head. His hair is so close, it brushes on my cheek. "They were horrible men while alive, and now they pay for it with torment for eternity."

"They tricked me." I feel the overwhelming need to defend myself against my stupidity.

"Of course they did. Did you really think you could trust souls of the damned?"

I shake my head and try to stop the tears threatening to flow from behind my lids. "I wanted to believe them."

Shayne turns to me, taking the glass from my hand and setting it on the ground. He reaches out until we're face to face, holding hands. His presence calms me and holds back my tears for the time being. "Did you get any answers?" he finally asks.

There it is. Hard in my chest. The sad truth. "Nothing. I didn't learn anything."

But Shayne doesn't take his eyes off me. They bore into mine, and flash red. I can't look away.

"Who am I?" he asks.

"Shayne. Hades. Lord of the Underworld. We've

been down that path," I say.

His eyes don't falter. "Who are you?"

I sigh in frustration, and move to get up, but his hands hold me in place. His mouth is so close to me, I feel the heat from his breath on my cheek.

"Who are you?"

I squeeze my eyes closed, trying to focus on his words. Everyone in Hell seems to know who I am. Shayne knows. Reese knows. Even naked Sisyphus knows. But I don't.

"Think. It's important. Who are you?"

He moves close, and a vein in his neck throbs. He waiting for an answer I don't have. For eighteen years, I haven't even known who I am.

Then, in my mind, I see my birthday present. The box with the red feather. And Tanni's voice rings in my head, but not with the haunting words of doom she's spoken to me in the past. I see her soulless eyes filled with fog. Like she's here in the room with us, but only in my mind.

Open the box. Free yourself.

I remember opening the box, finding the feather inside. The swirl of Greek letters. The wave of emotions which flew through me when I opened it. I relax and give myself over to the secrets once contained in the box, and the truth takes shape in my mind.

I open my eyes, and see Shayne's gaze has shifted from determination to hope. He's trying to draw the word from my mouth.

"I'm Persephone," I say.

It comes out solid. All at once. I am Persephone. The box had held the secret, and now the secret is out. The truth is finally free.

Shayne takes me toward him, and every fantasy I've imagined since I met him comes to life. I've known him and been with him for eternity, and being with him now fills a piece of me which has been missing for the last eighteen years. And I'm never going to let it go again. Our kisses start soft, but as the fire crackles in front of us, I throw away any bit of hesitation. The heat rises until there's no stopping either of us.

Chapter 36

Confusion

I lean back into Shayne and watch the fire.
Persephone. I play the sounds over in my mind. Four
syllables. Melodic. Exotic. And Shayne seems to like it.
He rubs my hair and keeps finding excuses to use it.

"Do you want more wine, Persephone?"

I shake my head. "No, I'm okay."

"Something to eat, Persephone?"

Again, I shake my head.

"Are you cold, Persephone?"

This is it. His arms are wrapped around me and
flames roar in the fireplace; he knows I'm not cold.

I turn to face him. "You're just trying to say it."

Shayne cocks his head. "Say what?"

I punch him lightly. "My name."

Shayne acts as if he's gotten the punch line to a joke.
"Oh…Persephone." He smiles. "I just haven't used it in
a long time."

The problem is that knowing my real name has only
made me more confused. "So I'm the Queen of the
Underworld."

"Next to my side." Shayne's breath is on my

shoulder. He leans into me and kisses my neck sending a ripple of chills through me once again. God, I love that.

I recover and look around the room, remembering how much I like it. "And I designed this room?"

Shayne nods. "I told you it was designed by someone with great taste."

"And so, we're…married?" It's weird even to say.

"Hmm…well…kind of."

I narrow my eyes. "What do you mean…kind of?"

"Think about it."

"I'm trying not to. It's making my head hurt." Because how can I be Persephone when I've been Piper my entire life?

"Maybe we can figure it out together." Shayne sits on a sofa and motions for me to sit next to him. Cerberus pads over and puts a head on each of us, begging for a bit of attention. "See, Cerberus remembers you."

I smile at Cerberus. "And I remember him. Though I'm not sure how."

"So what do you remember?" Shayne asks.

I sink back into the red leather and force myself to think. "I remember growing up. For the last eighteen years. As Piper."

"And what else?" He's hoping for something more. "Do you remember when we met?"

I sigh. "I don't know. I remember being Persephone.

Being part of this world. But it's like it was another life. A part of my past but not a part of Piper."

An image from ages ago plays there before my eyes like a movie on the tube. Of a mountain and a hidden area away from my mom. Even back then, she never wanted me to leave her. She thought I should stay by her side always. Earth was warm then, too, but my mom controlled the seasons. Winters were cold, and summers bright. But there were no extremes. No Global Warming. Plants prospered and flourished and flowered and bloomed. And I infused life into them just by my mere presence.

My mom tried to trust me. She let me venture out into the wide open spaces. And maybe I felt oppressed then, too, because I left her every chance I got. I had friends who met me and helped me sneak away. I had other gods vying for my attention. And though I toyed around with the idea of one day picking one to spend my life with, not Hermes and not Hephaestus and not Ares drew my interest. Though Ares was always the most persistent.

I saw my mom in the morning. She told me she would be spending the day traveling the earth in Apollo's chariot. As the goddess of all living plants, my mom had responsibilities way bigger than most of the other immortals. And so she left, and I met my friends in the meadow.

"Have you heard the rumors?" Peisinoe said.

"What rumors?" Aglaope asked.

I leaned forward, wanting to catch their excitement. After all, it wasn't every day my mom left me alone.

"The Underworld is leaking into our Earth," Peisinoe said.

"Leaking?" I asked.

Peisinoe moved her head forward so all four of our heads nearly touched. "They say monsters are coming out into the world."

Thelxiepeia put her hand to her mouth. "Monsters!"

Gods, she was always such a drama queen.

Peisinoe nodded. "Through the caves around Mount Othrys. They're coming out into our world. The gods are all trying to control them."

I covered my mouth. "My mom should know. She's out there."

Aglaope looked over at me. "Persephone, that's what your mom is doing today. She's checking to see if the rumors are true."

Aglaope had taken every opportunity possible to make me feel stupid. Of the three, Peisinoe was the only true friend.

I shook my head. "She's just on a random patrol." But the idea made sense. Monsters escaping might be momentous enough for my mom to leave me alone.

Aglaope tossed her hair over her shoulder. "You are so naïve, Persephone."

"I am not," I said, even though I knew it was true.

But with my mom controlling my every step, how could I not be? "What caves, anyway?"

And Peisinoe told me.

I waited until they left; I made an excuse about needing to help some dogwood trees blossom. And then I started walking. Maybe I was naïve. And overprotected. And if so, then what better way to begin my escape from that shell than to see exactly where these monsters were coming from anyway? Maybe I could help stop them.

It had taken over an hour to get to the caves. Not only was it through scrub and rocks, but it was halfway up a hill and hidden behind a couple boulders. In fact, I almost gave up on finding it entirely, but then I felt the waves of heat. And I followed them until I found the mouth of the cave.

It took a bit of convincing myself, but I finally summoned the courage to go inside. I took one step and then another and entered the blackness.

"Haven't you heard the rumors? There are monsters around."

I turned at the sound of the voice even though it was too dark to see. "I'm not scared of monsters," I said, though my heart went into overdrive.

He laughed. "Really? Then why is your voice shaking?"

Deep breath. Whatever I'd gotten myself into here, I was a goddess. I could handle anything thrown my way. "I'm just cold," I lied.

Another laugh. "Maybe you should come closer then."

And I walked closer.

He took one of my hands, and electricity shot though my entire body evaporating any chills or fear trying to hide inside me.

Now, back in his home, I run a hand through Shayne's inky hair, remembering it was longer when we first met. But otherwise, he looks exactly the same. Immortal. And perfect. "I remember. My mom was furious when she found out."

Shayne laughs. "And nothing ever changes, does it."

Things had only gotten worse. "She started the rumor," I say. "She said you'd kidnapped and raped me."

"And she turned your friends into Sirens," Shayne says. "They never got over that."

They hated me afterward, even Peisinoe, spinning the kidnap and rape story out of control. Everyone believed it.

I shake my head, remembering my mom's ensuing wrath. The barrenness of the earth for months at a time. The droughts. The ice storms that froze the earth over. That she knew I wanted to be with Hades made her actions all the more extreme.

"My mom never changes," I say. "But I still don't get how I'm Persephone and Piper."

Shayne takes a sip of wine. "And I don't have that

answer."

"So who does?" I ask.

Shayne sets his glass down on the end table and reaches to pet Cerberus again. "I'd start with your mother or father."

My memories are coming back, filling in the gaps. "My mother is Demeter."

Shayne nods. "Who still hates me, I might add."

"Let her," I say. I'd much rather spend eternity with Shayne than with my mom. I felt that way from the minute I met Hades so long ago, and it had driven my mom crazy.

Shayne nods, and his eyes flicker red amid the brown. "I will. And how about your father?"

"My father." I can't say it. I think of the man from the barbeque dinner. The man whose face looked so much like my own. It's too much. Too hard to believe.

So Shayne says it for me. "Zeus. King of the gods."

I work my mind around this fact. My father is the king of the gods. Not the king of Earth or the sea or even of the Underworld like Shayne. He is the king of all other kings. The ruler of everyone and everything. And I am his daughter. Every god on earth should bend toward his will—with *should* being the operative word here.

As memories flow back to me, I remember plenty of times when gods defied him. I remember plenty of times when I defied him. But I also remember talking endlessly with him over a campfire or by a mountain lake or in the dense trees of a jungle. My father never told me what to do and when to do it. He gave me advice and let me make my own decisions, so unlike my mom and her domination. She controlled everything from the number of ears of corn a stalk might sprout to how long I could spend in the gardens away from her each day. If nothing has changed with my mom, I'm willing to bet nothing has changed with my father either.

"He made up the thing about the pomegranate," I say, remembering the story my father told my mom after one of my visits to the Underworld.

Shayne nods. "Definitely a victory for us."

Zeus lied. That was all there was to it. He made up the whole superstition that food couldn't be eaten in the Underworld. And that if it was, the person who'd eaten it could never leave again. He told my mom I'd eaten six pomegranate seeds and had to stay in the Underworld one month out of the year for each seed I'd eaten. That she should be thankful I could return at all. That he was doing her a favor.

My mom was livid. She threw Earth into the coldest winter it had seen since the Ice Age. And my mom couldn't set foot in the Underworld, so Zeus never had to worry about her finding out the truth. I married Hades, and we lived together for half of each year in bliss, while my mom tormented the world above.

"Did she ever find out the truth?" I ask.

Shayne finishes off the rest of his wine. "I can't imagine who would have ever told her any differently. And she did let you keep coming."

She did. Even though it pained her each and every time. She adored me all spring and summer and then mourned me when I left. And I endured her all spring and summer, losing myself in the plants and flowers on Earth, and then rejoiced when I departed.

"They'll have answers," I say.

Shayne smiles, but there's a hint of sadness in his dark eyes. "They should. All I know is you've been gone from Hell for eighteen years now, and all of the Underworld is suffering as a result."

My suspicions are confirmed. "Because of me."

Shayne pushes some of my out-of-control hair behind my ear. "Yeah, because we missed you."

We walk back to the River Acheron, and it's as if lenses have been lifted, making a world where I feel comfortable turn into a world where I belong. The Underworld is as much a part of me as Shayne is. Love for it is rooted in all parts of my body. I ache when I think of all the time I've spent away. Time in which monsters have grown strong and boundaries have weakened.

When we reach the banks of the river, Charon's face breaks into a smile. I run over and hug him, never wanting to let him go. He's been my friend since the first time Hades brought me down here, thousands of years ago. He talked to me when Hades was gone. He listened to me blather on about anything, only stopping me when souls demanded his attention. He treated me like a part of Hell even before I was.

"I've missed you so much." Charon has been like a father to me. I love him as sure as I'm Persephone.

When we pull apart, tears run down his face, and his already milky eyes seem translucent. "And I've missed you, my Queen." He seems to have a hard time getting the words out, and before I can think, he's hugging me again like he wants to make sure I won't vanish.

My Queen. I was Queen of the Underworld. I remember walking the fields of Elysium and the meadows of Asphodel by myself, maintaining order and keeping control. And I even remember Tartarus. Delivering punishment to those damned. I think of Sisyphus and Tantalus and Pirithous. Punishment is deserved for evil like theirs.

Tantalus cut up his own son and served him in soup to the gods—to my own mother who actually ate it, which explains her aversion to meat.

Pirithous tried to steal me from the Underworld to make me his bride.

Sisyphus carved up travelers and guests for pleasure, keeping them alive as long as possible to prolong their suffering.

They deserved their fates in Tartarus. And I was happy to ensure their eternal torment. I delivered their sentences with pleasure.

Charon gives my hand a final squeeze and then takes us across the river. I look to the bubbling sorrows, and realize I can see faces with them now, not just hear words. I see Randy Conner's face with his sadness. I see Councilman Rendon; he wants another chance. I see deaths and miseries and longings, all left behind. But the sorrows don't tug on me as before. I dip my hand into the water, knowing the monsters won't harm me, letting them come to me and trying to offer calmness in return. And when my hand touches the water, the monsters disperse, and the mad, frenzied bubbling of the sorrows stops. Within seconds, the River Acheron is calm.

Shayne and Charon both stare at me.

"The water hasn't been calm in eighteen years, Piper."

I smile at my name, and Shayne starts laughing.

He puts up his hands in compromise. "I'll call you whatever you want." And then he motions back out to the water. We're bumping into the dock now, the boat causing the only ripples on the now smooth surface. "Just remember, we need you down here. I need you down here."

When we step out, he holds me, and I never want to leave. "I want to be here. Forever."

Shayne laughs. "And this is the root of the whole problem. It always has been."

I pull back and look at him. "What do you mean?"

Shayne rolls his eyes. "Talk to your parents. But just promise me one thing."

I nod. I'd promise Shayne anything. "What?"

"Promise me you'll come back."

It's my turn to laugh. "Promise you'll take me."

Shayne smiles, and more than anything I want to be with him for eternity.

I smile and give him a kiss. And then I'm moving through the earth and the silver divide again, rising up from Hell back to the Botanical Haven above.

Chapter 37

Awake

I check the clock on my FON; it's Sunday afternoon. While it felt like an eternity in the Underworld, it's only been about twelve hours of real time. And aside from me, the Botanical Haven is empty; my mom isn't home.

My parents are gods. I am a god.

I look at the plants in the Botanical Haven around me and realize, from the changes in weather we've been having, half are on the verge of dying. A raw humidity presses in from all sides; the glass is so wet with condensation, I can't see out. At the sink in the back, I fill a glass of water for myself, drinking the whole thing and refilling it before turning to the plants. They need moisture, so I throw open some windows. When I open the window, I notice dark clouds hanging in the west over the Hill Country. But they aren't moving. They stay still like a threat that could descend on Austin in a second.

The heat pumps in through the windows, and I'm moved by the powers inside me. Around me, life returns to everything. Leaves grow, and flowers bloom. I change them with a mere thought in my mind. Pinks become blues. Yellows become reds. Life blossoms and flourishes, limbs grow to the ceiling, and roots dig out of pots and reach for the floor. The Botanical Haven is a thing alive and under my control. It flexes and bends to my will. I grow vines around the railings and hang flowers from the rafters. Fruit blossoms and then bursts into being on orange and cherry and avocado trees. Vines produce tomatoes and kumquats and black grapes. It's a power I've always had though I've never known how to harness it like this.

A knock on the door shakes me from my zone. My mind immediately flies to Reese, coming to visit again. Knowing my mom isn't home somehow. He knows I'm Persephone. He's been waiting for me to find out. He's been courting me forever, since even before I knew Shayne. And of all the gods who'd pursued me before Shayne, Ares never gave up. Once I made my decision, Hermes and Hephaestus and Apollo acquiesced and recognized me as Queen of the Underworld. But Ares remained unwavering. Biding his time. Always nearby.

I glance around a tall tree and look through the glass. But I don't see Reese. I see Chloe. I rush to the door, unlock it, and throw it open. Chloe's standing there with her arms wrapped around herself, shivering even though sweat beads down her face and arms. The humidity's so thick, the air around her seems hazy.

"Chloe!"

She doesn't move. I grab her and try to pull her in,

and she finally lets me. I take her upstairs, drape a blanket across her bare arms even though it's well over a hundred, and start some coffee brewing. It's only when she's sitting there at the table that she finally seems to realize where she is.

"Piper."

"Hi." I fill a cup of steaming coffee and slide it over to her. "You're shaking."

Chloe nods. "My body can't seem to keep up with the temperature changes."

My mind can't seem to keep up with anything. "It's like autumn is coming," I say.

I try to think of something to keep the conversation going. Having Chloe here with me soothes something deep inside me. Like everything else about my life is off but Chloe is still the same. She's just been freaked out recently; that's all. She's getting better. "If autumn is coming, that'll blow a lot of scientists' global warming theories right out of the water."

"My mom says people used to play in snow," Chloe says. "They skated and made angels."

I think of the frozen River Cocytus, of doing just that. "It sounds like fun, Chloe. Maybe if we went far enough north—"

Chloe smoothes the top of her bandana. "You think there's still snow anywhere?"

I want to tell her about kissing Shayne on the snowy banks of the river. I want to tell her about blowing icy breath. And trees with icicles. And a glacier beyond the ocean. I want to tell Chloe everything. "I'm sure there is. I think there are winter wonderlands just waiting for us."

She pats my hands. "That sounds so nice, Piper. Like paradise."

"Yeah," I say. "Just like paradise." I'm trying to find a way to start. To explain the oddities which have become my life.

But Chloe doesn't give me the chance. Instead, she looks at her arm. "My tattoo keeps changing."

I'm looking at it, too. Pure black. Ebony. And it spells out a Greek word I read clearly as *Fate*.

"It's probably just the light," I say.

Chloe's holding her coffee cup with both hands, but she hasn't taken a sip. I pick up mine and put my lips to it, hoping she'll take my lead and do the same. But she sits there unmoving, her eyes still fixed on my arm.

"Did you know Hannah Reed is pregnant?"

So Chloe's heard about the classroom incident, also. I'm sure it's all over the school by now. "Yeah, I was there when she told everyone."

"Do you think she'll keep the baby?"

I try to grasp what Chloe is saying. "Yeah, I think she'll keep it. She misses Randy a lot."

Chloe nods and finally takes her eyes off my arm and looks at me directly in the face. "Randy misses her, too. I asked him about the baby." She sets the coffee mug down in front of her.

I hold my breath. Chloe's been talking to Randy Conner again from the dead. But Randy is in Asphodel; he shouldn't have any memories of who he is.

"He wants me to tell Hannah to keep the baby." And then Chloe's hand flies out like lightning and grabs mine. "But what if she doesn't listen?"

I don't look down, but her grip is icy. "You can't control other people, Chloe. You can't make her keep it."

Her clutch loosens. "Do you think the baby would go to Hell? Do you think Hannah would go to Hell?"

I pry my wrist out of her hand, and she hardly seems to notice. I don't want to think about Hannah or her baby. I want to stop this conversation now and get back to Chloe. To me. To us. "Hannah will keep the baby."

Please, Hannah, keep the baby. Because I don't want Shayne to have to judge something so small and innocent. The way I used to help him judge all souls which came to the Underworld so long ago. He's had to judge alone for the last eighteen years. He's had no one to share the burden with.

This seems to be good enough for Chloe. "Randy asked me to do something for him."

I hold my breath. "Something like what?"

Chloe picks up her coffee. Finally. She takes a long sip, the steam pouring out around her lips. "He asked me to kill his father."

I'm right to hold my breath. I'm afraid to move. I wish I could snap my fingers and make this whole encounter go away. Make Chloe normal again. I think I should have let her die on the creek side.

"So I did."

"No, Chloe, you didn't."

"Yeah, I did." She says it as calmly as if she's telling me about a lecture she fell asleep in. Like she couldn't care less.

"No." I breathe it out. Chloe can't be a murderer. I know what happens to murderers in Hell. Not that Randy's father wouldn't deserve death. If he did make it to the Underworld, I'd place him in the chamber with Aeacus and Tantalus and Pirithous. I'd strip the skin from his body and then set him to burn for eternity. I'd feed his eyes to Tantalus and cut his hands off so he could never hit anyone again. And I'd visit him every week to make sure things hadn't become too bearable for him.

"Yes," Chloe says.

I shake my head. "Please tell me you're lying, Chloe. Please. Just tell me you're lying." Persephone passes judgment on murderers. I know what will happen. I have designed those punishments myself.

Chloe laughs. "Don't worry. No one will ever know."

I'll know. And that's worse than anyone else.

"You didn't do it."

But Chloe nods, and whether she did or didn't, she believes she did which is almost as bad. "Randy asked me to. He told me how to do it. It's why I'm still here, Piper."

"What do you mean, why you're still here?" Her words are like crazy words spinning around in my head. How can everything have changed so much in such a short time?

Chloe shrugs. "It's why I didn't die. I needed to do this. It's why Thanatos didn't take me."

She says the name Thanatos, assuming I know who she's talking about. I do. He's the winged man who collects souls and brings them to the banks of the River Acheron. But I pretend I don't know. "Who?"

"Death. I saw him there. That day by the creek. But he left me, and I knew there was a reason. And killing Randy's father was the reason. Don't you see that, Piper? God, it makes such sense now."

She saw Death, but she acted like she didn't? Or did she only remember him afterward?

"I think you need some sleep, Chloe."

Chloe sets down her coffee cup, now halfway empty and still steaming. "Yeah. You're right." She stands up and heads for the stairs, leaving me there at the table. "But I just thought you'd want to know."

I watch her leave. I do want to know. And I don't want to know. And I know whatever else I do in life, I cannot let Chloe end up with an eternity in Tartarus because of my selfishness. No matter what.

Chapter 38

Choices

The more I think about Chloe, the more certain I am she didn't do it. She did not kill Randy Conner's father. He may be an abusive monster, and he may deserve to die a slow, painful death and suffer an eternity in Tartarus, but Chloe did not kill him.

It turns out I am wrong—partly. When I get to school Monday morning, the word is out. Randy's father is dead. One of the terrorist groups made good on its threat. They planted a bomb under the steel struts of a downtown dome and then blew it up. Hundreds of people had died in the explosion and in the fires that came afterward, and Randy's father had been one of them. And now they're threatening to blow up more if the city doesn't dismantle all the disperser missiles.

It was a terrorist casualty. Chloe could not have been responsible. She didn't do it.

The humidity from the day before has doubled, and smoke from the fires mixes with it. It feels like we're living in a giant brick oven. It feels like every bit of rain that poured down during the hurricane has lifted into the air and hangs there smothering the city of Austin.

Normally, I'd text my mom to see what the city council plans to do in response to the terrorist threat, but today is not a normal day, and my life is far from normal.

I head to first period, trying to do the things I'm expected to do, but how can I when everything has changed? I'm not even the person I thought I was. My life to this point has been some kind of fabrication.

The tube is already on when I get to class. That kid from our school is being interviewed, the sophomore who claimed he could predict when the next heat bubble was coming. He's sitting by a table with a giant piece of equipment on it that looks like some kind of satellite dish connected to a coffee maker. I have to wonder where he got the materials to make it.

The camera zooms out, and I recognize the city council chambers. It's a full room except for my mom and, of course, Councilman Rendon. Wherever my mom is, she's even missing the council meeting.

"So what you're saying is that you were approached by one of these terrorist organizations?" the acting councilman asks the kid. My mom had mentioned Councilman Morse taking over in the interim until elections were complete, but this seems way early for her to be having news conferences. Is she power hungry just like Rendon was?

The kid, whose name—Toby Garcia—flashes below him on the screen, nods. "That's right. They came to my house Friday night when everyone was sleeping. They grabbed me from my bed and started asking me all sorts of questions."

"What kind of questions?" Morse asks.

Toby pats the equipment beside him. "Well, they wanted to know all about the HB Predictor."

The words *Heat Bubble Predictor* flash on the screen.

Morse nods to encourage him to continue.

"So I told them about it. Told them how it can predict the bubbles."

"But it didn't work this week, did it?" Morse asks, and the way she annunciates it, it's like she's almost happy the HB predictor is flawed.

"Something else happened," Toby says. "Something happened to change the weather. Because a bubble was coming; I guarantee it."

Morse looks down at her notes and nods. "Yes. Fine. So tell us, after that what happened?"

"They told me they wanted me to work for them. They wanted me to predict the bubbles so they could cause extra destruction when the bubbles were coming."

This just feels off. Terrorist groups normally do the things they do because they think it will help their cause, even if it normally ends up happening in a destructive sort of way. I glance around the council chamber again and wonder where my mom is. Why isn't she watching this, too?

"What did you tell them?" Morse says.

Toby Garcia looks directly in the cameras, and not

an inch of fear shows in his eyes. "I told them to get screwed. That I'd never help their psycho organization."

When the show cuts to commercial, I get a bathroom pass and leave. I can't take it anymore. All people are going to do is talk about the terrorist attack anyway. I need answers. My mom's not home, but I don't want to hear her lies anyway. Our relationship is built on lies. My blood boils when I think of her. What I need is to find my dad.

I walk out to the breezeway, and when the heat and smoke hit me, I embrace them, letting them soak into me. The heat of the earth is not enough to bother me. I've dared the fires of the River Phlegethon and the torments of Tartarus. But it's still laughable. I don't know who I am. How can Piper be Persephone?

I head to the concrete bleachers around the soccer field, and even though there's plenty of shade covering them, I find a spot out in the sun. It burns my legs when I sit, but I force myself to tolerate it. Down below, there's a man in a baseball cap spreading chalk on the fake grass. Mr. Kaiser's talked about how fields used to be made from real grass before the Global Heating Crisis, but now they'd never waste water for such an unnecessary purpose.

The man moves in a line, heading away from me. He reaches the end, then turns around, and heads back, a few yards over. When he's almost done with the line, he looks up at me as if he knows I've been watching. And then he waves.

My father. He's heard me asking for him even though I haven't uttered a word. I wave back, unsure if I should go meet him.

But he puts up his hand. "I'll be right up. Just give me a second to finish this line." His words find their way to me even though he's far away.

I've given him eighteen years; another minute or two shouldn't matter. So I nod in acknowledgement, and rest my elbows on my knees to wait.

Zeus finishes the line, and then the chalk canister disappears into thin air. He looks at me and smiles and then climbs the bleachers to sit by me.

"Talk about humidity…"

It's the second time we've spoken, and again he starts the conversation by talking about the weather. I want to start it by talking about me. "Who am I, Dad?"

He smiles. "You're my daughter Persephone." He grins at me, and it's so infectious, I want to join in with him. But I resist the urge, instead holding my face as impassive as I possibly can.

I smirk. "Yes, I've managed to figure out that much on my own."

"So what do you need me for?"

"To tell me the rest. To tell me what I don't know."

"Like…?"

"Like who is Piper?" It's an obvious question, but there's been no obvious answer I can figure out.

"You haven't talked to your mom yet?" Zeus asks.

"My mom's been gone all weekend. I thought she might be with you." And a spark of worry creeps inside me.

"The assembly of gods found out what she did, and they brought her in for questioning. Lots of the gods are unhappy about the last eighteen years."

"Will she be back?" I ask, not sure what answer I want.

"Eventually," Zeus says. "But right now it's just you and me."

"And by me, do you mean Persephone or Piper?"

Zeus takes off his baseball cap and holds it in his hands. His skin is tanned to a perfect shade of gold contrasting against his platinum hair. "How about both?"

I nod. "That's a good place to start."

"You are Persephone."

"Fine. But I remember the last eighteen years of my life as Piper."

"That's because eighteen years ago, your mother did the unspeakable."

I know what he's talking about as soon as he says it. "She killed a phoenix." But I'm still not sure how it relates to me.

Zeus nods. "She sacrificed a phoenix. When Hermes brought you back from the Underworld, she sacrificed a phoenix, and you were reborn as Piper. A brand new baby from the ashes of Persephone and the bird itself."

The blood drains from my face. I know I'm staring at him, but I can't get my mind around what he's saying. "Sacrificed a phoenix?" My tattoo. Sacrifice. The answer has been on my arm this whole time.

"It's a horrible sin, but one containing the power of rebirth. The bird died, and Persephone died—for a time. But then she came back. As you."

"So my mother killed the phoenix?"

And my mother killed me.

My mother is the one who belongs in Tartarus.

"She hid you from us. Locked your identity away inside a box crafted by Hephaestus himself."

A box. My mind flies to the gift I received on my birthday.

Zeus continues. "It wasn't until the first time September came and you didn't show up in the Underworld that I realized what she did. Nobody did. But by then it was way too late."

I blow out a breath slowly, trying to calm my voice and keep it from shaking. "I never went back, did I?"

"No." Zeus looks up at the sun which is moving behind a cloud. "And autumn never came. Nor did winter."

The pieces of the truth move together and take shape. "You mean the Global Heating Crisis is entirely because of me?" It doesn't even sound real.

But Zeus looks at me and chuckles. "Well, of course. If you never go away, then your mother has no reason to make Earth change seasons. It's year round summer as far as she's concerned." He wipes his forehead. "And a year round sauna for everyone else."

"So you're saying if I go back to the Underworld, fall and winter will come?" Could it really be that easy?

"Things are pretty out of whack right now," he says. "It may take a bit of settling. But once all the climactic changes get in order, then yeah. You don't even have to go back to the Underworld. You just have to reside in the domain of another god where your mom can't get to you."

The domain of another god. "Like when I went to visit Shayne?"

Zeus nods. "Exactly. But don't think you have to be stuck with Hades. Your options are wide open."

I narrow my eyes. "What do you mean? I love Shayne."

Zeus rolls his eyes. "Don't overrate love. I'd be remiss if I didn't mention you have choices."

Is my father telling me to sleep around? Or am I totally misinterpreting him? "What choices?"

Zeus flicks his hands. "Well, how about Ares for starters?"

"Reese?"

"Well, sure. He's my son. He's a good looking kid. And let's face it: he's been pining for you since day one.

Seriously, I figured with the arguments he and Hades used to have, we'd be looking at another world war."

With Ares vying for the Underworld, it seems the next world war may start there.

"He's a little on the pushy side." And I realize so, too, is Zeus, king of the gods.

"But he thinks you're gorgeous. Not to mention, he's loved you as long as Hades."

Ares was pushy ages ago. And Ares is pushy now. Not much has changed.

"I just think you should talk to him," Zeus says. "Maybe when we're done talking."

I shake my head. "I don't have anything to say to him."

Zeus makes a dismissive gesture with his hands. "Suit yourself. But he's waiting for you over by the greenhouses just so you know."

"I'm not interested in Reese," I say to make sure he's clear on it. But the thought that Reese is waiting to talk to me right now makes butterflies start moving around in my stomach.

Zeus pretends to think some more. "I guess there's always Hermes. He's a good kid."

The family tree in my mind plays before me. "Hermes is your son, too."

Zeus nods and smiles. "I have lots of kids. It makes the wife a bit on the crazy jealous side, but I'm king of the gods. What does she expect?"

I can't believe my father is telling me this. And worse, he doesn't seem to want to stop.

"Or there's Apollo. His twin sister might hunt you down, but you'd have fun before it ended."

"Hunt me down?"

"I'm sure Hephaestus will be bothering you soon enough too, once he finds out where you are. Although that would just have to be an affair on the side. Aphrodite may not like her ugly husband, but that doesn't mean she wants you running around with him either."

"Why does it seem like you don't want me to be with Shayne?" To me, Shayne seems like the obvious answer.

Zeus pinches my cheek like I'm a five-year-old. Which I am not.

"Because I just can't stand the thought of my darling daughter running around with all those monsters and fires, doling out torture to everyone who happens to kill thy neighbor. Change might agree with you."

"I liked being the Queen of the Underworld." And I love being with Shayne.

Zeus points upward. "But think of the sun with Apollo. Or far away battles with Ares. There'd be plenty of death to be had with Ares in charge. Or Hermes, carrying messages around the world. You could see Japan."

"Or the Underworld, with Shayne."

Zeus exhales in disgust. "Yes, or the Underworld

with Shayne. Just talk to Reese."

"No." I sit back, letting the bleachers support me. "What about my mom?"

"Ah, the lovely Demeter. I've always had a sweet spot for her—even with all her peculiarities."

"Will she go to Tartarus?" I've been told more than once the price for killing a phoenix.

Zeus laughs, but it's not funny to me. I don't want to see my mom there even if she has been the most over-protective, overbearing mother in the whole wide world.

"She should."

"Will she?"

Zeus puts up his hands in defeat. "The assembly's split on it currently. There are some who would love nothing more than to strip her rank and cast her into Tartarus."

"But not everyone?"

"Not everyone. There are others who recognize that what she did, she did for love. And they want her to resume her role here on Earth."

Love. My mom has a strange way of showing it. "Send her home so I can talk to her," I say.

Zeus nods. "I think that's a good idea." He stands to walk away. "And don't forget…"

I scowl because I know what he's going to say.

"…talk to Ares."

Chapter 39

Betrayal

I have no intention of talking to Reese. I tell myself this the entire time I'm walking toward the greenhouses on the outskirts of the school property. It's like my mind and my body are at odds. I try to justify my actions by telling myself that the only thing I'm going to say to Reese is that I never want to talk to him again. And then he'll leave me alone, and I can have a future with Shayne.

Reese is waiting for me, leaning against a brick wall, and I know the second I see him that me being here is a huge mistake. I should leave, but before my legs can process this command, he's there beside me, and his smell hits me like simmering ambrosia. Intoxicates me.

He takes my hand, and though my mind screams at me to yank it away, I don't, instead letting him hold it as we walk.

"I told you I wouldn't wait forever, and now I don't have to."

His arm is next to mine, and I can feel the sweat from his bare shoulder mingling with my own.

I try to relax, but something about his voice sends shivers through my body. And his smell is amazing. I take another breath and let it course through me. It makes me think everything is normal—that everything will be okay.

Reese opens the door to one of the greenhouses, and we go inside and sit on a bench. It's foggy from the humidity, and I can't see the world outside through the glass. I sit there for a few seconds just breathing him in.

"My life started again when you opened the box, Persephone." He slides closer to me, pressing his leg against mine.

I shake my head, still trying to sort out the truth— if there is any truth floating around the strange stories I'm hearing. It's like I'm finally getting every answer I wanted, and it's too much to process. "Why did opening the box matter so much?"

His breath is hot; it's on my ear as he speaks. I don't pull away. His finger traces the line of my face.

"Only you could open it," he says. "Deceit made it that way. You opened the box and freed your identity. I felt it the second it hit the air. And I came to you the very next day."

I remember the day I met Reese. The same day I met Shayne. Just after my eighteenth birthday. "Who gave me the box? Who is Melina?"

Reese shrugs, and his muscles harden next to me, and I want to reach and touch them. "Aphrodite, though I think she was trying to kill you."

"Kill me?"

"She loves me," Reese says. "She always has."

"Do you love her?" I force the words out of my mouth. As absurd as the thought seems, I don't want Reese to love anyone but me. But I also think I hate him.

"She's nothing next to you."

I can't help but glance around. Can Aphrodite hear him? Will she smite me on the spot? "Reese—"

"Shhhh…" Reese whispers in my ear. "You can be with me forever, Persephone." He puts a hand on my leg, and a jolt runs through me, making every thought in my brain run off to the shadows.

"Forever?" I repeat. And his scent hits me hard. I fight it for a second—it's like a drug—but the smell is powerful, and it takes over. I inhale, and exhilaration moves into my lungs. It reaches every muscle in my body as his scent makes its way through my blood.

Reese nods, tickling my leg with his fingers.

I quiver under his touch and breathe deeply again.

His words are music in my ear, lulling me exactly where I want to go. "Forget about your mom. You can live in my world. We can be together like we should have been together so long ago."

But I shake my head. "My mom will never let me." And I'm not sure I will let me. Reese is lethal, but the thought of being near him for eternity empties my mind of every rational thought and makes my head spin. And there's something else niggling in my mind, but it won't take shape.

Reese smiles and rubs my leg sending a fresh wave of chills up me. "I'll take care of your mom."

I'm possessed, and the overwhelming urge to kiss Reese takes over me, and I lean into him. When his lips meet mine, I never want us to be apart. He separates his lips, and his tongue explores my mouth, and I let him and explore him, too.

His hands are rubbing me. Moving up my thighs. I want so badly to be with him. I want to feel this way for always. I tip my head back, and he kisses my neck, sending electricity down my chest and stomach. I spread my legs, and his hand begins to move, and I know I've felt this way before. I want to feel this way again. I ache to be with him. I want him to be a part of me. And when his fingers just barely reach me, I remember.

"Shayne."

It's like a whisper in my mind, but I say it aloud.

"No. Don't worry about him." And Reese's lips are on mine again.

"Shayne." I say it again this time, louder, and when the word comes out of my mouth, Reese's hand stops briefly, barely grazing me. I want Shayne. Not Reese. It's like a fog has been clouding my mind, but I'm trying to make it lift.

"Shayne tricked you, Persephone." His hand retreats slightly though, and rubs my thigh again, willing me to relax my legs.

An ache inside me wants to. To let him take me. Like

I let Shayne. But Shayne is who I should be with. "No. I want—"

Reese's mouth moves to mine again, but this time it's fierce. His lips press on me, and I can't breathe. But I'm kissing him back all the same with equal ferocity to his own. His hand on my leg begins again, and his other hand moves up my stomach, sliding under my shirt, until it finds my nipple, hard and waiting.

I gasp when he touches it. But I know this is wrong. Why am I letting him do this? It's so not right.

"I want you to stop." I don't want him to stop. I want him to keep going. At least right now I do.

But Reese doesn't stop.

"I want you to stop." Louder this time. I can't do this. I won't do this.

When he pulls back, it takes every bit of effort I have to not reach for him again. I'm breathing so hard, it comes out in gasps. And my heart is pounding with enough force I can see my eyes beating.

"Oh, gods, Persephone. Please just give me a chance. I can be everything and more to you than Hades. I can make you feel like a woman. To live above the earth. And what does Hades have to offer you? Life in Hell? Torturing and burning. Dead souls everywhere. Is that what you really want? If it is, I can give you that, too."

I'm dying to be with Reese. To let him have his chance. But it's all wrong, and my mind screams it at me over and over.

"I love Shayne."

"Love! He's lied to you. Tricked you."

I shake my head. "Shayne wouldn't do that." But a fresh wave of Reese's intoxicating smell enters my nose, and his words shift around and weave into something that makes sense.

"Why don't you ask him what he's been doing with Chloe? You think you're the only girl Hades is looking at?"

"Chloe?" I can't believe Reese's words.

But he nods. "Why do you think she's acting so strangely? She can't look you in the eye. She's sleeping with your boyfriend every chance she gets."

"Not Chloe. She wouldn't do that." But I remember Chloe and her sheets. The ones she'd cut to shreds because they'd felt dirty. Not to mention how distant she's been and her dates she's told me nothing about.

"She would. Over and over. Why do you think Hades saved her?"

"Because he loves me."

Reese jumps to his feet. "Wrong, Piper. Because he wanted to have her for himself."

I get up and move away, turning around so my back is to him. "You're wrong."

I hear him coming behind me. His hands are on my bare shoulders, and he leans into my ear. "I'm not wrong. And you know it." And he nibbles on my earlobe, sending a fresh wave of desire on top of the hurt I'm feeling from Shayne's lies. The lies which all fit together now. I can see them burning clearly in my mind like a hideous jigsaw puzzle. Reese's scent gives me perfect clarity.

I lean back into Reese, letting his hands rub me. Explore me. And then he turns me around and kisses me again, and it's all I can do to not drop to the floor right there on top of him. His breath tastes like wine, and I go after it, trying to draw as much of it into myself as I can. His hands move everywhere, and I don't stop them. Reese is willing to tell me the truth. And Shayne has lied to me. Shayne is with Chloe. Shayne doesn't want me.

"Yes, Persephone. Be mine. I'll love you forever. Protect you from your mother. You'll never have to go back with her. We can be together always. Side by side." His lips move to my neck and then farther down, pushing aside the strap of my shirt.

But when I see him, the top of his head, the color of his hair, I know I'm not ready. I moved too fast with Shayne which it turns out was a huge mistake. And I don't want to make that mistake again.

"I can't." I force his aroma from my nostrils and speak the words as flat as I can.

Reese keeps kissing. Rubbing. Ignoring me.

"I'm not ready."

He looks up, and his hands stop. "Great Zeus. If

you're not ready, then I don't know who is."

I shake my head, my brain and my body fighting inside me. Wanting him. Not wanting him. "I'm not ready. I need time to think."

Reese drops his hands, and his face hardens. "When then?"

I shrug, taking a step backward. Away from his smell. "I don't know."

Our eyes meet, and Reese looks hard at me. "Don't take too long."

I close my eyes and shake my head. "I won't."

And then he moves toward me again and kisses me. I fight to keep the smell from overpowering me, but the kiss is deep and sweet, and I don't pull away.

But he does. "Something to remember me by." He steps back, moving toward the door and opening it. "If you need me, just call my name. I am at your disposal."

When the door finally closes behind him, I fall to the ground, trying to get a hold on the flood of emotions moving through me. I want Reese so badly, yet I want Shayne, too. But Shayne doesn't want me. It's Chloe he wants. Not me. Chloe.

I throw the door open once Reese is gone to try to clear the air. As his scent evaporates, I'm convinced I must be crazy. I don't want Reese. Reese cannot be trusted. He's drugging me with his scent. That's all it is, just more lies. It's an entire world that can't be trusted, and I've fallen into it.

Chapter 40

Blame

I run back into the school because I have to talk to Chloe. I refuse to believe what Reese said about her and Shayne, but I just have to hear it from her lips.

"meet me in the auditorium," I text her. They don't use the eco A/C in the afternoon to cool it, so no one will be there.

"k," she texts back. Just like that.

I sit on the stage and wait for her. She looks up at me when she walks in and smiles almost like the old Chloe I used to know. The happy Chloe who took me to get a tattoo. The one who tied a present for me with a red ribbon. I try to smile back. My heart knows Reese's words can't be true, but lingering thoughts in my mind keep making me think *what if.*

The curtain's drawn, and it's hot as a sauna, but we have the entire place to ourselves. My stomach convulses every time I think about bringing up her and Shayne, about confronting her—especially since she seems so normal now. But I have to.

She beats me to the punch. "So, Piper, is there anything you're not telling me?" She says it so normally, like we've been hanging out as if nothing's happened. As if the last time I saw her she hadn't told me she killed Randy Conner's dad.

It's a fair question. But in my defense, Chloe has not been in any state to tell anything. I've wanted to tell her everything. To have her help me. Give me advice. Things that friends do.

"Like what?"

Chloe reaches behind her head, untying her gray bandana. "Oh, I don't know. Has anything unusual happened recently?"

She knows. Has Shayne told her who I am? Have they really been together? Blood rushes to my head, pounding in my ears. But I keep my face as normal as possible.

I purse my lips. "Why do you ask?"

Her eyes flash to me, and for a split second, I see the ghost Chloe inside. The one who nearly died at the creek. But then it's gone, and this new deceiver Chloe is back. "I just heard a couple things, that's all."

I try to keep my expression from changing. "From who?"

"That guy, Shayne." She reties the bandana, but it's off center. Chloe never ties her bandana off center.

My heart stops when I hear his name. "What did he say?" I realize I'm holding my breath, waiting for her to answer.

"He said you've been keeping secrets from me."

"Secrets?" I whisper the word in response.

Chloe nods. "Yeah, secrets. Like things you should have told me."

I shake my head and push the image of Chloe and Shayne out of my mind. It's not real. "You haven't been around, Chloe. You've been sick or not taking my calls. It's like you've been a ghost." And now the ghost is gone—replaced by some alien creature that looks like Chloe but acts nothing like her.

"It doesn't matter, Piper. Best friends don't keep secrets." Her eyes rip into me when she says it, and what I thought was a smile turns into a sneer.

I stand up, taking a few steps backward. I've had just about enough of the whole world turning crazy on me. It was bad enough when Chloe acted like a phantom. Now I almost wish I hadn't saved her. "Who are you to talk about keeping secrets? You've been sleeping with my boyfriend." I spit out the lie to test her.

Chloe laughs, showing her teeth, and I hate her.

"Your boyfriend. I don't remember Shayne saying he was your boyfriend. And anyway, you're the one who went on a date with Reese. You knew I liked him, yet you still went on the date."

My heart sinks. She doesn't deny a thing. Doesn't even flinch. Her lack of denial confirms every worst fear I have. Was this all my punishment for going on a date with Reese? Is this how Chloe has decided to get even? I can't trust Chloe, and I can't trust Shayne, and I can't trust my mom. And I sure as hell can't trust Reese; he scares the crap out of me.

Chloe stands and pulls off her bandana. She tosses her head and shakes her hair until it's fallen into loose waves around her shoulders. And then she begins to rub her hands up and down her sides. "He's so perfect and so warm. God, he makes me feel so good."

I stare at her, unable to move my eyes. They're glued on her like I'm being forced to watch an execution. I think Chloe's gone crazy.

"He told me he loves me." Her hands glide over her hips, and she sways to unheard music. Images of Chloe and Shayne, naked and lying together, flash before me. They're wrapped around each other. They're kissing. He's running his hands through her hair. He's moving on top of her. I want to banish the images, but they hold their position.

I want Chloe to die.

And then she looks at me and smiles, her hands caressing herself, as if she's imagining Shayne's hands on her. Rubbing parts of her I know he's rubbed. Her eyes close, and her lips part, and I think of his lips kissing her. Lips I thought only wanted to kiss me.

"He wants me so much, Piper." She licks her lips and her teeth. "Do you know how good it feels to be wanted so badly?"

I thought I did. I thought that was how Shayne wanted me. But Chloe's taken every bit of that dream and smashed it under her foot.

"And he's promised me the world, Piper. All for me. He's perfect. Do you know what he said to me?"

I don't want to know, but the words escape anyway in a voice so soft I wish she doesn't hear it. "What?"

Chloe's eyes open, and she looks at me, pupils so small I'm sure she isn't bothering to even see me. "He said I'll be his queen. His queen! He knew it would always be me." And then she licks her lips again and smiles.

I can't take anymore. I turn so I don't have to see another second of Chloe's madness and Shayne's betrayal, and I run, tearing through the curtains on the stage and then down the aisle. Trying to get away from her. Trying to get away from the hideous truth.

Chapter 41

Jealousy

I head out of school, shielding my eyes from the blazing sun. The row of black clouds still hangs in the west, but it's closer than it was before, and the air almost feels electric. All this is because of me. The seasons are stagnant because of me. It's eternal summer because of me. Why does it have to be my responsibility anyway? My burden. As if my life falling apart isn't enough.

I remember standing here talking to Shayne. I think of his arms around me, taking me to the Underworld, and sadness crushes me. I want so much to trust Shayne. Maybe Chloe lied; she has to have lied. I want to trust him, but now I also want to hate him.

I hop on the first shuttle that comes by the school, not caring where it takes me; what does it matter anyway? My life feels like it's over. I get the brief feeling that someone's following me, but when I scan the people on the shuttle, no one looks familiar. It's just a sea of people trying to survive the Global Heating Crisis. A sea of people doomed to slowly incinerate if nothing changes.

I've only just turned back to the front when

someone taps me on the shoulder. I turn to see Melina.

"Did you get dumped, Piper?"

I want to punch her. "Just shut up, okay."

"Oh, poor, Piper. She isn't getting everything she wants for once." Melina laughs.

I clench my fingernails into my palms. "Was I supposed to die, Melina? Was the box supposed to kill me?"

She presses her pouty lips together. "That would have been ideal."

"Ideal! For whom?"

Melina laughs and leans forward on the bench seat so her lips are only inches from mine. I hold my position. I am not going to back down from her. She may be a goddess, but so am I.

"Why for me, of course. What a dumb question."

I glare at her. "What have I ever done to you?"

Scorn flickers across her beautiful face, but she seems to catch herself and erases it quickly, replacing it with her standard serenity. "Piper. Persephone. What haven't you done? Here I am the goddess of love and beauty, yet you've taken the hearts of the only two men I could call my own."

"Your own?" My mind processes this. "Ares and Hades?"

Melina mocks my apparent stupidity. "Ares, of course. But then there's my cripple husband Hephaestus. He pined over the box holding your identity, worshipping it like a golden idol. I watched him for years, going to the altar, praying for your release. His prayers are the only reason I knew what was in the box in the first place. The precious secret. Your mother and Apate didn't tell anyone but him—and him only because he crafted the box and kept it safe. But all it takes is one weak link. So I stole it from him and gave it to you."

I fix my eyes on her, trying not to let anything show on my face. I can't believe my mom had worked with the goddess of deceit. Apate defines untrustworthy. My mom should know this. "But I didn't die, did I?"

Melina shakes her head. "It seems Apate has earned her name as goddess of deceit. Whoever opened the box should have burned in Tartarus, but Apate crossed even your mother, allowing that one person would be able to open the box."

"The person whose identity was stored inside," I say.

Melina nods. "That's right. You. And instead of an existence in Tartarus, which would have simplified my life beyond belief, now here you are once again trying to steal my true love."

"Not Shayne," I say. Inwardly, I laugh. If we're talking about stealing true loves, maybe she should talk to Chloe instead.

"Of course not Shayne," Melina says. "What a bore. Though I'm sure he, like every other man, would do just about anything to have me. Anything. You do know how men are, don't you, Piper?"

I'm flooded with relief when she denies wanting Shayne. "How are men?" I ask.

"They're selfish. And greedy. And all they care about is the conquest. Take your precious Shayne for example. Do you really think all he's been doing for the last eighteen years is pining away for you?"

I bite my lip. Actually this is exactly what I thought. Exactly what Shayne led me to believe.

She must see my answer in my eyes. "Don't fool yourself, Piper. Shayne is just like every other man. He doesn't care about you."

"You're wrong," I say. "You're just angry because Reese wants me."

Scorn fills in her eyes. "Reese doesn't want you. And Shayne doesn't want you. You're nothing, Piper. You're a fallen goddess. You aren't worthy of someone like Reese's attention. And if you ever think for a minute that Shayne will be true to you, you're wrong. No one will ever be true to you. You don't deserve anything."

She may be the goddess of beauty, but every word coming out of Melina's mouth is filled with ugliness. But her words dig deep and burrow inside me. "Why are you acting like this?" I say. In my past life, I remember talking to Aphrodite on occasion, and though maybe we weren't the best of friends, she never even came close to exhibiting the contempt she's showing now. "I never did anything to you."

Melina's perfect lips press into a perfect smile. And

then she leans closer to me and whispers in my ear. "Yes, you did, Piper. You didn't die."

I've had enough. I stand up so I can get off at the next stop. How can she possibly call herself the goddess of love? She knows nothing of love. Only jealousy and hatred, both of which seem to be directed at me.

"Oh, guess what I heard, Piper?" she calls out to me.

I take the bait and turn. "What?"

"Your friend from school, Randy Conner…"

"What about him?" I ask, and I get a sick feeling in my stomach. Because as soon as I ask the question, I see the answer. I see into the Underworld and into Tartarus. And there is Randy, standing on the banks of the river of fire. He's been moved from Asphodel and put in Tartarus. Guilt for his father's death covers him in a layer of red. As I watch, he steps through the wall of fire which makes up the boundary. He screams in a cry so heart rending, my own nerves feel like they are on fire. And then he's gone.

Melina smile. "Yeah. I thought you'd want to know about one more life you've screwed up."

I turn away from her and get off the bus.

I need to save Randy Conner. If I never do anything else of worth with my new miserable life, I plan to save him from the torture of Tartarus. I'll go back to the Underworld. I'll talk to Shayne and sort things out. He can clear up everything. This mess with Randy Conner. The untruth of his infidelity and Chloe's betrayal. I'm about to call out for him but stop myself as an image of Chloe wrapped in his embrace forms in my mind. I squeeze my eyes shut, trying to force it away. It's not true. It just can't be true. But the image persists, and I remain silent.

I look at the clouds and start to walk toward them. And like they're responding to me, they move closer with each step I take. Closer to me and closer to Austin. I head up the rocky cliff that overlooks the Colorado River, and I watch them. Dare them to come any nearer. Almost in response, lightning streaks through the clouds parallel to the horizon.

It's late afternoon, and there are a few college kids hanging around under a canopy, listening to music. They look over at me, and one of them waves. I wave back, remembering my visit to the Drag with Chloe to get our tattoos. To think I planned on being one of those kids. On leading a normal life. The Fates had been against me from the start.

One of the guys smiles, and motions me over. "Come join us. We've got plenty to share."

I look to the bottle of liquor he's holding, and honestly, a part of me is tempted. To grab hold of something normal from this world and hang onto it.

"We don't bite," the girl calls. "And anyway, Dylan here needs a date." She points to the boy on her right who gives me an inviting grin. Then she leans over and kisses the other guy full on the mouth until all three of them roll back laughing. Oh my god, they lead such normal lives, even amid the Global Heating Crisis. They don't have to worry about any of the craziness filling my world.

I shake my head, and they wave as I walk away. Behind me, I know the clouds follow. The wind starts to pick up, and darkness extends its fingers until it surrounds me on three sides. Lightning fills the sky again, but there's not a rain drop in sight. The storm coming is pure electricity. It's been brewing since my most recent trip to the Underworld, and any minute, it's going to strike.

Once I'm out of the college kids' sight, I sink down to the hard-packed dirt and rocks. I have to save Randy, but I can't bring myself to call for Shayne. I don't want his help. I still hear the music and laughter in the background as I scoot toward the edge of the cliff and look down. The water is so far receded that rocks and sand nearly reach the middle from both sides, leaving a thin ribbon of stagnant brown wetness in between. It's the only way I've known the river. Slow. Dead. Empty.

If I go away, will everything change? Will autumn return and winter come? Will the Global Heating Crisis really end?

"You're Persephone."

I whip around at Chloe's voice, and see her standing there. She must've followed me on the shuttle. But it's not the taunting, horrible Chloe from the auditorium come to tell me she's sleeping with my boyfriend. It's the withdrawn Chloe. The one who's almost died. And neither of them is the one I really want to see. I want my old Chloe back. I want Shayne back.

I turn to the overlook, away from her, and watch the sky. "Yeah. So what?"

I feel her sit down next to me, leaving space in between us.

"You didn't tell me."

I shake my head, not knowing if she's looking at me. "You never gave me the chance."

We sit there not speaking for a while. I'm not going to start up a conversation with her, and she seems to be trying to figure out what to say. If she even has anything to say. Lightning strikes again, straight down to the earth this time. It hits the bridge crossing the river with a crack so loud, the whole ground shakes.

"Why did you save me?"

I turn, and Chloe's looking at me. Her eyes contain a sorrow I never used to see. The Chloe I got a tattoo with never showed sadness. She was all fun. And adventure. She is not this Chloe.

I saved you because I love you, I want to say. But it won't come to my mouth. "I didn't save you. Shayne did."

But Chloe shakes her head. "No. It was you. I remember."

I turn back to the cliff, picking up a rock and tossing

it over. It clatters on the rocky outcrop, skipping vertically until it stops. Far below, what little water is left ripples in the wind.

"What's going to happen to me when I die?" She sounds like a child asking a random curiosity about the world.

I laugh, still keeping my eyes away from her. "You won't die, Chloe. You can be Queen of the Underworld."

I hear Chloe suck in. "Are you kidding? That's you."

I whip my head around to face her. "That was me, Chloe, until you slept with Shayne."

Chloe shrinks under my words, and for a second, I can't believe this Chloe and the Chloe from the auditorium are the same person.

"I don't think it was really Shayne." She puts her head in her hands. "I just don't know what happened."

I avert my eyes and pick up another rock. "I'm not going back to the Underworld."

"You have to, Piper."

"Really? I'm not sure I read that rule."

"The Underworld needs you."

I snort. "Please. What do you know about what the Underworld needs?"

Chloe grabs my arm. "But I need you there, Piper. For when I die."

I yank my arm away and toss the rock over the cliff. "You're not going to die."

But she nods. "Yeah. I am. Fate told me so. And I'm scared."

I stand up, walking a few steps away. The wind's blowing hard enough now my hair is flying in every single direction possible. I pull it back with one fist. "You don't know what you're talking about."

"I need you there to help me. I can't handle eternity in Tartarus."

"You don't have to worry about Tartarus. Randy Conner's taking care of that for you. He managed to get all the blame."

Chloe looks at me and blinks her eyes a few times. "He did?" She shakes her head. "But that's not right. Not fair."

I scowl at her, thinking of Shayne. "So why don't you ask the Lord of the Underworld about it?" How can I save Randy Conner now? I can't even save myself.

"It should be me. Not Randy." Chloe stands up now, and fear creeps onto her face.

So what? Let her be scared. "Why don't you offer yourself up in his place then if you think it's so unfair?"

She shakes her head, and her bandana slips off center. "I told the terrorists I wouldn't join. Said I didn't want any part of blowing up a dome. But they used me anyway, and the next thing I knew, Randy's dad was really dead."

"Randy asked you to kill him."

"I didn't mean to do anything. I swear." Chloe

presses her hands against her face. "But Randy shouldn't get the blame."

I shrug. "No, he shouldn't. Maybe if you go explain things, everything will be all right."

Chloe looks up then, taking her hands away. "Yeah, maybe. But I'm scared."

I nod. "You should be." I know I'm not comforting her, but I don't care.

Chloe bites her lip, and my eyes meet hers. "I'm so sorry for everything, Piper."

A gust of wind blows, and she turns away from me, looking out toward the barren water. Before I realize what she's going to do, she puts her hands up into the wind and jumps.

Chapter 42

Sacrifice

Chloe falls, and I run to the edge, but she's already gone. I'm too slow. My stomach tightens into a knot so hard and full of disbelief, I can't stand it. I lunge out on the cliff, but stop myself, unable to go beyond the rim.

Chloe will die.

I heard the words before and tried to stop them, but it was useless. Chloe is dead, and there is nothing I can do about it. Maybe there was never anything I could really do about it except postpone it.

"No! No! No!" I'm staring over the side, but I can't bring myself to actually look for her body. She's dead. She's gone. And though she's killed herself, I feel like I've pushed her. "Please come back. Don't leave me." I want the old Chloe here with me now. I want us to be friends, before my knowledge of phoenixes or the Underworld or Persephone ever came back to me. "Please, Chloe."

Lightning cracks, and this time it strikes a building across on the other shore. In seconds, the building catches fire, and smoke fills the air.

Off to the side, I hear the college kids coming

toward me. Did they hear me screaming? Did I scream? I can't face them or anyone. Before they can reach me, I run the other way.

Chloe cannot be dead.

Chloe will die.

It was her fate, and she knew it. But what is my fate? To be a curse to everyone I know?

I will not have it.

I direct all my thoughts to the Underworld. Not to travel there, but to command there. I was once the Queen of the Underworld. I should have power. And I want that power back if only for this one decision.

I see the Underworld before me. I rule it.

"Randy and Chloe will be moved to the Elysian Fields," I command. I have no idea if I even vocalize it. But I know I will make it happen with my sheer will. I may not be able to count on Shayne to do it for me, so I will do it myself.

The ground underneath me seems to quake at my words. I think for a second it will split and swallow me whole. Maybe I will have to take their places in Tartarus. Maybe this act will ensure Chloe and Shayne being together. But whatever the cost, I accept it.

"Now," I say. "Put them in Elysium."

The ground trembles one more time, and I feel it happen. I feel their souls move from the fires of Tartarus to paradise. My best friend may be dead, but now she's in her rightful place in paradise. It's where she should have been last week. I shudder from the power I've exerted. I've done it. Chloe and Randy are going to be okay. They'll have paradise forever.

I turn my mind from the Underworld back to the world around me. I run down the embankment, heading out into the street. I don't know where to go. I love Shayne. And I want to be with him now more than anything. But the image of Shayne and Chloe drops back in my mind. I stop and force it away and focus on the earth.

It's still hot as a sauna, but the wind is blowing so hard, it's almost pushing me over. The lightning is a storm of light and sound, striking everything it can. Sirens explode in the air, and smoke is thick. I run in the direction of the Botanical Haven, because if my mom is somehow responsible for this weather, I have to make her stop. It's killing the earth.

My legs pound; I run forever. I'm almost there. Sirens and wind are rampant around me, and lightning is striking everything in sight. It cracks so close it feels like it's next to me, and one of the Spanish Oaks in our yard splits in half and falls to the ground.

Another branch falls, and it smacks onto the glass roof of the Botanical Haven. I hold my breath even though the glass is shatterproof because it hits with such force.

The glass holds.

The rest of the world isn't as lucky as we are. I can

only imagine how this lightning storm is wrecking downtown Austin. Wrecking the world.

Chloe flashes through my mind, jumping over the side of the cliff. I ache at the thought of her and Shayne together, but I've paid the price for my mistakes.

I run across the rocks that make up our yard and pull the door open. My mom is inside, clipping dead leaves off the plants like everything in the world is as it should be. How could she be so oblivious to the earth outside the Botanical Haven when she's always claimed to love it? The leaves drop to the floor at her feet like the branches outside. I slam the door shut behind me to let her know I'm home. I need to confront her, and it has to start here with her killing everything around her for her own selfish needs.

The wind beats on the glass walls and ceiling, but I try to filter it out. But another branch slams into the roof, and I jump. The glass groans under the weight but holds.

"Why did you do it, Mom?"

She has her scissors in her hand, hanging down at her side, her gloves still on. "What?"

"Kill the phoenix. Why did you take me from the Underworld?"

The smile evaporates from her face like the mist sprayed over our hot Earth. "Who told you that?"

I shake my head. "It doesn't matter. I know—that's what matters."

Her eyes narrow, and her face turns red. "It does matter. Nobody was allowed to speak of it. Whoever told you will go to Tartarus."

"You've lied to me my entire life."

"Ares told you, didn't he?"

"Ares didn't tell me."

Her eyes are wild, moving around the room, looking for something or someone to blame. "He did. I know it."

I uncross my arms and take a step closer to her. "You don't know anything. You killed a phoenix and me at the same time."

My mom shakes her head. "No! I would never kill you. Someone has been lying to you. I love you."

"Love me! You killed me, and then, when I was reborn as Piper, you hid me away from everything I ever knew."

"You're wrong. It wasn't like that at all."

"You never even told me who my father really was."

My mom's hand flies to her mouth. "You know about that?"

I nod. "I know everything, Mom. Everything. I know who you are. Who I am. Who I used to be."

"But how—?"

"I loved Hades, and you took me away." When I say his name, I think of Chloe and Shayne. It can't be true. "Everything was perfect, and you ruined it all." Tears well up inside my eyes, but I refuse to let them fall.

"Perfect! How can you even say that? I was forced to be away from you for half the year. My precious daughter. And you never even seemed to mind."

"I belonged in Hell as much as I belonged here. My place was as Queen of the Underworld."

"Your place was here with me." She moves back, and her eyes bulge out of her head. They aren't focused on me. They don't focus on anything. There's sweat beading down her face, catching in her hair. "With your mother. Not off in some godsforsaken place damning souls for eternity. You should have been among the living. Not wandering around underground with no one to keep you company but ghosts."

"I had Shayne." And I want Shayne now.

My mom raises her eyebrows. "Yes, you had Shayne. But that's hardly a reason to spend half the year away from your mother."

"Was he really that bad, Mom? Couldn't you have just tried to get along?"

My mom stops cutting since all the leaves are gone. "Of course he was that bad. He couldn't stand to be around me. He was rude to me and arrogant. He showed me absolutely no respect."

My mouth falls open. I can't believe she's saying this. "But he was good to me. And I loved him."

My mom throws down the scissors, smashing them into the ground. "Good to you? He took you away from me." Overhead, the glass creaks again, and then the branch is too much. An entire section of the roof comes down off to my right raining glass in a glittering shower.

"Yes, he took me away from you, but he treated me like a queen."

My mom doesn't even seem to notice the roof. "So what? Any god could do that."

My mind flashes to Reese, but I push him aside. I don't need him coming into this conversation.

"I didn't want any god. I wanted Shayne. But you ruined all that." I dig my fingers into the soil of a nearby plant and grab a clump, smashing it in my fist. "You ruined everything. You're selfish, Mom. You've always been nothing but selfish. But let me tell you something. I'm grown up now. I make my own decisions. I will not be under your control any longer. You don't own me."

She meets my eyes then, and we hold them there. Her gaze bores into me, but I maintain the hold, not wanting to look away. Refusing to back down.

"You will obey me, Piper." Each word comes out slowly. Methodically. Like she's making a plan even as she says it.

I shake my head. "No, I won't."

"You will go upstairs and pack your things. We're leaving. Right now. We'll hide, and no one will find us again."

"No."

She moves to me to grab my wrist, but I'm faster. I

grab hers instead. I clench as tight as I can, hard enough to break it if she were mortal.

"Do you dare to defy your mother? Are you forgetting who I am?"

I grab tighter, holding until I feel the pulse in her arm. "Who?"

My mother stands a little taller. "I am a goddess."

I let go of her hand, thrusting it down to her side. "And so am I."

She stares at me, her mouth opening, but nothing comes out. Around us, the wind from the storm whips through the hole in the roof.

"Mom, do you know what the punishment for killing a phoenix is?"

My mom looks down, picking up the bucket of water by her feet. It's left a wet ring on the tile and drips when she raises it.

"It's life in Tartarus, Mom. Did you know that?"

She nods, still looking down.

I think about my visit to Tartarus. My horrible meal with Aeacus, Tantalus, and Pirithous. A meal that might have been my last. "Have you ever been to Tartarus?"

My mom lets out a bark of a laugh, but it's laced with fear. "Of course not."

"It's the most horrible place imaginable. Even worse, in fact. I've been there—as Piper. I should send you there myself. But even after everything you've done, I will never let you end up there."

The bucket of water falls, and I realize my mom is crying. I stand there, holding my resolve, but her crying tears at my heart. I try to be strong. I try to stay angry. But when I can't listen any longer, I move to her and catch her in a hug.

"I only did what I thought best for you, Piper. Best for us."

She's shaking under me. "Well, you screwed up, Mom. And now everything's falling apart."

She stops crying and pulls back to look at me. "I can get help." Her eyes are wide as if she believes the statement. "I can get Apate to help. She'll know what to do."

I stare at her, trying to keep my eyes impassive. "Mom, you can't trust the goddess of deceit."

But she nods her head. "Yes, Piper. I can. She helped me before. With you. I never intended to go through with my end of the bargain. I wasn't going to lose you again. So we came up with the idea of the box. To hide you from Hades and Ares."

I throw up my hands. "The box! How could you ever think that was a good idea?" The image of the box flashes in my mind, and I get the overwhelming urge to smash it against the wall.

My mom grabs my hands. "It kept you hidden from the gods for eighteen years. Until you opened it." Her eyes narrow. "Which you never should have been allowed to do."

"But I did, Mom. Don't you see? Apate tricked you.

You thought you could tuck away your secrets forever. But she tricked you, and I opened it."

My mom shakes her head. "No. There must have been some weakness. Apate swore to me it would work. We'll get her help now. Get away from here. No one will ever know."

I tear my hands away from hers and meet her wide eyes with a cold stare. "But I know, Mom. And I have no intention of ever being part of your games again."

My mom walks closer to me, but I don't want her sympathy. I don't want anything from her.

"I was just trying to help," she says. "When Ares came to me with the idea—"

My eyes nearly pop out of my head. "Ares! He came to you?"

My mom nods. "Of course. I never would have known about the power of the phoenix sacrifice if not for him. He was the one I made the bargain with in the first place."

Something clicks far in the back of my mind, but it's nearly silent.

"Ares told you about the phoenix?" My heart has started beating like a drum, pounding so hard I'm sure it'll come out of my chest.

"Ares came up with the idea. We planned it all out. But nobody could be told. Not your father. Not Hades. And certainly not you. Everything had to be just perfect."

Ares knew about the phoenix. It was his idea.

"What happened?" I'm trying to stay calm, but something is building inside me, trying to come out.

My mom pulls off her gloves and tosses then on a plant stand. "We waited until you were due home. And when Hermes brought you back, we acted. We took you to Phoenicia, to the Well of the Phoenix."

"I fought you." I remember this like it was yesterday. Standing by the well. Being forced to drink from the water. And flames. Lots and lots of flames.

My mom nods. "Yes, you fought. But Ares managed to control you. He has this way of calming people. Getting them to do what he wants."

It settles on me; I know only too well about Reese's power. It's the power that overcomes me every time he's near. "He drugged me."

My mom shrugs. "Drugs. Power. Call it what you want. We needed your cooperation."

How my mother could be a part of her own daughter's abduction and drugging and death is beyond me. "I drank the water. And there was fire."

"Yes, Piper."

She moves toward me and reaches out, but I slap her hand away. This is not my mother. She's a demon in the body of my mother.

My mom lowers her hand. "Ares killed the phoenix, then. It had to be done just right. With flames and a knife made of pure gold. Hephaestus himself crafted it, though he had no idea why."

"Reese killed the phoenix?" I say.

"Yes. Without him, I never would have been able to do everything. You were still fighting, but as soon as the bird burst into flame, so did you. And then you were reborn to me and free of Hades forever."

It's like I'm watching my past life through the eyes of someone else. I cannot fathom how my mother could have done this. "And Reese's involvement—"

"What? What about my involvement?"

I turn to see the door wide open, and Reese standing there, watching us. Outside, the wind howls, and the air is filled with smoke.

"You're responsible for everything. Everything."

His smile only grows.

"Every single thing that's happened has been your fault. The phoenix. My death. Taking me away from the life I loved."

Reese spreads his arms, like he thinks I'm going to run over and hug him. "But look at everything you have in your future." And then his smell hits me hard, and I know it's a drug.

I cannot let it overcome me. I cannot let go. I back away, putting distance between him and me, but he takes two steps forward for every step I take back.

"Stay away from me!" I scream it at him, fighting to keep the aroma from entering me.

But he still comes. "You promised, Piper. You said

you'd give us a chance." He's close now, and I'm up against a wall.

I look to my mom. She's standing there, watching, not seeming to process that I'm being threatened. "Help me, Mom."

My mom looks at Reese. He's next to her now on his advance toward me. Behind me, I feel the glass of the wall against my skin. And the thick scent of wine enters my nose. I force it out but know I need to breathe.

My mom shifts, and I think she's going to do something to stop him. But then she actually presses her lips into a thin smile. "But maybe I was wrong, Piper," she says. "Maybe being with him will solve all our problems."

I shake my head. She's under his spell. "Can't you see it, Mom? He's tricking you. You aren't in control. He is."

"Half of the assembly backs him," she says. "And he's waited so long."

I look from her to Reese.

He nods. "Thousands of years, Piper. I've loved you since the day I first saw you."

"He'll let us all stay together. We won't have to worry about the Underworld," my mom says. "I can come with you when you need to go away."

Every word out of her mouth makes me sick. A sudden coldness hits me as reality sinks in. I have no control. I have nothing. Even my own mother has betrayed me.

"I've waited for you, Persephone. I've waited so long. Forever. It's been worse than eternity in Tartarus without you. Torture every time I see you." He takes a step and then another, until I realize he's only a foot away.

"I don't want you." I force the words out, even against the intoxication I feel seeping through me.

"That's crazy." He reaches out and touches me.

I yank my arm back. "I don't want you. Not now. Not then."

Reese steps close. "You do. You want me more than life itself. I see it in your eyes. I can smell it on you. You want me with every inch of your glorious body." He grabs my arm now and holds it, his grip tightening until it hurts.

My body is dying to go to him. To give in to his words. Words I know are true. And words I know are planted by him, but I don't care.

"Yes, Piper. Come to me. Be with me forever."

My legs betray me, carrying me forward. But some part of my brain stops them, until I'm held rigid by my own internal battle.

"I don't want you." I can only get out a whisper now.

He's leaning toward me. His smell is in my nose. In my mouth. I can't fight it. I don't want to fight it anymore. I just want to give in to what I know is right.

"Yes." I whisper the word.

Reese smiles, and his eyes meet mine. And in them, I see the deception, masked behind sapphire irises. He's coming for me. And I can't stop him alone.

"Shayne." I call him, praying he'll come. Because I don't think I'll have a second chance.

"He won't come," Reese says. And then his lips are on mine, and I close my eyes.

Chapter 43

Darkness

Reese's kiss is hot and hard, and I feel like he's about to devour me. My mind fills with fog, and even though my brain screams against me, I kiss him back. But then, with a sudden motion, he flies across the room, landing on his back.

The door bangs open, and a breeze blows into the room, clearing away the drug that is Reese. I look around, but don't see anything. And then a familiar hand touches me on the cheek, stroking it gently.

"Shayne?" He's come.

I feel him but don't see him anywhere. And then his lips are on mine, and I know everything I thought about him is wrong. I love him more than life itself. He's my perfect soulmate, and I'll never belong with another. The assembly of gods be damned.

"Shhhh," he whispers in my ear. "I'm sorry I took so long."

I still don't see him, but he's here, and his invisible presence moves away from me; I know he's heading for Reese.

"Ares!" Shayne's voice booms across the Botanical

Haven.

Reese is on the ground, but he jumps to his feet, and a grin filled with malevolence covers his face.

How could I ever have kissed him?

"Nobody invited you to this party, Hades," Reese says.

I look at my mom, who's glancing around, trying to find Shayne, not looking at me.

"Piper invited me." His voice comes from a different location now. He's moving around. And he's invisible.

Reese jumps out toward the voice, but when he reaches out and closes his arms, they come up empty.

"Looking for something, Ares?" Shayne's voice again, now coming from near the register.

Reese whips around. "Why don't you take off your helmet and fight like you aren't a coward."

Helmet. Of course. Shayne has his Helm of Darkness on. No one can see through it. Not even the gods.

"Cowards drug their victims, Ares. If you're looking for a coward, you should check the mirror." And when Shayne finishes talking, a giant palm tree lifts and flies through the air, hitting Reese on the back so hard he slams into the register.

But Reese is expecting it. The terra cotta pot shatters on the hard tiles, and he spins, flinging my mom's scissors which he's picked up from the ground.

They fly through the air, stick in something invisible, and vanish. And I hear Shayne's gasp of pain. He's been hit.

"Ah ha." Reese is smiling now, walking toward the spot where Shayne is. "Maybe you can keep the helmet on after all." He punches out, but his fist keeps going, hitting nothing but air.

"I want you to leave Piper alone. Forever."

Reese looks toward me. "Piper wants to be with me."

I shake my head. "No! I don't."

But Reese licks his lips. "You seemed to want to be with me in the greenhouse."

"Shut up!" I scream, willing him to stop.

He turns away, his eyes roving the room for Shayne. "Do you know how sweet your Piper tastes? How hard her nipples are when she's excited?"

"I can't stand you!" I want it to not be true. For me to never have done anything with him. And I don't want Shayne to hear. My face is hot, and everything around me is starting to turn red. "You're a monster."

But Reese is having too much fun to stop. "You didn't seem to think so when we were together."

"We were never together!" I want Shayne to know, whether true or not, I was not a willing party.

A bucket slams into the back of Reese's head, wiping the smile off his face. He falls to the ground, but lands in a crouched position, like a lion ready to pounce.

"It's time you let someone else have a turn, Hades. Let someone else show her how it feels to be a woman."

I shake my head. The only person I want—I've ever wanted—is Shayne. "I would rot in Tartarus before I'd be with you." I take my own scissors and pitch them at Reese, but he springs off the ground, and I miss him by inches. And then I feel a slight brush on my cheek, and my hair moves aside. I turn, but it's gone.

It's only when I notice the drops of blood on the ground that I know Shayne is in trouble. Each a footstep apart and moving across the room. And before I can warn him, Reese notices, too, and he pounces, landing on top of an invisible form, so it looks like he's levitating in the air.

Shayne pops into visibility, and Reese tosses the Helm of Darkness across the room where it clatters to the ground near my mom who's still standing there, watching like she's placed money on a boxing match and needs to see who will win.

Reese and Shayne fight, rolling around in a battle I fear will end in only hurt. The struggle is a blur of flailing limbs and electricity mimicking the storm outside. I want to go in and stop it but know I can't. Shayne has Reese in a throat lock so tight that Reese's head begins to turn white. He manages to throw Shayne off, gasping for air as he stands up. And then he's back on Shayne, pressing Shayne's head together with the flats of his hands. And Reese turns him to face me.